Simple

Short

Stories

II

To further tingle the imagination

Simple
Short
Stories
II

To further tingle the imagination

by

K.J.Goss

Simple Short Stories II
To further tingle the imagination
Copyright © 2016 by Ken Goss
All rights reserved

ISBN Number: 978-0-9960140-8-3

Acknowledgments

As always my thanks to my wife, Jeanne, for her encouragement to pursue my imagination and her patience for all the time I take to write along with my two fingered typing.

A very special thanks to a dear friend, Nan Gwin, who generously volunteered to edit my drafts and correct my grammatical errors along with my spelling. Her words of encouragement helped spark my enthusiasm.

Contents

Return to El Dorado

by

K.J.Goss

Return to El Dorado

I really don't know how many people are into antiques. For me it's a passing interest, only every now and then. I always find them fascinating to look at and think about the history they represent, but that's about the extent of it. My financial involvement has been almost nothing. A few items over many years was my total investment. Even at that, the treasures I have were because I liked them, not to have them as a financial investment. However, I periodically wander into antique shops just to browse, and see what stimulates my imagination, which of course has led me to this tale of discovery.

It was mid-winter, snow covering most everything in sight. The roads were clear enough for limited driving so for a change of pace, and to shake off some cabin fever, I decided on a short ride. A relatively local antique shop was my target destination. It was known to have a good reputation and was a rather large place spanning two floors of an old mill building. The perfect place to lose a couple of hours.

I wandered for quite some time unattended which made the visit relaxing until a small walled off section in a back corner drew my attention. There, on the crowded shelves was various statuary that seemed, to my uneducated eye to be of South American origin.

One item in particular drew me like a magnet. There was really nothing special about it. It appeared to be a jungle cat of sorts, with no clear identification. The cat was poised on it's hind legs, it's front paws on a tree trunk as if ready to climb. There was other jungle underbrush and grasses surrounding both tree and cat. The carving seemed to be of stone and was sizeable at about fourteen inches high, a foot long and carrying a width of approximately eight inches. The carving, though crude, left no doubt as to it's identification, though I could not name the type of stone it was carved from. I stood mesmerized. I don't know what it was, but it was drawing me in, more and more. I was shaken out of my trance by the owner of the shop.

"Nice sculpture." he said laying his hands on a small Inca type figurine carved out of jade. "Especially compared to the piece of junk next to it."

It was that piece of junk I was looking at. I was now back to reality, but an unknown force emanating from that junk rock still held me in it's tentacles. So as not to be rude, I reached out and picked up the jade piece. It truly was beautiful.

"I can let you have that for four hundred dollars. It 's probably worth more but I'd like to clear up some shelf space." came the used car pitch.

"That's a bit much for my pocketbook." I answered thinking it was probably only worth two hundred dollars, " But you can clear off more shelf space by selling that."

I pointed to the roughly carved cat statue.

"Oh, that piece of junk. I don't even know why or how that got mixed in with this shelf, but the dealer brought it in all together. Even he said it couldn't be worth much."

The pull of the cat seemed to grow even stronger.

"How much are you asking?" I finally managed.

"You really serious ?" the owner inquired.

"I thought it was something I could stick in the garden." I lied in answer. "It might look good there."

"Tell you what." he said excitedly. "I'll let you have it for thirty bucks just to get it out of here."

"I'll take it." I said hurriedly. "I have just the spot in my herb garden," I fibbed again.

I handed the man three ten's and left before he could change his mind.

Driving home with my prize on the seat next to me I thought about my rash move. I was not usually an impulse buyer. I really don't know what possessed me. It was almost as if I had no control of myself.

I stopped about halfway home and viewed my junk treasure. The more I looked at it the more I liked it. Holding it in my hands gave me a strange feeling. I felt like it was talking to me. I don't exactly know what it was about the carving but I genuinely fancied it. It made me happy and I don't know why. I can't tell you when I last felt this good about something. I finally was able to pull away from my prize purchase and continue my drive home making a quick stop for Chinese take out. I was too excited and not in the mood for cooking. I arrived back at my hideaway in the woods making a mental note to myself to do some more snow blowing now that it had at last stopped. Not today though, I was too wrapped up in my amazing new find. Even if it turned out not to be an antique I was still pleased with myself.

Setting my precious find in the center of the kitchen table I stared at it from all angles while stuffing my face with Egg Foo Yong. I decided the carving definitely needed cleaning and I mentally made it a priority for first thing tomorrow, which was Monday and a workday but being self employed had it's advantages. I studied my statue in great detail, even going so far as to do some reading on the internet, trying to find drawings or articles on the cat like figure, but no such luck. Resigning myself to the fact it was not antique I did not feel disappointed. Regardless, I still liked it and felt a magnetic draw to it.

I carefully moved it to the fireplace mantle before calling it a night   greatly looking forward to tomorrow.

I awoke the next morning still tired. I know I slept through the night but the sleep was not restful. There were constant dreams. Dreams of steaming jungle, screeching cats, slithering snakes and malaria infested mosquitoes. Not just one dream but a continuous flow of scenes all oriented around jungle settings. A refreshing shower worked wonders and from there I headed for some chilled orange juice. I wasn't really hungry for a full breakfast but I did manage to down almost a full quart of juice.

The anticipation of working with my new carving did more to wake me up than anything else. I gently removed it from the mantle and carried it to the kitchen table. I sat there taking in every detail for twenty minutes before I realized that I wasn't getting anything done.

Being that it was carved from stone I figured a little water couldn't hurt it. I found an old tooth brush and prepared a small bowl of warm water and proceeded to do a careful cleanup. I was truly surprised at the amount of age and dirt I was removing. Some color appeared here and there. Faded though it was, it was color nonetheless. My hopes started to rise as to it's age. I recalled seeing these faded color distortion types in museums. I tried to tone down my enthusiasm; after all, it was too early to tell anything yet.

I suddenly became more meticulous in my scrubbing, working that tooth brush into every crevice I could find. Some Q-tips also aided in the process. I sat back after an hour of cleaning, satisfied with my handwork. It was then I spotted some cotton lint caught on a grass spike. On closer inspection I discovered the jagged edge of a broken spike. It was obvious this caused the tear from the cotton swab. Using a pair of tweezers from my trusty pocket knife I carefully picked off the lint. At first I thought it was my imagination, but after double checking, that broken grass spike was loose.

"Too bad." I thought. "My perfect statue now has a flaw."

Stupid as it may sound, I felt bad. Wanting to assess how bad the damage was I probed again with the tweezers with the aide of a magnifying glass. It was loose alright yet it appeared to have been done on purpose. It did not make much sense to me why something should have been built or carved that way. I carried it carefully out to the garage and work bench where there was a goose neck lamp. Perhaps more light would help me discover it's mystery. I picked and poked with a dental pick from my tool box until suddenly I heard a faint click.

"It sounded like a small lock click." I thought. "That's crazy though, I'm just letting my imagination run away again."

Or was I ? The whole figure of the cat was now loose. Worried that I had broken my special treasure I sat back taking my hands away. Annoyed at myself and puzzled by what I had done I mentally scolded myself. It was then I noticed what appeared to be a seam along the bottom edge. I had not seen this earlier. I moved the light showing a different angle. The seam was now very apparent and ran around about eighty percent of the base. I gently reached for the cat to see how loose it was. In moving it closer to me the cat lifted from the base. The seam was just that, a seam. The whole top of my statue was moving up at an angle. It finally stopped at about a forty five degree angle. My heart was now pounding as I was breathing rapidly. I was looking at a hidden compartment. Aged sepia colored paper was staring back at me. It looked dried and fragile so much so that I dared not touch it. I just sat there mesmerized. My mind was racing with all sorts of scenarios. I don't know how much time went by but I sat there frozen in place. Feeling slightly embarrassed I looked around to make sure no one was looking which was, again, me being silly. I was in my own garage with the door closed. Nevertheless I closed the statue's secret door, covered it with an old rag and swiftly returned to the house making sure I locked the door behind me. Safely inside I placed the cat carving on the kitchen table. My silliness still had me under it's control as I proceeded to close the blinds. Now I even laughed at myself. You would have to be ten feet tall to look in the kitchen window. I turned the overhead light on and went to the cat. Carefully opening the lock once again and lifting the cat I was facing what appeared to be very old paper. I felt myself get all tingly. One part of me wanted to grab the paper instantly while the other me argued about leaving it untouched. Like all of us, human curiosity won out. I ever so gently reached over and lightly touched the paper. It did not crumble or disintegrate.

"I guess that's a good thing." I thought.

Thinking my fingers would be more gentle than tweezers I lifted the paper from it's crypt. It was brittle, though not as bad as I anticipated.. The paper was rolled not folded and there were multiple pages. My breathing increased again as I took my hands away to stop the shaking. I felt a few deep breaths to calm myself were in order. When I had recovered enough I reached for the roll of papers and slowly began to unroll them. It felt brittle and stiff but did manage to unwind. Using the sugar bowl as a weight on the top I slowly unrolled the papers weighting the other end also with an old cookbook that was within reach. Still apprehensive about touching it too much I let the papers lie under the makeshift weights while staring wide eyed at the writing. The ink was fading. It was obviously black at one time, now having turned reddish brown with age almost fading into the yellow sepia of the paper. Then the sudden truth hit me. It was Spanish. Apparently, by what I was seeing it was written rather rapidly. My Spanish being relegated to ordering ham an eggs or beer, left me with the massive challenge of translating. My heart sank, my mind racing still. I scanned the text unhurried and finally saw the words that almost stopped my heart. It was unmistakable. About halfway down the page it stood out. ***"El Dorado"***

Could this be ? Naaa. Just some joke I reasoned. From my readings of years ago it was determined that El Dorado was just a myth perpetuated by the greed of early explorers.

There were five pages total, four of text, the fifth being a crudely drawn map. I put the map aside momentarily concentrating on the hand written letter. The writing was small and looked rushed. Being written in Spanish certainly did not help any. The last page was signed but to me it was undecipherable, at least for now. The only thing I could read was the date. As scribbled as it was, there was no doubt about it.

"Marso" or March, 1541.

The hand that held the paper was now trembling, so much so that I could no longer read anything not that I could read the Spanish anyway. I replaced the papers on the table and stared into empty space. This was either the all time greatest practical joke or truly the map for El Dorado.

I finally calmed down, physically anyway, and studied the map somewhat. It really was a crude drawing which indicated nothing to me. I realized I would have to do a detailed study and comparison with some real maps of South America.

Putting the map aside, I refocused on the written text. Every now and then I could make out a simple word but even that did not tell me a story. I definitely needed help.

"What kind of help do I get ?" I asked myself aloud.

That got me to thinking of all kinds of scenarios. A professional translator would open up other problems. Suppose it is real, a real map and a real story. Then someone else would know about it and then the rumors would spread. It would no longer be exclusive.

Whoa, look at me, already I'm acting like the first explorers I read about. Apparently this greed for gold does take over one's soul. I don't want it to affect me that seriously, nevertheless keeping it quiet for a while I think is in order. Where does that leave me ? Translating it myself posed a gigantic task. I could probably do it but how long will it take ? Putting pieces out to different people might be one avenue to consider, though even that could put out too much information which may prompt questions.

My mind ,yet in a quandary, turned to the job of putting the pages front to front and back to back under the heavy weight of some large books. The next phase would be to copy them to use as work copies rather than take a chance of damaging or destroying them.

Once the weights were taken care of I fixed myself a pot of coffee and sat staring out the window into the woods. My mind wandered to South America where I was now following the map to find El Dorado. I would naturally have to keep a journal so I could write about my exploits after the great discovery. I gradually came back to the real world feeling a bit embarrassed. I had not even translated the letter yet, not only that but I didn't know where to start. So much for writing a book.

I remembered my daughter took four years of Spanish for her high school requirement. Though she was now married and moved out I still had many boxes of her things stored away in the basement. Perhaps some of her old school books may be there. I poured a second cup of coffee and headed for the cellar. Luck was with me for a change, I found several of her old books. At least it was a start. I felt better now and could see a plan forming. My next step was the local library where I managed to find a couple of books on the language and a few historical accounts of early explorers. Now armed with source material I gave myself the rest of the day for starting my research and translation. I was actually starting to feel good about this, but I did caution myself against getting too excited over the wrong things.

I reproduced two copies of each page including the map, then made a flat wooden folder for the originals and secured them in my safe.

I collected the things I thought necessary, settled myself at the kitchen table to enjoy the sun, and started the translation process. After struggling for awhile I found it necessary to not only get my large magnifying light but to also make enlarged copies of the text pages. The next three hours flew by but proved fruitful. I was definitely making headway. Key words and phrases were coming to light. I did not have a story yet since I was working on all four pages or actually just sections of them that were the most easily read. I felt pleased with the days efforts and collected the research papers and tucked them away in the safe for the night. I closed up the cat carving returning it to the mantle. Because of my work schedule it would be a few days before I could continue my Spanish lessons.

~ ~ ~ ~ ~ ~

It was difficult to keep my mind on my professional work. I was forever drifting to the map and papers. At night my dreams were jungle bound. As luck would have it whenever I turned the radio on for comforting music to help me concentrate on the work at hand, inevitably it would be a classical Spanish piece. I was being consumed by El Dorado. Against my better judgement I finished my present assignment and closed my studio. I decided an early vacation was the only answer. I figured once I had the mystery decoded my curiosity would then be sated and I could resume a sense of normalcy to my life. Little did I know at the time what adventures lay ahead.

Having set my new goal and now with unrestricted time my anxiety eased as I worked non-stop in my decoding quest.

Hours passed into days exposing more and more of my mysterious letter. I was becoming more convinced that this was a genuine sixteenth century tale.

My first week was filled with visits to four different libraries including the local college. I devoured every article or book I could find on the early Spanish explorations of El Dorado. The internet was also some help. My final thrust was maps of all sorts from Central to South America, at all scales and sizes. At the end of the week I was quite tired and at the same time so exhilarated that I did not want to stop my studies. I gave myself a break though and treated myself to dinner on Saturday evening. A few glasses of wine, with dinner allowed me to relax just enough to sit back and review my weeks efforts. Now even the crudely drawn map was showing definite points. I planned to do some comparisons for my next task. I needed a break from the letter translations.

I did manage with only a few hours work to narrow down an area of specific interest. Once I added some information from the books and the stories of individuals I felt sure I could pinpoint the exact area in question.

The start of the second week put me back to the translation issues. I was becoming excited again knowing the end was in sight. I could feel the story coming alive. There were still a few words I could not make out because of blurred ink blots or that just plain faded with age. This was of little concern to me because once the main letter was totally exposed those missing words should
fill themselves in, or at least their meaning.

I looked at the unbelievable stack of books around the room and laughed, yet I actually used everyone of them. A few more hours of, week two had me convinced me I was finished with the letter. All that was left was to assemble all my notes and actually write the letter. As much as I wanted to rush into it, I dared not. After all, after four hundred plus years what's the hurry. I relaxed with a cup of coffee before starting my final step.

~ ~ ~ ~ ~ ~ ~

THE LETTER

To whoever finds this if I do not survive.
My name is Armondo Luis De Aponti......
I joined the expedition of Don Pedro Fernandez de Lugo in Spain in 1535. This was to be for the exploration and search for golden treasures. The stories of unlimited golden treasures abound. All with this expedition are anticipating unfound wealth, both for King and country and, of course, for personal gain. Our experience here did not live up to our expectations. The hardships we endured, no man should have to be exposed to. The seas were extremely rough on the voyage to this God forsaken place but were trivial next to our experiences of the jungle. If it was not for the promise of gold I don't believe any of us would have stayed. The heat has been oppressive, the rains endless and destructive and the food lacking in both quality and quantity. The local inhabitants are unfriendly and aggressive, the jungle unforgiving and impenetrable and filled with untold creatures bent on the destruction of anything that moved, man being their most favored meal. The mosquito's carry the fever of death that one cannot escape . The bite of a snake is a welcome relief from the suffering of the fever. I have seen the strongest of men reduced to human skeletons barely covered with flesh. I pray the Almighty to have mercy on me and allow me to see home again, though I believe mine and the others prayers have been in vain. There is no relief from this living cruelty.

In early February we set out from Santa Marta. There were forty three of us. This was meant to be an advanced scouting expedition to locate EL Dorado. Whether a lake or city was not known. There were rumors of both. The jungle surrounds took an early toll on our small party. Snakes and jungle cats killed four of our number the first day out. Constant attacks by the local savages whittled us down to just a handful before the week was done. We persevered under the command of Hernan Perez de Quesada and despite our heavy losses of men, horses and food, fortune finally smiled on us. The gold we had been seeking was there for our eyes to behold. El Dorado was both a city and lake. The title also referred to a man. A king whose body was covered in gold dust daily. Since we were so few *in number the Indians did not fear us. They fed us and made us welcome. After ten days surrounded by nothing but gold we five chose to go back to Santa Marta to tell our tale and return with more men and pack horses to transport the gold. We each carried as much golden pieces as we could to prove our story. The journey back was even more exhausting. A muddy swamp claimed Miguel and Hernando and most of our golden treasure. We became totally lost for four or five days, I do not really remember how long it was, in some of the heaviest rain I have ever witnessed. Fever's pain drove Jose mad so much so he took his own life. With only two of us left we forged on totally dependant on each other. The stress and strain of our uncontrollable situation claimed Guilliamo and he died in my arms. I cursed him for leaving me alone and did not bother to bury him. I was determined not to give up and so continued with blind dead reckoning in my chosen direction. With each passing hour my weakness grew. I managed to eat some grubs and found a few yucca plants which I devoured as fast as I could. The heavy rains supplied water, that is if I could corral it before it became tainted. My clothes were all but ripped from my body, my feet, now shoeless, were swollen and bloody. The final hours of my trek were actually on my hands and knees until all went blank. I was found only a few meters from the town of Santa Marta barely alive. I was told it was three whole days before I regained consciousness. Many more weeks passed before I was totally coherent. I tried to tell my story but no one believed me. They all thought I had truly lost my mind which they had seen so many others do because of the effects of the jungle. I was tolerated and treated like the court jester.*

Other expeditions left to continue the search for El Dorado none of which would pay attention to my map. I then vowed to be their clown until I felt recovered enough to set off and retrieve my hidden treasures. This gold was sacred to the native inhabitants. Not for the value we put on it nor for a monetary exchange. It was for ceremonial use and common everyday affairs. It was pretty which seemed to be it's only attraction. They could take it or leave it. They could not understand our greed for this metal. It was just there for decoration. But it was still sacred enough for them to try and hide it from the crazed white man. Thus the legend started. When we the conquering Spanish, could not find any gold where we, thought it should be we would burn their towns and take their food and eventually kill or enslave them. Even these practices did not yield us any treasures.

Being treated as an outcast by my own people prompted me to write this. I found this old carving and reworked it to make this hiding place should I not survive to claim the gold for myself. The map is the best I could do with what little was available to me. I had no way of measuring, so the distance and the direction are the best I could gather from the sun and star positions, and my weakening memory. The travel times may change depending in how fast and easily you travel through the jungle. I know it is a crude map but I will stake my life on it's accuracy. I fear I will not get my second chance at El Dorado. Good luck and God Speed to whoever finds this.

By my hand on this nineteenth day of Marso, 1541.

Armondo Luis de Aponti.

~ ~ ~ ~ ~ ~

I sat quietly, tightly clutching that last page. My mind was awash with feelings of excitement, empathy and sorrow. What tortures Armondo endured. So close to fulfilling his wildest dreams only to see it disappear like a wisp of cloud.

Now my problem was what to do. From the studies I just put myself through I would judge the documents to be genuine based on the names of the town and it's leaders. The records of the volunteer party names also stood up to scrutiny. Do I now risk my life and future on a dream that perhaps may not be real ? Do I face the risks of the jungle or drug cartels who now pervade those same South American lands. That risk is probably even greater than the natural hazzards of the jungle. A trek like this is much too risky to do alone but who do I ask to join me and what reason do I give ? Do I mention El Dorado and accept criticism, or do I fabricate a story and act surprised at our find. If that's the case what do we do with the gold ? Who is the rightful owner ? It certainly isn't me.

Then there is the secondary problem, where do I get the money to pay for such an adventure. Plane fare, boat fare, guides, equipment, food, porters, living expenses etc. Even the Spanish explorers were being backed by the king of Spain. My savings amounts to about six hundred dollars, which will get me absolutely nowhere. I let these thoughts weave back and forth in my mind for a while until I found the courage to dismiss them temporarily.

Before making any kind of final decision further map study was necessary. I put aside all the text information and refilled the table with assorted up to date maps and Armondo's hand drawn map. The start was obvious. We had the town name from his letter. After some difficult translation I realized some confusing markings on the map were indicating a day's march. From there it was figuring how did a days march equate to distance marked. With much interpretation effort of both large and small scale maps along side the survivors map, I picked a standard. It wasn't great but it was a start. Making up jungle pictures in my mind and gauging travel hazards and hacking out a path I set off on an imaginary journey. By making comparisons with today's contour maps and the hand drawn pictures I was able to start in a south southwest direction. The standard I had picked of two and one half miles a day sort of worked. I realized I would have to adjust this one way or the other as my journey continued. I was able to match a few landmarks with the modern topographic maps, which in turn allowed me to adjust my distance traveled base. Excitement was building inside again as I saw a route unfolding.

I stayed with this process for the rest of the day gaining confidence that I was on the right track in my interpretation of Armondo's drawings. I followed what I determined to be the Magdalena River heading inland in a S.SW. direction. My mind wanted to jump ahead to make conclusions but with much inner struggle I remained true to the slow and steady pace of the tortoise and continued step by very slow step of the interpretive process of Armondo's map. I was exposing more symbols and actually matching them to the topo map. In the present direction I was pointing to Bogata, Columbia. For whatever reason I was hoping to stay away from Columbia, yet now I was aimed right at the heart. In spite of my fears I stayed with the interpretation work.

I took a small break from the map to refer again to some of the journals written by early explorers. They indirectly confirmed I was on target. I was making for the Cordillera's. There were numerous references to these mountains and the Cundinamarca plateau by many different expeditions, all coming from different directions.

Back to the map with even more confidence, I felt renewed. Armondo's journey must have been months considering the time period.

Most likely a year or more. The historical journals I had gathered information from all referenced long jungle treks to and from unfulfilled destinations. Many hours additional of map transferences finally yielded a finished map. At least I hoped it did. Now that I had a pinpointed location did not mean I would find any gold. After all we're looking at a span of roughly four hundred and sixty years. The local people had learned to hide their gold from the Spanish and English also. It is a very real possibility that they moved it to hide elsewhere, or slowly pieces were found and by now, had totally disappeared. To be optimistic, perhaps foolishly, it may have remained hidden all these years. If that's the case, where ? Well, being it is a mountainous region, a cave sounded logical. That was easy to say, but I seem to be forgetting over four hundred years of change in topography. Earth quakes and tremors, flash floods, people searching, land slides, this could be the proverbial needle in a very large haystack. Enough with the maps, back to the journal studies. Perhaps even more library visits.

I decided against additional libraries. I felt these original diary entries from dozens upon dozens of explorers were adequate. They all ruled out the amazon area along with Venezuela. By now I pretty much convinced myself that the Cordillera area and the Cundinamarca Plateau was the **X** marks the spot I should go to. I called it quits for the night and slept with dreams of the jungle.

The next day was blue sky and sunshine. I felt good about myself after the massive bundle of work I had accomplished. Reflecting on the past two weeks I mentally took inventory of where I stood. I had the letter and was pleased with my translation results. I had the map which I was convinced were real. I had piles of research papers which was quite an education. Lastly but certainly not least I had the desire and inclination to launch the search for El Dorado, it's mysterious legend and treasures. And there ended my dreams. It's funny how the lack of money can really put a damper on things. Oh well, such is life. Now that I have been slapped back to reality, I would just have to set a new goal for myself to try and put money aside for a trip to South America. This obviously will give me time to do the proper planning necessary for such an adventure.

I was excited yet very disappointed. How often does one come across an historical treasure like this. I dare not even share the find yet for obvious reasons. Having finally resolved myself to the fact that I had to wait before any further pursuit, I turned my attention back to my business. If I wanted to save money I would have to work for it. I buried myself in my chosen profession to the point I was working seven days a week. I managed to pick up a few new industrial accounts which were quite lucrative, both in dollars and reputation. El Dorado was still on my mind but fast becoming more distant with each passing day. I was consumed by my work.

A few months passed, my savings were growing fast, not enough to do anything yet, but growing nonetheless. At last, giving myself a break, I quit work at a normal time rather than the usual nine thirty or ten o'clock as had been my habit of late. Over dinner and a glass of wine I went through a pile of mail I had not touched for a week or more. A rather thick envelope caught my eye. The return address was Tekler College, Tucson, Arizona. I remember a friend of mine of many years ago had mentioned some interest in it which I hastily dismissed because there was nothing there for me. It was a small college specializing in archeology. The envelope contained a long hand written letter along with a newspaper clipping and copies of pages from various books and a map. Much to my surprise the letter was from that very same old friend, Peter Tobias. He was a professor of Inca studies at the college and was involved in a project about a newly discovered Inca ruin. He was heading up an expedition for preliminary excavation of the new find. He remembered my casual interest of years ago in photographing such a project, and was extending an invitation for me to join the team. It was to be fully funded by the college. My only expense would be my air fare to Arizona and personal clothing.

Reading further referenced the map. It was located near Bogata, Columbia. My excitement soared. I even caught myself yelling out loud. Embarrassed once again I gazed around the room to make sure no one heard me. I could not believe my good fortune. I looked at the post mark on the envelope and saw it was dated five days ago. I hoped I wasn't too late as I reached for the phone.

My conversation went well with Pete, and it was determined I had eleven days to get to Arizona. I poured a second glass of wine to celebrate while mentally making some plans.

The next few days I spent finishing up work projects preparing to close up shop for an indefinite period. I returned library books and reorganized my notes and paperwork which I then secured in my safe. I neatened up and made two copies of my map without annotations. I kept them on a separate overlay sheet. I hid one set in different pockets of my wallet and the other set buried amongst my photo equipment. I decided not to tell Peter about my quest unless it was absolutely necessary. Once we were there perhaps I could figure a way to get out on my own for a few days.

I kept my anticipation in check somewhat by keeping busy with the details of packing and planning. By the time my departure date rolled around I was more than ready.

The flight to Arizona was boring but I was enthusiastically met by Peter. We talked over old times on the ride to the hotel where I met the rest of the team. I rounded out the group of seven professionals and four student undergrads. We were to meet a guide the next day in Bogata. The guide, I found out later, was of Inca ancestry. He was from the area we were going to study and was a part- time professor at the University in Bogata. After an enjoyable dinner we all turned in early knowing tomorrow was a big day.

Peter had chartered a private plane to take us to Bogata because of all the gear we were taking. The flight was only about four and a half hours and was quite pleasant. It gave me a chance to get better acquainted with the team. Suburban's were waiting for us when we landed in Bogata along with the guide Amelio. We spent the night at a motel just outside of the city and prepared for an early start the next day.

Once on our way I was able to glance at Peter's maps during our ride on the first part of our journey. We were going in the direction of my special location. Not the exact spot but very close. Everything was working out so well in my favor I started to wonder what was going to go drastically wrong and how soon. One man can't be this lucky.

By the end of the day we were more than halfway to the new site. We had just traveled more than one hundred and fifty miles. I laughed silently as I made a mental comparison to Armondo's torturous trek of weeks and months to get this far. Most of what was once impenetrable jungle was now a network of roads, some only a donkey cart wide, but roads nonetheless.

We stopped for the night. It wasn't really camping though. There was a large wooden building that easily housed us all.
We cooked and ate outside under a broken down wooden canopy. That evening before bedding down I got to view Pete's location map again. I quietly made a comparison with the map copy from my wallet. Our two locations couldn't have been more than three or four miles apart as the crow flies. The Cordillera's basically run north east - south west. Pete's ruin location was south west of the range while my X spot was north east. I realized that the three or four miles would be quite a few hours walk up and over the mountain range. What did please me though was the fact that a town ruin so near to my X did lend credibility to the map and letter. I returned the map to Peter and thanked him for letting me familiarize myself with the area. I really was looking forward to photographically recording this new find.

Back in the trucks the next day put us about ninety percent toward our destination; from here on we would hike. The trucks could go no further. In fact, after unloading they turned back to Bogota immediately.

We camped for the night and planned our trek into the jungle. It was kind of restful that night listening to the distant jungle sounds of the varied birds, bugs and animals. I was doubly excited with the new ruin project and my golden quest, but I still found comfort and relaxation in the surrounding darkness.

Our next days journey into the dampness of the jungle was somewhat difficult but nothing, I'm sure, like Armondo's or any of the earlier explorers of the fifteen hundreds. I was so enthusiastic about just being there, the few hardships we encountered were not enough for me to even be concerned about. I almost did not notice them. The others commented on my exhilaration and said they wished they had my energy. Little did they know of my motivation.

We made camp early though we knew there was only a short distance left before we were at the ruin site. A short distance, yes, but it would have put us there after dark. It was an easy evening, pleasant conversation and all around fun. I checked my camera equipment and left it easily accessible so that I could record our entrance to the lost town. One by one we all crawled into our mosquito proof sleeping tents and were lulled to sleep by the jungle 's din.

The team was awake with the sun, filled with anticipation. Camp was dismantled in record time anxious to be on our way. Three and a half hours later Peter introduced us to the hidden ruin. Hidden it was, too. We saw nothing but the same jungle we had for the last few day's. Disappointment showed as all turned to stare at Peter. He smiled, almost laughed, as he gazed at ten somewhat confused people.

"You're not looking." was his only answer.

I and the others turned to further scan the jungle. Suddenly, like a fog clearing from our brains, things began to appear. It was like the movie *"Brigadoon"*, the mist cleared and the town grew before their eyes.

As expected the jungle had reclaimed it's own. Between the tangled web of vines and roots, bits of houses showed. The more you looked the more you saw. Fifty or so yards in front of us was a well hidden massive stone structure, the jungle still doing its best to swallow it.

Remembering my assignment I quickly assembled the camera gear necessary and began shooting in every direction. Finally controlling my initial excitement, I slowed my pace to record in a journal what I had just photographed; direction ,time, object etc., the usual information for proper documentation for such a scientific project.

An hour later, once our initial curiosity was satisfied, the group professionalism became apparent once again. Camp was established to it's full extent; storage, cooking, sleeping and working areas were made as comfortable and permanent as possible which pretty much filled the rest of that day. Before retiring for the night, we all wandered like tourists in different groups "OOO-ing and AHH-ING" at different discoveries. Tomorrow our more scientific work would begin.

For the next week work was non-stop, tedious and slow going at times, but all in all quite rewarding. The work was so non-stop that even though we were so close to my golden treasure I did not have time to dwell on it.

Actual dating of the town would have to wait for better lab conditions but consensus put everything to the fifteen hundreds. The stone structure, it's use still unknown, was of particular interest. Some jungle thicket had been cleared away revealing work beyond imagination. Precisely fitted stones, rubbed smooth, roughly four by six feet in size, weighing who knows what, all put together without mortar of any kind, an engineering feat we have not successfully figured out.

The first week behind us, it was decided to take a break for a few days to catch up on the much needed written documentation. I was elated at hearing this. Perhaps this could be my perfect opportunity. I went to my sleeping area pretending to be working on my equipment while I thought out my plan.

The closer study of the terrain I conducted a few days ago allowed me to adjust my times. Instead of the original estimate of four hours I now figured it could be done in three. The major problem I faced now was whether or not I would be allowed to go alone, and the need for a possible overnight. I certainly did not want to put the project at risk but I needed an answer to the letter. I felt I owed it to Armondo. I wandered away from camp, not far, but I wanted time to think my way out of my self made confusion. I had my camera with me and started taking some shots of the local flora. After a while I was joined by our guide, Amelio.

"I've always been interested in photography but some how was too busy with other loves to pursue it." he said starting a casual conversation.

"And I've always been interested in archeology but had the same problem. I spent so much time learning my craft I didn't have time for other pursuits." I commented.

"Probably typical of a lot of folk." Amelio replied.

Idea's began to pop into my head. I continued shooting various scenes but tried to steer our conversation in a more favorable direction for me.

"I realize the importance of written documentation in archeology and my part is pretty much up to date. So I thought I would wander off on my own in search of photo ops. What can you tell me about that Plateau over there and what's on the other side ?" I asked Amelio innocently.

He replied willingly, as if happy for the engagement..

"It's pretty peaceful over there now, not a well traveled area. Folk lore and legend from hundreds of years ago spoke of the Plateau as a sacred place. Some myth's still exist about it as the great hiding place of Inca treasure."

"That's really interesting" I said not having to pretend my interest. "What do you think ? Any truth to the legends ?

He smiled quite genuinely answering,

"The academic in me say's they are just that, legends or stories. The Inca ancestry in me wants to believe they're true. We may not have much recorded history, but our oral history has been retold for over a thousand years. As a child I can remember my grandmother telling some of those tales. Word for word they have not changed in all that retelling."

"So you believe that there is hidden gold somewhere ?" I politely interrupted.

"I'm not sure about the actual gold or treasure but I do believe in the oral history that has been handed down."

He paused and looked at me seriously almost as if he were reading my mind.

"As far as wandering off on your own I would not recommend it." Letting that sink in, he looked directly at me and probably sensed my disappointment. "But if you really want to go." He paused, "I could be your guide since I am familiar with the area. I'm sure Peter would have no objection if we went together."

He caught me a little off guard with his statement. I was obviously excited but my thoughts quickly changed. I did not want to betray my secret. How do I pursue this now? I certainly did not want to be rude and refuse his gracious offer. Oh well, perhaps I can work something out when we get there.

"That would be great Amelio. I guess we'll need permission from Peter though before we go scooting away." I replied.

"Good." Amelio answered. "We can check with Peter when we get back. Now how about explaining to me the use of the different lens's you keep changing back and forth."

I smiled in answer thankful for the change in subject matter. The rest of the day went well. We spoke of Inca history and the ins and outs of Photography. I felt an inner connection with Amelio. He gazed at me sometimes as if he could see into my very soul. It was almost as if he already knew my secret, yet down deep inside I knew I could trust him. I still argued with myself on that though.

Peter had no problem with us going off on a tour, in fact he encouraged it. He did not wish to see me get bored with the same mundane routine. Personally I don't think any one would get bored looking at Inca ancient History.

Early the next morning Amelio and I prepared our packs with food and other necessities for our short journey. Peter even suggested we take one of the rifle's with us just in case. Of course we also had our cell phones if we could catch a signal.

We left camp at seven and I was right, we arrived at my chosen location by ten A.M. Amelio noticed I kept checking my G.P.S. and finally became curious enough to ask why. I made up a quick story about making sure we could find our way back to camp without a problem. He accepted the answer although I could tell he really didn't believe it.

While we rested he related one of his stories from the Inca traditional oral history. It was of the Spaniards of the fifteen hundreds, their thirst for gold and the ravaging destruction and murder they promulgated in their quest. His ancestors, he said were always hiding their possessions so as not to lose their complete history and life story. He went on to relate that there were one or two men who actually saw the hidden treasure and did escape to the north coast. Whether or not they lived to tell others was unknown. Then looking directly at me as if he already knew, gave the last sentence of his tale.

"This is the very spot as legend has told of the final resting place of our lost history."

There was a long silence between us but we held eye contact. I knew then I had to share my secret.

"I know." I said quietly. "I also know one of those Spaniards did survive for a while."

Amelio, half smiled as a worried look clouded his eyes. I immediately followed with,

"Your secret still remains a secret."

Now smiling a full expression, "Until now ?" he added as a question.

"Until now." I confirmed.

I settled myself comfortably on a rock and related the story of the letter. He was as fascinated as I upon hearing of my experience with the carving and translation. I myself felt better having shared my burden. Not that it was really a burden but I guess I did not realize how much of a mental weight it was. I even knew Amelio was the perfect one to share with. Who better than one of Inca ancestry and discipline.

We continued talking for a couple of hours, each of us feeling the bond that was forming between us. We agreed to stay overnight and worked briefly on a quick camp setup. Satisfied with our efforts we put some time in looking for some sort of cave entrance.
We laughingly joked with each other reminding ourselves we were searching for something that no one has found for almost four hundred and fifty years. In reality it was pretty funny. I don't know what we were thinking of. We stopped at dusk, fixed a quick supper and crawled into our sleeping bags.

Amelio was instantly out like a light while my mind became suddenly alive. I tried all sorts of scenarios to mentally find the treasure. We looked for a cave entrance, but why a cave entrance ? Perhaps it's underground covered with many feet of dirt over the past four hundred years. Perhaps there was no real treasure, maybe the whole thing truly is a myth. These and other ideas went round and round in my head in a giant loop. My mind even drifted back to the carving that started this whole thing. I was confusing myself again, wanting to find this elusive golden piece of history and yet not wanting to upset a part of the Inca history they fought so long, at a great loss, to keep hidden. Checking my watch it was after two in the morning so I re-tuned my mind to the sounds of the night and was able to drift off to sleep.

Amelio was up early full of energy while I walked around in

a fog. We discussed my thoughts of last night over a light breakfast and he agreed with all my scenarios. He ran the same thoughts that morning while I slept. We cleaned up breakfast and continued our search among the rocks. Two back breaking hours passed when a dark opening showed itself after the removal of a few large stones. Amelio and I sat there staring eagerly. Could this be it ? Was this the door to history ? We probed a bit deeper into a zig-zag thin portal that did not seem to end. A sudden flush overcame me and I stopped. Amelio, who was behind me said nothing. I turned out my pocket flashlight and just stood there breathing deeply. A few moments of silence was finally broken by a calm voice. It was mine.

"We don't belong here." we both heard me say. The next sound I heard was Amelio moving towards the light of the entrance. It took us five or six minutes to make it completely out to the sunlight. As I exited the narrow passage I was met by the warm smile of Amelio.

"I knew you couldn't go through with it." he said softly.

I sheepishly smiled in return.

"Let history remain history." I said. "Why disturb the dead. Let them live on in our memories."

"I always thought you had Inca blood in your veins." laughed Amelio.

I   felt a little embarrassed, yet I was pleased with myself.

Without a word between us we worked at replacing rocks to cover the entrance. We continued our silence as we broke camp and started our journey back to Peter and the newly discovered town. After an hour of silent walking, Amelio, without looking at me, said softly;

"We have some small explosives with us packed away. We shall return soon and make sure the entrance is closed for ever."

In a matching voice I answered,

"Good idea."

By the time we reached camp we had resumed normal composure and were discussing our adventurous day and the many pictures I had taken of plant and animal life. Peter welcomed us back and was pleased that we had a productive hike.

We picked up our normal routine work of studying the four hundred plus year old settlement as if nothing had changed. Amelio and I however remained close friends having shared such a sacred secret.

The team worked tirelessly over the next six weeks with new and exciting discoveries every day. The site added invaluable amounts of knowledge to the Inca history as we knew it. It was with much sadness and disappointment that we closed camp and put the site to rest for the season. Next season would encompass a much more detailed excavation. Peter had prepared a preliminary report for the Columbian Government Department of

Antiquities to be followed up with a more comprehensive research paper after all notes were consolidated back at the college.

Amelio and I found time to return to the Plateau and seal, we hoped forever, the legend of El Dorado.

We kept in touch for years with both visits and letters. By mutual agreement I preserved the letter as a historical document to go to Amelio and /or The Columbian Department of Antiquities upon my death, however, the map I burned with much regret. As much as it hurt to do so I know it was for the better.

In my mind I had found El Dorado and no other person could claim that.

Thank you Armondo.

The End.

The Storm

by
K.J. Goss

The Storm

Mike Cassady climbed out of his Peterbilt tractor shielding his eyes from the wind blown snow as he made his way to the diner. Dawn was just becoming evident, darkness prevailing longer than usual because of the storm. He guessed the snow to be about fifteen or sixteen inches as he struggled to keep his footing. When he opened the door a wind gust nearly took it off the hinges along with his arm. With some extra effort he managed to pull it closed, but not before a few inches of snow covered the floor.

"Thanks for the extra snow Mike, I was beginning to run out of ice." quipped Susan, the auburn haired woman behind the counter. She was owner, chief cook, waitress and dish washer of this popular truck stop diner. It was called *"Welcome to the Nowhere Diner"* because of it's location in the middle of nowhere on a sparsely traveled road in Converse County Wyoming.

Mike welcomed the enveloping warmth as he unbuttoned his heavy wool jacket. He sat down at the counter and Susan already had a mug of black coffee waiting.

Mike was a regular at the diner for almost three years now as were the other five patrons scattered throughout. Sitting next to Mike was Hank Wilson who had his own small appliance repair. Five stools away was Tom Hurley, a local realtor who really didn't have much to sell but he did know the area well having grown up here.

Big Ed Grimes poked his head out from the kitchen pass-through window;

"The usual Mike? He asked. "Looks like you could use a good meal."

"You're right Ed, do you know where I can get one?"

Susan let out a low chuckle, as did everyone else.

Big Ed grunted and turned to his grill. Ed was a retired trucker but helped out now and then to give Susan some relief.

Seated in a small corner booth was Alice Reynolds, the local mail carrier for this rural route. Mike waved to her and she returned the greeting without taking her head out of the newspaper.

In a booth at the opposite end of the eatery from Alice was Tim Fuller, the deputy sheriff for the area. He was trying to call on his radio with obviously not much success. Rounding out the regulars was Pete Lomax, a local farm boy out joy riding on his over priced ski mobile. Mike then caught site of an unfamiliar face almost hidden in one of the middle booths. He was a young sailor flipping through the juke box selections. He later found out the navy man was thumbing a ride home. He was on a thirty day leave and got caught in the storm.

Susan served Mike his usual breakfast of bacon and eggs, pancakes and sausage along with a few slices of toast. Setting the platter down she inquired;

"Anything on the radio about the storm."

"The last I heard was about twenty minutes ago." answered Mike. "After that I lost all contact, Nothing but static. The report was that they are now calling this a major blizzard and depending where you are we should expect accumulations in excess of three feet. It's supposed to continue for at least another twenty four hours, perhaps more."

"Looks like you have company for the day Susan." remarked Tom. "What about you Mike? You sticking around?"

"I was trying to make it home for my wife's birthday tonight, but that's still another eight hour drive under the best of conditions. I'll see what it's like after I eat." Mike mumbled , his mouth full of breakfast.

"Don't waste your time Mike." called Tim Fuller. "I managed to get through for a short message and the road is closed about three miles ahead."

"Oh great." grunted Mike. "I'll have to call Julie and give her a rain check on dinner."

"That would be a nice gesture." volunteered Susan, "But the phones are out. Right now we are cut off from the world. Not to worry though, we have plenty of food and a backup generator."

"What about Pete and his ski doodle thing or whatever you call it." asked Alice. "Perhaps he can get some place and let people know that we're okay."

"Ski - Mobile." Grumbled Pete, sensitive about his beloved toy. "It's called a ski - mobile and that's what I have it for. I can go anywhere when you guys can't " he bragged. "It's a good idea though, I'll get right to it." he said putting on his coat.

"Wait a minute." Tom Hurley said. He removed a pad and pen from his shirt pocket. "Pass this around and everyone can write their telephone number down and he can drop it off at the Sheriff's office." Having said that he turned to Tim Fuller. "Any luck yet with the radio?"

"Naaa." answered Tim disgustedly. "Apparently the storm is interfering with the signals. Oh well, I didn't want to go anywhere today anyhow." he smiled.

Pete, now fully geared up with helmet and gloves walked to the door;

"See you later." he said in a show off tone of voice.

The open door let in more snow before Mike was able to pull it closed.

"Got a mop Sue? I'll clean this up for you." he asked.

"Don't worry Mike, I'm way ahead of you." said Big Ed, mop in hand.

"I'm glad to see they finally found something you were suited for." joked Mike.

Big Ed made a fake swing at Mike with the mop then turned to the job at hand.

When Ed finished mopping all applauded as he took an exaggerated bow.

Susan with a fake frustrated look said to herself, but loud enough for all to hear,

"It looks like it's going to be a long day."

~ ~ ~ ~ ~ ~

Upon Pete's exit the rest gathered around the counter area where Susan stood. Hank spoke first with what seemed to be on everyone's mind.

"As long as we are all going to be together for a while is there anything we can do to make it easier on you Sue."

The others nodded affirmatively.

"Thanks guys, There's nothing I can think of right now. Remember I've been running this place by my self for a long time. I think I can handle eight people. Especially since you are all friends," she added lovingly.

The door swung open scattering winters snow on the floor again. A tall snowman entered, shaking snow off himself as he did so. It was a very humble Pete Lomax.

"My ski machine won't start and I think the Battery is dead now.

"So I guess we really are isolated." said Tom verbalizing the obvious.

Hank quickly joined in reaching for his coat and gloves.

"Come on Pete, I'll give you a hand. We'll take the battery out and bring it in here. Perhaps I can rig something up with the generator and get it charged."

Winters chill entered the diner again as they exited. Mike and Big Ed comically fought over mopping the floor. While they horsed around Susan did the mopping herself.

"Thanks guys." She remarked politely as she walked to the back room mop in hand. The young sailor followed her.

"Let me do that for you Mam. Wringing out mops is one of my specialities. After almost a year at sea you get used to certain things."

He smiled and gently took the mop from her.

"Why thank you sailor." she returned the smile with genuine warmth.

"As long as we're going to be held hostage by this storm for a while, first names I think, would be more appropriate. I'm Susan and you are?" She extended her hand.

"Sean, Ma'm, Sean Finnegan." He shyly shook her hand.

"Well I'm pleased to meet you Sean Finnegan. You can consider this your home for a while. Relax and enjoy. At least you'll be warm and dry." Susan laughed. "Come and meet the gang or should I say your fellow hostages."

Coffee was poured as introductions were made.

"What do you do in the Navy, son." questioned Tom Hurley.

"I'm in the fire control section, which means we take care of the aiming accuracy the big guns."

"No kidding." Tom answered in surprise. "That's what I did way back in Viet Nam. I'm sure things are a whole lot different now."

The two drifted over to a booth and were soon deep into exchanging experiences.

~ ~ ~ ~ ~ ~

Snow and cold filled the doorway as Hank and Pete rushed to get inside.

"Man it sure is getting worse out there. You can't even see to walk." Hank blurted out.

Mike helped pull the door shut while Sean went for the mop.

Pete's extreme frustration was evident as he grumbled that they had no success with his transportation.

Susan had hot coffee waiting by the time their jackets were off. All this time Tim Fuller had been glued to his radio.

"I do have some news folks, but I'm afraid it's not great. I still can't get any calls out, however I did catch a static filled weather forecast. The major storm center has yet to arrive and snow accumulations are feared to be beyond measurement at this time."

Serious concern was now evident on everyone's face.

Tim addressing Susan in a serious business tone, remarked;

"Looks like we may be here for more than just a day Susan. I think we should take inventory of the necessities."

"Aren't we being business like." chided Mike, which managed

to bring a smile to Tim.

"**He's** right though." added Big Ed. Our delivery was supposed to be today."

"**O**kay Ed, let's see what we can come up with." Susan gave a quick look around. "There are nine of us." She and Ed returned to the kitchen.

"**W**hat next big guy?" questioned Mike deferring authority to the obvious emergency training.

Tim gave a partial laugh and continued.

"**I** was just thinking that if any of us had any type of emergency gear in our vehicles it might be prudent to have it in here with us."

All agreed and proceeded to reach for their coats.

"**I** suggest we do it in pairs. You know that safety in numbers thing." added Tim.

Alice agreed to go with Tom and Hank, while Pete paired up with Mike. Tim and Sean teamed up to round it out. The teams took turns weathering the elements so that the door would always be manned.

In the meantime, Susan and Big Ed compiled an inventory they were satisfied would last close to a week. The fuel tank had been topped off the day before and the generator was in good working order. In under two hours all were safely settled in the warmth of "The Nowhere Diner". Under the circumstances the mood was jovial. Even Sean was fitting in like a regular. Lunch was light, with each conscious of the possible food rationing. By three o'clock most were napping quietly, the snow depth having already reached over four feet.

Darkness overcame the diner but the howling winds and blowing snow were still in force.

"**H**ow about a nice dinner at seven folks. Big Ed is preparing a nice pot roast with gravy and sundry veggie's. And believe it or not this ones on me." smiled Susan happily. "We may not all be where we want to be but let's make the best of the situation."

"**I**'ll even throw in a bottle of wine with dinner ." Mike volunteered. "It's obvious I'm not going to make my wife's birthday tonight. I'll pick up another tomorrow on my way home."

The diner was alive again as if nothing had occurred. Sean picked some soft background tunes during dinner that added to the festive mood. The much enjoyed meal lasted almost two and one half hours after which the group shared in the cleanup. Susan was in a greatly relaxed mood because she had so little to do. The friendly conversation slowly died down as each patron chose a resting place that would do for the night. The continuing howling winds acted like a narcotic allowing sleep to take over.

Except for a few grunts and snores the night passed without a major crisis.

~ ~ ~ ~ ~ ~

Mike was the first to awaken with daylight. Because the windows were frosted over a view of outside conditions was not possible. Proceeding to the men's rest room he was able to open the small window and glance outside. It was still snowing and quite heavily too. The wind was still gusting, though not as severe as the last night. He could see little else through the tiny window.

"I'll try the door later after the others are up." he thought to himself.

Returning to the front he found Susan preparing a fresh urn of coffee. Eventually others stirred and except for a few creaks in the bones none were worse for the wear. It wasn't their bed at home but it was sleep.

"We survived the night ." Tim reported "But still no luck with the radio."

The smell of bacon and eggs revived the rest of the guests and again the diner was alive with quiet chatter.

After the second cup of coffee Mike decided a more detailed look to the outside was due. Pete Lomax offered to join him, still worried about his snow machine.

Pete, being young and a bit egocentric, his motorcycle and snow machine were all he seemed to care about. He was basically a decent person, just a tad self absorbed with his own importance.

Sean and Hank stood by with the mop as Mike pushed open the door. Some wind but no snow entered the diner. The pair exited quickly and Mike pushed the door shut. As he and Pete turned from the door they sort of froze in place. They were facing a wall of snow. This they expected but they did not expect what they were actually seeing. The snow wall was a good fifty feet or so from the diner. Part of the road was visible as was the whole parking area around the building. There was no more than three inches of snow covering the immediate building area while the wall surrounding that had to be eight or ten feet high.

It was then the greater shock hit them. There were no vehicles. Only Mike's Peterbilt tractor remained. The fifty one foot trailer was missing as were the Sheriff's car, the ski-mobile, the mail truck and other private vehicles. They were totally walled in by snow. The only clearing was the fifty foot spacing around the perimeter of the diner. Mike and Pete stared at each other not knowing what to say. They each wandered in different directions searching. Searching for the cars mostly but searching for hints of what had happened. After completing a circle around the diner they met by the door. They shrugged their shoulders at each other and went inside. Those inside looked up and ceased talking waiting with anticipation for news of the storm. Mike, not knowing how to say it just blurted out;

"The cars are gone. They're all gone except my cab."

-26-

Everyone chuckled at this. Susan added;

"With this much snow, I'm sure everything is buried. Naturally everything is gone."

"Wait, this is not a joke. Mike is being serious." said Pete Lomax in his oh so serious voice. "The cars are gone and so is the snow by the building."

"What do you mean, no snow by the building." piped in Tom. "It's been snowing like crazy all night."

"See for yourself." said Mike. "We are not making this up."

Sean was the first to head for the door followed by a grumbling Big Ed. By the time the door was open all were crowded around. Ed stepped outside and suddenly stopped.

"What the hell?"

The others filed out and the same reaction was repeated. Disbelief silenced the chatter. Hank started to walk around when Mike announced,

"Pete and I already did that. There's nothing there."

"This is freaking me out." said Alice. "Besides it's cold. I'm going back inside."

Everyone followed except for Hank.

"I'll be there in a minute." he said staring up at the white wall in front of him.

Back in the warmth, questions abounded.

"This reminds me of the old TV shows like Twilight Zone or Outer Limits." commented Big Ed.

"This is no time for being funny." said Alice in a scolding tone.

"Okay folks, calm down, I'm sure there is an explanation for this." answered Tim Fuller trying to sound official again. "Swirling winds could very well account for the lack of snow around the diner. Things like this have happened before."

"Yeah! But can you account for the cars disappearing." Big Ed added.

"Well- - - - No- - - - ." Tim hesitated, "But I'm sure there must be a logical explanation."

"Yeah, like the Twilight Zone." Ed threw back

"Knock it off Ed." pleaded Alice. "I'm nervous enough as it is." She left the rear booth and moved up closer and slid in with Tom.

Everyone then realized she was truly upset but were gracious enough not to make an issue of it.

"I just made another pot of fresh coffee." Volunteered Susan to lighten the air. "Please help yourself. I'm not going to stand on formalities today."

Minor conversations continued for a while for lack of

anything better to do. Sean sat quietly sketching portraits. Alice nervously doodled on a napkin, mostly ripping it, but it kept her busy.

Mike pulled Susan aside commenting;

"What's up with Alice. I've known her for years and I've never seen her like this. She's usually steady as a rock."

I know." Susan whispered, "It's not like her at all. It's not just today, though, for the past week or so she has been acting strange. Some one said her ex was back in town. I wonder if - - -"

Mike cut her short "Perhaps you're right. If I remember correctly that breakup was a rough one."

Susan nodded in agreement saying, "Let's give her some space." as she turned to walk away.

Big Ed poked his head out from the kitchen;

"Hey Hank! As long as you're here why not take a look at my big mixer. It's been acting up lately."He looked both ways and called again "Hank ?"

Tim gazed up from his radio. Looking around he also called "Hank ? Anybody seen Hank."

"I don't think he came in from outside yet." Mike answered.

Pete volunteered to get him. He threw on his coat and quickly pushed through the door. In a little less than a minute he returned.

"Did Hank come in while I was gone ?"

Everybody 's attention went to Pete.

"No one came in." answered Tim. "Why ?"

"Because He's not outside, that's why." Pete answered looking serious again.

"He was out there with all of us before." Remarked Tom.

As he spoke Alice reached for his hand and grasped it tightly.

"He's got to be out there." Tim said. "I'll go with you and we'll look again."

"Okay." answered Pete, "But I already checked around the building."

"Fine, but let's do it anyway." Tim answered in his official tone.

They exited the diner and proceeded to call out Hank's name. Not hearing an answer Tim pointed to Pete indicating he move one way while he went the opposite direction around the diner. They met in the back neither having seen Hank. They completed their circles and met back at the front door with no results.

"There weren't even foot prints." commented Tim.

They quickly reentered the diner. As all looked up, Alice was the first to speak;

"Where's Hank ?" distress showing in her voice.

"We didn't see him outside." Tim said calmly.

"Maybe he's in the men's room." said Big Ed knowing he wasn't.

"I've already checked that twice." replied Tom. "Perhaps he is in the kitchen." returned Big Ed.

"Oh my God. What's happening." screamed out Alice. "Are we all going to die? "

She was physically shaking now. Susan took Tom's place next to her enfolding her in her arms.

"Shush now. There is no need to get upset."

"But every thing's disappearing. Even people now." Alice said in a quivering voice. "Whose next." she screamed.

Susan holding Alice tighter turned her head to Big Ed.

"Get the brandy from the desk in the office Ed."

He turned to do as he was bid, jokingly complaining.

"You never let me drink in the morning."

"But that's your trouble Ed, you don't know when to stop." chided Mike.

"And you do ?' Ed answered sarcastically.

"Just get the brandy Ed." added Susan slightly annoyed as Ed pushed into the kitchen.

"Mike, can I see you a moment ?" asked Tim.

Mike walked to the end of the diner where Tim had his radio. Tim wasted no time and started speaking as Mike approached.

"I don't know what's going on but we are going to have to try and maintain calm until we can figure this out."

"I agree." Mike replied. "But figure what out? "

Tim just starred at Mike with no comment. Alice could still be heard sobbing into Susan's shoulder. Sean wandered to the juke box hoping to lighten the mood somewhat.

"Good idea." said Pete as he joined him.

The tune they picked was lively without being noisy and it did interrupt the darkness of the mood. Sean joined the ladies while Tom and Pete decided to plan with Tim. Big Ed returned to the kitchen thinking about preparing some lunch or dinner or whatever. People would be hungry sooner or later.

Upon seeing Big Ed going to the grill Susan yelled to him;

"Ed I think we still have a few steaks left in the cooler. Let's break them out and give everyone a treat today."

Turning back to the seating area Susan added ,

"On me folks, and I'm sure we can throw in a few baked potato's."

The men thanked her with smiles and nod's. Sean must have had some kind of influence on Alice because she seemed calmer now and was actually smiling. Tim continually tried the radio with no results. The sudden sound of a breaking bottle caught everybody's attention. Susan, glancing at the kitchen, with annoyance in her tone, said;

"Can't you be more careful Ed. That's the second time this week."

There was no further sound from the kitchen. Susan tried again.

"Ed ?" After a pause she continued. "Are you alright Ed....Ed.?"

By now Tim and Mike were headed for the back of the diner each calling Ed.

Entering the kitchen they observed a half gallon milk bottle and it's contents spread out on the floor. There was no sign of Big Ed, nor was there any sign of tracks from the spill area. The two men starred at each other in bewilderment. Susan was heard again.   "Everything alright back there? "

"Yeah." Mike yelled in answer. 'Just a broken bottle of milk"

"And no Ed." whispered Tim so only Mike could hear.

"What do we do now ?" Mike asked.

"Let's at least look around a little." Tim replied.

The pair proceeded to make a thorough search of the kitchen, store rooms and even the walk in cooler. They drew a blank in all places. Although the back door was locked and barred they unlatched it and checked outside only to find nothing. They resealed the door as Mike commented.

"Why bother, it apparently doesn't matter." Tim's face remained serious as if in deep thought.

Finally coming out of his meditative state he muttered,

"I guess we have to tell the others." and turned toward the seating area. The two exited the kitchen and Susan inquired;

"Is Ed okay?"

Tim hesitated for a moment, then answered quietly.

"We don't know. He's not there."

"What do you mean he's not there? " screamed Alice hysterically.

She repeated her question now shaking uncontrollably.

Sean and Susan grabbed her simultaneously hoping to calm her.

"Leave me alone." she screamed again pulling away from Sean and burying her face into Susan's shoulder sobbing.

"We're all going to die, we're all going to die." she repeatedly cried.

"Shut up Alice." came a deep loud voice from across the room.

The usually meek and quiet realtor was now red faced and shouting.

"Don't you think we are all just as concerned. Becoming hysterical is not going to change the situation or help any of us, so just keep your emotions to yourself."

By now all eyes were on Tom, including Alice. She cowered deeper into Susan's shoulder wiping her eyes with a napkin.

"That's enough Tom." Spoke Tim firmly without raising his voice. "We are all concerned about our predicament, but there is no need to lose our heads. That will only defeat us before we start. We need to keep calm heads and cool tempers if we want to get to the bottom of this. There has to be a logical answer and we will get nowhere if we fight each other."

Everyone remained quiet and acknowledged Tim's council. Even Alice muffled her sobbing.

Pete Lomax broke the silence,

"I for one want to do another tour around the outside. Maybe my ski-mobile is buried in that wall of snow."

"I don't think any of us should do anything alone." answered Tim looking directly at Pete.

"I really don't care what you say Tim, I'm going outside." Pete replied reaching for his coat.

"I think Tim's right." joined Tom Fuller. "I'll go with you Pete. I need some fresh air anyway."

The pair left the diner without another word.

Mike glanced at Susan still holding Alice close. Susan's eyes told Mike to leave Alice alone for a while longer. His eyes moved to Alice who was staring back but not seeing.

Outside Pete walked to Mike's Peterbilt cab with Tom following close behind.

"I sure would like to know why all our vehicles disappeared but not Mike's truck." commented Pete.

"Are you saying that you think Mike has something to do with all this ?" asked Tom.

"I didn't really say that , I just find it strange that all is gone except his truck. Answered Pete.

"Don't forget, his trailer is gone." reminded Tom.

"Yeah, I forgot about that." mumbled Pete.

His eyes then switched to the snow wall.

"That's strange, what's that ?" He was walking to a slight discoloration of the wall. With his gloved hand he dug into the snow. The off color remained. Using both hands now he dug deeper. Now at a depth about fifteen inches he could still see color. Moving to his right he continued to claw at the wall until he finally came to white. Tom joined him remarking that it was probably nothing. He pointed to the bare ground area nearby.

"Look here, this red clay is what most likely stained the snow."

Embarrassed, Pete answered; "I guess you're right. I'm trying too hard to find answers."

"We all are kid. Then again maybe you're on to something. Let's walk the perimeter again keeping a close eye on the snow wall. Who knows, perhaps we can get a clue of some kind."   "We already did that twice." Pete replied a little annoyed.

"I know." Tom continued, "But you were looking for people then. I really think we should concentrate on the snow. Who knows, It's worth a try. I also think we should heed Tim"s advice and stick together.."

"I guess so." muttered Pete, not liking being told what to do.

Together they started keeping close to the wall, eyes searching and at a slow pace.

Sean took the obvious hint and left Alice alone with Susan. He wandered back to Tim and his radio setup.

"This is a hell of a way to spend a leave." He said jokingly.

"It's better than being in harm's way." answered Tim.

"I don't know with this situation I think I'd rather be back aboard ship." returned Sean.

"I guess you're right." smiled Tim.

To kill time Mike joined Tim and Sean making small talk.

"I was in the Navy myself once." said Mike. "Maybe we can compare ships.

Sean smiled and the two sat in the next booth up from the radio. Quiet conversation took over the diner and all appeared normal.

~ ~ ~ ~ ~ ~

A cold breeze entered with the door opening as Pete Lomax rushed in.

"Close the door." shouted Susan.

"Shut the door Tom." Pete repeated turning around.
"Tom ?" he called.

Pete stopped removing his jacket taking a further step towards the open door.

"Tom ?" he called again raising his voice.

Now Mike and Sean were right behind him. Pete repeated his call this time yelling. All three were outside now.
Mike pointed to the ground.

"Look here." he said seriously. "The second set of footprints stop about fifteen feet shy of the door."

"TOM." All three shouted

Silence still reigned.

"Let's get back inside quick." Mike yelled pushing the other two ahead of him and pulling the door shut when he was in.

Alice started in again.

"Didn't I tell you, we're all going to die We're lost, this is the end. No one is going to help us."

She repeated this over and over with a few quivering screams thrown in.

"Calm down and shut up Alice." Tim said in a stern voice. "Getting hysterical is not helping anyone."

Alice glanced up with glaring eyes that looked as if they could melt steel, but she did remain quiet.

"What happened to Tom ?" questioned Tim

"I don't know, he was right behind me." answered Pete. "We walked the perimeter and yes, we did it together." he added sarcastically. "We were scanning the snow wall in detail looking for anything out of the ordinary. Tom thought maybe we could pick up some sort of clue."

"The only clue is we're all doomed. It's just a matter of time." Alice mumbled.

Tim cast a shut up glance at her again.

"We were never out of each other's sight until we turned to come back inside." Pete continued. "He was still talking when I opened the door."

Pete's demeanor had changed. His know it all attitude had been replaced with an uneasiness not familiar to him.

"Any luck with the radio yet ?" Mike inquired.

"Not really." Tim commented. "When I do get any sound it's just static.

"Yeah, that's all I got on my CB in the truck."

"By the way Mike your beloved truck is still out there." Pete muttered sharply.

Mike looked at him but chose to ignore the remark.

"Coffee anyone ?" Susan suggested happily trying to change the room's mood.

"A drink would be more appropriate." Mike added.

"I don't have enough for everyone." quipped Susan, "Besides I'm keeping that for myself." she smiled.

"Okay, from now on no one does anything alone." announced Tim.

"What if I have to go pee ?" questioned Susan jokingly.

"That goes for that also. Take Alice with you." Tim shot back returning Alice's cold stare. He followed up with; "Any other comments? "

"Yeah, I wish I was back aboard ship." said Sean with a smile.

This did generate a grin from Tim.

"Tell you what Mr. Navy man." said Susan as she walked to Sean and hooked her arm into his, "You come and watch me throw some lunch together and then I'll watch you swab my deck. That should get rid of some of that homesickness."

"What ever you say Ma'm." answered Sean allowing himself to be led to the kitchen.

Pete turned and headed to where Alice was sitting.

"Spare me your pity." she said annoyed. "I don't need help from anyone. I'll be hysterical all by myself."

With a hurt look Pete stopped. He looked at Alice, hurt still showing and quietly muttered, "I wasn't here to pity you, I just wanted some company."

As Pete turned to go, Alice followed softly with;

"Sorry kid, come sit down. We can commiserate together."

Tim and Mike remained at the radio making small talk and trying to come up with some sort of explanation.

"I need a quick break." Tim said making for the rest room.

"Hold on." Mike quickly replied. "Your rules. Some one has to go with you."

"I know what I said but you can see the door right there. Can't be more than ten or twelve feet away. You can watch the door from here."

Realizing Tim was being stubborn Mike let him have his way. "Okay." Mike returned, "But yell if you notice anything unusual."

"Yeah, yeah." was Tim's reply pushing open the bathroom door.

Mike turned his attention back to the radio antenna pointing it in different directions. Laughter was coming from the kitchen which caused Alice to remark sarcastically;

"How can anyone have fun in this situation? "

Peter Lomax followed with, "I guess some people just don't consider this very seriously. I hate to admit it, but right now I'm scared."

It was now Alice's turn to comfort as she stretched out her hand and gently touched Pete's arm. Quickly changing her mood she yelled down to Mike;

"I thought you were supposed to be watching Tim. It doesn't take that long to pee."

Alerted by her call Mike went and knocked on the men's room door while calling,

"Tim, What's taking so long ? You okay ?"

He was answered with silence. He called again as he opened the door. The room was empty. Mike even looked behind the door. There was no sign of Tim or even a struggle of any kind. He exited the room wearing a sheepish expression.

"**He's** gone." he announced.

"**I** thought you were supposed to keep an eye on him." yelled Pete angrily, his frustration peaking.

"**See** didn't I tell you." shouted Alice. "We're all going to die."

Susan poked her head out of the pass through and with a firm and somewhat annoyed voice directed at Alice said, "Will you knock it off. We are all on edge. You're just making it worse."

Stunned at being spoken to this way Alice glared back at Susan but without comment.

All attention was shifted back to Mike who was no longer there.

"**Mike** ?" Susan called. Pete started up from his seat,;

"**Maybe** he went into the men's room." He yelled Mike's name as he rushed to the rest room. He repeated his call, somewhat panicky this time as he slammed open the bathroom door.
The water was running in the sink but the room was empty. Pete backed out, visibly shaking now and screaming,

"**Mike, Mike, Mike.**– Mike's gone too. What do we do now. Alice was right, we're all gonna die. We have to do something. What are we gonna do. We have to get out of here."

Sean and Susan were soon at his side. Susan wrapped her arms around Pete in an effort to calm him. Sean stood in front of him grasping his hands toward the same end.

"**Now** maybe you'll listen to me." sneered Alice with a wicked grin. Susan turned her head glaring at Alice not saying a word but Alice recognized the message and returned her eyes to the newspaper sporting a sly grin.

Peter Lomax was almost in tears and now trembling.

"**Sean,** in the bottom left drawer of the desk in the office you will find a bottle of brandy. I think he could use some. I think we could all use some." commanded Susan

Without thinking Sean ran through the kitchen toward the back office. As he disappeared from view Alice in a *(I told you so)* voice stated;

"**You** shouldn't have let him go alone you know. You may never see him again."

Susan glared as before. The minutes passed in silence. Pete was sobbing softly into Susan's shoulder, slightly calmer than he was earlier. You could see the concern building in Susan's eyes as she looked at the clock knowing that she may have just sent him to his death.

Six minutes passed with no sign of Sean.

"Where's your little sailor boy now sweety." wickedly sneered Alice.

Come with us." ordered Susan. "The three of us together will check in the kitchen."

"What's the use deary. He's probably gone just like the rest of them." Smiled Alice.

"Just get up and shut up" ordered Susan angrily.

Alice annoyed at Susan's tone, did stand up, however slowly, and maintained her smile. The trio made their way to the kitchen with Alice laughing and mumbling incoherent remarks all the way. Pete started calling Sean's name but as they all suspected there was no reply.

"I told you so." uttered Alice now knowing she was in control. "I knew he was gone before we came in here because I'm the one who made him go away. Now you will both do what I say for a change."

"What do you mean by that ?" asked Susan quickly.

"Don't be so naive, sweety. Who do you think has been in charge all along." answered Alice haughtily.

"And what do you mean by that ?" Susan repeated more challengingly.

"You humans are so ignorant. You haven't figured any of this out yet. I don't know why we even bother coming to places like this." said Alice, her very uncivil attitude showing it's ugly head. It's a waste of my valuable time. I wish they would give me assignments to equal my talents."

Pete and Susan were both looking confused now. They stared at each other questioningly.

"Come on kids, why are you being so stupid. Can't you tell when you are facing your superiors? " Alice continued.

"Certainly not in manners." replied Susan as a challenge.

"Oh so you do have a little spunk left in you. Don't sass me young one. I have dissolved better challengers than you."

Pete, who was normally not very confrontational, had enough of Alice and stepped forward to restrain her. Alice laughed at his movement and extended her arm full length barely touching his chest sending him awkwardly backwards, slamming him into the counter. Susan was instantly at his side. Pete recovered looking rather embarrassed.

"You people are pathetic. Will you never learn anything? " Alice sneered again.

"Okay Miss Control Freak, if we are so stupid, why don't you enlighten us? " Susan threw out as a challenge again, hoping to buy some time.

Alice hesitated not liking the challenges. Her silence lasted more than a minute.

"Okay earthling, I'll enlighten you, for all the good it's going to do. Then I'll watch you slowly dissolve into nothing so I can hear you suffer. I'm tired of playing these silly games. I'll explain what would have been obvious to intelligent beings. Hopefully your putty like minds will be able to comprehend."

Alice was half laughing, almost evilly, while she was saying this.

"You see we are an advanced people, who in my opinion shouldn't be bothering with the likes of you. But my governor's wish is to pursue studys of inferior beings. I have been assigned this galaxy. I will not go into details of my mission however. In your particular case I think I will just dematerialize you slowly for my entertainment. There should be no loss to your world with your absence. This storm you see is just my way of making my job a little more exciting. I like to see my inferiors struggle in their lack of intelligence. It amuses me. And you Mr. Hero." Alice turned her attention to Pete. "I'm going to allow you to join her in the land of disassembled molecules. Now do either of you beings have any other questions? " she asked pleased with herself.

"Oh don't look so sad you two." using a sing song voice, "Just think how nice your world will be without you in it."

Laughing at her own attempt at humor Alice then retrieved a dull silver looking tube from her coat. Pushing a few buttons a low hum emanated from the tube.

"Now my friends, it's time to slowly say goodbye."

Pointing the mysterious tube at the bewildered pair and laughing Alice pushed the large blue colored button.

Awaiting their unknown fate Pete and Susan looked at each other, not with fear but with admiration.

They waited- - - , Nothing happened.

A look of shock took possession of Alice's face. Hurriedly she pushed the trigger button a second time. Nothing happened. Panic was now in her eyes.

"Having problems Ankur 3."

It was Mike's voice as he appeared in the kitchen doorway.
"YOU !" was Alice's startled answer.
"But how ? I disassembled you ! I broke you into atoms.
Alice was now showing actual fear.
"How did you know my title ? Who are you ?"
"I am Zandok 2, your superior and overseer."
"Why are you here. You were not assigned this galaxy. You are supposed to be in the Fetis 3 quadrant."
Confused once again, Susan and Pete watched intently what was taking place before them. Alice or Ankur 3 was shaken, trying to come to terms about the situation facing her. Regaining her composure and putting false courage in her voice she challenged Mike.

"You have no right to be here. You are abusing your authority. The Grand Council shall hear about this in my report."

Pleased with herself she gained confidence with her words thus continuing her verbal assault.

"Now stand aside, and let me fulfill my job."

Zandok 2, not threatened in the least, moved even closer to Alice or Ankur 3.

"That is the very problem Ankur 3. You are not completing your assignments as given. Threatening and dematerializing study subjects is not your assignment. And as for the Grand Council, they have harbored suspicions of you for quite sometime. That is the reason I am here, and from what I have seen so far those suspicions are well founded."

Frightened and pale Ankur 3 was silent. Her eyes were constantly moving now as if looking for an escape avenue, though she knew it was a useless effort.

"Ankur 3, it is you who is abusing your position. You have been dematerializing all of your study subjects. You have been falsifying your study records. You have been interfering with these peoples lives. That is not your mission. Our's is a non interfering study project. These beings have done you no harm. I am surprised at your behavior Ankur 3. Surprised and disappointed. Because of your training record I supported your appointment to this elevated position. I can see now, after these last few days what a miscalculation in judgement we have made. I must say your act was extremely convincing. How well you pretended to be upset and concerned. Your sobbing method was well portrayed. One would almost think it was real. That much effort should have been put into compassion for these beings not disdain.

"But they are all so stupid and backward." Alice reported disgustedly. "Why should we bother with such ignorance? "

"You may not remember Ankur 3, but we were once as these subjects and the Ancient Ones helped us become what we now are. When these beings are ready we will do the same for them."

"Why should we wait, we can extinguish them all and move on to a more worthwhile project." Alice was now smiling. "Join me, help me dissolve these last two and no one will know ." proposed the pseudo Alice.

"The others will know." answered Zandok 2.

"What others." slipped Alice.

"The beings you thought you eliminated earlier." replied Zandok 2 calmly. "I was able to neutralize your unit before you used it on the other subjects as I will do again if necessary.

A flush drained Alice's complexion, hate filling her eyes. Then as she watched, one by one, wisps of vapor appeared. Out of each stepped the missing diner patrons until all five were present. Stunned, they looked around at each other in utter bewilderment, not quite cognizant of their surroundings.

Frightened and obviously shaking, Ankur 3 ran to the door while pointing her weapon at Mike. She hastily pushed the main button which failed to produce any result. She looked down at the weapon mystified as Zandok 2 fired his. The nine diner people watched, unbelieving, as Ankur 3, who they knew as Alice, vaporized into nothingness.

Frightened, but ready to move against Mike or Zandok, the five absentees were stopped by Susan.

"Wait, I can explain." she yelled.

Zandok 2 was not concerned by the threat but allowed Susan, along with Pete, to outline the present circumstances. They listened to the explanation, their eyes constantly shifting from Susan and Pete to Mike. But now there were two Mikes.

Tim interrupted;

"Alice ! What about Alice ?"

He seemed very upset.

"Your Alice is quite safe and perfectly alright. She will be joining us shortly."

"But she disappeared right before our eyes." said Hank.

"What you saw being dematerialized was Ankur 3. She also is safely demobilized. She is now restrained back on our mother ship. Her actions will be dealt with by our Grand Council."

The atmosphere was calmer now but confusion still showed on every one's face. The other Mike (aka Zandok 2) spoke softly.

"There is usually no need for explanations of our actions. Our study procedure has been harmless and totally undetectable. But in light of the present circumstances I feel an obligation to answer your questioning minds. I, too, would feel as you had the situation been reversed. Please sit, all of you. You are in no danger any more."

As the group moved to various locations to seat themselves a vaporous mist appeared again returning the real Alice to her friends. Susan immediately went to her softly whispering;

"I'll explain this all later. Sit with me. Everything is alright."

When all were seated comfortably Zandok 2 resumed speaking.

"I know this seems rather bizarre to you and I will try to clarify everything for you. As you have already determined I am not of your world. I come from a galaxy far beyond your knowledge.
Our mission, I assume you also have figured out, is purely a fact gathering, non - interfering study project. There are many habitable worlds in this universe and I'm sure there are others we have not discovered. We are only trying to determine status of advancement both morally and scientifically. We have no goal of conquering and subjugation. To what final end are we using

these study's we do not even know ourselves. You do not have anything to fear from us. I doubt travel between our two worlds will ever come about. The distance is far too great. We have been in what you could call suspended animation for over three hundred of your years just to get here. Our normal procedure is to only take one being at a time. Usually some one who is alone. We perform both mental and physical scans to procure data which we feel show's growth maturity and then return that person to exactly where we found them. There is no memory recall what so ever from this procedure. When I leave, even you, will recall no knowledge of these last few days. Your lives will be as normal as if none of this took place."

"How did you replace us in our body's." asked Mike who felt funny talking to himself.

"We developed the ability to morph our own physical being into any form we wish to copy. We do not take over your body's or minds. We scan you minds so that we may emulate everything you do, so that we appear to be the real thing. In this particular case, our Ankur 3 obviously turned rogue. Normally you would never have been aware of our existence. I, as you already know was able to neutralize anything she did in order to keep you safe. By the way all your vehicles will be returned safely. No harm was done. I realize this has been a quick explanation but because of Ankur's antics I am behind schedule and I must take my leave. Good luck. I wish you all a very peaceful future."

Zandok 2 started fading away as pixels on a computer screen until he was non - existent. The nine people of the diner drifted off to sleep.

~ ~ ~ ~ ~ ~

Mike Cassady climbed out of his Peterbilt tractor shielding his eye from the wind blown snow as he made his way to the diner. Dawn was just becoming evident, darkness prevailing longer than usual because of the storm. He guessed the snow to be about fifteen or sixteen inches as he struggled to keep his footing. As he opened the door a wind gust nearly took it off the hinges along with his arm. With some extra effort he managed to pull it closed, but not before a few inches of snow covered the floor.

"Thanks for the extra snow Mike, I was beginning to run out of ice." Quipped Susan, the auburn haired woman behind the counter. She was owner, chief cook, waitress and dishwasher of this popular truck stop diner. It was called the "Welcome to the Nowhere Diner" because of it's location in the middle of nowhere on a sparsely traveled road in Converse County, Wyoming.

Mike welcomed the enveloping warmth as he unbuttoned his heavy wool jacket. He sat at the counter and Susan had a mug of black coffee waiting.

Big Ed Grimes poked his head out from the kitchen pass

through:

"**S**ome weather out there , huh Mike ? Being snowed in like this in an isolated diner reminds me of a "Twilight Zone" type story from years ago. You know aliens and all that.

"**D**on't be silly Ed." said Alice, the local rural mail carrier. "Things like that don't happen in real life."

-41-

The End

The Perfect Christmas

BY
Ken Goss

THE PERFECT CHRISTMAS

Many years ago, I don't recall exactly how many, I learned a valued lesson I'll never forget. It was one of those things you read about in stories, or hear from a church pulpit. Hearing or reading about love, sharing, humility and happiness sounds all well and good, but for the most part they are just as quickly ignored or forgotten. After all they are just stories, stories to think about and perhaps aspire to. The emulation of such things could help you to be a better person, at least I'm sure that is the intent of such teachings.

To actually witness such happenings is truly a humbling experience.

This all came about through my daughter who worked for a family preservation agency in the county she lived in, in another state.

She spoke highly of this single mother of three, whose husband died in an accident three or four years ago, who was struggling to keep her family together and was holding two jobs in order to attain this goal. Oh, there was assistance from the county and state, but not nearly enough to help turn the lady's life around. She worked tirelessly to make ends meet, yet as she made a little extra money to try and move forward, in turn, that much more was withheld by the state assistance. She was walking up a down escalator and getting nowhere. This catch twenty two, however did not dampen this woman's enthusiasm or deter her determination to move upward.

It being Christmas time, my daughter was making her holiday rounds and asked if I cared to join her. I immediately said yes. I wanted very much to meet this "Wonder Woman".

Thirty some odd minutes later we were parked in front of a small, in much need of repair, house in a not too nice neighborhood. Despite the needed attention to the physical structure, it's appearance was neat and orderly. The yard and grounds were clean and picked up. It was so well

groomed it almost seemed out of place for the surrounding neighborhood.
I smiled to myself, actually pleased to see what was before me. My daughter
smiled at me smiling, knowing what I was feeling.

We approached the front door and knocked quietly. Within
seconds we saw a curtain pushed aside at a front window and were greeted
with the animated faces of a girl and a boy. A shriek of recognition for my
daughter could be heard through the closed door. Moments later the door
opened as we were welcomed by a not unattractive woman of early thirties I
guessed. She wore a genuine smile as she greeted my daughter with a hug that
could only be given with love. I was introduced, and she took my hand with
the warmth of her affection and it passed to me and instantly touched my
heart. She appeared actually happy that I had come with my daughter. Her
three children stood quietly behind her sporting grins from ear to ear. Each,
it turn was presented to me proudly, and each in turn greeted me in their own
way showing true warmth. I guessed the ages of the two girls and one boy at
approximately seven, nine and eleven, the boy being in the middle. Their
manners and behavior was the first thing that showed.

As the children escorted us to the living room, I could not
help but notice the cleanliness and neatness of the house interior. Don't get
me wrong, it was a well lived in house as any house with three kids would be,
but even the disorder of toys had a neatness about them.
Upon entering the living room I beheld a most beautiful sight.
A Christmas tree decorated like I had never seen before.
"We cut it ourselves." volunteered the boy.
"We all helped." added his little sister.
"It was a family outing. We always make it an old fashioned
Christmas." explained the proud mother.

The tree itself was a little sparse. I made it out to be about
six feet and held only one set of very old colored lights. But the beauty of the
tree was it's decorations. I counted only a half dozen glass balls, all the rest
were handmade ornaments. Not just hastily thrown together paper things
either. They were carefully hand crafted with precise care. Wood, plastic,
soda cans, aluminum foil and paint of many colors were changed into the
beauty before me. There were log cabins, birds, butterflies snow flakes and
stars. Real ginger bread cookies and cardboard candy canes, gold and silver
foil chains topped off this master piece of design. It's presentation was
literally breathtaking. Rockefeller Center Plaza had nothing on this tree.
In the corner, next to the tree, was a scene that topped it all.
A creche obviously, made by hand, had it's own place of honor. The stable

was made of twigs and sticks, most likely from their own yard, yet assembled with a reality that drew you in. The figures of the Holy Family, the Kings shepherds and even the animals were cut from cardboard. The detail was drawn and painted with the love and care of true artist's. I had never seen such love and perfection put into old scraps of cardboard.

I was awestruck as was my daughter. The extremely proud mother stood there, her three children gathered about her and all four with beaming smiles.

"We made this collection of ornaments over many years, we add some each year. The children take great pride in their artistic talents." the mother, Lisa, I believe was her name, commented.

"As well they should." I replied softly. I felt my chest swell as if I was sharing their pride.

Lisa then directed the oldest girl to make tea for their guests.

"That's not necessary." I said politely. " We shouldn't be interrupting your day like this."

"Nonsense." Lisa smiled. "We don't have guests very often, so please let us pamper you."

The children animatedly agreed with mom.

Tea was served with great style along with a platter of homemade Christmas cookies.

We stayed for a while with each child telling stories of how they made their presents, of course without revealing too much detail to give away the secret of the precious gifts. I was totally taken in by this family's spirit and true love.

As we were getting ready to leave, Lisa spoke of how people commented on them as to how poor they were.

"If we are, we are not aware of it." she said.

The eldest of the children remarked sincerely;

"How can we be poor, when we have all this." she emphasized her words with a wide sweep of her open arms.

We said our goodbyes with warm hugs and kisses and finally left. Out side I looked at my daughter and gently remarked,

"I almost did not want to leave."

"I knew you would feel that way." she answered.

The ride back to her house was quiet, neither of us wanting to break the mood of what we experienced.

Later that day I suggested to my daughter we go shopping for some gifts and toys for the three children to give them a merry Christmas. We convinced each other, which was not hard to do, that this would be a good thing and off we went to the nearest shopping mall.

Back home with our newly purchased treasures we proceeded to wrap them as gayly as we could. Our plan of attack was discussed while we wrapped. I would go to Lisa's early Christmas morning and leave the goodies at the front door as quietly as possible and disappear before they realized anything.

Feeling good about ourselves we toasted Christmas with some eggnog and went to bed thinking of Santa.

I slept a little later than I planned but was still early enough for my Santa Clause visit. Arriving at Lisa's at about a quarter to six, I parked a few houses away and continued on foot. I tiptoed up the front steps but as I gained the top step of the porch I could hear voices and laughter inside the house. I stood there quietly listening. I felt a little guilty about prying into their privacy but I could not help myself. Christmas music was playing in the background mixed with a lot of ooo's and ahhh's. This was one of the happiest Christmas's I can ever recall. True happiness. I found myself humbled. I was trying to give them a merry Christmas but instead they gave me a Christmas I will never forget.

I looked at the packages in my arms and thought about the others still in the car. I made up my mind then and there not to give them the wrapped gifts. Why commercialize their Christmas. They were already in possession of the perfect Christmas. I could not improve on what they had nor did I want to try.

I silently left contemplating the lesson I had learned. On the way back to my daughter's I passed a local hospital and anonymously left the gifts at the children's ward. I actually felt better for having done so.

Since then my Christmas's have become much less commercial and much, much more satisfying. Giving, loving and sharing doesn't cost a single penny.

The End.

Another Day

by
K.J.Goss

Another Day

It was dark and stormy in the city and as usual I was out walking in it. Of course it was dark, it was night time. I was meandering by the river looking at the stars which were not visible since it was stormy. I decided to wander on to one of the docks, however since I was looking for the stars I failed to see the sign saying closed for repairs. The next thing I knew I was plunged into icy cold waters deep into darkness. It was then I remembered it was January, hence accounting for the icy cold waters. I recovered myself and saw a light above and I pulled hard at the water up to the light. I soared up through the surface at a great speed, and in doing so hit my head on the bookshelf mounted on the wall above my bed. Obviously my dream got the better of me.

I reached up to my head only to feel a large open gash from which copious amounts of blood, my blood, flowed. Looking at the fast staining bed clothes I realized that perhaps I needed medical attention. Lucky for me I lived in this big city and a hospital was only two blocks away.

I quickly threw some clothes on and headed for the elevator of my apartment building. I pushed open the doors, again failing to see the sign saying **"DO NOT USE"** and proceeded to fall three floors down. The angels were with me though; my fall was broken by the cables and gears connected to the top of the elevator car. Still, I considered myself lucky, I remained with one good leg and I believe only my one wrist was broken.

I managed to make it to the street and figured a taxi might be in order. It only took twenty minutes to flag one down. The cab driver, obviously in a hurry, started to take off before I was completely in the car. The open door hit my right side and pushed me out of, and down onto the curb. The rear wheel caught the ankle of my good leg, ran over it, and crushed the bone. Not one prone to ill spirits, I figured it could have been worse.

With a forced smile I continued on my way, crawling the best I could. I was amazed at how any dirty looks and nasty comments I didn't receive. The most difficult part was getting up the ten steps into the hospital building itself.

At last obtaining my goal, I was picked up by some attendants and put on a Gurney and wheeled to a private screening room. Luck was with me again, I only had to wait two and a half hours, then was transferred to another area.

The crying out and moaning awakened me somewhat. It was enough though to realize I was in the delivery room. The angels were still with me, it only took another hour to convince them I was not there to have a baby. They were more than willing then to present me with their bill and politely discharge me. I really have no comments on the hospital food, I guess I wasn't there long enough to rate a meal.

Back on the streets of my beloved city, I just started counting my blessings when this young man in a ski mask pulled a knife and demanded my wallet. Well, the first thing he saw in my wallet was the hospital bill. He moved closer, looked me over carefully, mumbled the words "I'm sorry.", reached into his pocket and gave me a one hundred dollar bill and turned and left. I felt better already.

Because of my appearance, I took a shortcut through an alley, crawling a little slower then I was before but I was making progress. I suddenly heard a noise above me and as I looked up a fire escape ladder came rushing down, caught my shoulder and flattened me to the ground. I started to move to get up when a large, booted foot came down hard on my back. Not to worry though, I don't think too many ribs were broken.

I continued on my way envisioning home and a good nights sleep. Once out of the alley I took up the direction of my apartment. As luck would have it I met with the local beat cop, who after a couple of swats with his night stick, told me to get off the street, he did not want any pan handlers on his beat.

It was slow going after that, yet , I did attain my goal. I reached the corner of my block where I met one of the lovely's of the evening. It was obvious she took pity on me because of my condition and after some light conversation she took my one hundred dollar bill on account, in case we should meet again in California. I had trouble figuring that one out because I live in New York.

I did make it home however, just as the sun was coming up. It was good to feel it's warmth on my face. I managed to successfully navigate my way to my apartment and once inside settled in me dried bloody bed. I thanked my lucky stars for such a wonderful night. It could have been much worse, I could have caught a cold being out in the rain.

Oh well! Tomorrow is another day.

The End

Family History

by
Ken Goss

Chapter 1

"It was bitter cold this Christmas night. Twas not a night for any man or Critter. The snow was stained red by the Blood of them whose shoes were broke through. Some of the men hadn't any shoes atal. They wrapped their swollen feet in rags if'n they could find any. We was heddin for the river. Twas the Delaware. The general wanted to crost it tonite so's we kin catch them murderin Hessions whilst they was sleepin. Looks like it's gonna be another hard nite. The rivers almost froze solid. Boats been ferryin men acrost for a couple a hours now. My turns cummin next. - - - - - - -

Sure am glad to be on land agin. Snow an all. At least it's not movin an rockin. The river water woulda froze a man as kwik as a shot. Them men from up Boston way sure know how to hand'l them boats. Ice an all. I guess it's cold up that way to. Looks like we're on the march agin. Gotta make Trenton afore sun up. - - - - - - - -.

We're splittin inta 2 collums now so's we kin attack from 2 directions at the same time. I'm in the one led by the

The door to the den opened quietly and an attractive woman of thirty three poked her head in.

"We're home Tom. How about some lunch."

There was no answer from the man deep in concentration of the surrounding old battered book he held carefully.

"Tom." said the woman a little louder as she walked further into the room.

The man still had not moved. Approaching closer, and reaching out to touch his shoulder, the woman spoke again with concern in her voice.

"Are you alright, Tom ?"

Shaken from his hypnotic state, the man looked up at his wife.

"Oh hi Hon, you're home."

"Are you alright, Tom." she repeated.

"Yeah, why ?" he answered.

"I called you a few times and you didn't budge. What's that you're reading and what's the big box ?

"Hi Dad, look what I just bought." said Tom junior holding up a new baseball glove. "Wow ! What's in the big box ?"

He reached down to move the box flap to get a better look.

"Be careful ! Don't touch that." was Tom Sr's slightly alarmed answer.

The young man quickly pulled his arm away, a confused expression now covering his face.

"Sorry son, I didn't mean to yell."

Looking up at his wife again and holding the old book a little higher he asked,

"Do you know what this is ?"

"Of course not, that's why I asked."

"This is a diary." he continued not really listening to what her answer was.

Turning his gaze to his son, "This is a piece of history." he went on.

Looking back to his wife again he added, "A piece of real history."

"Fine, so you found an old book.: answered Carleen. I'm going to fix some lunch." she said uninterested as she turned to move away.

"No wait Hon." Tom said excitedly. "Let me explain. Sit

down both of you, please."

Mother and son looked at each other a bit confused but did as he asked. Tom anxiously went on before they were even settled.

"UPS delivered this box while you were out shopping. I was a bit curious myself, because I wasn't expecting anything. When I opened the box I found this letter."

He very carefully put the ragged book down in his lap and reached in the box for the letter. A three named law firm was imprinted on the envelope.

"It seems that when my great grand father passed away in two thousand three, can you imagine he was ninety nine years old," he interrupted himself, "Well anyway, it apparently took forever to locate his will and settle his estate. I didn't know he even had anything. Unfortunately I never even knew the man."

Turning to his son he said,

"Try not to let that happen to you Son. Always keep in touch with family."

Carleen, showing a slight sign of impatience said,

"Get on with it Tom, I have lunch to make.

Ignoring her remark and with excitement still in his voice he continued,

"He really didn't have much. Most of what he did have went to pay expenses after his death. His most precious possession was what's in this box."

"It looks like just some papers and a few old books." said Tom Jr.

"Exactly." answered his father. "But *what* old books." he said emphasizing the what. "These are diary's. Old diary's, written by my great, great, great, oh I don't know how many greats to go back that far, but written by mine, and yours Son, an ancestor during the Revolutionary War."

Picking up the book from his lap again, he opened it and read aloud the same page he was reading when they interrupted him. He paused at the same place and looked up at his wife and son.

"That general he's talking about is George Washington. My ancestor knew and fought with George Washington."

When he repeated the name of Washington you could detect a note of reverence in his voice.

"Now really Tom, aren't you going a little too far. I know you read a lot of Revolutionary War history, and admire George Washington, but now it's like you are trying to make a wish come true."

Tom gazed at his wife with a look of hurt in his eyes.

"But I'm not making this up. There are all sorts of letters, documents and papers here."

He was frantically looking through a pile of envelopes while talking.

"Here, this is what I was looking for. This is a letter from some sort of expert historian certifying Washington's signature on a document. I haven't found the document in question yet, but I'm sure it must be in here."

Carleen took the envelope, opened and read it.

"Dad ?" asked Tom Jr. "Can I look at one of the diary's?"

"Of course Son but be very careful. They're a bit on the fragile side." answered the father.

Carleen finished reading the report and commented,

"I guess you do have something to be excited about."

She viewed the box with a totally different attitude now as she also reached for one of the diary's.

"Listen to this." Tommy almost shouted excitedly.

"*January, I don't know what, 1780.*

We bin on haff rations for a cupple a weeks now. Some days we don't git bread, some days we don't git meat. Some days we don't git either. This winter is colder'n Valley Forge was back in 77. They said we were at Morristown Hites. My farm is in Morristown, but this sure don't look anything like it. They said we was totally out of food now, so we have to git it from the people in the countryside. I volinteered some of my cows and grain. The General hisself signed my certificate for payment after the war. I even got to go git it. It was sure nice to see my wife and children agin. Even for those few days -

- - - -

It's gitten even colder now. We was told that New York Bay was froze solid but we don't even have enuff powder to make an attak."

"**I** don't remember anything like that in the history books in school." remarked Tommy with surprise and concern in his voice.

"**I'**m not surprised." answered Tom. "Today they just seem to gloss over the real facts and only concentrate on a few dates."

"**D**on't go getting cynical again Tom." interrupted Carleen

"**B**ut it's true." countered Tom. "Our own history is being lost and replaced by global concerns."

Suddenly changing the subject he said as if surprised,

"**T**hat must be it. George Washington's signature on

the certificate of payment. That's probably the reason for the authentication letter."

Tom immediately started going through the box, sorting envelopes, papers and diary's.

"**W**ell, while you're doing that I'll go fix lunch. We still have to eat you know." said Carleen as she headed for the kitchen.

Chapter 2

"Listen to this one Dad." as Tommy read another diary.

> "*January, 1777.   Them Hessions is not even human. They are only fighting for money and spoils. All kinds of reports has come in of them rapin the women folk, murderin woman and children alike. They burn barns and houses of purely innocent folk. They are even killin farm animals, not to eat but just for fun. Some of the red- coats are startin to be just like them. They drink and laff while they're killin. The people in Jersey are finally startin to come around to our patriotic cause.. We must defeat them British and save our freedom.*"

"I never heard about that either." Tommy repeated.

"You know there are libraries and many books about the Revolutionary War, Tom" answered his father. "I'm sure there is even information on line. Try looking for Washington Irving books about George Washington and the war."

"Why cant I just read these diary's ?" questioned Tommy.

"You can and should." Tom returned. "We all should, but I'm sure they don't cover everything. These are just one man's experience and viewpoint. Remember there are always many sides to a story. Especially one as big as the War for our independence from Britain. The more sides to a story you get the better your understanding of the issue.

"Yes Dad." was Tommy's reply said sort of disgustedly as if he was annoyed at being preached to.

"Sorry Tommy. I didn't mean to go off on a lecture." apologized Tom Sr. "I think we can all have fun and learn something from these diary's. This is what real history is all about.

"Believe it or not I really am interested and excited about this Dad."

Suddenly Toms eyes grew larger and in a raised slightly raised voice he interrupted,

"Here it is. This is the certificate they were talking about, In order to feed the army, Congress authorized the issue of certificates to the civilians who were willing to share their crops and livestock. These certificates specified the quantity of goods and terms of payment. The goods being the animals for meat or grains for bread and so on. This one", he held up the paper in his hand, "was the one given to our ancestor."

Tom opened the envelope slowly while Tommy anxiously looked on. Gently, he unfolded the paper and there it was.
George Washington's own written signature. The two stared at the paper in total silence. Carleen's soft shout of "Lunch is ready." shook them out of their trance. They smiled at each other, excitement in their eyes. Tommy jumped up running to the kitchen happily yelling,

"We found it, Mom. Dad found the certificate. We have the real George Washington autograph."

"Calm down Tommy." was Carleen's cautioning retort. "You don't have to shout the walls down."

"Sorry Mom, but you should see it. It's as clear as if it was just written."

Tom Sr. Followed Tommy to the kitchen at a slower pace carefully carrying the paper as if it were fragile glass. Carleen looked at it and was also brought under it's spell. All three were in silent contemplation. After many seconds passed, Tom carefully refolded the precious paper and returned it to it's protective envelope.

"Let's eat." he said. "I'll be right back, I'm going to put this away in the den for now."

As he returned to the kitchen, Tommy asked with a mouth full of roast beef sandwich,

"Can I shake dem to schoool."

"No you can not, and don't talk with your mouth full." corrected Carleen.

Tommy lowered his eyes disappointed. Tom looked at his son

while making himself a sandwich.

"At least not just yet." he continued what Carleen had said. "We have a lot of work to do first."

Not waiting for any other comments he explained his thinking.

"We have not yet looked at or read everything. There are papers and envelopes unopened I think I would like to make an inventory of what's there and put it in order of date, or category of subject matter.

"Can I help." interrupted Tommy enthusiastically.

"Of course you can, I would hope that both of you would." was Tom's reply.

"It might be fun at that." added Carleen. "I was never much of a history buff, but this is really a personal history now. You always said you wanted to do a genealogy search. This is a great start."

The three Chadwick's finished lunch joking and smiling, anxious to start their new project.

Chapter 3

Tom and Tommy headed back to the den while Carleen straightened up the kitchen. She joined them only moments later. As they settled around the box, Tom quietly spoke,

"I don't think we should mention this to anybody just yet. At least until we have the whole story of what's in this box."

"I agree." smiled Carleen.

Both Tom and Carleen looked at Tommy. He looked back at his parents smiling and said,

"I know you're right, but it's not going to be easy. It's not every day one finds out they have a connection with our first president. I promise Dad, but I can't wait to read one of these dairy's in school. Oh heck, I want to read all of them."

The family laughingly set about their new task. Tom and Carleen started with the papers and envelopes while Tommy carefully tried to put the diary's in order of date. Quite some time was passed in silence as they became absorbed in history. Real history. Finally Carleen spoke quietly,

"Look at this Tom. It's a letter your great, great, great whatever grandfather wrote about not cashing in the food voucher. He also indicates another paper somewhere hoping to start a family history of keeping his story alive. I guess the government still owes you some money." she added jokingly.

"Oh, wow ! How much do you think we'll get ?" questioned Tommy, his eyes all aglow.

"Absolutely nothing." Tom answered firmly. "These papers are priceless."

"I know that Dad. I was only joking." said Tommy laughing.

Tom smiled back and sort of thinking out loud added,

"I wonder though, what they would be worth, especially after all these years. What with interest and inflation for lets say two hundred and thirty two years. We could pay for Tommy's college, buy a new car, take a long vacation - - - - - - ."

"Dad," said Tommy seriously now. "I was only kidding. You

can't sell George Washington's signature. That's a family treasure. Some day my treasure or my son's treasure. I won't let you do it. It wouldn't be - - - - - - -."

Tom Sr. interrupted , "Whoa, slow down boy. Now who's serious and whose joking."

Tommy looked at his father a little embarrassed and then started laughing. All three were soon laughing.

"Let me see that ?" asked Tom holding his hand out to his wife.

Carleen handed the letter and envelope to him and then turned her attention to the box to retrieve another treasure.

"Benedict Arnold, Dad, Benedict Arnold. This one talks about Benedict Arnold." without taking a breath, Tommy began to read aloud.

"Sept, 1780. Am still with the General. Now in New York. Heard Rumors today that General Benedict Arnold tried to sell out the fort at West Point and now has retreated to the British. They caught a redcoat Major Andre' who was spy'n with Arnold. The General's not going to be happy about this. He really admired Benedict Arnold and all he had done for the cause. Don't know why this happened yet. Looks like they're gonna hang that Major Andre'

Tommy paused to comment,
"Wow Dad, this is just like being there."

Carleen could also feel the change in herself as she got caught up in the excitement. *"What a wonderful way to learn history."* She thought to herself.

The rest of the afternoon into early evening passed without notice. Some progress was made but there was still a lot to do. Most of the papers were organized by date, but only a few had thoroughly been read. Tommy found that not all the diary's were just the Revolutionary War. There were some from other generations which really peaked everyone's interest.

"Oh my." exclaimed Carleen. "It's seven fifteen already. I forgot all about supper."

"Who cares. This has been fun." chimed in Tommy.

Tom Sr. sat back and stretched.

"Why don't I just get some Chinese take out. It's too late for you to start fussing now. We can leave everything just the way it is and pick it up again tomorrow."

"That would be great." Carleen responded. "And thank you." she moved to her husband and kissed him on the cheek. "I'll set the table while you're gone. Come on Tommy, that's enough for today. You can help me in the kitchen, besides the garbage has to go out."

"Aw Mom." Tommy whined as he got to his feet.

Carleen gave him a soft pat on his butt as he walked past her.

"I'm going, I'm going." he laughingly complained.

Chapter 4

Having returned with their take away supper, Tom went to the fridge to retrieve a beer while Carleen spread out the containers on the table. Tommy was already biting into an egg roll as he inquired about the next step.

"I'm glad tomorrow's Sunday so we can continue with the diary's but where do we go from here."

"I'm not rushing into anything just yet. These papers have been held by the family for over two hundred years, so what's the hurry. And hurry to do what ?" answered Tom with his question.

"I don't know." returned Tommy, "Maybe it really is worth something."

"But why would we want to sell our family history ?" Tom again questioned. "One thing at a time, first we have to find out what we really have and next you have to pass the fried rice."

Tommy smiled and pushed the carton towards his father.

"You know." said Carleen quietly, "If all these diary's really contain that much history, you could always write a book."

Both father and son looked at each other as if to say *"why didn't I think of that."*

Tommy immediately chimed in with, "And we can title it. ***Tom Chadwick Jr.'s amazing family history***, in three volumes."

"And since when did all of this become your's ?" inquired Tom Sr. "I'm not dead yet you know."

"Well I am the rightful heir." answered Tommy with a put on snobby attitude.

"Since when did I get cut out of all this." Tom asked again.

"Now cut it out you two." Carleen scolded, "Or I'll put away your toy's and send you both to your room's.

"You wouldn't dare." remarked Tom with a mock look of shock on his face.

"You better watch out Dad, I think Mom's just mean enough to do it." Tommy mumbled.

"Just for that young man you will get no dessert."

admonished Carleen trying to look serious.

"See Dad, didn't I tell you she was mean." mumbled Tommy again.

The three finished their meal in a much relaxed and jovial manner. All agreed not to do any more reading this night and instead watched an old movie on TV.

Chapter 5

Sunrise the next morning found Tommy already up, dressed and carefully dusting the old diary's as he put them in chronological order. He had set up the folding card table in a corner near the book shelf for easy access but still out of the way. Tom Sr. stood quietly at the room entrance proudly watching his son.

"He handled those old books even more gently than I do." he thought to himself.

He found this rather unique in this day and age of computers, for a thirteen year old boy to take such an interest in his nations history. *"I guess George Washington still held influence over people even two hundred plus years later."* he thought again.

Sensing he was being watched, Tommy turned towards the door,

"Oh hi Dad. I hope you don't mind, I wanted to get an early start."

"Good morning Son. No I don't mind. I'm rather proud that you have taken such an interest."

Tommy felt a little embarrassed but was also pleased at his father's comments. To get out of the uneasiness he felt, Tommy matter of factly stated,

"I already put the coffee on for you Dad."

"Thanks Tommy, why don't you join me in the kitchen and we can talk."

"Sure Dad." answered young Tom, "I'm just about finished here anyway."

In the kitchen Tommy poured a large glass of orange juice while his father filled his favorite mug with coffee.

"Sit down Son." Tom motioned to his son while seating himself. Tommy sat down, sipped at his juice, all the time studying his father.

"What's up Dad, why so serious."

"Well, I was thinking myself to sleep last night and reflecting on what your Mother said." Tom answered staring at the dark coffee in his cup.

"About what ?" inquired Tommy quietly.

Looking directly into his son's eyes Tom continues,

"What would you think about writing a book ?"

Excitement flashed in the young boy's eyes.

"Really Dad !! That's great. I can help you do research. I'm already working on putting the journals in order. I can go to the library too and read some other history books so we can make a comparison. We can reprint George Washington's signature and maybe find some pictures to use. And then we can - - - - - ."

Tom Sr. interrupted his son.

"Whoa boy, slow down. You've got the book already published and I haven't even finished my coffee.

Looking at his Dad a little embarrassed Tommy put his head down quietly mumbling, "Sorry Dad."

Reaching across the table and gently squeezing his son's arm, Tom lovingly said

"Nothing to be embarrassed about Son, I'm overwhelmed by your enthusiasm. I wasn't meaning to put you down."

Like the flip of a switch Tommy was fired up again.

"When do we start ?" he queried

"It's just an idea." answered Tom. "Lets wait and discuss this with your Mother."

"Discuss what ?" Carleen soft voice was heard from behind them. "What are you two plotting now." leaning over to plant a gentle kiss on her son's forehead.

"The book, Mom. We're gonna write a book. We're gonna do research and get pictures and - - - -."

Carleen cut him short questioning,

"Gonna ? Your gonna write a book when you can't even speak correctly." she said smiling.

"Aw , you know what I mean, Mom." Tommy replied laughingly.

Carleen poured herself a cup of coffee and joined her two favorite men at the table.

"Now tell me what's **going** on." She emphasized the word going while looking directly at her son with a smile. She then turned her gaze to her husband waiting for his reply.

"Well, you mentioned yesterday about a book and I did a lot of thinking about that in bed last night. I think the idea has merit. Based on the few things Tommy read from the diaries, it would be looking at history from a whole new angle. It would not be interpretive. It would be actual from one who was there. The political cause and effect would not be foremost, but the results of those of John Q. Citizen would be evident, showing a whole new side of our struggle for independence."

"**W**ow ! you did do some serious thinking last night." commented Carleen.

"**Y**eah Dad, even I understand what you mean." added Tommy "Besides it being a history book, it can be a warm family story of how history can and has affected an average person not really involved in politics.

The boy's parents looked at each other with barely detectable smiles, seeing their son a whole new light. A new growth step toward adult maturity had just taken place right before their eyes. One that could actually be seen for a change, instead of having taken place some where along the line without notice. They both realized that saying something about this would just embarrass the boy, so they both proudly accepted his adult comment.

"**E**xactly, Tommy, that's exactly it in a nutshell. Our early history under a different light." Tom continued.

Carleen joined in cautiously, "It looks like we are setting ourselves up for a humongous task. Do you realize what this is going to involve."

"**I** know." replied Tom, This is no two week or two month project."

" **I** figure it for a minimum of at least two years. More than likely three years possibly heading into a forth." added Tommy with a very serious look on his face.

Again the proud parents gazed at each other almost not knowing what to say.

Young Tom picked up on this pause and with a half smile on his lips innocently said,

"**I** did a lot of thinking about this last night also, and I for one think we should do this. We owe it to our ancestors who took the time to record this.

"**T**hen it's decided." Carleen said firmly, touching her Son's arm and looking directly at her husband. I did some thinking too you know."

"**I** agree." Tom said proudly "We can start planning right after breakfast."

Young Tom's sudden adult maturity melted away as he got up and danced around,

"**Y**ippee ! We're gonna write a book, we're gonna write a book." he laughingly emphasized gonna in front of his Mother as he narrowly escaped her loving swat at his rear end.

Chapter 6

Tom Sr. and Jr. repaired to the den while Carleen, humming quietly, put her attention toward fixing breakfast.

"This should be a good celebratory breakfast." she thought to herself, pleased with the recent decision.

Tom Sr. started sorting through envelopes again, not really looking for anything in particular, just sort of killing time until breakfast. Tommy picked a diary at random from the just sorted collection and opened it somewhere in the middle and read to himself.

"August, 1777. I have bin assigned escort duty for the General hisself and we went to Phillydelfia. That's where I met a new officer. a very young Frenchman. He can't be more'n 20 year old. It looks like General Washington has taken a liken to him, and even is puttin him up in his own house. I think his name is Lafayette."

"Listen to this Dad." said Tommy as he reread the paragraph."

When he finished the short entry he commented,

"The more I read, the more I feel like I'm actually there."

"I understand Son. I feel the same way. We are reading about our family and actually are reliving their history. Our history."

"I feel a little embarrassed to say this." admitted Tommy. "But I get a funny feeling inside of me when I read these things."

"So do I Son, so do I. I think they call that pride and patriotism."

Breaking the spell of nostalgia, Tom finally spoke.

"Let's go have some breakfast."

Carleen was still humming a bright upbeat melody when they reached the kitchen.

"Oh good I was just about to call you." she said with a happy lilt.

"Wow ! Mom, you out did yourself this morning," Tommy volunteered as he looked over the festive table. "What's the special occasion ?"

"It's not every day or every family that decides to write a book, so I thought we would celebrate a little.

The two males with beaming smiles sat down to their feast. In between bites and swallows Tommy relayed to his Mother what he had just read.

"Imagine that, my great, great whatever actually met Lafayette."

"I'm sure there will be many more surprises to come by the time we finish reading those journals." returned Carleen

"I believe it's eight." chimed in Tom Sr.

"Eight what." asked Tommy.

"Eight greats. I believe it's eight greats back to the ancestor in question," answered Tom.

"Eight to me or eight to you." queried Tommy again.

"Eight to you Son, I think Tom said hesitantly. Oh well we'll figure it out later by doing the proper math. It will also depend on what the journals say."

"What do the journals have to do with it." Tommy asked inquisitively

"Not every one gets married and has children at the same age Tommy. Some one could have married later in life or earlier for that matter." answered the father.

"Oh I see." Tommy continued. That could have thrown the whole generation thing off. I didn't think of that.

Tom Sr. turned to his wife saying,

"Really great breakfast Hon, and just for that, in order to extend our celebration, we'll all go out to dinner tonight."

Carleen moved to her husband and kissing him lightly on the cheek said,

"That's wonderful Tom, that will leave us the whole day to plan and organize."

"Exactly my thought." Tom replied, "and as I mentioned earlier we first must identify all that we have. Tell you what Tommy and I will help you clean up the kitchen, that way all three of us can take our time in the den and figure out where we're going with this project. Come on Tommy, I'll wash and you dry while your Mom put things away."

"Sure Dad." Tommy answered without complaint, although he was really anxious to get back to reading the diary's.

Quick work was made of the dishes and cleanup and the trio casually made their way to the den and history. Tom Sr. had refilled his coffee mug and now sipped at it while reading the contents of some envelopes. Carleen busied herself with other envelopes trying for chronological order. Tommy headed right for the diary's. Taking one at random he read.

> *"We had no bombproof shelters but even with the constant stream of shells, bursting above us and raining down on us, not a man flinched or left his post. It was realized the flag high atop the fort acted like a sighting marker for the British guns. We then took cover against the outside walls of The fort for better protection. All the shells were bursting inside the walls. A bomb a minute fell from the British guns for hour after hour. I have to move now.*
> *T.C. 13 Sept. 1814."*

Confused by the date, Tommy quickly thumbed through additional pages until he saw an entry that rang a loud bell in his head.

"Francis Scott Key." he yelled aloud." "Francis Scott Key, Dad, look Mom Francis Scott Key, this journal is from the War of 1812." Our family is really rolling in history. We're a famous family and I never knew it."

Looking at each other and smiling excitedly, Tom and Carleen then turned their attention to their overly enthusiastic son.

Calm down Tommy, you'll give yourself a stroke and that would make me very unhappy." said Carleen.

"Take a deep breath and relax and show us what you found."

added Tom.

"Sorry Mom, Dad but I just can't believe all that I'm reading." Tommy said with excitement still in his voice. "I didn't go in order, I just grabbed a book, opened it in the middle and started reading. I didn't realize I was in the war of 1812 until I saw the date on the bottom of what I read. He must be talking about Fort McHenry. Maybe he even knew Francis Scott Key."

"I suppose he could have." answered Tom Sr. Read us what you just read."

Tommy did as he was asked and when he finished he added "Wow! I wonder if he was scared. I think I would be."

"Let me see that journal." asked Tom reaching his hand out.

The journal was passed and Tommy said "Wow." again as he obviously thought about what he had just read.

"With the initials "TC" I guess it could be another relative. Tell you what though - - - - from now on let's try to do this in order. That way we can make our notes accordingly, which will make it easier when we actually start to write something."

"I know you're right Dad, but this stuff is just so interesting." replied Tommy.

"Let's make a compromise." chimed in Carleen. "You go in date order while we're working together, then on your own time later you can jump ahead."

Young Tom was wide eyed and wide smiles at this suggestion, while Tom Sr. semi reluctantly gave his approval. He really did not want to dampen his Son's enthusiasm. The three worked tirelessly not even watching the clock. The large Breakfast fared them well. They all agreed around two o'clock in the afternoon that cookies and milk would suffice till their dinner out. Another two and a half hours found them all about read out. Deciding to get cleaned up and ready for dinner, Tom and Carleen left the den. Tommy chose to read one more diary entry, again choosing a book at random.

"Oct. 19, 1781. Today Lord Cornwallis surrendered Yorktown. I was lucky to be in the General's guard. Cornwallis did not come out but sent an aide. So the general hisself would not accept the sword but sent one of his aide's, Major General Lincoln. Then all the British troops

He sat for a while day dreaming of what he had just read. His mother's voice disturbed his reverie,

"Come on Tommy, clean up and change your clothes."

"Coming Mom." he answered.

He returned the diary to it's place in the stack and headed for his room. While washing and changing, his mind was all astir.

"Imagine." he thought, "Spending a couple of years with George Washington. Even under those harsh conditions. Just being there would be a thrill. Then having the foresight to keep a journal of everyday events which may not have seemed much then. But now. Wow! Real history with a personal touch."

Tommy made a silent promise to himself then to start a journal of his own." Who knows, perhaps someday I could be someone else's history."

Chapter 7

The Chadwick's had a relaxing, enjoyable dinner at one of the better restaurants in town. They kept the conversation light, although each in their own way were thinking about the history they suddenly found themselves immersed in. Particularly Tommy. He was determined to carry on this Chadwick tradition of diary's. He wondered what future events lay ahead that would put him also in history's light. He was anxious to get back to reading other journals to see what other stories would be revealed. A whole new meaning of the world and his life had been opened to him.

The drive home was pleasant and quiet, each still in their own world of thought. Arriving home they went their separate directions, then almost simultaneously drifted back to the den as if some strange force was drawing them in. They laughed at this common attraction, and all agreed to keep it short this night. Tomorrow was a work and school day.

Tommy picked up the very first diary, at least the one he thought was first, strictly going by date. Picking up a pad and pencil, he settled himself in a corner chair and prepared to take notes as he read.

"Nov. 15, 1753 — I am with a very young British Major. I think Washington is his name. I was hired as a hunter to go with this Major on some kind of mission to the French. We spent 8 or 10 days trudging through freezing rain and snow afore reaching Logstown. Rested here 5 days afore goin on to Vernango. Finally on Dec. 4. arrived to meet with French. Traveled agin to Presque Isle on Lake Erie. Arrived

Young Tom sat there totally mesmerized. He was staring at the journal page but not seeing. Not one note had been taken. He almost could not believe what he read. Long moments passed before he snapped out of his trance. Looking over to his Father and in a serious voice said.

"Nine, Dad."

Not really listening Tom replied,

"Oh is it nine o"clock already." and continued studying the document before him.

"No Dad, it's nine generations." Tommy said a little more firmly.

"Oh good Son, you figured it out." Tom again replied, his preoccupation obvious.

"That's not what I mean Dad. I found another generation. This is before the French and Indian War."

Tom finally looked up.

"Did you say the French and Indian war ? But Washington was still young then."

"But Dad, this **is** about Washington. Another of our ancestors was also with Washington, when he was a young British officer." explained young Tom.

"Let me see that." said Tom holding out his hand.

The book was passed. Tom studied it for a few minutes, then thinking out loud said,

"E.C., signed E.C., Well the C. Fits if it's referring to the same last name. I wonder? Tommy hand me a journal from the middle of the stack and one of the last ones too."

Tom Jr. did as he was asked. Tom thumbed through each of the two journals commenting every now and then with a non - distinguishable "UM". Finally, closing both books and handing them back to Tommy, who replaced them back in their proper place in the stacks. Looking directly at Tommy He said,

"I wonder if anybody took the time to record each generation by name. It seems all of the entries are signed by the same last initial. A "C" like our last name."

"Is this what you're looking for."asked Carleen holding a few hand written pages paper clipped together.. "I just opened this envelope as you asked about recording generations."Tom reached for the papers and scanned each one quickly.

"That's exactly what I'm looking for." he answered."This will save us a ton of work on our own. We will have to confirm it though for our own satisfaction and accuracy."

"Confirm what, Dad." queried Tommy.

"Our genealogy Son. Something I've wanted to do for a long time but never got around to it. One of our ancestors has started it for us.. Now let's see E.C., ah yes, here it is."

"Ebenezer Chadwick 1721 — 1763."

"I hope he wasn't like Scrooge." joked Tommy.

All three laughed softly then Tom continued,

"This looks like a pretty complete list, but as I said, we should do some further verification, but not tonight. This is too big a job to be done in a short time. It's already late and we all have work and school tomorrow.

There was no real argument with this. They straightened up their respective piles and stacks of papers and books and headed for the living room and a little relaxing TV before bed.

"Do we have any ice cream left, Mom." asked Tommy.

"How could you, Tommy, after what you ate tonight." was Carleen's answer with a smile.

"I think I'll join Tommy if you have enough." added Tom.

"I don't know about you two." laughed Carleen as she went to the kitchen.

Chapter 8

The next few weeks found the Chadwicks falling into a regular routine. Tommy, home from school would immediately take care of his chores, do his school work then willingly drift to the den to his beloved diary's. His note taking was improving greatly bit still, his favorite past time was reading from the journals. As he had vowed to himself, his own journal started to collect daily entry's.

Both Tom and Carleen developed similar routines. Normal household chores, then back to research in the den. The evenings were usually quiet with each of the Chadwicks absorbed in their own phase of research. On one particular Wednesday night the dull quiet was interrupted by Carleen's soft voice,

"**B**ingo" she said, "We just hit a small jackpot."

This of course drew the attention of both Tom's.

On her lap was a ten by thirteen manilla envelope, marked personal correspondence .It contained a half dozen or so individual envelopes. The one opened in her hand was what she was referring to.

"**W**hat's the jackpot, Hon." tom asked.

"Listen to this." Carleen answered excitedly,

"My dear Mr. Rufus Chadwick,

'It was with the greatest of pleasure that I was in receipt of your correspondence of the twenty third of August. My thoughts have been with you as I fondly reflect on our times together, both in hardship and pleasure. That the Almighty Power above has protected you through our young country's

The three sat in total silence at the end of Carleen's reading, Tommy, after a long pause, was the first to speak,

"Wow! Not only did he serve with George Washington, but actually knew him well enough to exchange letters with him."

"It also shows that besides being a great man and a leader of our country, he was a humble man who was not above the common soldier." said Carleen.

She and her son turned their attention to Tom, who as of yet, had not said a word. He remained motionless as if in a trance.

"Tom ? Softly whispered Carleen, "Are you alright ?"

He gently turned his head to look at his wife, his eyes showing the slightest hint of dampness. Realizing his emotions had been piqued, She gently reached out and touched his hand. He smiled hesitantly, as a tear rolled from the corner of his eye. He squeezed her hand in return drawing himself back to reality. Young Tommy, also caught up in the moment, could detect the wetness growing in his own eyes. Embarrassed by this swelling of pride, he stood, softly saying,

"I'm going to get a drink of juice, anybody want anything ?"

Not waiting for an answer he left the den.

Tommy's movement broke the spell that had captured the room.

"I'm alright Hon." Tom spoke, "It's just that - - - - ."

"I know sweetheart, I know." whispered Carleen, squeezing his hand again and then withdrawing hers to fuss with the papers. To give Tom more recovery time, Carleen put the envelope and letter aside, stood and announced,

"I think I'll join Tommy in something to drink.

Tom, content in being alone, momentarily allowed himself to drift again, putting himself in the shoes of his ancestor and conversing with his longtime idol. Finally coming back to the present
he yelled toward the kitchen,

"Bring me back a drink also, please."

Moments later Carleen and Tommy returned, each carrying their chosen beverage and Carleen holding an additional glass.

"I think this again calls for a mini celebration." she said as she handed Tom a snifter of cognac.

Tom smiling, at Carleen, accepted the glass saying,

"Your choice could not have been more perfect."

He raised it in toast and said,

"To George Washington and Rufus Chadwick."

Following suit, Mother and Son raised their glasses, then all three sipped their refreshment. Tom fully recovered said ,

"This really is a jackpot. This letter deserves special handling. Perhaps some sort of protective frame. What do you think ?"

Tommy quickly answered,

"Maybe we should frame a copy and keep the original in a place of safety."

Tom and Carleen, again proud of their Son's growing knowledge and maturity, both smiled and replied in unison,

"Great idea." which brought a chuckle from all three.

Tom carefully refolded the letter and returned it to it's envelope and handed it back to his wife.

"Anything else of importance in those other envelopes." he asked.

"I don't know yet, this was the first thing I opened." she replied.

Putting a small check mark on the corner of the envelope, she slipped it back into the larger brown one. Her attention went to the remaining unopened ones. Tom returned to what he was doing, while Tommy engaged himself with his stack of diary's. Opening one of the early diary's he again became intrigued by what he read.

May 10, 1775.— Young Major Washington was made Aide-de-Camp to General Braddock. Though the General does

Tommy closed the book and whispered aloud to himself,

"Wow ! By the time I finish reading all these diary's I'll know more than anybody about our early history."

"Did you say something Tommy." asked Tom.

`"Not really, Dad." answered Tommy, "I was sort of mumbling to myself. Our friend Ebenezer just met Benjamin Franklin. I'm telling you Dad, this is so much better than what we get in school."

"I realize that, Tommy, but don't knock school too much. Education goes both ways. School gives you the basics. If it stirs your interest in something, it is up to you to pursue it through other sources, and other sources are out there. You may have to dig to find them but they are available. What you're getting here is a very personal touch to just one subject.

"I know Dad, I guess that's what makes it so much fun."

Carleen interrupted, "I hate to put a damper on your fun Tommy, but I think we've all had enough excitement for tonight."

Reluctantly Tommy put away his notes and diaries. He kissed his Mother good night, said "Nite Dad," to his Father and taking the stairs two at a time went up to his room. In bed he turned out the light, and lay there in the dark placing himself back in 1755 with Washington and Franklin.

Chapter 9

Social studies and History were two of Tommy's favorite subjects in school. Now in his freshman year in high school he was looking forward to deeper studies of American History. Even more so now since the diaries arrived. With great eagerness did he leave for school this day, knowing they were going to start on the Revolutionary War period today. In class, causes for the war were quickly outlined. Tommy thought these were touched on too briefly, but for now let it go. Principal players and their causes was discussed next. Missing from this list was George Washington. The Chadwick family research showed this not to be the case. Not just because of the journals, but the additional reading they had undertaken to fill in the story as presented in the journal. Young Tommy questioned this in class and felt he did not get a satisfactory answer. Not wanting to reveal the diary information per his Father's request, again he let this pass. He also did not mention this at home.

A few days later, now well into the Revolutionary War, a statement was made about Valley Forge being the coldest time for General Washington and his troops. Tommy's enthusiasm for the truth led him to again question this. His teacher, a Mrs. Porter, politely listened to Tommy's interruption before answering,

"That's a very interesting statement Tommy, but how can you argue with a book of history."

"But I know it's wrong, Mrs. Porter, and I thought history books were supposed to give the true story." he said.

"So now you're an expert on something that happened some two hundred and thirty years ago."

Not one to give up when he was right, Tommy politely countered with,

"I can't tell you how I know, I just know."

This drew a laughs from some classmates, but Tommy didn't care.

"I suggest Tommy that you take your seat and we'll discuss this further after class." Mrs. Porter said nicely but firmly.

Tommy, having been raised with a strong ethic of respect for others, said "Yes Mam. And quietly took his seat.

When the class was over and the others were leaving, Mrs. Porter asked Tommy to stay. As the room emptied and just the two remained she looked at Tommy and said,

"Okay, Tommy, what's this all about. You're not one who usually disrupts my class. And what's this foolishness about you arguing the facts in a history book."

Tommy answered hesitantly,

"I'm not trying to be a smart aleck, Mrs. Porter, but there are certain things I know are wrong in the book."

Mrs. Porter patiently countered with,

"Alright, if you say the information is wrong, on what facts or information do you base your statement."

Tommy realized she was being fair and giving him a chance.

"Well, I can't really tell you that, I just know it's wrong."

With a small sign of annoyance in her voice, Mrs. Porter replied,"I'm really surprised at your behavior, Tommy. You have never acted this way before. I'm letting you know right up front that I'm going to have to call your parents unless you can explain yourself better."

She paused, waiting for an answer. Tommy just sat there, his eyes avoiding hers, thinking,

"I promised Dad I wouldn't say anything about the diary."

Mrs. Porter waited a few minutes, then finally stated,

"Okay Tommy, I'm a little disappointed in you. You may leave now, but I will be calling your folks tonight.

Chapter 10

Tommy attended his last two classes but was quiet and not paying much attention. He welcomed the final bell signaling the end of the school day. He went straight home not stopping to play ball with his friends. He had never been in trouble before and could feel the anxiety building in him. He talked aloud to himself on the way home finally convincing himself that he had done no wrong and had no need to worry about any consequences. Arriving home, he did his chores and homework then went into the den, which seemed to be his favorite room of late. He picked a diary at random and read.

"June, 1775 — Am with General Washington. We left New Jersey and now in New York. Today heard about Bunker's Hill up in Massachusetts. Looks like the shootin war has started. The General now impatient to get there. I heard he is Commander in Chief of all the colony's troops. This Washington looks like a true Commander. He is rather tall and has a very stately appearance. More later. R.C."

He made some notes, then also remembered his own journal. Locating his book he made some entry's regarding today's school class. Satisfied with what he had written, he closed his own diary and reached for another old diary.

Tommy closed the diary in his lap and like his father drifted into a daydream about being with Washington. His Mother's greeting from the other room shook him out of his reverie.

"How was school today." she inquired.

"Well, okay I guess." Tommy answered hesitantly.

"What do you mean, I guess." Carleen asked as she entered the den.

Again Tommy hesitated,

"I got into a little trouble in class today, and I'll tell you about it, but I would rather wait for Dad to come home so I can tell you both together."

Carleen looked at her son, quietly concerned, but gave way to his request. She knew her son well enough to respect his feelings.

"Okay, if that's what you want. I'm going to start dinner, you can give me a hand by setting the table." she returned trying not to show too much concern.

Tommy was thankful of his Mother's reaction. It helped take the edge off some of his anxiety.

It was close to six o'clock when Tom got home.

"Sorry I'm a little late Hon." he said as he entered the kitchen. "There was an accident on Bridge Street which really tied up traffic for a while."

Carleen kissed her husband smiling,

"Wash up, dinner is ready. Tommy," she called, "We can eat now, Dad is home.

Tommy did not answer but walked quietly to the table and sat down. Tom Sr. joined Mother and Son and said,

"Hi sport, how was your day."

"Alright."was Tommy's quiet answer not looking at his father.

Tom returned with,

"What's up sport, you look like you just lost your best friend."

Tommy stared up at his Father, not having touched his food yet.

"I guess I may as well tell you now that you're both here."

"Okay, so tell us." Tom said , still being cheerful.

Carleen reached out and touched Tom's arm lightly as if to quiet him.

"Well" — Tommy said hesitating somewhat. "I sort of got into some trouble in school today."

"Oh !" Tom remarked looking a little more serious now.

"It was in History class." young Tom continued. "I made a comment that didn't agree with the book, but I didn't say what source I used to back it up. Mrs. Porter kept me after class for a while, but I still would not answer her. You said not to tell anybody about the diaries. Well, any how she said she was going to call you tonight. I'm sorry."

"Oh, is that all." said Carleen." You looked so down all afternoon, I thought it was something more serious."

"But it is serious, Mom, I've never been in trouble before."answered Tommy.

"And you're still not in any trouble." said Tom with a smile. "Don't worry, I'll take care of the whole thing when Mrs. Porter calls. Now go ahead and eat your dinner. We can't have our chief researcher starving himself. We have a book to write."

Tommy's mood changed and his anxiety disappeared. He went right into telling about what he had read in the diaries earlier. Carleen squeezed her husbands arm. They looked at each other softly, almost undetectably. She withdrew her arm and both proceeded to eat.
Dinner atmosphere was pretty normal from then on.

After dinner the two men repaired to the den while
Carleen finished up in the kitchen. She joined the others in the den just as the telephone rang. Tom went to answer it. Tommy froze, his anxiety returning. Carleen saw this and sat next to him saying,

"It's alright, you have nothing to be upset about.

A few minutes later Tom returned to the den.

"It's all set, Mrs. Porter will join us here on Saturday afternoon."

"Here !" said Tommy with alarm, "Mrs. Porter is coming here. What if somebody sees her ? I'll be as good as dead with my friends."

"Don't worry, We'll sneak her in the back door." quipped Tom.

"Very funny." smiled Tommy in return. "Does she have to come here ?"

"Yes Tommy. I think it is important she know's where your answers came from." answered his Dad.

"But you said not to tell anybody about the diaries." complained Tommy.

"Yes, and I still mean that." said Tom.

Carleen interjected,

"What your father means Tommy, is sometimes things are unavoidable and I'm sure Mrs. Porter can be trusted to keep out little secret for a while, or do you want her to go on with the wrong impression of you."

"No, I guess not." said Tommy calming down, and then adding,"I hope none of the guys see her here."

Tom and Carleen laughed quietly at this, then turned their attention to their respective piles of papers. Tommy feeling much better about his troubles sort of half smiled as he reached for another diary.

" Aug. 29, 1776 — Providence was With us tonight. On General Washington's orders, nine thousand men, and all their munitions of war were evacuated from Long Island, lest they be surrounded by the British. Late evening, under cover of fog and under the very noses of the British ships and troops they crossed to New York. The General hisself was at the ferry point, supervising everything. All went well. By daybreak the fog cleared, and the whole transfer was complete. General Washington was with the last to cross to the city. I sure was afraid to be the last ones to cross. R.C."

Tommy closed the journal, letting his imagination take over as he drifted into a daydream of how it must have been. How thousands of men and equipment crossed silently from Long Island to New York or Manhattan Island. The British, literally only a few hundred yards ,away totally unaware. He could feel the small boat rock with each pull of the oar, and listened to the water lap quietly at the sides, while not being able to see more than a few yards away. His Father's voice interrupted his trip across the water.

"Well, how about it." he heard.

"How about what ?" Tommy asked hazily.

"I asked if you wanted ice cream." Tom answered.

"Oh, sure." Tommy replied, fully awake now. "I'll even get it." Not waiting for any other remarks he started for the kitchen, thinking how lucky he was compared to our first patriots. He stood in the kitchen for awhile not knowing what he was there for. Carleen's voice awakened him again.

"What are you doing, making the ice cream by hand.?"

"Be right there." Tommy replied slightly embarrassed.

He returned with the ice cream for the three of them and they chatted about meaningless things while eating. Tommy eventually excused himself, said his good nights, and went up to his room, his mind again drifting back to Washington and the river crossing. Sleep finally overtook his dream state and the night passed.

Chapter 11

The next few days remained uneventful. The family continued their daily routine never tiring of the research that tied them to the house. Saturday arrived with sunshine, but a cloud of shadows dampened Tommy's spirits. Mrs. Porter was coming this afternoon. He was almost hoping for rain. The chances were better for his friends not to be around if it was raining. He could feel the anxiety building, the more he dwelled on Mrs. Porter. While he dressed, he tried to think of something else.

"Enough daydreaming." he told himself and headed downstairs to the kitchen.

Carleen greeted her son with,

"Good morning sleepyhead. I thought you were going to sleep the whole day away."

"I guess I was tired." smiled Tommy in answer. "Right now I know I'm hungry."

Tom Sr. Joined the conversation with,

"Have your breakfast and then right after join me outside. There's a few chores we have to get done before Mrs. Porter arrives this afternoon."

Tommy's facial expression changed instantly as he looked at his Father and said,

"Don't remind me." in a very gloomy voice.

Tom glared back at his son.

"I would suggest you change your attitude. She's not the enemy you know." he said in a calm but stern voice."

"I know Dad. I'm sorry, It's just that - - - - -"

Tom interrupted his son,

"I know how you feel Tommy but you did nothing wrong and you're not in any kind of trouble. And stop worrying about your friends."he added.

"If you try really hard, you might find her to be a nice person." joined in Carleen, smiling.

Tommy smiled uncontrollably at his Mother and mumbled,

"I know Mom, I know."

Gazing again at his Mother and with more life in his voice Tommy asked,

"What's for breakfast."

Still smiling, Carleen answered,

"The condemned man can have anything he wants for his last meal."

Tom followed immediately with,

"Eat hardy my son fore this afternoon you hang."

"Very funny guys, very funny." Tommy shot back laughingly

Tom Sr. Headed for the garage laughing.

Tommy then realized that he actually felt better *"I really did nothing wrong."* he thought to himself, feeling his mood on the upswing. He finished his plate of bacon and eggs his Mom
provided and set out for the garage.

A few hours later, tired and dirty, but proud of what they had accomplished, both father and son had a light lunch and went straight for their respective showers to clean up. They dressed and met downstairs again with twenty minutes to spare before the arrival of Tommy's teacher. Tommy could feel the tension building again as he watched the clock tic away. One minute before Two o'clock the doorbell rang. Tommy could feel himself stiffen as his Mother answered the door. Moments later she returned to the living room followed by Tommy's teacher. Both men stood as the women entered the room.

"Tom this is Mrs. Porter." said Carleen.

"My pleasure." stated Tom as he gently shook her hand.

"So nice to meet you, Mr. Chadwick." She returned and turning her head toward Tommy, Mrs. Porter smiled and added a very pleasant, "Hello Tommy."

Tommy answered with a quiet Hello trying to avoid her eyes.

Carleen, indicating a comfortable chair saying

"Please sit down. Can I get you a cup of tea."

"That would be lovely." answered Mrs. Porter.

Carleen turned toward the kitchen saying,

"I'll just be a moment."

Tom proceeded with some polite talk just to kill some time awaiting Carleen's return.

It was really only moments when she reentered the living room with a tray holding the tea and a few cookies.

Tommy sat quietly in the corner of the couch thinking, *:Let's get this over with in a hurry."*

Carleen seated herself comfortably and got right to the point,

"Tommy told us what happened in class and we understand

your concern."

Tom then politely interrupted,

"I think we can show you something that will explain his behavior."

"Please don't take me the wrong way." answered Mrs. Porter. Tommy is a very good student and his behavior is not a problem. His challenging attitude sort of took me by surprise. I never saw him like that before, and when he refused to answer my questions, well naturally I became concerned"

"I'm afraid I'm to blame for that Mrs. Porter." said Tom. "You see I told him not to say anything about his source of information not realizing that this would have affected his work in school, and for that I apologize."

Looking a bit confused Mrs. Porter answered,

"I don't think I quite understand."

Tom smiling, stood and said,

"Please follow me I'd like to show you something." as he turned and walked to the den.

Mrs. Porter stood, as did Carleen. Carleen nudged Tommy,

"You too Tommy, after all this involves you most of all." she said.

"Yes Mom I'm coming." he answered reluctantly.

Trying to be as inconspicuous as possible he allowed everyone else to enter the den first and then tried to blend in with a corner.

"Have a seat." Tom indicated to Mrs. Porter who was observing all the boxes, books and papers as she sat down. "What you see before you Mrs. Porter is living history." Seeing a still questioning look on her face, he continued, "This will all be a lot clearer in a moment, please bear with me. I'm not trying to be mysterious. Tommy, why don't you read for Mrs. Porter, about the topic that started this misunderstanding."

Tommy could feel his face burning with embarrassment. He felt uncomfortable being the all of a sudden center of attention. Never the less he moved to the stack of diary's on the card table. It took a few moments to locate the book and passage in question. Once he found it he turned and read aloud. Finally after reaching the sentence of concern he paused looking up at Mrs. Porter. *"She even looks interested."* he thought. His attention was refocused again as he heard his father urging,

"Go ahead Tommy, finish it."

Tommy read the sentence slowly and clearly.

"This winter is colder'n Valley Forge was back in '77"

Tommy again hesitated slightly before reading the rest of the diary entry in a normal tone and speed. Upon finishing he closed the book and looked directly at Mrs. Porter feeling sure and confident again. She smiled back at him but her eyes still betrayed her confused and questioning thoughts. Tom immediately took over the conversation.

"What you just heard, Mrs. Porter, was a diary entry. A diary entry from 1777. An actual first person account of what went on that given day." Pointing to where Tommy was standing, he added, "That table is holding journals and diary's going back as far as the French and Indian War. They are diary's kept by our ancestors throughout our nations history. It seems that the Chadwick family of old has kept an up close and personal view of our country's evolution and growth. No judgements or opinions, just the recording of events as they happened. Tommy was watching Mrs. Porter's face as his father spoke. Her eyes were concentrating on the stack of journals on the card table. Her mouth was partially opened as if to speak, but no words escaped. Her face betrayed her interest and wonderment combined. Even Tommy could read the change enveloping his teacher. Tom stopped speaking as Mrs. Porter stood and walked to the table where Tommy was as if drawn by some mysterious force. As she neared Tommy, her left hand extended itself toward the book Tommy had read. Without exchanging words the student relinquished the diary to the teacher. She caressed it as if drawing out its contents by osmosis. Tom was quiet now. All eyes were on Mrs. Porter as she opened the book and read silently. The diary's spell had captured another. Total silence lasted for almost five minutes. Smiles and glances were exchanged by all three Chadwicks. Mrs. Porter finally closed the book. Looking directly into Tommy's eyes she struggled to find words,

"I - - - - I - - - - don't know what to say. I almost feel like crying to have been privileged to read something so intimate and personal." She paused, then added "And what makes it even more beautiful is its historical significance."

She returned to her seat still clutching the diary and sat in silence as if contemplating her next words. Looking directly into Tommy's eyes she quietly said

"Why didn't you say something."

Before the boy could answer Tom broke the spell.

"As I said earlier, I'm the one to blame for that Mrs. Porter. I told him not to say anything to any body before we further researched what we had here."

"What you have here Mr. Chadwick, interrupted the teacher, is a gold mine of history. If all these books are, as the passages I've just read, it's obvious we still have history to learn."

Tommy enthusiastically chimed in,

"Oh ! They are all like that, Mrs. Porter. When you read them it's like you are really there."

As he continued speaking his shyness completely disappeared and he became more animated,

"And it's not just the revolution. It's all kinds of history. My ancestor actually knew George Washington and they even wrote letters to one another."

Whoa ! Slow down boy." directed Tom. "Calm down, we are all right here."

"Sorry Dad." answered Tommy. "Sorry Mrs. Porter."

"It's okay Tommy. I completely understand your excitement."returned Mrs. Porter beaming a warm smile. "I share that excitement also."

Turning again to Tommy's parents she continued,

"Obviously we have no problem here with Tommy other than some over enthusiasm which is totally understandable. I'm sorry to have bothered you but my students mean a lot to me."

"I'm very pleased with your concern Mrs Porter, correcting herself *"We* are very pleased with your concern, and there is no need to apologize. It's nice to know that you care that much." Carleen stated

Mrs. Porter stood and said,

"No need to take up any more of your time."

"Please stay." said Tom. "That is if you have the time, and perhaps we can discuss the diary's some more.

"Yes please stay." added Carleen. "Can I get you some more tea."

"To be honest with you, I'd love to discuss these diary's some more." still tightly clutching the one she held. Looking at Carleen she added, "And yes, I would love some more tea."

"I'll get the tea Mom." said Tommy as he stood and started for the kitchen.

"Why thank you dear." answered Carleen. "I'll have another cup also."

"While you're at Sport, coffee would be great." added Tom.

"You got it Dad." Tommy yelled back from halfway to the kitchen.

"I think your excitement has even made Tommy happy" suggested Carleen smiling.

"Yes he was a bit apprehensive about your visit." said Tom quietly.

"I'm sure he was, but I'm used to that by now, although most of my visits are not this pleasant." remarked Mrs. Porter.

Tom, with half laughter in his voice said,

"You know you can put the book down. It will make drinking

your tea a little easier."

"I'm sure you're right."answered Mrs.Porter laughingly, "But I feel like I'm under its spell. I still can't believe what I'm holding is actual history. Not that it's any of my business but what do you plan to do with this fortuitous find."

"Well we are still in a bit of shock ourselves, but after some thorough verification we were toying with the idea of a book." said Tom.

"What a fabulous idea. Funny, because that's just what was going through my mind as I was reading." commented Mrs Porter.

"Tommy is just thrilled with the idea. I've never seen such genuine enthusiasm in a young boy before." interjected Carleen.

Just then Tom Jr. reentered the room with the tray of beverages. Going directly to his teacher first, smiling broadly he said,

"Here's your tea Mrs. Porter."

She, in turn, with as big a smile answered,

"Why thank you Tommy, how nice of you."

Tom and Carleen were grinning at each other, both thinking of Tommy's change in attitude from just a short while ago. Tommy then served his parents and lastly himself pouring his soda in a glass rather then drinking from the can. Again Tom and Carleen quietly grinned at each other. Before he even sat down, young Tom spoke directly to his teacher.

"Did Dad tell you that we are going to write a book using the diary's. I've already started doing some research, both on line and at the library."

"Yes Tommy, we were just talking about that." she responded. "Would it be okay if I read another passage ?"

"Yes Mam." was Tommy's quick answer, not waiting for his parents approval, who again quietly smiled at each other. "Could you read it out loud so we can all enjoy it ?"

"Of course Tommy if that's what you would like." remarked Mrs. Porter.

Picking a journal at random that had not been read before he handed it to what now seemed to be his favorite teacher and retired to a chair in the corner. Mrs. Porter opened the diary and proceeded to read.

Jan, 1779 - - - Am with the General
in Philadelphia. Bin here most of the winter.
He has been tryin to git the Congress to give
more supply's and troops. The General
hisself is disgusted with the congress attitude.

She paused here, then quietly closed the book holding it tightly in her hands. A dampness in her eyes was visible and the room was silent. Young Tom was the first to interrupt,

"Isn't it great, Mrs. Porter, it really is just like being there." he said in an excited voice.

"You're right Tommy, it is. I've always enjoyed history, but I had no idea it could be this exciting." Turning to his parents she continued, "Reading about the revolution has always fascinated me, but reading it as a first person account is beyond my wildest imagination. I know this is a lot to ask, but do you think it possible for me to be part of this in some way. After being teased in this way I don't think I have the patience to wait for the book."

"Tommy was now sporting a big smile as his father answered.

"We do want to keep this as quiet as possible for now, but I was considering the same thing. I'm sure you could be of invaluable help to us. I must ask however, your promise of total confidentiality."

"I totally understand and you have my word on that. I would feel exactly the same if this were my family history. Oh dear look at the time, my husband will think I've deserted him. I really must be going now. Thank you so much for sharing this with me and I so look forward to working with you in what ever way I can."

The good-bye pleasantries continued as they all headed for the door. Just as the door was opening Tommy looked seriously at Mrs. Porter asking,

"Ah - h - h Mrs. Porter do you think a - a - - ."
Anticipating his thoughts she interrupted him.

"**D**on't worry Tommy, your reputation is safe. You will receive no special attention in my class because of this. We will still be teacher and student."

Tommy was now beaming a broad smile, although a bit embarrassed about having asked this. Carleen lovingly ran her hand through her son's hair in a caressing manner, she also sporting a smile. The three Chadwicks watched as Mrs. Porter dashed to her car trying to avoid the rain as much as possible.

As the door closed and the three walked back to the den Tom addressed his son,

"**W**ell sport, what do you think of your teacher now ?"

"**W**hat can I say, I guess she really is nice after all." Tommy answered.

Carleen gently put her arm around her son's shoulder and softly said,

"**S**ee, when you do the right thing and are honest about it you will never really be in trouble. It may sound idealistic, but give it a try and you will find that it works."

"**I** guess you're right Mom. I know I sure feel a lot better now."

She gave his arm a little extra squeeze before releasing him as he continued with,

"**W**hat's for dinner tonight, I'm starving."

"**N**othing." she chided, "Your father and I decided the three of us should go on a diet, starting today."

Tommy gave his mother a surprised, double take look as he spurted out "**No way.**"

Carleen laughed at his reactions but eased his tensions by saying,

"**W**ell being as late as it is I didn't really have time to prepare anything, so I thought we would just have soup and a sandwich if that will suit you."

"**T**hat's just fine with me." Tommy answered

"**M**e also Hon, In fact I'll give you a hand." said Tom Sr. As he followed his wife to the kitchen.

Dinner was quite pleasant, with the conversation light. The clean up was easy and the three retired to the living room.

"**I**nstead of TV tonight I think I'll just go to my room and read and maybe drift off to sleep early for a change." remarked Tommy.

"**T**hat's not a bad idea." commented Tom. "It's already almost eight and I'm a bit weary myself. It's been a long week."

"**A** fine thing, my two favorite men deserting me and leaving me all alone." said Carleen, playing on their sympathy.

Tom looked at Carleen and said,
I'm sorry Hon, I didn't mean to - - - -.''
She cut him off with a smile,
"Go ahead you two, this will give me time to catch up on
some letter writing. I'll be up later on."

Tommy was up early and being Sunday there was no school,
for which he was thankful. With his parents still sleeping, the house was quiet,
He made a quick stop at the kitchen for some orange juice, then headed for the
den for some quiet undisturbed reading. Tommy grabbed a diary at random,
made himself comfortable and proceeded to read.

August, 12, 1784 – I was humbled today by a visitor I received for a few hours. The Marquis de Lafayette honored my small house with his presence. We spoke of our time serving with the General hisself. He relayed to me he was on his way to visit the General after an appointed visit in Philadelphia. I could not believe a man of his presence would grace me with such a visit. We found a mutuality in our fondness and respect for the General. The children spoke of his visit for many days. To have known two such men gave me no end of pride. RC.

"Wow, this is really something." Tommy said aloud to
himself when he finished reading the page. I remember that Rufus was friends
with Washington, and I remember that he saw Lafayette. But now to read that
he was actually visited by General Lafayette, this is some family history. This
is really gonna," he paused, "going to be," he corrected himself thinking back
to what his Mom said, "some book. This is really writing itself. Boy ! I
wonder what other family has ever had a history like ours."
"Who are you talking to sport ?" said Tom Sr. Softly so as not
to startle his son.
Turning to his Father, Tommy said,
"Oh, Hi Dad, do you know what I just read. No, I was just
talking to myself. This journal has more about Lafayette. I didn't think you

would be up this early. Our ancestor was friends with him also."

"Whoa, slow down boy. Let's talk about one subject at a time." cautioned Dad.

"I'm sorry Dad, but I just get excited when I read these journals." commented Tommy. I was just asking myself what other family could have a history like ours, especially documented so well."

"There goes that maturity level again." Tom Sr. thought. *"My boy is growing right before my eyes."*

Speaking directly to his son Tom said,

"Tell you what son, let's me grab a cup of coffee and then we can chat and you can fill me in on what you just read."

"Is this a private party, or can anyone join in." inquired Carleen as she entered the den.

"Morning Mom." answered Tommy. "Sit with us and listen to what I just read, it's about - - - ."

"Hold on Tommy." interrupted Tom Sr. Let's both get settled with coffee first and then you can have our undivided attention."

"Okay, Dad, sorry." said a sheepish Tom Jr.

He sat reading the journal passage waiting for the return of his parents. Over coffee and juice they all enjoyed the visit with the Marquis de Lafayette.

The rest of the day, in fact the rest of the week became routine. Work, school, chores and cataloguing would seem boring to some, but to the Chadwicks the thrill of this new challenge of a possible book made the time fly.

Weeks passed, and as promised, Mrs Porter became an active partner in research and preliminary writing. At the end of the school year in June, she broke the news that she would no longer be part of the project. Her husband had been transferred to the West Coast and she would be going with him. She was hoping to get a teaching job once they settled in somewhere in California.

The three Chadwicks, particularly Tommy, were extremely disappointed at the lose of Helen Porter. She had become a regular household fixture on weekends. Tommy had taken a strong liking to her and they got along surprisingly well. They managed to maintain their teacher, student relationship and Tommy's secret was
never discovered by his friends. He felt he had the best of both worlds. The family held a small farewell party for her a few days before she moved, thanking her for her devotion to their family history. She had been most helpful in their research.

Most of July was taken up correlating their paper work piles and chronologically sorting the information gathered. Satisfied with their progress, a self reward was promised. A trip to Washington D.C. and the Smithsonian Institute for a final verification of George Washington's signature. Before leaving for D.C. Tom Sr. Purchased fire proof storage boxes, enough to house their accumulated mass of paper work and of course the treasured journals. Only one remained unsecured, which they planned to take with them backing up the story of George Washington's signature.

-93-

Chapter 12

The drive to the nations capital was pleasant and non eventful. Tommy occupied himself with additional readings from the journal they brought along.

> *1780 – Winter – The General hisself did not want to take food and supplies from the people and only did so under worst conditions. In doing so left them with a certificate for payment to be paid by the congress. Knowin our plight and hardship the folks here in Jersey were most generous in sharin what they could. RC.*

"I guess we can be proud of our New Jersey ancestors." said Tommy after reading the passage aloud. I'll bet most folks don't even know about such things."

"You're right Tommy", answered his father. "And the general history books in schools probably don't even mention it. You have to do additional research on your own to learn the real story of the hardships our young country faced."

Carleen looked out the car window and smiled, proud of her son's interest in his family history.

Tommy, somewhat reluctantly, put aside the journal to focus his attention out the car window to see the sights. This was his first visit to the nations capital, the city was named after the man whom his ancestor knew personally. His face beamed with the pride of this fact. Reaching the hotel, they checked in. Since their appointment with the Smithsonian wasn't till the next day, this left them time for some quick sight seeing before dark. They had dinner at a nice quiet restaurant and walked back to the hotel and settled in for the night.

Chapter 13

Up early and excited, the Chadwicks had the hotel's continental breakfast as they dressed and prepared for their Smithsonian visit. Tommy privately wished he had more journals to read, but did understand the necessity of having them securely locked at home.

"Oh well." He thought, "We'll only be here a couple of days."

He finished dressing with time to spare before their appointment so he turned to his own journal to update their progress in the verification process.

Leaving their own car at the hotel garage, the three took a cab to their appointment to save time and hassle. Unless you are familiar with the layout, driving in the DC area can be a nightmare.

Arriving a few minutes early they were shown to the third floor office of a Mr. Stensen. Casual introductions took place and coffee was offered.

"I understand you have something you want verification on." Said Mr. Stensen.

"Yeah ! We have George Washington's signature." blurted out Tommy enthusiastically.

"Whoa, calm down boy, you don't want to frighten the man." Tom Sr. reprimanded quietly.

"Sorry Dad, sorry Mr. Stensen."

"It's alright son, it's refreshing to see youthful enthusiasm for our nations history." commented Mr. Stensen.

"Okay, what exactly do you have." Stensen asked.

Tom Sr. Reached to the inside pocket of his jacket, retrieved an envelope but chose to hold it in his hand unopened.

"Perhaps I should give you a little background first, as to how this came into our possession." said Tom.

"I think that would be quiet appropriate." returned Mr. Stensen.

Tom Sr. Related a brief history leading up to this visit to the

Smithsonian with a few overzealous comments being put forth by Tom Jr., who seemed unable to control his excitement. Mark Stensen showed no irritation or annoyance at Tommy's honest enthusiasm, in fact he smiled when ever Tommy spoke. This helped Tom Sr. relax somewhat, and of course Carleen beamed with pride for both her men.

With the story ended and Tommy finally settled in his seat, Tom Sr. Handed the envelope to Mr. Stensen, who in turn, with careful and practiced hands opened it. He gently slid the paper from it's protection and unfolded it. He studied and read it silently for a bout three minutes which was a week and a half in Tommy's mind.

"I could have read the whole history of the revolutionary war by now." He thought to himself, however he did remain silent.

At long last Mark Stensen looked up, removed his glasses and said,

"I've seen a lot of George Washington signatures and to me this looks like the genuine article, however I'm not the true expert. With your permission I'll take this down the Hall to Bill Hanson, our resident Washington expert.

"Well yes, I guess that would be alright." Tom said turning to his wife and son who nodded in the affirmative. We want the best verification possible."

" Then if you will excuse me, I'll only be a moment." said Mr. Stensen, and left the room. No sooner had he exited when Tommy was all aglow again with words flowing.

"This is it Dad, Now we can really get to work on the book. I have a lot of research already outlined for the beginning and we can continue to collect stuff as we go. The we can. . . ."

Tom held up his hand, palm towards his son, indicating his interruption.

"Not now son, these things should be discussed in a more private place where we can really focus our attention on what is necessary.

Tommy, looking slightly disappointed, answered,

"Sorry Dad, I was just - - - -."

Tom Sr. Interrupted again.

"I'm not scolding you Tommy, it's just that this isn't the time or place."

As he finished his sentence Mark Stensen reentered his office.

"It looks promising but Bill will need a little more time for a comparative study. It should only be a couple of hours at most. In the meantime could I interest you folk in a tour of some of the working parts of our facility and then perhaps some lunch in our cafeteria."

"The three Chadwicks, all smiling, readily accepted and soon were following Mr. Stensen down a long corridor with openings to various work rooms with tables and files. The map room was of particular interest to young Tommy. He was able to see some of the actual maps used by those who fought for our independence.

"Maybe one of these was actually held by George Washington or even The Marques De Lafayette." He thought to himself.

"Can people get copies of these ?" he asked Mr. Stensen.

"Yes you can Tommy. Many people doing research projects on the War of Independence for books or articles for studies do just that." he answered.

Tommy, because of his unbound enthusiasm was going to ask something else, but looked at his Dad and thought better of it and remained silent. He decided he would try to keep his questions simple or very general.

Their abbreviated tour was extremely interesting and the trio of soon to be storytellers now found themselves entering the cafeteria. They were surprised by the variety of choices but all chose a light fare planning on dinner out that night. Conversation during lunch centered on the historical preservation work the Smithsonian was involved with. Tommy was surprisingly quiet but was absorbing every word for his own future knowledge and use. Time was flying by. It was already one fifteen and as the group was preparing to get up from the table, Mark Stensen's cell phone jingled a quiet and pleasant tone.

"Excuse me." he said flipping open the phone to answer it.

"We were just finishing lunch. Okay, we'll see you in a few." he was heard to say. Looking at the Chadwicks, Mark said, :That was bill. He says he's ready to meet with us back at my office, so if you will follow me." Mr, Stensen turned to the exit of the cafeteria, the Chadwicks following.

Chapter 14

They had just settled comfortably in Stensen's office when Bill entered, envelope in hand. Introductions were made to the Chadwicks, anticipation on their faces.

"Might as well get right to it." Bill said. "The signature is the genuine article."

Tom, Carleen and Tommy were now sporting beaming smiles

"But." Mr. Hanson continued. "I'm afraid I have to report that the document is a phony."

Smiles were now replaced by concerned confusion and questioning looks.

"It can't be" blurted out Tommy, only to be hushed by Tom's comforting touch.

"It's one of the best copies I've seen in years, nevertheless it is still just a copy."

"Are you sure ?" questioned Tom.

"Quite positive, I'm afraid. This paper has only been produced in the last few years. The ink also is of recent manufacture. Where did you get this ?"

Tom hesitated for a moment and again stopped young Tom from speaking. The look in Tommy's moisture filled eyes was
almost challenging, but he knew by his father's touch he had to remain silent.

Tom still hesitant, slowly explained the story to Bill and Mark. He, even though reluctantly, produced the journal from his briefcase to back up the truth of the story. After a cursory viewing of the journal, Bill's eyes sparkled as if he had just discovered gold. With a smile on his face and excitement in his voice he said,

"Without even testing I know this is the real thing. I've been doing these studies for over thirty years and I know true historical documents when I see them. You are a very lucky family to have this kind of history in your possession."

"We have many journals like this that tell the story of the whole War of Independence." Tom stated.

"And the war of 1812." Tommy excitedly added.

"And others beyond that." Carleen volunteered.

"I don't understand how just that document could be a phony." Tom queried. "Can I see that please ?"

Bill handed Tom the envelope and said,

"Oh! By the way the envelope is not the original either, but it is well over a hundred years old."

Tom, still obviously concerned, removed the document from the envelope while Mark Stensen turned on the small light table on his desk. Tom placed the paper on the table and looked at it closely. It did seem different but he thought it might just be his imagination and the power of suggestion. Bill noticed his confusion and proceeded to point out the things indicating that it was a copy, such as the folds not being worn and the ink in the folds not being cracked.

Tom looked at Mr. Hanson asking,

"You said this paper was only recently manufactured. How can that Be ? These journals and documents have been in our possession for many month's and have not been out of our sight."

"Here let me show you one more thing that proves that this is a copy." said Bill as he reached for a small magnifying glass.

Focusing on one corner of the paper he continued.

"See this small jagged line ? Apparently at one time a small piece was ripped off or fell off because of age and or handling, but this document has the corner in tact. This was copied with that piece missing. I'm sorry Mr. Chadwick, but this is only a copy and not worth anything except to tell the story of these certificates. We have a few here on file and they are quite valuable."

Tom sat down again showing his utter disappointment. Tommy quickly brushed away a tear trying to hide it from the others. The room was now silent.

"I have that piece." Carleen stated firmly.

Everyone looked at her, not quite comprehending what she had just said.

"What do you mean, you have that piece ?" questioned Tom.

"Could you explain that ?" followed Bill Hanson.

"Of course I can." smiled Carleen. "When we first received the journals and other papers and we opened this particular document, I noticed that corner piece was still in the envelope. Wanting this certificate to be complete as possible, I carefully removed it and placed it in one of those acid free whatchamacallit envelopes."

"Archival." volunteered Bill

"Yes that's it. Archival envelopes. Thank you. I

thought it might be valuable to the integrity of the piece."

"You thought right, Mrs. Chadwick." said Mark Stensen. Carleen looked at Tom, who had a troubled look on his face.

"You don't seem very happy about this, Tom. I thought I was doing the right thing."

"It was Hon. You did the right thing and I'm glad you had that foresight but something else is bothering me right now."

"I think I know what you're going to say Dad." interrupted Tommy. What good is that little piece if this is only a copy."

"Exactly, Tommy" said Tom.

The room went silent.

"Do you have that piece with you Mrs. Chadwick ?" asked Mr. Hanson.

"As a matter of fact I do. I thought perhaps you might need it to show the whole document."

"May I see it." Bill Hanson further asked.

"Yes Carleen answered. "It's right here in my purse."

She opened her purse and withdrew the archival envelope and offered it to him. He once again turned to the light box where the document still lay and with small pocket tweezers reached for the corner piece. Over laying it on the copy he studied it with a magnifying loop.

"It fits exactly." not really surprised, he stated.

Looking up he put the small piece back into it's protective cover and said,

"I want to run some age tests on this back in the lab, I'll be back shortly." and with that, turned and exited Mark's office.

Tommy watched as Bill Hanson walked out with a very disturbed look about him. A look of hurt and not understanding what was going through his mind. The start of tears could be seen again no matter how hard he fought them back. Carleen, observing her son's change , became concerned.

"What is it Tommy ? Why are you so upset, it's only a piece of paper." She asked.

Tommy was now more visibly upset. A few tears rolled down his cheeks. Besides being hurt, he looked angry.

"Mrs. Porter ! She stole it from us. She stole George Washington from us."

Tommy was now shaking with tears and hurt. Carleen moved to her son and enclosed her arms about him, hoping to comfort him.

"I thought she was our friend." Tommy cried. "But she stole from us. We trusted her and she stole from us."

Tommy wrenched himself from Carleen's embrace and moved to the window, his back to everyone. Carleen made a motion to follow her son only to be held back by her husband.

"Let him be." Said Tom. "It's all part of growing up."

Reluctantly she resumed her seat.

Tom, he's hurting." pleaded Carleen.

"Let him be for the moment, he needs his own time. He will work it out by himself." Said Tom.

Carleen resigned herself to her husband's plea. Her mothering instinct was to enfold and protect her young but down deep inside she knew Tom was right. Her son had to grow on his own, the hard way. It seemed an awkward moment for all but was excepted without comment.

The awkward mood was gratefully shattered when Bill Hanson reentered the room.

"It's original all right." he said excitedly. "Definitely late eighteenth century. The document you have or had was the real thing."

He handed the corner piece back to Carleen. She thanked Bill and turned again to her son.

"You don't know that Tommy. You don't know that Mrs. Porter took that certificate."

"Who else could it be." interjected Tom. "No one but she even knew we had these journals and letters."

Both Mark Stensen and Bill Hanson were looking confused. Mark, out of curiosity, asked who was Mrs. Porter.

"Tommy's history teacher." answered Tom Sr. I may as well complete the whole story for you gentleman. What I told you before was only about half."

Tom sat back and proceeded to fill in the missing pieces and it did capture the interest of both of the Smithsonian men. Before he finished there was a quick knock on the office door, then it opened. A man in a white lab coat stepped into the room.

"Sorry to interrupt, but I just remembered something that may be of interest to you. That small corner piece you just brought to the lab triggered something in my mind. I saw that exact same document before. About three weeks ago a man brought it in for authentication. I think you were busy elsewhere that day Mark. Well, anyway, we ran the usual tests and yes it was an original certificate. It was during the testing that I noticed the missing corner."

"Did you say anything to this man about it." asked Bill.

"Now that I think of it, no, I didn't. I was going to but the conversation took another direction and I guess it slipped my mind. He seemed more interested in it's worth than anything else."

"I'm glad you forgot Jack, that will be a big help to us and thank you Jack, we'll probably get back to you later."

"You know where to find me." he said and closed the door behind him.

Tommy was facing the group again with interest in his expression.

"Mr. Porter." He said in a clear tone.

"You're most likely correct in that assumption, Son." said his dad.

Tom continued the story of the journals to the point of having Tommy read a passage. He proudly did so without any sign of tears.

> *1777 – We rested at Perkiomen Creek for a couple a days. We got some reenforcements from Rhode Island troops and almost a thousand from Virginia, Maryland and Pennsylvania. We are moving to Philadelfy next. – RC.*

He finished with his own remark,

"This was written by my ancestor who was there with George Washington. He was with him during the whole war. They even became friends and wrote letters after the war."

Beaming a broad smile now, he looked directly at Mark and Bill. They in turn smiled acknowledging the boy's pride.

"Well." said Mark." You have more then convinced us of the legitimacy of these journals. Perhaps we can be of help to retrieve your documents, and in turn let us at least have a more in depth look at the Diaries.

Tom's comfort level with these two gentlemen rose about two hundred percent. Turning to Carleen and Tommy, who were both smiling and nodding their approval, he answered affirmatively.

In thinking back to the offer of help, he asked,

"How can you be of help if you don't mind me asking ?"

"Of course not." mark answered. "That's part of our job, keeping track of legitimate history. To start with can you give me a detailed description of this Mrs. Porter."

"Yes, we can." said Tom Sr. "We worked very closely with her for a couple of month's."

Tom then proceeded to write a description of Helen Porter with welcomed prompts from Carleen. After handing the paper to Mark, Tommy piped up with,

"I can go one better than that. How about a picture ?

Her photo along with all the other teachers is in the high school yearbook every year. We can E-mail you a copy as soon as we get home.

Smiles went all around the room at young Tom's thoughtful suggestion. Mark then asked Bill,

"Get a hold of Jack again and see what info he can provide us on the man who brought in the certificate."

"I'll go down and see him myself right now." he replied and exited the office.

Still a little confused Tom inquired again as to how these descriptions were going to help. Seating himself at his desk, Mark went on to explain.

"Historical documents are big business in this country these days. For that matter it's big business world wide. Documents such as your's go for big bucks at auctions. Sometimes at pawn dealers but the really big money is at auctions. Good auction houses are as good at authentication as we are. Perhaps sometimes better. The best part about this story is they look out for each other and are for the most part honest and legitimate. After all this is how they make their money. They are very good at spotting phony stuff and are excellent at reading people. There are very few shady auction dealers. Of course they do exist but they usually don't last too long. Anyhow, getting back to my point, these auction houses maintain close connections with each other and with us and various State Historical Societies. We will send out descriptions of the people and of the document. If and when it shows up at auction we will know instantly. The auctioneers will continue negotiation as usual so that the perpetrators are none the wiser. The rightful owner, in this case, you, then has the time to make the decision as to what to do as far as recovery of his property and pursuing legal action, if that is your choice."

Tom Chadwick Sr. Sat back in his chair, sighing,

"I had no idea this could be that involved."

"When we're dealing with such large sums of money, you would be surprised how complex these situations can get." replied Mark.

Tommy and Carleen started to speak simultaneously. They laughed, and Tommy conceded to his Mother.

"May I ask what kind of money you are talking about with this certificate ?" she asked.

Tommy smiled and quietly stated that he was going to ask the same thing. He now stood behind his mother's chair his hand lightly resting on her shoulder.

"I was getting to that." answered Mark. "As I said earlier, collecting historical documents is quite popular now. In the case of your documents, it can be valued two ways. First of all, since it has never been turned in, it is still redeemable by congress. Of course you must have proper documentation as to lineage of the original owner, which I'm sure you can do. Your journal history alone would be sufficient evidence."

The three Chadwicks smiled at this, proud of their books.

"As to the actual sum, it would be based on the going price of 1777 for the goods exchanged. Now comes the real fun. The accrued interest would then be calculated for the last two hundred and , what is it. Thirty two years. That would be it's worth today."

"Wow." exclaimed Tommy quietly, trying to do the math in his head. He gave up on that quickly realizing he would need a calculator, or even better yet, a computer.

"That's one value." continued Mr. Stenson, "And only you could collect that. The second is more readily available to anyone holding the certificate. That of course is the auction houses. Bidding on such a paper as this is, with George Washington's signature, would probably start around five or ten thousand dollars. I personally suspect this would most likely sell for an excess of one hundred and fifty thousand dollars. Perhaps even more based on it's state of preservation. Taking that one step further, that collection of diaries and journals you say you have could easily be valued in the millions."

Tom and Carleen appeared breathless for the moment. Tommy, in his usual uninhibited manner, stated.

"There's even a higher value than that available to us."

Questioningly, Carleen, Tom and Mark looked at Tommy for further clarification.

"And what would that be." Mark asked, sudden surprise in his voice.

Tommy answered with an air of confidence, in a serious tone, **"Family History."**

These two words seemed to echo in the room as if to say his family was not for sale. Carleens eyes dampened as she rose from her seat and turned and embraced her son, unashamedly saying,

"I love you."

Tom, almost embarrassed with pride spoke directly to Mr. Stensen.

"Well ! There's your answer. He just made our final decision for us."

Mark smiled, obviously emotionally touched and stated.

"I couldn't agree more. That is a most difficult decision and the best one I've heard in years."

Tommy, still in serious voice asked;

"Can I read something else ? I promise I'll be quiet after that."

"Go right ahead Tommy. I wouldn't want to stop you now, anyway." Mark replied.

Now the center of attention, Tommy proceeded.

"George Washington didn't write this, Thomas Paine did, but

General Washington read it to his troops on Christmas eve 1776 just before crossing the Delaware to attack Trenton.

Christmas eve — 1776 — The General is determined to take Trenton by surprise. In order to do that we all has to do our jobs and do um right. So the General passed out copies of a writing by this Tom Paine fella, so the officers could read it to the men. The General hisself read it to those closest to him. Later he let me barry it so's I could copy it in this Diary.

"These are the times that try men's souls. The summer soldier and the sunshine patriot will, in this crisis, shrink from the service of their country; but he that stands it now, deserves the love and thanks of man and woman. Tyranny, like hell, is not easily conquered; yet we have this consolation with us, that the harder the conflict, the more glorious the triumph."

He read this to stir the troops and it sure worked. RC.

Tommy paused for a moment, cleared his throat and said,
"George Washington read that to the troops. My ancestor was there to hear it from his own lips and he stayed with Washington throughout the whole war. This is part of our history, my history, my family history. This family history has no price."

His voice was shaking with emotion now, and almost challenging. He closed the diary and held it closely to his chest.

Tom Sr. now stood, walked to his son and hugged him tightly saying,

"And no one ever will put a price on it Son."

The quiet of the moment was shattered by the office door suddenly opened as Bill returned. All were smiling which prompted Bill to ask,

"Did I miss a party or something."

No party, Bill but what you did miss was a wonderful moment in the preservation of American History." answered Mark.
Mark went on to say, "Never mind, I'll tell you later."

Dismissing it Bill said: "Jack gave me all he had, name address and what seemed to be a pretty good description."

"What about a phone number ?" Mark inquired.

"No, no phone number. The story is, he just moved and the phone was not connected yet." replied Bill.

"Well this is enough for a start. Let's get this right out to the network. We'll follow it up again later when we get the photo of Helen Porter." said Mark

Bill shook hands with the Chadwicks and left the office again. Turning to the family again, Mark spoke with true sincerity when he said.

"I know now you must feel but we will do everything we can to help you retrieve your certificate. Unfortunately, there is nothing more that can be done right now except hope for the best. Relying on this network of dealers we have, should, in time, be able to turn up some information. Don't give up. I'm sure young Tom here won't let you give up."

Mark extended his hand to Tommy;

"It's has been my privilege to meet you Tommy and I hope we meet again. Perhaps you would like to work here in the future. It is people like you who make it worthwhile preserving history. I personally thank you for that."

Carleen felt that swelling in her chest again as she looked at her son. This time it was her eyes that moistened.

Goodbys were exchanged and the Chadwick family returned to the hotel. They chose to keep a positive attitude and promised each other that all would turnout okay.

Chapter 15

        The return trip to Morristown was quiet. Each of the three Chadwicks wrapped in their own thoughts about the meeting in D.C..   They kept the chatter light avoiding stirring emotions. Tom concentrating on driving, Carleen mentioned a point of interest periodically, not that there is much scenery on the Jersey Pike, and Tommy played a mental collect the license plate game on and off. One more diary story would help pass the time he thought. He read aloud for all to hear;

> *"January 2, 1777 – Twas just outside of Princeton. We heard heavy fire and came upon some of General Mercer's troops retreating. Mercer was down and bayoneted real bad by the British.   The General hisself spurred his horse and charged into the enemy's direct fire waving his hat. The men seeing Washington and his white horse charging, turned and rallied and won the day. The General didn't get one scratch." RC.*

        "I don't think I'll ever tire of reading these diaries." he said closing the book. "I think we should get to work right away on writing this story. At least get it started. I can't wait to read more of the journals about the Revolution. I wonder what the Civil War journals are like. Boy ! We sure have some history in our family.

        Tom and Carleen were smiling listening to their son's animated voice. His excitement over the books would help him recover from the shock of Helen Porter's betrayal.

        Settled at home again and back to the routine of research, took up most of Tommy's time which he gladly welcomed.

As promised Tommy located the yearbook and Tom Sr. E-mailed Helen Porter's picture to Mark Stensen. Tommy became so involved in the research that he had to be encouraged by both parents to join his friends periodically before summer was over. With mixed feelings, he did just that, enjoying both equally.

Having a soda one day after a ball game, some of his friends were talking of having met their math teacher's husband, and how he was not what they expected. Their conversation then went on to wondering what other teachers spouses were like. This was the perfect opportunity for Tommy to slip in Mrs. Porter's name to the discussion without alarm.

"I met him once." said his friend Andy. "He was nice enough I guess, but not as nice as Mrs. Porter.

"What did he look like." asked Carl, another ball playing friend.

"*Good.*" thought Tommy, "*I'm totally free now from any connection.*"

Andy went on to answer, "He's kinda hard to describe. There was really nothing outstanding about his features.

I did see his picture in the paper a few day later though, having something to do with the Rotary in town. Who pays attention to that stuff.

"*Bingo.*" thought Tommy again who then asked innocently;

"Really ? When was that ?"

"I don't exactly remember, I guess about a week or so before school closed."

Tommy changed the subject then so as not to raise any questions of why he was asking.

Nearing late afternoon, the boys broke up and went their separate ways. They would meet again the next day for another game. Tommy rode his bike home as fast as he could.

Carleen listened quietly to Tommy's exciting find.

"Your father will be glad to hear this." she said although , deep inside she wanted to give Helen Porter the benefit of the doubt. She still found it hard to believe that Mrs. Porter would have taken the certificate to copy. "Your father is very busy at work this week, so perhaps I can go to the newspaper office or the library tomorrow and see what I can find."

"That would be great, Mom. I have another ball game tomorrow, besides I don't want to let on to the guys what we're doing."

"That's a good thing." Carleen replied. "Why don't you shower before dinner. You're so dirty, that except for your voice I did not recognize you."

"Aww Mom !" Tommy gently complained.

"Scoot." Was her reply. Tommy headed upstairs and Carleen happily took on the dinner duties.

After three helpings at dinner, Tommy retired to the

den for some quiet reading. Tonight he decided he needed a change of venue, so he moved forward in the stack of journals to find something else on the War of 1812. Finding the appropriate years, he read;

"24 August, 1814 — It was a little after 9 o'clock in the evening when them redcoats set fire to the Capital. Flames were every where. They lit up the whole night sky. The flames even left their mark on the stone bald eagle carving, the symbol of our new young country. The heat was so intense it was melting glass and destroying stone. The flames of destruction literally lasted the whole night. I did not want to watch this deliberate destruction but I could not turn away. Must leave now, more later." TC.

"Wow." He said quietly as he sat back in the recliner and closed his eyes. Drifting into dreamland he was suddenly there. The burning of Washington was happening before his eyes. The heat was intense. He could feel it's power even standing almost a half a mile away. Soldiers with torches were everywhere indiscriminately setting fire to any structure they came upon. Public buildings or private houses were equal in the eyes of the British. Burn it all was their goal. Tommy's heart filled with hurt as he watched the Capital burn to nothing more then ashes. Hearing a noise behind him, he turned to meet two British soldiers running at him. One held a torch, the other a rifle brandishing a long bayonet aimed straight at his heart. Tommy sat straight up dripping with sweat, ready to cry out.

It took a while to realize where he was and slowly he calmed down. It was a dream but it was so real he could feel himself still shaking. He put the book down and was thankful that no one had witnessed his frightful experience.

      " **M**aybe I should go and see if Mom needs help with the dishes, That should calm me down." he said aloud.

Chapter   16

Carleen was successful at the library and was able to make a copy unnoticed. It wasn't very good but she thought they may be able to enhance it at the Smithsonian. She mailed it off that same afternoon, rather then losing anymore detail via E-mail.

The last couple of weeks of summer vacation swiftly disappeared. Tommy sort of looked forward to his return to school although he knew it would cut down on his research time. These and other thoughts he continued to put in his own journal.

"Not as exciting as my ancestors notes." he thought, "But I'm still young yet."

The first week in October, the phone rang at the Chadwick household. It was seven thirty and they had just finished cleaning up dinner dishes. Tom was walking by as it rang.

"Hello Mr. Stensen, I was wondering if we were going to hear from you."

Both Carleen and Tommy's ears perked up at hearing Tom's words. They stopped what they were doing and moved closer to Tom.

"Really ! That is good news." Carleen and Tommy looked at each other, anticipation building. They could only hear one side of the conversation, but their imaginations were running wild. The conversation went on for about five minutes.

"Okay Mark, we won't do or say a thing until we hear from you again. Have a good evening and thanks for the update."

Tom hung up the receiver but didn't utter a word, turned and walked to the den, sat in his recliner and buried his head in the newspaper. Tommy and Carleen quickly followed.

"Tom ! Dad !" They said in unison.

"Um." Was the only reply they received from behind the paper wall.

Carleen moved closer and grabbed the newspaper and pulled it away revealing a laughing, smiling face.

"You rat." Said Carleen, just for that you get no ice cream later."

"That's cruel." He answered.

"I told you she could be mean, Dad, but you deserved that." joined Tommy.

"Did you want to see me about something." Tom inquired still smiling.

"Keep it up and you won't even get dinner tomorrow."

"Okay you win." Tom replied. With a more serious tone he continued;

"Someone turned up at Sotheby's Auction House in Boston, and yes, it was Mr. Porter."

Carleen's hopes for an innocent Helen Porter were suddenly dashed. Tommy also looked a little sad.

"He's brought the certificate in to place it in auction. Sotheby's is using delaying tactics just as Mark and Bill said they would. The police and Federal authorities have been notified. Furthermore, Mr. Porter has been suspected of similar actions before but was never caught. They feel, this time, because of our documentation, that they can finally put an end to his scams. We have to sit tight now till they contact us."

"So we can get our certificate back to where it belongs." said a serious Tommy.

"Why so sad sport, I thought you would be happy about this ?" Tom said.

"Oh, I am Dad, it's just that - - - ."

"I know son, Mrs. Porter. You have to realize that things happen sometimes that are beyond our control. This will not be the first time you will experience disappointment."

Carleen put her hand on her son's shoulder,

"Just remember we are always here for you."

To lighten the moment she then declared,

"Okay, ice cream all around."

Smiles appeared again as Carleen turned towards the kitchen.

At school the following day the bell rang ending fifth period History. History had always been Tommy's favorite, but now seemed rather boring after having been so involved with actual living history. His daydreams almost made him miss the periods end. He suddenly jumped up from his seat and headed for the door when Miss Tarant called to him.

"Tommy ! Could I speak with you for a moment."

He turned and walked to the teachers desk wondering what he had done now.

"Yes Miss Tarant ?" he questioned.

"We don't have much time now but would you please see me at the end of the day before you go home."

"Okay." was Tommy's puzzled answer.

"Don't forget now, it's very important." Miss Tarant's eyes were looking directly into his checking to see that he understood.

"I won't forget Miss Tarant. I'll see you after school."

Tommy left the room trying to figure out what she wanted. He had done nothing wrong as far as he knew.

"Oh well, math is next and that I have to pay attention to." he thought.

The rest of the school day passed pretty normally with Tommy not thinking much of the meeting with his history teacher. He was too involved with his classes and socializing in between. When the final bell rang he went to his locker, checked to see that he had the necessary books for homework, then walked straight to miss Tarant's class.

Miss Sarah Tarant was at her desk when Tommy entered the room. She looked up as if surprised saying,

"Oh good, Tommy, you remembered. Please close the door."

He was puzzled about the door but did as she asked then took a seat directly in front of her desk. He looked at Miss Tarant and noticed that she was a bit nervous and her face was quite serious. He remained silent.

"Tommy, what I'm about to say must not leave this room except go directly to your parents."

Tommy felt completely lost by this statement but continued to listen. She reached into her large leather briefcase and withdrew a brown manila envelope. It was a five by seven envelope

and heavily sealed with reenforced packing tape. She handed it to Tommy.

"Take this home to your parents. They are to open it together with you present. Please do not lose it. It is very important."

She relaxed somewhat now and smiled.

"Remember we never spoke."

She handed him a book that had been sitting on her desk.

"Take this book that you are borrowing from me in case anyone saw us together in here. You can return it another day whenever you want. You had best go now. I'll see you in class tomorrow."

"Miss Tarant turned her attention back to the papers she was marking ignoring Tommy as he left the room.

He left the building and while walking to the bike rack glanced at the book she had given him. It was titled, "George Washington's

First War." Tommy thought this rather ironic but dismissed it quickly. His curiosity was concentrating on the mystery envelope.

Tommy unlocked his bike and started home. He purposely did not rush to get home.

"What's the use." he thought. *"We can't open the envelope till Dad gets home."*

He knew he had done nothing wrong, so he put the envelope out of his mind and started thinking about the book they were preparing to write.

"I think a good way to start would be with one of the journal entries." he said out loud talking to himself. "Something dynamic, that would grab the reader's attention right away. Then we can blend a story, no, the start of a story into that particular diary

entry, highlighting the dates. Yeah ! That's it. Maybe I'll just go ahead and write my own start, then show it to Mom and Dad."

Pleased with himself, he whistled a few tunes on the rest of the way home.

Carleen heard Tommy slamming the door as usual and called out;

"I'm in the den, Tommy."

He made his way to the den dropping his school books on the stairs as he passed. He kissed his Mom on the cheek and she noticed the brown envelope he was holding.

"What's that you've got." she inquired matter of factly.

"It's from Miss Tarant, my history teacher." He answered handing the envelope to his mother. Carleen was instantly concerned.

"Oh no ! Tommy, did you get into trouble in school again ?" she asked.

"No Mom, it's nothing like that." Tommy was quick to answer. He then related the whole mysterious story to her.

"Well then, let's open this and find out what this is all about." stated Carleen.

"No Mom, we can't." said Tommy, putting his hand out touching his mother. "She was very specific and emphatic about her instructions. We have to wait for Dad."

Following Miss Tarant's instructions obviously meant a lot to her son so she conceded and put the envelope on the table with the journals. Looking at her son with a slight smile she said,

"Are you sure you're not in trouble again."

"Positive Mom, trust me, I am not in any trouble." Tommy answered, also smiling. "I'm going to do my homework ,
while we're waiting for Dad." he remarked as he left the den.

Alone again, Carleen glanced at the envelope noticing how

well sealed it was. It is rather mysterious." she thought, and went back to her own reading.

Tom arrived home from work his usual time, throwing the car keys on the table by the door, he went straight to the den. He leaned down to kiss his wife and noticed the well taped brown envelope.

"What's this." He asked curiously.

"That's the mystery of the day." Carleen replied. "Before you open it we have to get Tommy."

She called Tommy, letting him know his father was home. A minute later Tommy entered the den and saw his father holding the brown envelope.

"So , Mom told you about the envelope." He said excitedly.

"No, I have not said a word yet. Tell your father what you told me earlier." she requested.

He repeated the same story for his father that he relayed to his mother, word for word.

"That does sound strange." Tom Sr. Said when Tommy finished.

Tom reached into his pocket for his small pocket knife;

"Well lets see what this whole thing is about."

The tape was finally slit across the top of the envelope. Tom placed the knife on the table and retrieved the paper within. Opening it, he glanced at the bottom.

"It's from Helen Porter." He said somewhat annoyed.

"Read it Tom, please." cried Carleen sympathetically.

"OH, alright." answered Tom in a disgusted manner.

Dear Tom, Carleen and particularly Tommy,

I know what you must all be thinking, especially since you put your trust in me. I can't blame you either, for whatever ill feelings you may harbor.

Please don't throw this letter away. At least listen to what I have to say, then you can decide what you may. I certainly did not want to betray your trust, but my very life depended on doing what I did.

My husband became obsessed by your

certificate. All he could think of was the money it would net him. I only mentioned it casually at the dinner table one evening. You know, about the diaries and the book you were planning and the research that I was assisting with.

His questions and probing for more information became relentless even to the point of physical abuse. My resigning from school, saying I was moving was only a ruse on my part. I just could not face the shame I felt. I was under constant surveillance, even when I was at your house. Either he or a partner were always outside watching. My cell phone was destroyed, I was almost never alone.

Please forgive me, I never meant to hurt you. All three of you have been so wonderful to me. I reached a point where I felt I had no choice. I feared for my life and still do.

My friend, Sarah or Miss Tarant as you know her Tommy, does not know the contents of this letter, nor do I want her to. It took me quite some time to get this message together because I was never really alone. She only agreed to get this to Tommy. In a way I fear for her also, if I'm ever found out.

Please, do what you have to from your end as if you had never met me. Act as if nothing ever happened, I fear for you also.

The receipt and reading of this letter is very important to me. All Tommy has to do is give Sarah an *affirmative nod of his head in class. I will then get the same message from her.*

> *Again please forgive me. Good Luck.*
> *With Love,*
> *Helen Porter.*

Tom put the letter down and sat back staring at it.
The wrinkles and dirt on the paper seemed to bear out her story of taking a long time to write. Some of the ink smears were probably caused by tears." he thought.

Carleen and Tommy were both blotting moistened eyes and trying not to show it.

"Tom, what are we going to do." Carleen anxiously pleaded.

"How can we help her, Dad." added Tommy, visibly upset "We have to help her." he pleaded.

"Don't worry Tommy, we will, but we have to be careful in doing so. It's obvious the woman has been through a lot already." was Tom's reply.

Tom left the den heading for the phone. Taking a card from his wallet he dialed the number. There was a pause, then

"Mark, Tom Chadwick here. I just received some information I thought you should know about."

Tom then read the letter. He listened to Mark's comments then answered;

"You got it. I'll do it right now, and yes we'll wait to hear from you."

Hanging up the phone he immediately turned on the FAX machine, inserted the letter and listened to the hum as the paper was copied. He returned to the den.

"Okay, we are to do just as Helen requested and pretend nothing happened. Tommy, tomorrow in school you give the nod to Miss Tarant and no more. Beyond that make believe she doesn't exist. Mark is getting in touch with the proper authorities, probably even the FBI. They will work everything from their end down rather then risk endangering Mrs Porter more than she already is.

"Tom, I'm worried." said Carleen.

Tom took her hand in his.

"It will be alright. We will be doing every thing we can. Right now, for us, that means doing nothing."

"Don't worry Mom, I'm right here with you." Tommy said as he put his arm around Carleens shoulder.

School the next day went as usual. Halfway through history class Tommy caught the eye of Miss Tarant and gave a barely perceptible nod. She was then distracted. Tommy was not upset by this, he would just bide his time.

Drifting off in a daydream he fancied himself involved in the intrigue of the spy game. He had to get this secret message to Sarah without being seen. He looked around the classroom trying to identify the enemy agent.

Ring -g -g -g -g -g.

The period was over and he abruptly came back to the real world . He purposely fumbled with his books so he could be the last to leave the class. As he neared the door Miss Tarant looked up from her desk, gave a slight nod and a wink. Tommy wanted to smile but thought better of it. In the hall on the way to his next class he thought, *"Mission accomplished."* He smiled and felt proud of himself and continued on to math. The thoughts of the spy game played with his mind throughout the rest of the day. It was only on the way home from school that he remembered this really wasn't a game for Mrs. Porter. He felt a little guilty of making a game out of something that surely was not a game to Helen Porter.

Chapter 17

Almost a week had passed since Tom's call to Mark Stensen. They heard of nothing new. They waited anxiously but patiently. Just before noon on Wednesday there was an impatient knock at the rear door of the Chadwick house.

"Oh my, did that boy forget his key again." said a slightly annoyed Carleen. She had been transplanting a house plant and had to drop everything to answer the door. She opened the door to the kitchen, words of reprimand on her lips, when she froze in place. She was staring at Helen Porter, her face half hidden in a hooded sweat jacket. In a tear shaken voice, Helen said;

"I didn't know where else to go."

Carleen reached for her and quickly pulled her into the house. Helen Porter fell into Carleens arms, sobbing uncontrollably. While gently trying to comfort her she pushed the hood from her head revealing severe bruises on the left side of her face and head. The hair was matted with dried blood and her left eye was blackened and quite swollen.

"Oh my God, Helen." said Carleen with a deep intake of breath.

Helen looked at Carleen through tear filled eyes and repeated,
"I didn't know where else to go."

"It's okay, It's okay, You're here now. You're safe now." Carleen answered as she held the throbbing body tightly.
"Shhhh, now." she said still comforting Helen, "Come sit, and let's get you cleaned up."

Carleen walked her to the table, pulled out a chair and sat her down. Warm water and a wash cloth were next. She carefully and gently tended to Helen's injuries. From her experience with her own son's falling mishaps she figured the wounds were several hours old. Doing the best she could to clean and dress them she finally said;

"You really need a doctor."

"Oh no ! I couldn't, not now. I may have been followed." said Helen in a startled voice as she looked up at her makeshift nurse.

"It's okay, you're safe now." soothed Carleen. "How about a cup of tea or would you like something stronger."

"Tea would be fine." Helen answered with a gratitude still shaking a little.

Carleen prepared the tea and while it was steeping asked,

"If you're up to it why don't you tell me what happened."

"Yes, yes I will." Answered Helen, "As soon as I stop shaking." she added trying a small smile.

She fiddled with her tea bag for a few nervous minutes. Carleen remained silent not wanting to push her distraught friend.

"It started early this morning, my husband caught me going through his briefcase. I was looking for the certificate. As it turned out it wasn't there. He had taken it to an auction place somewhere in Boston.

"We know, Sotheby's." volunteered Carleen. "We have been keeping track of it for a couple of weeks."

Helen seemed pleased with this information and went on with her story.

"He became violently angry when he caught me and you can see the results of his temper. The auction house had been in touch with him and he left for Boston again this morning, but not before his partner was there to watch over me."

"How did you get away." Carleen inquired.

With a light laugh, Helen continued,

"I don't know where I got the courage, but I managed to hit him on the back of the head with a table lamp and ran. I hid in the kitchen broom closet after opening the back door. He wasn't down very long when he came after me. Seeing the open door he ran out. In a few minutes I heard his car start and he pulled out of the driveway. I waited a few more minutes, then ran out and through a neighbors yard. You were the only one I could think of to go to. I'm sorry I did now because he will probably come here looking for me. I feel I have put you in danger now. I'd better go."

Helen attempted to get up as Carleen grabbed her hand,

"You'll do no such thing. You are safe here and you will stay here. Tommy will be home from school soon and in the meantime I'll call Tom. You come with me while I call."

The two women went to the living room where the phone was. Carleen started to dial while Helen gazed absently out the window. Carleen then heard a quick intake of breath and Helen say,

"There he is. That silver car a few houses down across the street."

Carleen put the phone down to join her friend at the window being careful not to be seen.

"Are you sure it's him ?" she asked.

"Yes I'm positive." answered Helen shaking again. "I remember the licence plate."

"That's good." said Carleen. "Now sit down while I call Tom."

The number was dialed but voice mail answered. Carleen left a quick message without detail. Becoming a bit worried herself she hung up the phone.

"What do we do now." Asked a crying Helen.

At that moment a key turned in the door and Tommy entered calling out,

"I'm home Mom."

Entering the living room he noticed Mrs. Porter's Bruises. Anger crossed his face instantly.

"It's okay Tommy, but I'm glad you're here."

"Hello Tommy." Helen said quietly looking embarrassed.

Carleen quickly outlined the story to her son including the car across the street. Listening to the explanation of what happened, Tommy could not take his eyes off Helen Porter. He didn't mean to make her uncomfortable, He just felt so sorry for her.
In his mind, it wasn't right for someone to do that to another person, especially a woman, and in particular, his teacher.

When Carleen finished her tale, Tommy, without saying a word turned and left the room, much to the surprise of both women. He returned moments later holding a baseball bat.

"If he comes in here we'll be ready for him." He stated firmly.

Carleen felt proud of her son again. There was no end to his heroic attitude, although she did caution:

"Now don't go doing anything foolish."

"Don't worry Mom, I'm staying right here till Dad gets here."

With that the phone rang. Carleen recognized Tom's office number and answered. She relayed the whole story to Tom, who reassured her all would be taken care of, including the car across the street. "It might take a half hour or so, so keep the doors locked.." and he ended the conversation.

"I just remembered." Tommy exclaimed out loud. I'm supposed to be at a baseball meeting at Andy's"

Without waiting for any comments he walked to the phone, bat still in hand, and dialed.

"Hello, Andy, this is Tommy. I just found out my Mom doesn't feel well and I don't want to leave her alone. Can we have the meeting here instead ? Good, see ya then."

He hung up the phone, looked at both women and said, "He won't try anything with a whole bunch of us here."

In ten minutes there were twelve boys aged thirteen to fifteen gathered

on the front lawn and in the driveway. "Here's your private security force."
he joked as he went outside to join his pals.

Now it was Helen Porter's turn to marvel at Tommy's
maturity and actions. Feeling a little less tense now they enjoyed a second cup
of tea.

Unnoticed by the boys a local power company truck, followed
by a car also bearing the company logo, parked both in front of and behind the
silver car across the street. In less than a minute the occupant of the silver car
was being escorted into the back of the truck. Tommy caught this act with a
side glance and smiled to himself. The two vehicles drove off leaving a
locked car on the street.

Tommy's baseball group fooled around for another half hour,
then broke up. Tommy reentered the house all smiles. Walking over to Mrs.
Porter he said proudly,

"Now you have nothing to worry about."

Helen Porter took Tommy's hand in her own,

"The world is a better place with you in it Tom."

With his cheeks turning red, he thought,

"Wow ! She called me Tom, she's talking to me like an
adult."

Carleen came over and kissed her son's cheek. Now he felt
himself really go crimson.

Chapter   18

Tom Sr. Came home shortly after they towed the car away that belonged to Helen's threat. One view of Mrs. Porter and he calmly but authoritatively said,

"Now that the immediate danger has passed, you are going to the emergency room."

Looking as if she was going to say something, Tom put his hand up adding, "And there will be no arguments."

Helen looked at Carleen and Tommy, who were both smiling and hesitantly said.

"I don't deserve this, but I put myself in your hands."

A single tear rolled down her cheek.

Tommy remained home to work on school work and monitor the phone in case Mr. Stensen called, while his Dad, Mom and Mrs. Porter went to the hospital. There wasn't much homework and he knew his folks would be gone for a few hours, so he retreated to the den. It had been a while since he buried himself in his diary's.

The thought, perhaps for a change, he would advance in the journals to the Civil War. Finding the necessary years he opened one at random.

"*November – 1863 We was goin afta General Braxton Bragg at Chattanooga, they sure have funny town names here in the South. General Grant has ordered us to build a supply line to town. We was builden bridges, and railroads and floating men and arms up the river right passed them rebels, who never seen us. Looks like we can win this one.*" JC

Tommy closed the diary and as was his usual habit, closed his eyes and put himself near Chattanooga. His imagination flew. He saw Grant and, at a distance saw, General Bragg on his horse. Tommy had read that the two Generals knew each other and that Grant had a lot of respect for Braxton Bragg, and that he was a good military man.

There was a loud thump nearby and Tommy sat bolt up right, eyes wide open. The diary had fallen off his lap to the floor.

"Just as well that it did." He thought, *"Otherwise I might have slept the afternoon away."*

Putting the book where it belonged in the stack, he went up to the spare bedroom to make sure everything was in order. Knowing his Mother she would insist Helen Porter stay with them tonight.

His parents and Helen returned a little after six o'clock. He noted that his Dad carried a small suitcase, obviously Helen's. Smiling, Tommy said to himself, *"Boy did I call that one right."*

"I noticed you had already prepared a stew for tonight,

Mom, so I went ahead and set the table for four of us."

"Why thank you Tommy, how thoughtful of you." Carleen answered.

Helen Porter looked a lot better than earlier in the day, Tommy noticed, then asked sincerely

"How are you Mrs. Porter."

"Much better now, thanks to all of you. One could not ask for better friends." She replied.

A little embarrassed again by her reply, Tommy decided to change the subject.

"We're getting a lot closer to an outline for the book since we saw you last."

"We are ?" quipped his father.

Ignoring his Dad's remark he went on to say,

"In fact I have started writing my own beginning for the book. I think it's going to be just Wow !"

It was now Carleens turn to poke at her son.

"It would be nice if your mother and father could have a part in this book." She said from the stove.

Deciding to keep the fun going for Helen's sake, Tommy shot back,

"Well, if we can have ice cream tonight, I just may let you."

Helen could see what a loving and together family this was and was pleased to be a small part of their lives. Perhaps, someday, she could have all this.

Dinner was enjoyable though simple. Conservation was kept light and no mention of Helen's ordeal seemed to be the unspoken order of the evening. When dinner was over, the men retired to the den while Helen insisted on doing her share in the kitchen with Carleen. It wasn't long before they joined the Chadwick men. The talk, of course, turned to George Washington and the diary's. All four were reading different years and making notes. Tommy, with his overworked enthusiasm would interrupt now and again to read a passage. It was fruitless to try and silence him

"Listen to this ." He said for the third time, and with out waiting he read,

(Month ?) 1780 – Word came today of the battle of King's Mountain. The British troops under Colonel Ferguson were routed by the Mountain Men from the Carolinas and Georgia. Over eight hundred British troops were taken prisoner. The General says, though it was only a small engagement, it may have turned the tide of the southern war. Cornwallis was all but checked." RC

Mrs. Porter having learned something herself spoke to Tommy before he could comment.

"You're right ,Tommy, that's not in the school history books either."

He smiled in answer.

"She beat me to it." He thought.

The clock was ticking and Tom finally said aloud what everyone was thinking,

"Obviously we won't get news from Boston tonight, so I suggest we all turn in."

No one argued the point and a clean up of papers and books ensued.

"What a pleasure it is to be doing this again." Helen commented, to herself, more than anyone else.

Chapter 19

Seven fifteen, breakfast was interrupted by the harsh sound, at least at that hour of the morning, of the telephone. Three of the four people at the table froze in place. Only Tom jumped to answer the ring.

"Yes, this is he.

"That's correct, Mr. Mark Stensen."

Now Carleen, Helen and Tommy were gathered at the archway to the living room listening intently to decipher the half of the conversation they could not hear.

"Yes we have the documentation he spoke of."

"Yes we can arrange that."

"We will be there by mid-afternoon."

"Okay, see you then."

"Thank you so much."

Tom put the receiver back in it's cradle. He turned to his three eavesdroppers smiling.

"It's over." he said. "I'm sorry, Helen, but Mr. Porter has been arrested."

"I'm not." she mumbled.

"Our document is safe, however we are to meet Mark and Bill at Southebys this afternoon along with the Federal Authorities. Once we show our evidence, George Washington will be home with us again. Speaking to Carleen directly, Tom said,

"We'll have to pack a quick overnight bag and get on the road ASAP."

"What about me Dad, I'm coming also, right ?" he questioned.

"It's a school day Tommy, besides we'll be gone two days, I thought you could stay with Andy."

Tommy's face showed bitter disappointment.

"Tom." Carleen said in a firm voice she rarely used, "If anyone deserves to go, it's Tommy. He's an "A" student and two days off will not hurt."

"Besides he can see all the Revolutionary history of Boston." threw in Helen knowing that this was none of her business.

Tom saw a look in Carleen's eyes that told him she was unmovable on this. He smiled and said,

"I know when I'm outnumbered."

Tommy beamed instantly.

Tom started for the breakfast table again then paused in front of Helen.

"Care to make this a foursome." He asked.

She paused, almost afraid to answer,

"Will I have to see my husband and what about the authorities ?"

You could detect a slight tremble in her voice.

"The answer to both is NO." Tom replied. "There are no charges against you."

Helen looked confused.

"We certainly are not going to press charges against you." interrupted Carleen.

"I would love to go with you." answered Helen, a tear in her eye again. "It seems that's all I have been doing lately." she added as she patted her eyes with a tissue.

Carleen put her arm around her shoulder as they continued on to the breakfast table.

They made quick work of breakfast, threw a few things in a suitcase and were off to Boston.

The visit to Boston and Southebys' was anti-climatic. The Federal Authorities accepted the Chadwick's documentation and released the certificate. It was learned that Mr. Porter was wanted in four states and various country's in Europe for Grand theft and fraud. Mark Stensen and Bill Hanson got their wish of reading some of the journals. The Southeby people were extremely disappointed about their chance of having the certificate. They graciously bowed to the pressure of Tommy's second well spoken speech on the preservation of "Family History". They admitted that no argument could be made against that kind of pride and sentiment.

The book now had it's title in all it's simplicity,

"FAMILY HISTORY"

When the book was published it read:

Family History
by
Tom, Carleen and Tom Chadwick
with
Special editing by Helen Porter

The End

The Mystery Bomber

by

K.J.Goss

The Mystery Bomber

Breaking news bulletin. April 16, 2012.

"Temple Beth El was just bombed. The building was totally destroyed. Casualties unknown as yet. Police at the scene. A two block radius has been cordoned off. Further details will be given as received."

~ ~ ~ ~ ~ ~

Marie McGowen knocked softly and pushed open the door immediately, not waiting for an answer.

"I'm sorry for disturbing you Mr. Hanlon, I know you're busy, but..."

"It's okay Marie, what is it? "

"The radio Sir, I just heard a news bulletin. The Temple Beth El had an explosion, The radio said bombed but I don't know how they knew that."

"Any casualties ?"

"I don't know Sir. The radio said it was too early to say."

"Let's hope not." was Dan Hanlon's answer.

Dan was the District Attorney for the city of Metrolia, and had been for just under a year. He was building a reputation for being tough on crime in the city of three and a half million.

He picked up the remote from his desk and switched on the large flat screen television across the room. Pictures of a flattened burned out building instantly flashed into view.

"Boy! The news people certainly don't waste any time." he said annoyed.

Marie just nodded her head, not saying a word. She was used to Dan's mumbled comments having been with him since he took office.

Dan watched and listened to the reports, speculations and witness interviews flowed for a few minutes then in anger switched off the TV. He started writing notes, and without looking up said;

"Marie get me the man in charge of whatever precinct that is and tell him to get his ass over here now! And without delays or excuses."

"Yes Sir, Mr. Hanlon. And that's the 8th Precinct Sir." answered Marie, her unmatched efficiency showing. She exited the office and softly closed the door.

~ ~ ~ ~ ~ ~

Fri. - April 16, 2012 - 1057 hours: The District Attorney's Office

"Come in." Dan Hanlon gruffly answered the knock on his office door.

A uniformed Police Lieutenant entered and before he could speak, Dan, not in the most courteous of tones spat out.

"What took you so long and where is Capt. Browning."

"On vacation, Sir." was the instant answer of Lt. Dunne almost at attention.

Finally looking up at the young police Lieutenant he softened his tone and directed him to a chair opposite his desk. Relaxing somewhat, but not knowing what to expect, Lt. Dunne spoke, carefully choosing his words.

"I assume this is about the Synagogue explosion."

"You assume right Lt.." was the serious answer. The D A paused for a moment, collecting his thoughts. "Look Lieutenant, before this gets out of hand I want you to put everything we've got into it. A.S.A.P. Spare no expense and no department. I'm sure I'll be hearing from the FBI, but before we get them involved let us do everything possible ourselves. I want this played down in the press, though I know that's difficult to do. Feed them only the basics. Let me take the heat from the press."

Dan Hanlon loved being in the limelight of the press. It was good for his career.

"The bomb squad is already at the site, Sir." Lt. Dunne interjected quickly.

"What about forensics ?" asked Dan.

"As soon as the fire is declared secure we'll get them there, Sir."

"And keep them there until they find something." ordered

Hanlon. "And keep me apprised of every thing that comes up." he added. "Day or night."

"Yes Sir." Dunne snapped back.

Dan Hanlon stood and stretched out his hand. The brief hand shake dismissed the Lieutenant.

~ ~ ~ ~ ~ ~

Fri. - April 16, 2012 - 1305 hours.   Avenue M - Synagogue Location

The smouldering ruins of Temple Beth El was an ugly reminder for everyone to witness. The damage, luckily enough, was confined to the free standing Synagogue which was flanked by a parking lot on one side and a wooded lot on the other and to the rear. Lt. Sean Dunne approached the plainclothes detective Sargent who was obviously running the preliminary investigation

"Hey Chuck." Sean called . "I know you've got your hands full ***BUT***" he emphasized the but, "I spoke with the DA earlier and...."

Chuck Broadhurst quickly interrupted, "From what I hear you were the first of a whole list. He sure is a go getter."

"**I** guess I don't have to repeat what I was told then." Sean said.

"**P**robably not. Let's just compare notes later before we make our reports." replied Chuck

Sgt. Dean Campbell from the bomb squad joined the pair.

"**G**etting right to the point - this was definitely the job of a Pro. This was no crack pot do it yourselfer."

Sean and Chuck became instantly serious.

"**T**errorist you think." asked Chuck speaking for both.

"**I**t's too early to tell and I wouldn't want to hazard a guess just yet. We have got to keep this quiet for a while. You know what a field day the press will have with it. We do not need public panic right now."

All three silently agreed.

"**G**otta go." Dean continued, "I just wanted to keep you up to date. We are no where near finished yet."

As they watched Dean walk back to the smokey brick and rubble, Chuck spoke matter of factly,

"**M**ight as well let these guys do what they're getting paid for. Talk to you later."

He followed Deans path.

~ ~ ~ ~ ~ ~

Lt. Dunne approached the uniformed Sargent who was already conversing with two patrolman.

"**S**gt., can I see you for a minute."

Redirecting his attention to the Lieutenant, Sgt. Dunston answered with a snappy, "Yes Sir." and added "Carry on boys, I'll see you later." to the uniformed men.

Once alone with the Sgt., Lt. Dunne picked up where he left off:

"**I**t's almost dark and I want three men here at all times, four if you think necessary. Recheck all perimeter tapes and barricades. No one comes near this place. Is that clear."

"**Y**es Sir." Sgt. Dunston repeated.

"**A**nd no talking to the press under any circumstances."

"**I** understand and will instruct the men accordingly."

I"ll work out the relief schedule as soon as I get back to the precinct. Remember, keep alert, we don't know what we are dealing with yet." said Sean Dunne as he turned back to his car.

Sgt. Dunston immediately returned to the other uniformed officers and began to set up the night patrol guidelines.

~ ~ ~ ~ ~ ~

Fri - April 16, 2012 - 2300 hours.   **The D.A.'s Office.**

The District attorney had just returned to his office and was turning on the TV and when he was joined by Police Commissioner, Bob Tierney.

"**Y**ou are just in time." said Dan, "Grab a seat."

"WKBX TV News update. Jim Hunter reporting.

"**T**he investigation is still ongoing regarding the bombing of temple Beth El. To date there have been no apparent leads as to suspects or reasons. The police are remaining tight lipped and the D A's office has not released any update yet. The surrounding area residents are naturally concerned, as voiced by one of the locals."

The camera switches to the on the street interview tape.

"No I wont give my name, who knows what can happen. The police presence here has not been the greatest so we beefed up our own

neighborhood watch. This is America. This is not supposed to happen here. This is definitely an anti Semitic act. We have to get this madman. I want to go on record saying- - - "

The ranting resident was cut off as the interviewer said;
"Sorry that's all we have time for, back to the studio and Jim Hunter."
In order not to make the local feel slighted the camera man/ interviewer said he would continue the interview for a possible later date airing and of course did not turn the camera on.
Dan Hanlon used the remote to turn off the wall mounted TV just as Jim Hunter was saying;
"And now the international news."
"Nothing more we can do tonight, might as well head home."

The two men left his office.

$\sim\sim\sim\sim\sim\sim$

Saturday. - April 17, 2012 - 1030 hours.   Avenue M - Synagogue Location

Sean Dunne had just joined Chuck Broadhurst and Dean Campbell at the Synagogue site. At this point Dean took control of the conversation.
"This is absolutely the most professional job I have ever seen in all my fourteen years on the bomb squad. Of course this is just a preliminary report, I know the DA wants an in depth written one as soon as possible. My guys have combed this place pretty well and there are no real leads. The remnants of wire and parts are common everyday materials that can be purchased anyplace. There must have been a timer of sorts, but not a trace to be found. This was obviously someone who really knew his profession."
"A terrorist or terrorist group." asked Chuck Broadhurst.
"I wish it were that simple." answered Campbell."I usually know their signature work Who ever built this is truly a master." Hanlon is not going to like that. He expects instant action," Lt. Dunne added. "Which really leaves us a big headache. We don't know where to look. Local terrorists, international terror groups, anti Semitic groups or just some nut case with a ax to grind. Where do we star?"
The uniformed Sgt. Dunston approached the trio.
"We canvassed five city blocks in all directions and so far

came up with zilch."

The head session continued for some time only to be interrupted by Jason Clark, a uniformed patrolman.

"Sorry to bust in like this, but I might have found something. Three sets of eyes instantly snapped on to the patrolman.
He paused for a moment, almost frightened by the sudden attention."

"This is my regular patrol route and as you know you get used to certain things and people. Well there's this homeless guy I see quite often on my rounds. He's been around for a year or more. He's quite harmless and actually a really nice guy. Well, anyway, Early this morning I saw him on Starret Street near the vacant lot. I think he sort of lives there. He nervously approached me saying he saw him, he knows who did it. But before I could press him any further there was a fender bender not more than fifty feet from us. I quickly told him to wait there, I'd be right back. Unfortunately when I did return, a mobile unit showed up to cover the accident, and then he was no where to be found. I'm sure I can find him, he's a regular around here."

Lt. Dunne addressed Sgt. Dunston.

"Get a replacement for—" he turned to the patrolman a question in his eyes.

"Clark Sir, Jason Clark," answered the patrolman.

"Get a replacement for Clark here. I want him on nothing but locating this drifter." And looking at Clark again, "Change into street clothes if you wish, but find him."

A dual "Yes Sir." was voiced by Dunston and Clark as they separated from the group.

Dunston directing Clark, "Give me ten minutes to get some one here then you can be on your way. Lt. Dunne has the D A on his back which rippled all the way down to us, so let's hope you can find your man."

"I'm sure I can Sarge. I'll check in with you later."

The pair separated.

~ ~ ~ ~ ~ ~

***Saturday April 17, 2012 - 2030 hours.*   Vicinity of Avenue M.**

Patrollman Jason Clark phoned in a report to headquarters, Attention Sgt. Dunston No luck yet. I'm going to get some sleep. I'll pick up again first thing in the morning. He usually hangs around the Catholic Church on Central St. On Sundays."

~ ~ ~ ~ ~ ~

Fire and police were massing at St Joachams Roman Catholic Church on Central Street which had just been imploded by a bomb or bombs and totally destroyed. The district Attorney arrived at the scene at 0345 hours. Approaching the fire chief already half yelling;

"Why wasn't I called earlier? "

Not threatened by this attitude Chief Thomas answered calmly,

"Our first duty is the protection of life and limb and the safty of any survivors Mr. Hanlon. Everything else is secondary Sir."

He sarcastically added the Sir.

Upon finishing his sentence he looked directly into Dan Hanlon"s eyes.

Suddenly aware of his rudeness Dan replied, half apologetically,

"Yes, yes you're right of course. It's just that this whole thing is very disturbing."

"Lt. Dunne is over there with the bomb squad boys." Thomas said pointing and turning away from Hanlon.

Dan drifted over to where Campbell and Dunne were standing.

"Anything yet ?" he asked trying to sound sincere.

"Not yet, Sir." Campbell answered showing his annoyance. "It's still too hot to get in there."

"Yes, of course it is. I guess I'm a little anxious." replied the D A who then shifted to Sean Dunne.

"How you doing with this homeless guy ? Any word yet ?"

"Not yet sir, but we're on it twenty four seven."

"This is really scary now. I can't help but think these two bombings are connected," Dan mumbled almost to himself.

"Did you say something, Sir ?" asked the Lieutenant.

"No, no, - just thinking aloud, I guess. Remember I want to know what ever info you get as soon as you get it. Keep me posted, I'll be at my office."

He turned and disappeared in the smoky mist without even really looking at the church ruins.

"I have a feeling he may be right." said Dean Campbell.

"You mean that the bombings are connected ?" asked Sean.

"Yeah, I'll know more positively once we can get in there.. If I have to be up in the middle of the night at least let me work so I don't feel like I'm wasting time."

"Okay !" commented Sean. "I'll let you be, I've got to talk to Broadhurst anyhow. He patted Dean's shoulder and left

~ ~ ~ ~ ~ ~

Sunday April 18 - 0620 hours: **Montgomery Ave, three blocks from Center St.**

"It's him, it's him, It's the same man," was all he kept saying." reported the patrolman who took over Jason Clark's shift. He said he would only talk to Jason and, while I tried to phone in he took off yelling, "Only Jason, only Jason." I tried to follow him but he just disappeared..Jason was about four blocks away at the time, he's on his way. I expect him any minute now. Yes Sir, we will keep you posted.

Tom Baxter switched his radio off and resumed his search for the possible witness. He did not wander too far for fear of missing Jason. Barely a minute passed when Clark in street clothes showed up. Tom recounted his meeting with the homeless man then the pair split up to once again take up the search.

~ ~ ~ ~ ~ ~

Sunday - April 18, 2012 - 1112 hours.   **Market St. (a few blocks from Ave. M)**

"Tom ? I found him. A side alley by Pat's Pork Palace on Market St.. But we're too late. Someone bashed his head in. Get the necessary people here. I'm going to stay with the body." Jason said.

"I would say he was facing his assailant from the looks of it. My preliminary guess would be a tire iron or crow bar, but I'll go with the tire iron. These indents on the skull fit the lug wrench side of a tire iron. I would also say the first blow did the job, the rest was just for effect. There's no trace of a tire iron either. His pockets were obviously gone through. I guess to make it look like a mugging." Broadhurst suggested as he ended his short report.

"Who would want to mug a down and out homeless person ?" asked Jason rhetorically to no one directly. He bent down and carefully picked up two well handled photo's. He handed them to Chuck Broadhurst.

"Check these for prints though you most likely will not find any. The woman was his wife who died years ago in a car accident, the other is his son, killed in Afghanistan about two years ago. He apparently could not take the double loss and it took it's toll on him. I'm not the detective, Sergeant, but I would say this was no mugging. I think he was silenced because he saw something he shouldn't have.

"You may be right Clark but don't let your emotions interfere with your judgement." replied the Sgt.

"I'm aware of that, Sgt. But just the same, after you're finished here I'd like to go over this alley my own way, I guess I was about his only friend. I'm not casting any aspersions here but part of me wants to see what I can do for him. He shouldn't just be forgotten."

"I understand Jason, and no offense taken, in fact I wish you luck. Keep me up to date with whatever your results are. We're almost finished here then the alley is yours. You can keep the tape barricades up as long as you need to."

"Thanks Sarge, and I will keep in touch." Jason answered.

~ ~ ~ ~ ~ ~ ~

Sunday - April 18, 2012 - 1345 hours **Market St. Alley.**

"Are you Jason Clark ?" asked the D.A. As he ducked under the yellow barricade tape.

"Yes Sir Mr. Hanlon." replied Jason.

"I understand you knew this vagrant that was killed."

Not liking the D.A.'s tone Jason answered with annoyance in his voice.

"He was not a vagrant Sir. He was a good man who had some rough breaks. He lost both his wife and son within a few years of each other and with the economy and job market the way it is he was one of the unfortunate the government doesn't care about."

He said this while looking directly into the eyes of Dan Hanlon. Having been swiftly put in his place Hanlon replied;

"I apologize. I obviously hit a nerve. I guess I shouldn't always be wearing a political persona. Let me start again. Was he a friend of yours ?"

Feeling somewhat satisfied Jason also softened his tone.

"I don't know if you would call him a friend in the true sense of the word, we came to know each other well because of my patrol route."

"Is that a smart thing to do ? You know, becoming overly friendly with people in a patrol zone ?"

Irritation again showed in Jason Clark's voice.

"It is a very smart thing to do Sir. The idea is to build confidence and trust with the people of your district. This insures full cooperation from the public when it's needed. Such as now. Hard assed tactics in a situation such as we face now will not garner any cooperation from the general public. And now is when we need it."

"Okay, okay, I surrender. I know when I've been put in my place. No offense was meant." offered the D.A.

"I'm sorry also Sir. It's just that I take my job seriously and yes I did consider Fred Johanson a true friend."

"So that was his name. I'm sorry for your loss Patrolman Clark but right now I'm concerned with a bigger problem."

"I realize that Sir, I think we are all concerned and are working towards the same end."

"And towards that end have you found anything to help us ?"

"No Sir, and that's too bad because the way Johanson spoke I'm sure he had something concrete to give us.

"It's a shame too. It's always the little people or the good ones that suffer from events that do not even involve them, such as your friend Johanson, here."

The two were interrupted by another voice.

"Sgt. Broadhurst said I might find you here." said Lt. Dunne and shifting his gaze acknowledged Dan Hanlon. His eyes moved back to Jason.

"Find anything worthwhile ?"

"No Sir, but I'm still looking."

Dan Hanlon, as he was wont to do took over the conversation.

"I know I probably should not be here interfering in this very early part of the investigation, but I feel I owe something to the public. I promised to clean their city of crime and violence and yet now we have back to back bombings of religious houses. I want to find the fiend behind this diabolical terror and keep my promise to the voters. I feel like I'm letting them down."

Lt. Dunne interjected,

"It's only been two days, Sir. No one should expect miracles. You're doing the best you can as we all are, but it is still rather early. Don't beat yourself up over something you have no personal control of."

"I know you're right Lt., but I just feel so helpless. Okay I'll leave you two alone for now, I have to prepare a talk for tonight's broadcast update. Please keep me in the loop.

D.A. Hanlon turned, ducking under the tape and disappeared around the corner. Lt. Dunne returned his gaze to Clark.

"I didn't have the heart to tell him the F.B.I. has been in contact. They are about to take over the whole investigation. Bombings of religious houses of worship are a no-no on their list. They are already looking into terrorist groups."

"**I** figured they wouldn't be too far away from this one." commented Jason. "I hope you don't mind Lt., the fact that I'm still here I mean. Sgt. Broadhurst said it would be okay if I continued to look."

"It's okay Clark. I know you were close to the victim, but after today you will have to take over your normal beat again. With these two bombings so close to each other we're becoming short handed."

"**I** understand Sir and thank you Sir. I'll report as normal tomorrow." replied the patrolman.

Lt. Dunne's cell phone buzzed and he responded quickly .He listened intently for a few seconds then shut his phone.

"**I** have to run Clark, good luck. Keep me posted." he said as he left the alley.

Jason Clark went right back to searching . Not knowing for what, but was still looking for anything at all. He walked the alley at least a dozen times, slowly and methodically making sure he left no corner or inch of flat ground unchecked. One last and final viewing he thought as he started again where the body was found. Moving ever so slowly, Jason scanned every square inch of ground. Suddenly something caught his eye. A lone cigarette butt , approximately seven feet from the body position. Ordinarily there would be nothing special about a cigarette stub but the paper on this one was still white. Everything else in the alley was brown with age and weather. It wasn't the ambulance or police scene crew, as there is no smoking at a crime scene. This cigarette had to be recently smoked. Jason gingerly picked it up with tweezers from his pocket knife and secured it in a small plastic bag. On close inspection he determined it was a hand rolled smoke. "It may be nothing." He thought. "But I think I'll just hold onto this.

Another half hours worth of deliberate searching convinced Patrolman Clark he had done all he could for now. He exited the alley and started walking to the precinct.

~ ~ ~ ~ ~ ~

Sunday - April 18, 2012 - 1540 hours. **8th Precinct, Sgt. Broadhurst desk.**

Chuck Broadhurst returned to his office which he shared with another squad detective, to find a note left by Jason Clark.

1410 hours. Sgt Broadhurst - Please call me at ext. 402 when you get a chance. - Patrolman Clark.

He chuckled to himself at the formality of Clark and at the same time

he knew it was professionally correct. He grabbed the phone and dialed 402.
It was answered on the second ring with Jason identifying himself. Chuck
agreed to meet him if it could be right away. Within minutes Jason Clark was
in the detective Sargent's office carefully removing a plastic envelope from his
uniform pocket

He explained how he came about the cigarette butt and asked the Sgt. If he
could hold onto it with whatever else his team collected. He then inquired
about keeping his little find quiet for now for personal reasons. Broadhurst
knew Clark to be a good cop and a decent person so he agreed without
question. He felt it was the least he could do knowing how he felt about Fred
Johanson, the one who was just murdered. Jason was thankful for
Broadhurst's cooperation in keeping his confidence. Each then went about
their own jobs.

~ ~ ~ ~ ~ ~

Monday - April 19, 2012 - 2000 hours. WKBX news room.

"This is Jim Hunter, WKBX news. We are bringing you a
special news update on the tragic bombing of two of our religious facilities.
I now turn the mic over to District Attorney Dan Hanlon who has jumped in
with both feet into this abhorrent disaster, and we already know of his record
on the crime cleanup in this city. – Mr. Hanlon." - - -

"Thank you Jim and thank you to this great station of both
radio and television.

"Citizens of Metrolia, we are faced with a dastardly disaster
that should not have darkened the worst places on this planet, let alone our fair
city. I can tell you right now this is not acceptable and will not be tolerated on
my watch. I have pulled together all the resources of this city and I promise
you this deed will not go unsolved and the guilty person or persons will be
brought to justice. We are already being assisted by the Federal Bureau of
Investigation. Please do not panic, carry on with your lives as always and I
know justice will prevail. I personally, with the cooperation of this station,
WKBX, guarantee quick and positive results. You're cooperation is also
asked and welcomed. If you know anything, please contact us day or night.
Your call will be held in the strictest confidence. I will personally keep you
posted as progress is made.

Thank you and Good Night, Stay safe."

"Great job Mr. Hanlon, we will keep an open mic for you

anytime you need it. Is there any other way in which we can assist you ?"
uttered Jim Hunter trying to further butter up the District Attorney.

"Not that I can think of at this time Jim, but thanks for the
offer and cooperation. You've always been a great help and we won't forget
it." replied Dan. The two men shook hands and Dan Hanlon left the building.

~ ~ ~ ~ ~ ~

**Tuesday - April 20, 2012 - 0600 hours. Center St. Across from St.
Joachmans R.C. church.**

This was Jason Clark's normal rotational day off and he took
this opportunity to follow a whim. He didn't know why he was here but had
a strange feeling that something had drawn him to the church site. He started
a methodical search of the area surrounding the church. Not the church site
itself. That was too messed up, what with the explosion, and fire and
investigative people. Just away from the well worked area such as where he
was right now, across the street . Jason was into his ground examination about
an hour when, there it was. A cigarette stub, the paper still very white. It was
near a tree trunk. A tree that would have made a perfect place to hide and
observe. Observe and not be observed. The magnifier showed it to be the
common roll your own paper, just as before. He knew this was nothing
concrete and held no credibility, but his gut feel was strong on this, especially
when he thought of Fred Johanson. He again pocketed the stub in a plastic
bag with identification as to when and where it was found. He would turn this
over to Broadhurst at a later date, Clark continued the search for one square
block around the church but turned up nothing else.

~ ~ ~ ~ ~ ~

Tuesday - April 20, 2012 - 1145 hours. The D.A.'s office.

Dan Hanlon approached his executive assistant's desk.
"No matter what you are working on put it aside. I'd like you

to join me for lunch. There are numerous reports I'm working on, and since we both have to eat, I thought you could take some dictation while we eat. That is of course, if you don't mind."

Marie McGowen, a not unattractive woman in her early fifty's, was the perfect stereotypical, ever efficient secretary. A professional woman both in and out of the office. What every executive wanted and Dan knew he was lucky to have found her.

"I don't mind at all Sir. It would be my pleasure to join you. Let me just get my book."

She joined him at the elevator. Dan made light conversation on the ride down in the elevator.

"I know I keep you quite busy and I'm pleased you could make time for my little whims like this."

"It is not a problem Sir. I'm glad I can be of assistance in any project you choose.

His car was parked some fifty feet away from the office building door. He reached into his pocket for the remote door opener and pushed the appropriate button. There was an instant blinding explosion. Powerful enough to push Dan and Marie against the building wall with Dan trying to shield Marie as best he could and still maintain his own balance. The late model sedan was totally inflamed with some smaller sputtering explosions still discharging. In less than two minutes a fire truck was there with the appropriate foam to put out the fire. Luckily the fire station was no more than one hundred yards away. A few passerby's were already assisting an older man who had been thrown to the ground by the blast impact. Both Dan and Marie were physically okay, upset slightly from the sight of the explosion but otherwise Okay. The usual procedures were under way within minutes by both the police and fire departments.

Dean Campbell was on his way to the scene with others from the bomb squad. An initial check up of the District Attorney and his secretary was clear and they returned to their office awaiting a visit from Sgt, Broadhurst. In the meantime one of the other office staff ordered a quick lunch for the D.A. and Marie from the local Deli and left to pick it up. They ate quietly during Broadhurst's interview after which Marie was sent home for the day.

Later in the afternoon Dan Hanlon made arrangements with Jim Hunter for another special news break for that evening's six o"clock news.

~ ~ ~ ~ ~ ~

Tuesday - April 20, 2012 - 1800 hours. **WKBX TV news.**

WKBX TV news update, Jim Hunter reporting:

"In the wake of the third bombing in four days we bring you a special report:

"At 11:54 this day , the District Attorney's car was blown up outside his office. Luckily for the city the D.A. was not in the car. I will now turn you over to Mr. Hanlon himself for a first person report. - Mr. Hanlon;"

"Thank you Jim and thanks again for the air time. And now for *YOU* - Mr. Mystery Bomber. Take a good look, I'm still here and I promise you, your days are numbered. I and this city have had about all we're going to take. You will be brought to justice one way or another. So far no one has been seriously injured. Turn yourself in now to me or the police, we can still consider leniency. If not I guarantee you we will catch you. Our full resources and that of the F.B.I. have been called into play so it is just a matter of time. Do this city and yourself a favor, turn yourself in and I promise you the utmost fairness of treatment. Please, I'm begging you, before someone receives serious injuries or even worse, the loss of life. If it's me you are after, contact me and I'll meet with you. I'm sure there's nothing we can't work out. You know where to find me.

Back to you Jim and thanks again for your cooperation."

"Well there you have it folks, straight from the man who truly cares for you and your city. This is Jim Hunter for WKBX news, stay tuned for the weather."

The studio sound now off Jim Hunter walked with Dan Hanlon toward the building exit.

~ ~ ~ ~ ~ ~

Wednesday - April 21, 2012 - 0400 hours. **The Muslem Mosque on Second Ave.**

-144-

Fire personnel were responding as were the police. The Mosque on Second Ave. on the south side of the city had imploded at 0354 hours. Residents, awakened by the explosion were gathering in the streets in all sorts of apparel, watching the burning remnants of the mosque. The police instantly pushed back observers and set up perimeter barriers. Dean Campbell and Sean Dunne arrived about the same time. Shortly thereafter they were joined by Captain Ted Harris in charge of the second precinct in which the mosque resided. Usually precinct jurisdiction is quite defined but under these unsettled conditions overlapping authorities was a welcome thing.

"Has anybody called Hanlon yet ?" asked Lt. Dunne.

Almost silent snickers and slight smiles appeared on all three faces.

"Okay, I'll have someone from the precinct call him as soon as I find my cell phone." replied Capt. Harris smiling, his cell phone in hand.

Campbell left the group to talk to the fire chief. He needed an estimate of time for when his bomb squad could start their work.

~ ~ ~ ~ ~ ~

Wednesday - April 21,2012 - 0715 hours. **2nd Ave. Mosque location.**

Both the D.A. and Police Commissioner arrived together looking all important as usual. They were doing their usual questioning, but at least this time D.A.Hanlon limited his interference with the actual working crew. Chuck Broadhurst was on the scene some twenty minutes later and purposely avoided Dan Hanlon. He sought out Lt. Dunne for an update comparison. They mutually agreed that a strategy meeting was in order. Sgt. Broadhurst politely pleaded that such a meeting would be without the D.A.. Sean Dunne smiled and had no problem with the request.

~ ~ ~ ~ ~ ~

Wednesday - April 21, 2912 - 1600 hours. **Interview room - 8th Precinct.**

Present:

Lt. Sean Dunne, Sgt. Chuck Broadhurst, Sgt. Dean Campbell, Capt. Ted Harris, 2nd. Precinct, Chief Ken Thomas, Fire Dept. #8, Sgt. Dunston, 8th Precinct, and Larry Thompson, F.B.I.

Lt. Dunne, standing in front of a chalk board, started things off.

"I want to keep this short and sweet. We are facing something that seems to be getting worse by the day. So let's break this down as best we can. We'll start with number 1, No deaths caused by the bombings." which he wrote on the board.

Sgt. Dunston volunteered, "What about the homeless guy? "

"True." answered Dunne, but his death was not directly caused by the bombing as tragic as it may have been."

Sean did add it to the blackboard.

Capt. Harris looked a bit confused. "What homeless guy ?"

LT. Dunne gave a brief synopsis of his death then continued:

"Anything from you Campbell ?"

"Yes, the chief and I have been comparing notes. Number 1 - All three were implosions. This is a practiced expert. Damage was very tightly restricted to the immediate area. Again this person or persons knew what he or she was doing. Number 2 - All explosions were at times when no people were around, as if planned that way on purpose. Is there some thought behind this ? Number 3 - We are dealing with a top notch expert. There is little to no residue, wire or parts to trace. Everything has been incinerated by the explosion and fire. Perhaps Larry can help along those lines." He briefly gazed at the FBI presence. "And 4th and last, at least for me, why all places of worship ? What's the connection ?"

Sgt. Broadhurst chimed in with,

"And what's the reason behind all this ? Trying not to kill people but blowing up buildings, not just buildings but places of worship."

"Okay, now back to our homeless man. Patrolman Clark was convinced that the man knew who the bomber was and was frightened. Unfortunately, if this was true, the bomber also knew he knew and eliminated his only witness.

Chuck Broadhurst spoke quietly;

"What about the D.A.'s car and why ?"

"Good question." commented Capt. Harris. "Unless he or they didn't like his TV and Radio comments."

"That would be my only guess." answered Sean. "And again no one was hurt."

"Back to the places of worship again." Capt. Harris joined in. Could it be that our bomber picked these places because he knew no one would be there in the wee hours? I realize it's not much of a trend, but it is a trend nonetheless, so do we take precautionary measures and start watching all houses of worship? "

"Do we even have enough people for such a task ?" joked Sgt.

Dunston. "There must be at least a hundred churches in this city."

"Not quite Matt." replied Lt. Dunne, "but there are a lot. It's actually not a bad idea. Let's check on our resources first. Ted can you take care of that ? We can be in touch again in the morning and see what we can set up."

Chuck Broadhurst was going to mention Jason Clark's little find of the cigarette paper but thought it might be a little premature. Even Jason seemed to want it kept quiet for now.

Larry Thompson sort of raised his hand to get attention.

"For a very quick summary let's see what we have here. You have a super expert bomb maker who leaves no traces. One tentative witness who has already been eliminated. A pattern of houses of worship with absolutely no connection to each other and not a single clue to hang your hat on."

"That pretty well sums it up." said Lt. Dunne.

"I thought it would." said Thompson. "I'm about due for vacation soon." he added smiling.

The room chuckled.

Any suggestions gentleman ?" asked Sean Dunne.

"Watching the other churches is a good start." commented Dunston.

"I'll run our list of expert bomb makers and also check with InterPol." added Agent Thompson of the F.B.I.

Chuck Broadhurst volunteered,

"Let's get bulletins out to the foot patrolmen for closer attention, especially around churches. Have them follow up on the slightest abnormal behavior. Being extra alert is about all we can do right now."

Other minor details were discussed and break up finally occurred at 1645 hours.

~ ~ ~ ~ ~ ~

Wednesday - April 21, 2012 - 1500 hours.   **Vicinity of 2nd. Ave Mosque.**

Jason Clark upon finishing his normal tour, rushed to the 2nd. Ave Mosque area. He wanted to check out his own theory of the bomber. He looked specifically for relatively hidden spots which one could observe the mosque from. Within forty minutes he found the very thing he was searching for. There next to an old tree trunk he found a very white cigarette butt. Picking it up carefully with tweezers and examining it with a glass determined again that it was self rolled. Giving it the plastic bag routine he tucked it away and continued his search just in case. As it turned out he was glad he did. No more than fifty yards he found another spot that fit the same specs and yet another cigarette stub. He was elated. Of course they had to be subjected to tests for a match but he felt at least it was something. This he would bring personally to Broadhurst. He trusted the detective Sgt. to keep his secret.

~ ~ ~ ~ ~ ~

Wednesday - April 21, 2012 - 1800 hours   WKBX   TV.

"This is your six o' clock news hour, Jim Hunter reporting with yet another bombing. Here is your District Attorney, Dan Hanlon.

"Thank you again Jim, this is getting to be a habit and a habit I do not like."

Looking directly at the camera, face distorted in anger, the District Attorney continued:

"Mr. Mystery Bomber, what is it that you want ? This has got to stop. Is it me you want ? Name the time and place and I will meet with you. I will be unarmed and unescorted. Please contact me. Give me your reasons for this destruction, we can work something out. Please I'm begging you. My telephone number is on the bottom of the screen. Contact me please. I promise you your call will not be traced. The next step is your's. "I'll be waiting."

Dan Hanlon slid the microphone back to Jim Hunter.

"You're putting yourself right out there. Do you think you should be doing that. It's like you're putting your life on the line and for what? " Jim commented.

"It's the least I can do for my city, Jim, let's let it go at that." answered Dan. "Thanks again for the use of the airwaves."

Dan Hanlon left the studio still looking upset.

~ ~ ~ ~ ~ ~

Thursday - April 22, 2012 - 0753 hours.   **WKBX studio's**

"News flash - WKBX Radio and TV.

"For the second time in as many day's the District Attorney's car was blown up. Only this time a death was reported. Marie McGowen, Mr. Hanlon's executive assistant was in the car at the time of the explosion. Mr. Hanlon has not made any comment at this time. He is obviously extremely upset. He is cooperating with the police as we speak and will give a detailed statement later today."

"In other local news - - - -" The TV was shut off.

$$\sim\sim\sim\sim\sim\sim$$

Thursday - April 22, 2012 - 0800 hrs.   The D. A.'s office.

Present were Lt. Sean Dunne, Police commissioner Robert Tierney, Sgt. Chuck Broadhurst and D.A. Hanlon.

Mr. Hanlon was giving an emotionally charged statement to the police presence.

"**W**e both came in early. In fact I picked her up, it was about five twenty. Her car was in the shop for service. We had a lot of work to catch up on. This bomber crisis was taking a lot of my time. It was going on seven thirty when we decided a little breakfast would do us good. She volunteered to go to Big Al's diner, so I let her use my car. The next thing I knew or heard was an explosion. I looked out my window and saw, - - - - I saw - -"

He paused to catch himself in some tears.

"**I**'m sorry, just give me a moment."

At this point Sgt. Dean Campbell entered the office. He quickly gauged the room's mood and remained silent.

The D.A. continued with what he saw and how he then rushed from the office down to the street. He paused again and sank down in the cushioned arm chair near his desk. The room remained silent for a few moments giving Dan time to recover himself. Lt. Dunne broke the silence.

"**W**hat have you got Dean ?"

"**N**ot much Lieutenant. Pretty much the same as last time, a quick but very professional job. Not much to recover as far as the body goes, but I'm sure there will be something the lab boys can do for positive identification."

Dean cut himself short after his glance at Hanlon's face. Hanlon showed obvious disturbance when the body of Marie was mentioned.

"**I**'ll finish this later." Campbell volunteered. "I have to check back with my crew."

He turned and exited the office as quietly as he had come in.

As the door closed Hanlon spoke;

"**I**'ll be okay gentlemen, I'm sure you have work to do. You can update me later in the day."

As all prepared to leave, "Bob can you stay awhile ?" added Dan.

The Police Commissioner remained.

~ ~ ~ ~ ~ ~ ~

Thursday - April 22, 2012 - 1400 hours.   **8th Precinct - Lt. Dunne's office.**

"Thanks for coming." said Dean Campbell addressing F.B.I. agent Larry Thompson. "I may have some information or at least a theory, that you can possibly help with."

"Let's hope I can. Right now I feel useless. It would be nice to contribute something." replied Thompson enthusiastically. "So let's have it."

Dean made himself comfortable in a chair near the desk.

"This second car bombing has been nagging me all day. Up until a little while ago I didn't know why."

"And now you do ?" asked Thompson.

"Yes, I think so and that's where you come in."

Dean now had Sean and Larry's undivided attention. Sgt. Campbell, aware of this , continued.

"We know we are dealing with a pro, but I think this now goes beyond that."

Dunne and Thompson caught each others eye with a confused expression.

"All three buildings and now the cars were implosions. If it were just the structures, that would be one thing. Contractors do it all the time to get rid of old buildings. But cars imploding ?, that's another whole different ball game. This person, who ever he or she is, does not want to cause collateral damage. All three buildings were at times when no one was around. The cars, however, were both daylight hours. They too were imploded. Except for the D.A.'s unfortunate secretary, no one else was injured. Today's implosion was so perfectly executed, there's hardly anything left of Ms. McGowen to identify. So my question to you, the F.B.I., is how many people have that kind of expertise and talent. Is this something you have records of or can find out about. Do we know who the world's best bombers are ?"

"That's some theory Dean, and it all seems to fit. Congratulations! " commented Lt. Dunne."

"Yes, we do keep track of such things and I'll get on it right away." was Larry's quick answer. My hats off to you also. May I use your phone ?"

Sean gave his approval with a wave of his arm towards the phone, then said,

"Nice piece of work Dean. Let's hope it pans out, we could use a break about now."

Larry quickly finished his preliminary set up and rejoined the others. Now that he had the attention of both again, Dean respectfully requested,

"Could we keep this on the QT for a while. To put it bluntly, keep Hanlon out of the loop for a while. With his penchant for notoriety and high lights, I wouldn't want this sort of info put on the airwaves. At this stage of the game we don't need to tip off our man. You are the first two I've told so far and there won't be too many others. At least not yet. I'll probably bring Broadhurst into the loop."

With sort of a smile Lt. Dunne replied,

"I can't fault you on that Dean, the D.A. sure does love the TV spotlight in spite of the threats to himself."

Thompson agreed and added that he should have some sort of information on Friday morning.

~~~~~~

Thursday - April 22, 2012 - 1530 hours.　　**8 th Precinct - Sgt. Broadhurst 's desk.**

Broadhurst was on the phone as Clark, in street clothes, approached his desk. Chuck indicated to the chair next to the desk and resumed talking on the phone. At last finished, he settled himself in his own chair.

"Good to see you again Jason, what can I do for you."

Without speaking he retrieved three plastic bags from his pocket.

"I already gave you one of these. I know it may not be anything and I'm not trying to interfere with your department, it's well." he paused, "well, sort of a hunch I have."

"There's nothing wrong with having hunches, I've been working with them my whole life. Okay so what's the story behind the cigarette butts."

Jason Clark went on to explain the how and why of the paper stubs and why he felt they were important. Because he went into detail, Sgt. Broadhurst patiently listened for the whole eight or ten minutes without interruption. He knew from his years of experience no detail should be overlooked no matter how silly some may sound. Jason finished and sat back
~~~~~~

with questioning eyes.

"You may have something there but of course as you said yourself we have to run tests first and personally I think it's worth doing."

Jason smiled and felt relieved that he didn't do all that work for nothing.

"I was going to ask you Sargent if we can keep this quiet. I don't want to be embarrassed if nothing comes of it."

"I have no problem honoring your request, but don't ever be embarrassed by having ideas or theory's. I'll get the lab working on this right away and with any luck we should have something by tomorrow afternoon. Let's keep our fingers crossed."

"Thanks Sarge. I really do feel strongly about this."

~ ~ ~ ~ ~ ~

***Friday - April 23, 2012 - 0940 hours.* Office of F.B.I. agent Larry Thompson.**

"Come in gentlemen and find a seat. Pardon the lack of amenities, the Feds don't give us field workers a very big budget for such things. Can I get anyone coffee?" All three waved off the coffee. Dunne and Campbell from yesterday afternoon's meetings were joined by Detective Sgt. Broadhurst.

"I'll get right to the point gentlemen. We did have some luck, but before you start celebrating let me give you the rest. For that level of sophistication it did narrow down the list. We came up with sixteen so far, at least that we know of. Out of that sixteen we can account for twelve that we're sure you can cross off your list. Four were old Russian KGB, five from China also accounted for, two in US Federal prisons and one with England's M I - 5. That leaves four and we're still working on them. One with the Navy Seals, two we have pinned to Al Kaida, and I think we can account for them, and last, a mid country contractor. We're waiting for confirmation on him."

The phone rang and Thompson grabbed it right away.

"Thompson." he said quietly. "Uh huh, okay, thanks." as he cradled the phone, "The contractor has been in the hospital for over a week with a broken leg."

"Scratch him." said Campbell.

"That leaves us with one Navy Seal and two terrorists and two in prison."commented Lt. Dunne. "We are right back where we started from."

"Not quite." Dean interrupted. "We still have the two Al

Kaida and the Navy Seal."

Larry joined with, "As I said before we think we can account for them, we're just waiting for a last confirm."

"Okay." said Dean, so we still have the Navy Seal."

The others looked at him as if disbelieving what he just said.

"I know you think I'm crazy, but other military personnel have gone rogue before and there is still yet one more possibility."

"What's that ?" Thompson asked.

"If he's that sophisticated an operator and a Seal, he had to learn from somebody. Chances are it was another Seal. Somebody, retired. Perhaps."

Thompson was already on the phone requesting additional info. His request finalized, he hung up the phone turning to the three policemen.

"It might take some time, Government security and all that, you know, the usual need to know stuff, but we'll get what we want. Probably not today though."

"I guess that's about it for us then, Back to the routine gentlemen." directed Lt. Dunne. "Oh, one other thing, Not a word to Hanlon about this. He's too free with info on the TV. I think we need to keep some secrecy if we're going to get anywhere with this."

All three men agreed. The meeting broke up with Broadhurst still keeping Jason Clark's secret. *"Now is not yet the time."* he thought. *"I want to give the kid some freedom on this, who knows perhaps he is onto something.* On the way back to headquarters Chuck Broadhurst left a text message for Clark on his personal cell phone.

"Clark, - - - Meet me when shift over - - Precinct parking lot - - your car. - - Broadhurst."

~ ~ ~ ~ ~ ~

Friday - April 23, 2012 - 1540 hours.   Precinct parking lot.

"Thanks for agreeing to this, I appreciate the effort." said Broadhurst as he and Clark drew closer to each other.

"No problem Sarge, Is something wrong ?"

"On the contrary, it's about your cigarette butts. I've been giving your theory some thought and I wanted to go a little further if you're willing to do a little more leg work."

"Sure Sarge, anything you need."

"I'm a little too well known to go where I want you to go, so I thought perhaps - - -."

Before Chuck even finished his sentence Jason was agreeing.

"What ever you want Sarge, I'm already involved and want to help in any way I can."

"Good, I'm glad, I figured I could count on you." replied Broadhurst. "I'll outline my idea then you tell me what you think of it. Do you know where the D.A. lives ?"

Clark nodded his head then stated;

"Yeah, in the Mayfair Apartment complex on twelfth Ave. They have their own private parking garage."

"That's the one." Chuck confirmed.

"Do you suspect Mr. Hanlon ?" questioned Jason with a suspicious look and a hidden smile on his face.

"No of course not." was the quick answer but someone had to have access to his car in order to place the bomb, and they did it twice."

"Oh, I get it Sarge, you want me to have a look and check for cigarette butts."

"Exactly." said Broadhurst. "You have these roll your own's at all the other sites so why not the car."

"I'm sorry I didn't think of that myself." Jason said apologetically. "I'll get right on it." he continued.

It was then Broadhurst cautioning;

"You have to do this quietly and carefully. No one must know, except you and I for now. Since the bombings he has uniformed watch dogs patrolling his residence area."

"I understand Sir." answered Clark returning to his formal training. "No one will ever know I'm there."

"Take all the time you need for this, Clark but do report back to me when ever you think you have something, no matter how crazy it may seem. Remember, not a word to anyone. Good Luck." Before Clark could respond Chuck Broadhurst turned and walked away in the direction of the precinct building. Jason stood there frozen for more than a minute before pulling himself out of his self induced mind trance. He slowly smiled to himself and walked in the opposite direction.

~ ~ ~ ~ ~ ~

Saturday - April 24, 2012 - 0420 hours   Buddist Temple -
Chinatown.
14th and Yang Sts.

The quiet of the early morning was shattered by a low rumbling explosion imploding this beloved Temple of the Chinatown section of Metrolia. Within forty seconds all was quiet again leaving the sacred building a mass of rubble, smoke and debris. By now even the flames have subsided. A true implosion leaving the perimeter area untouched. The neighborhood soon became congested with the usual fire and police equipment and personnel and of course, onlookers. Lt. Robert Lawson was on the scene about the same time Lt. Dunne arrived. They nodded in recognition of each other but remained silent. Dean Campbell arrived soon after, lightly complaining about getting this solved soon because he was losing too much sleep with these middle of the night calls. An hour later Broadhurst shows up as grumpy as Campbell. Chuck immediately loaned himself to the Fifth Precinct Detective squad. He wondered to himself how long it would take Clark to start his usual cigarette stub patrol.

It was going on 0600 hours when D. A. Hanlon appeared with his usual *"Okay, I'm in control now."* attitude which most everybody ignores except the press. He met with Dunne and Larson spouting that we must step up the investigation before this ***"WACKO"*** destroys the whole city. Lt. Dunne assured Hanlon everything possible was being done and that they were making progress.

"**Then** why haven't I been filled in with this progress." Hanlon asked angrily.

"**Because** Sir." Dunne answered in a firm professional voice. "The areas we are checking are extremely sensitive regarding security and the fewer people in the know the better our chances of decent results."

Red faced and extremely irate, Hanlon returned with;

"**We'll** just see about that Lieutenant. A word with commissioner Tierney might just straighten this out.."

Dan Hanlon stomped away.

With a half smile Lt. Larson joked,

"**You** sure know how to live dangerously. I'll back you up on this one and I'm sure everyone else will also. Most of us are fed up with his power hungry childish behavior."

With the absence of the D.A., routine, yet positive police work went on uninterrupted. Broadhurst, having finished with the Fifth Precinct team returned to his car to leave and noticed a familiar figure across the street from the destroyed building. He wasn't totally sure but thought it was Jason Clark in street clothes.

As the police sedan pulled away into traffic Patrolman Jason Clark thought he recognized Sgt. Chuck Broadhurst behind the wheel but made no attempt to wave or give signal of that recognition. He methodically went about his search. Once he found an observation point that was difficult to observe luck was again with him. The very white paper of a cigarette stub showed itself. *"I just add this to my collection."* He thought happy with his find. *"Now on to Hanlon's garage. It should be a good time especially with the D.A. now out and about. I'll change into my uniform first in case there*

~ ~ ~ ~ ~ ~

Monday - April 26, 2012 - 1015 hours.   Office of F.B.I. agent
Larry Thompson
Present: Lt. Sean Dunne, Sgt. Chuck
Broadhurst, Sgt. Dean Campbell & Capt.
Ted Harris, 2nd.. Precinct.

Larry Thompson started with;

"**W**ell gentlemen we have been somewhat successful, but it left us with good news and bad news. The good news is that we were able to trace the records of the Navy Seals. And yes there was such a bomb expert who taught our present day man. Unfortunately he was KIA in Afghanistan two years ago. In checking further some of the Seal personnel were most helpful and remembered another man who taught the KIA.. He was active during the Iraq war, ninety one or ninety two I think. He was considered by the Seals to be a genious when it came to implosions."

All heads looked at each other with the same thing in mind.
"Perhaps we're on to something."

The letdown showed as soon as Larry continued.

"**A**gain we're apparently out of luck. He went MIA in ninety two or ninety three. There has been no trace of him since. We even tried a finger print match up. To date nothing has showed, and that's almost twenty years. I guess we can count that one out."

"**I** wouldn't jump to that so fast." commented Dean Campbell.
He could be with Al Quada and perhaps here right now.
Four incredible looks now stared at Dean. No one wanted to hear what they just heard but they also did not disbelieve it.

"**O**kay, we won't write that one off." Larry quipped. "Which brings us back to zero again. Well maybe not quite zero but no real active leads."

"**W**ell gentlemen, any suggestions." asked Lt. Dunne.

There was a few moments of silence before Sgt. Chuck Broadhurst finally spoke.

"**I** may or may not have further information that we have not touched on yet."

"**E**xactly what do you mean by that Sargent ? Are you holding out something that we should know ? That's not like you Sgt."

"**I** know Sir, but please bear with me on this. I'm holding someone elses confidence on this and don't want to betray it. I promise by tomorrow I will have something concrete, one way or the other."

"Okay." replied Dunne not really angry. He himself has been in similar situations. "Just don't make a habit of it yet." he smiled.

Dunne then turned to Thompson.

"Nice work Larry. I hope we can keep these lines open with you. Who knows we may need some more Navy Seal info. I appreciate your staying with us on this."

"No problem." Larry shot back. "That's why they pay me the big bucks."

Of course harassing remarks followed as the meeting broke up.

~ ~ ~ ~ ~ ~

Monday - April 26, 2012 - 1630 hours.   Broadhurst's Office.

"Glad you could make it Clark." Chuck addressed as Clark entered his office.

"I was just about to call you when I got your message. There's something we have to discuss." answered Jason.

"Probably the same thing that's on my mind." said Broadhurst. "You first Jason, I'm sure I'll find what you have to say very interesting.

Jason was a bit confused by his statement but let it go as he started to give his report.

"I started my usual search pattern across the street from the Buddist Temple, I was looking for that perfect place where one could observe the Temple and not be observed while doing so. Like all the others there was such a place and as before I found a relatively fresh cigarette stub. And yes, it was a roll your own."

Jason handed Broadhurst the plastic bag.

"I then went to the D.A.'s garage."

"Did you encounter any problem there ?"

"No Sir, I thought if I wore my uniform I would have fewer problems, which was the case. I located Mr. Hanlon's assigned parking space and immediately found a cigarette stub. A fresh one. While putting it in a plastic bag I spotted two more, all within twenty feet of his car."

"Good work Clark. Is that it ?"

"Well - - - not exactly Sir. But, ah, I'm, ah, not exactly sure how to say this."

"Don't hold back son. Spill everything. This is important

police work we're talking about. And what ever you say do not be embarrassed about it. The smallest thing can be of the greatest help sometimes."

"Yes Sir and thank you Sir."

Jason paused to put his thoughts in order.

"First of all Sir, I would like to see my finds tested in the lab for a match or matches. I believe Sir they will all match. Then I would ask if it is possible to do a DNA test on the stubs. You know from lip saliva or hand and finger oil."

Broadhurst was paying close attention to young Jason. He thought of himself as a young patrolman seventeen years ago.

Clark paused again for a few moments. It was obvious he was going through some sort of internal struggle, and was trying to figure out how to say what he really wanted to say.

"I'm no detective Sir. I've only been with the force for just over two years."

"Yes and I'm familiar with your record. Both at the Academy and here." interrupted the Sargent.

"Well Sir, I've had my own theory and it has bothered me for some time. I just can't dismiss it any more."

"And that theory is ?"urged Broadhurst.

Speaking hesitantly and shyly Jason went on.

"Well my sister in law has mentioned a few things to me over the last few month's that just don't add up Sir. Things that really should not have taken place."

"What has your sister in law got to do with this ?" asked the Sargent with slight annoyance. Jason looked at Chuck Broadhurst directly in the eye, his own eyes damp with the start of tears.

"My sister in law is, or was, Marie McGowen. Her husband was my older brother by my mothers first marriage. Her husband died and she remarried. My father also died in a car accident about ten years ago. My brother was killed in Afghanistan three years ago. Marie and I stayed close in spite of the age difference. We confided in each other. Sir I believe she was killed on purpose and I believe the District Attorney is responsible."

"Hold on Jason, do you realize what you are saying. Accusations like that could get you into serious trouble." Chuck cautioned.

"I know Sir, that's why I'm here. I know you're a good man. I've watched you work. You are fair and determined and I believe even you have some misgivings with the D.A.."

Both were silent now. Chuck sat back in his chair, a wry smile on his lips.

"You're very observant Clark, but let's face reality. To pursue such an avenue we need incontrovertible truth. Do we have that yet ? Do you have that ?' It must be something solid. Extremely solid to offset the mass of public opinion he has on his side at the moment."

"Sir, before we dismiss this may I continue with my feelings."

"Of course Jason and I'm not dismissing anything."

"Well Sir, the night before Marie was killed she called me and was very disturbed. She said she came across something shocking but before she was able to say any more we were disconnected. The line went dead. It's not like she hung up, it felt like the wire was cut."

"Broadhurst was taking notes. We can check on that." He said. What else do you have ?"

"I tried calling again but just got a busy signal. I waited a while then went to her apartment. There was no one home. For what ever reason I dismissed it and figured she went out for the evening. I know now I should have pursued it further."

"Yes you should have and you should have reported it to me." Chuck answered in a mildly stern voice. "So far none of this is enough to make any kind of accusation."

"Then there's my homeless friend. Not much time had passed since I reported that he may have seen something till we found him dead. Mr. Hanlon then appeared in the alley where we found him while I was searching for clues. He was acting curiously strange and inquired if I found anything. At that point I hadn't. I didn't find the cigarette stub until after he left."

"And again I will remind you this is all barely circumstantial. And what's with the cigarette stuff. The D.A. doesn't even smoke." Chuck emphasized.

"How do we know that ?" Jason quickly returned.

"Broadhurst started to say something but thought better of it. He knew Jason Clark was being sincere.

"Okay Jason, what do you want me to do ?"

"To start with Sarge, could we get the cigarettes tested for match and a DNA sample if present. Then somehow we'll get a DNA sample from Hanlon."

"Alright Jason, we'll do the test. Just be aware we can not accuse any one yet. We really have nothing to go on."

"We will Sir, if it takes me ten years, I'll get what we need."

"I believe you mean that Jason. Just remember no more hold outs. You know better. I will support you all the way. Don't worry, I'll put a rush on these tests and let you know ASAP. We're going to need a sample of DNA from the D.A. if the test is going to be meaningful."

"Can do and will do Sir, just give me a few days." replied Jason as he left the office.

~ ~ ~ ~ ~ ~

Monday - April 26, 2012 - 1930 hours   Metrolia Center Park.

Unnoticed by most, two men in plain clothes were having a casual conversation on a park bench. Sgt. Chuck Broadhurst had just finished filling in all the details of Jason Clarks story to Lt. Dunne. Both men had become fond of Patrolman Clark and were not going to come down too hard on him for holding back information. Of course Dean Campbell and Larry Thompson would be notified of this latest development and it was then that Larry suggested a finger print match between Hanlon and the MIA Navy Seal. All agreed it was a great idea. It was also agreed that this be handled with the utmost secrecy. The fewer people in on it the better the chance for success. The two men eventually departed the park in opposite directions.

~ ~ ~ ~ ~ ~

Tuesday - April 27, 2012 - 1030 hours   8th Precinct meeting room.

District Attorney Hanlon just finished addressing most of the day shift of the 8th Precinct personnel and left the room taking with him his all important demeanor. Quietly and unnoticed Patrolman Clark managed to secret away the water glass Hanlon drank from and without hesitation delivered it to Sgt. Broadhurst.

~ ~ ~ ~ ~ ~

Tuesday - April 27, 2012 - 1400 hours.   Police Commissioner
Tierney's Office

"Now gentlemen what's this I hear about you not cooperating with the District Attorney." queried Com. Tierney addressing Lt.'s Dunne and Larson. "After all isn't he doing his best to help clean up this city."

Lt. Dunne sat up straight and directed his eyes at Bob Tierney.

"It was not a matter of non- cooperation Sir." Dunne said firmly but professionally. "It was a matter of need to know, and in my professional opinion he did not need to know at that particular time. Our investigation is ongoing and making progress. The District Attorney's questions were also at the site of the Buddhist Temple bombing which had occurred only an hour and a half earlier. His timing could not have been more wrong. Now to relate to you exactly what I told Mr. Hanlon, the area's we are pursuing are extremely sensitive regarding security, both national and local, and the fewer people know the better our chances of decent results. District Attorney Hanlon seems to have a penchant for giving out too much information on his television spot lights. Now if there is nothing else Sir we both have very busy schedules."

Lt. Dunne stood followed quickly by Lt. Larson.

"No - - er - - No, that will be all gentlemen. Thanks for stopping by."

Lt.'s Dunne and Larson exited the office. Neither spoke a word till they hit the street.

"There's nothing like bulling your way through a tight spot." commented Larson.

"Sometimes certain things are necessary. How he ever got elected Police Commissioner I'll never know." Sean answered

~ ~ ~ ~ ~ ~

Wednesday - April 28, 2912 - 0945 hours.   Police Comm:
Tierney's Office

"What do you mean there was nothing you could do. You're the Police Commissioner, you tell them what to do, not the other way around." berated an irate District Attorney. "I believe they are with holding information from me and I want to know why."

"They did mention Government security reasons and I can understand their concern." suggested Comm. Tierney.

"Bull" answered the D. A. Rather emphatically. He turned to leave saying;

"I guess I'll have to do your job too."

~ ~ ~ ~ ~ ~

Thursday - April 29, 2012 - 1030 hours.   F.B.I. Office
. Present:
Lt. Dunne, Sgt. Broadhurst,
Sgt. Campbell, Larry
Thompson.

Lt. Dunne not wasting time immediately retold Broadhurst's report of Jason Clark. Chuck interrupted a few times with a detail or two missed by Dunne. Both Dean and Thompson were extremely interested. Lt.

Dunne finished with,

"Now gentlemen, now that we're all on the same page, where do we go from here.

Dean spoke right up with;

"In doing our finger print check I came across D. A. Hanlon's file. He has no finger prints.

Confused looks showed on the other three men.

"What I meant to say is the prints on file, which by the way is marked, "Fingers Burned. In Fire Years Ago" could be used for future checkups but will match nothing from the past. My personal opinion is they were surgically altered not burned off. It is possible, not often does it occur, but it is possible. If the techniques ever get's perfected Police work as we know it will be in big trouble."

The room was silent as Larry's statement was digested.

"So the possibility exists that Hanlon could be that MIA." Broadhurst posited. "That's really a long shot but how do we check up on something like that ?"

The room went quiet again. Larry Thompson broke the quiet;

"I'll start a background check on Hanlon and see how far back we can get."

"His teeth." yelled out Dean. "Navy Seals keep accurate records on everything about every man including teeth."

"I can probably get that." said Larry "But what about Hanlon ?"

"The best we can do now is a very quiet check into Hanlon's personal life." Dean suggested. "Which will not be easy."

Again silence was repeated. This time it was Broadhurst who spoke up.

"Did Hanlon get a replacement yet for Marie McGowen ?"

"As of late yesterday she was not yet replaced.." answered Dunne. "Why, what did you have in mind ?"

"Well, We put watch dogs around his apartment and garage, right."

"Correct." replied Dunne. "But he refused a personal body guard."

"I know that, but a watch dog at his office he really can't say no to. He can play it up big when he hits the TV station again. So we supply him with a police woman with secretarial skills. Perhaps his daily schedule and routine may show up something. She can down play her Police job with him and pretend she really would enjoy working a normal job for a change."

Smiles went all around the room.

"He's just vain enough to buy it." replies Sean. "Do you have anyone in mind ?"

"As a matter of fact I do. We can borrow her from the Fifth

Precinct. I worked with her once before, about a year ago on special assignment. She will be perfect for the job. You would never know she was a trained Police Woman.”

"Gentlemen, what do you think ?”

There were nods of approval all around.

"Good, I'll get this set up ASAP.”

"What about a tail on Hanlon.” Dean inquired firmly.

"I was thinking the same thing.” joined Chuck.

"I agree.” Dunne replied. "The problem is that he has spent so much time bugging all the precincts he's very familiar with faces.

"How about some of our people ?” Larry asked. "This is much too important not to do everything we can.”

"You've got yourself a deal. I'll take all the help I can get.” answered the Lieutenant.

"Okay, give me a couple of hours to get this set up.” Thompson replied.

Dunne added; "Call me on my private cell when it's a go.” He handed him a paper with his number on it. "Thanks Gentlemen, There's not much more we can do for the moment, just remember, keep this quiet and stay in touch.

They left Larry's office one by one heading in different directions.

~ ~ ~ ~ ~ ~

Thursday - April 29, 2012   1140 hours.   Sgt, Broadhurst's Office.

As Chuck entered his office he noticed the blinking light on his phone indicating a waiting message. He pushed the button as he sat down.

"Sgt. Broadhurst this is Patrolman Clark. If possible I would like to meet you in the Media Room at sixteen hundred hours. If I don't hear back from you I'll assume it's a go. Thank You.”

With a smile on his lips Chuck deleted the recording.

~ ~ ~ ~ ~ ~

Thursday - April 29, 1612 - hours   Media room. 8th Precinct.

As Chuck Broadhurst entered the room he was addressed immediately by Jason Clark.

"Thank you sir for coming on such short notice. I just had to show you something. For a few days now something was tugging at the back of my brain. This morning I finally remembered. The tape I'm about to show you is from last fall. It was the Metrolia Autumn Fair Days held at the

-163-

football stadium.."

Jason pushed the start button on the remote and the screen came alive. It was the usual fair stuff, kids rides etc. Jason fast forwarded to the oxen event. Back at regular speed you could see one of the officials in a checkered farm shirt and levi's. It was D.A. Hanlon. The camera zoomed in and Clark hit pause.

"Okay, what am I supposed to be looking at." asked Chuck.

"His shirt pocket, Sir."

Jason zoomed in even closer. You could now see a small bulge in the pocket and a double string hanging out of the top of the pocket.

"That's a loose tobacco pouch, Sir.

He fast forwarded again to the concert stage area. The camera man was slowly scanning the audience. Toward the side and back of the stage stood Dan Hanlon rolling a cigarette. Jason paused so Broadhurst could get a good long look. When he returned to normal speed the pair watched as Hanlon finished rolling and proceeded to light up. The camera now moved to the on stage performers. The screen went blank. Broadhurst was now smiling.

"Great work Clark. I also have some good news. Your cigarette stubs all match up and there is a DNA match to Hanlon's water glass. Looks like your hunch paid off. But you do also realize of course, that alone is not solid enough. It just shows he was at the scene."

"Don't you worry Sir, we'll get him." Jason said with a strong air of confidence." then quietly mumbled to himself, *I'll get that son of a bitch if it takes the rest of my life."*

"I'll pass this info back to the rest of the team." said Chuck. "Remember we are keeping this all very quiet. Thanks again."

~ ~ ~ ~ ~ ~

Friday - April 30, 2012 - 0900 hours   District Attorney's Office

Lt. Dunne along with Police Woman Susan Stuart entered D.A. Hanlon's office and were greeted by a somewhat surprised Dan Hanlon.

"What can I do for you Dunne." The D.A. asked

"It's rather what I can do for you Sir. We recently had a meeting with the Police Commissioner and Mayor and it was decided that with these bombings and two attempts on your life already that you should have some Police protection."

"Don't I have any say in this." Hanlon spat out somewhat annoyed.

"I'm afraid not this time Sir. You were unavailable when we had the meeting Sir." answered Dunne. We are all aware of your feelings on protection, but this is for the benefit of the town. We don't want to lose you

Sir."

"Even though it almost turned his stomach to say it playing to Hanlon's ego always worked." Dunne thought.

"This is Sgt. Susan Stuart. She is extremely qualified and as an added bonus her secretarial skills are beyond questioning. Until you get a permanent replacement for Ms. McGowen she should fill in nicely."

"As far as anyone is concerned Sir, I am just a temporary secretary.' Added Susan Stuart.

"Well as long as it's the town's wishes I guess it will be okay, temporarily, of course. But I still do not want a body guard outside the office. Who knows if the bomber wanted to contact me I couldn't very well negotiate with a body guard around." answered Hanlon.

"We are sensitive to your feelings on that and respect your wishes Sir."

"Good, now if there is nothing further Lieutenant I do have other things to attend to."

Hanlon turned to Susan and pointed to a stack of papers saying, not too nicely,

"File those and then I'll have some dictation later."

Being the ultimate professional Susan smiled and said "Yes Sir." and went right to work.

~ ~ ~ ~ ~ ~

Friday - April 30, 2012 - 1400 hours.   Police Lab.

"Hi, I'm District Attorney Hanlon."

"Yes Sir, Mr Hanlon, I recognize you from the TV newscasts." answered Scotty McDermott. "What can I do for you."

A small smile appeared on Dan's face pleased at the recognition.

"Oh, I was just wondering how the tests relating to the bombings were coming along." the D.A. fished.

"Pretty well actually." Scotty answered innocently. "The tests on all those roll your own cigarette's all match up. They also match the sample DNA provided."

"Oh, really and who's the DNA from ?" Hanlon asked casually.

"I'm just the lab guy, they usually don't give me details." Scotty said with a laugh.

Hanlon laughed along and said thanks and left.

Scotty was quickly occupied with his work again thinking nothing of the conversation.

$$\sim\sim\sim\sim\sim\sim$$

Friday - April 30, 2012 - 1815 hours   Office of Larry Thompson,
F.B.I.

Susan Stuart, first checking to make sure she was not followed, entered the building that housed the F.B.I. office of Larry Thompson. She instantly recognized two faces. That of Sgt. Broadhurst and Lt. Dunne. She was then introduced to Larry Thompson.

"Luck was with us on this one." she said. "Hanlon was out for a while this afternoon and his appointment book was on my desk. As I said luck was on our side. Five months ago he had a dental appointment."

She handed Broadhurst a paper with the necessary information. Chuck in turn handed it over to Larry.

"I'll get on this right away. By the way when Hanlon went out this afternoon, around two-ish I think, He went to the Police Lab."

Sean, Chuck and Susan looked at each other alarm in their eyes. Larry picked up on this right away.

"**Damn**." he said aloud.

"**Damn** is right." repeated Sean.

Chuck slightly more alarmed turned to leave,

"**I**'ve got to get hold of Jason right away. I'll check in with you later."

Larry, now also becoming more alarmed, rushed to the phone. "I'll double up my men watching him just in case."

"Susan, perhaps you can fill in Lt. Larson while I head back to my own Precinct. Remember, the fewer people that know the better."

$$\sim\sim\sim\sim\sim\sim\sim$$

Friday - April 30, 2012 - 1910 hours.   Market St. Side alley by
Pat's Pork Palace

"**I**'m so glad you could make it Patrolman Clark." said the D.A. quietly.

"Not a problem Sir." answered Jason. "You said you wanted to see me about some information on Fred Johanson, but why down here Sir.

"**Because** this is where he was killed wasn't it ?"

"Yes Sir, but I ask why here at night."

Ignoring Jason, Dan Hanlon continued.

"If I'm correct it was you who said this Johanson had information to give you regarding some bombings."

"Yes Sir it was. He trusted me."

"Isn't that nice, a homeless drunk trusted you. You must feel so proud." Hanlon said in a nasty, sarcastic way.

Jason could feel himself go tense. *"No I must not let* that show." he thought. *"He must think I don't know anything."*

"Do you feel proud, Patrolman Clark. ?" Not letting him answer, he answered for him. "Of course you do. Did your friend the Bum tell you anything Jason or are you just trying to be the hero? Oh, I know all about you and your cigarette butts. What are they going to tell you ? Only that someone in a city of three plus million people walked down the street smoking. Oh wow what a discovery. Perhaps they will make you a detective because of your brilliant skills."

The D.A. was laughing now. He could not seem to contain himself.

"He really is a sick man." Jason thought to himself. *"But I can't let him know anything yet. He's just baiting me now."*

"I don't know what you mean Sir. Why would they make me a detective. I'm very happy with the job I have."

"Oh, come now Jason. You don't mind that I call you Jason, do you ? Of course not, that's you name. Solving the mystery of the bombings of late would make you a big man. Okay , so what did your vagrant friend tell you he saw."

"As I said Sir, he didn't get a chance to tell me anything. He was killed before I met up with him."

Still trying to play innocent Jason asked,

"What is this all about Sir ? Why did you want to see me here ?"

"You really don't know , do you ? You poor stupid little man. And to think I was worried about you."

"I don't understand Sir. Why would you be worried about me. We hardly know each other."

Hanlon was laughing again.

"This really is funny, I was worried about nothing. No matter, it will all be over soon."

"What will all be over soon Sir." Jason pursued.

"The bombings, stupid, the bombings."

"You mean you know who did them Sir ? That's wonderful. Have there been any arrests yet ?"

"You really are dumb, Clark. Do you even know how dumb you are ? How did you ever get to be a policeman ? Yes I know who did them and no there will be no arrests, because I did them stupid. Me, District Attorney Dan Hanlon, ridding the city of crime.

It will also be me who puts a stop to it. I personally will apprehend the mystery bomber who unfortunately will be killed in the process."

"But why are you doing this. You must have a reason."

"Of course I have a reason stupid, otherwise why would I be risking my career. It certainly is clear I didn't have to worry about you. You have got to be the world's biggest idiot. I'll even tell you because you will not be around to stop me."

"Why won't I be around, I have no plans to go any place."

Shut up stupid. I can't believe any one could be this dumb. You see I'm going to be the next Governor and after that, who knows what will be next.   By solving this dastardly crime my popularity will be unstoppable. Don't you see the people will just love me."

"But doesn't it bother you to know that you have killed people to do this ?" pleaded Jason.

"What people ?" Hanlon answered in a very despicable tone. "They were insignificant. Your homeless vagrant friend was useless and meant nothing, as did that prissy little typist. Both useless to the world. I don't know why people like that even exist. And that goes for you also my puny little friend who likes playing at being a policeman. You think you are going to stop me after I've come this far. I think not."

It was now Dan Hanlon withdrew his hand from his pocket holding a small .32 cal. Revolver.

Jason doing an excellent job at keeping his composure after hearing the remarks about Fred Johanson and Marie McGowen, just smiled and said;

"You're a sick man Mr. Hanlon. We may be able to get you some help."

Dan Hanlon laughed out loud, "You're going to get me some help! That's very funny Mr. Clark. Very funny indeed. I don't need your help or anyone else's. It's the world who needs my help and will soon have it. So how are you going to stop me ?"

Hanlon was still laughing but almost in a silly manner by now.

"Well to start with I have this whole conversation on tape."

Dan's face turned dead serious for a few seconds till he smiled again.

"Thank you for telling me Mr. Smarty Detective. I should have no problem disposing of that."

Suddenly a deeper, unrecognized voice from behind was heard.

"And will you dispose of me that easily also Mr. Hanlon. Oh, by the way don't make any sudden moves, I really don't want to have to shoot you."

Dan's facial expression was pure terror now. He turned slowly towards the direction of the strange voice. As he did so Jason quietly stepped back into the shadows. A second strange voice was now speaking from the left of the D.A..

"It's over Mr. Hanlon. Why don't you put the gun down and relax. We don't want to hurt you."

"No, No you can't do this to me. I'm your Governor. That's not right. You must obey your Governor. I'll do good things for you."

The first stranger spoke again to the right of Hanlon.

"Put the gun down Governor. We're here to help you."

Jason Clark, unseen was now next to Dan Hanlon and reached for the .32 revolver. Without resistance Dan released the gun.

"You don't need the gun Governor."

"No, no, of course you're right. The Governor has the Police to do his work for him. Good job men. This should put a stop to the bomber. The city will be safe now, thanks to me."

The two F.B.I. agents approached to take D.A. Hanlon into custody. The appropriate calls were made and soon the instrumental men of the investigation showed up at the alley. The story was reconstructed and reports filled out. The formal debriefing meeting was scheduled for the next morning at 0900 hours,

~ ~ ~ ~ ~ ~

Saturday - May 1, 2012 - 0900 hours.   8th. Precinct Meeting Room.

"Gentlemen and Lady." Lt. Dunne started off.

Susan Stuart nodded her head in thanks for the recognition.

"This sure has been a week of Hell, but thanks to good old fashioned Police work, and a few hunches, the worst is behind us. Thanks to our training and zeal we earned our money on this one. Each of you should be proud of the contribution you made. Our special thanks to the F.B.I. men at the end having Clark's back."

"You don't know how much I was counting on that Sir." Jason interrupted. "I didn't have too much time to make the necessary contacts before I met Mr. Hanlon."

Larry Thompson raised his hand with a paper in it.

"Yes Larry go ahead." said Sean Dunne.

'This is the final Navy Seal report I received late yesterday afternoon. Thanks to Susan's speedy work, about the Dentist and today's fast computers, we have a match up. Dan Hanlon or should I say Dave Hanson is our MIA expert Bomber. What he was doing for the past twenty years we haven't a clue. Perhaps he himself can shed some light on that, if he becomes coherent again. We should pay attention to that incoherence also. It's not the first time that act has been used to get away with something."

"You're just full of good news." Broadhurst said with a smile.

"How did you know to be prepared for that final meeting with Hanlon, Clark ?" Inquired Lt. Dunne

"I had also met with Scotty at the lab after Hanlon and he told me what he shared with him. He honestly did not know of the quiet ban on the report. I tried to play stupid with Hanlon to see haw far it would get me."

"And you played it very well, I must say." said the F.B.I. agent Jackson who was tailing Hanlon. "You had me totally convinced you really were stupid. I began to wonder how you ever got on the force. I thought I was going to be completely alone on that capture." He was smiling as he said it.

Jason in turn smiled along with everyone on Jackson's remark.

"What's going to happen now." asked Jason.

"We won't know that until the Doc's get finished with him." answered Dunne. At least we can breath easier for now.

When the meeting finally ended and all the paper work was completed, Sgt. Broadhurst took Jason aside and offered to get him a transfer to the detective Squad.

"No thanks." was Jason's answer. "I'm quite satisfied just being a beat cop.

The End.

"My Grandfather"

by
K.J.Goss

"My Grandfather"

Chapter 1

I always felt close to my Grandfather when I was young, at least up to my early teens. Then what seemed like overnight, he changed. He no longer took an interest in much of anything.

As a child I would sit with him and watch the "Grand Old Brooklyn Dodgers" on a giant ten inch television while he smoked a long cigar. I remember he had a large, and I mean large, brandy snifter next to his chair which held the paper bands from the cigars. My cousin and I called them rings and he would always give us some when we went to visit. Come to think of it, I still have one of those rings as a keepsake.

Now that I'm just about the age he was then, I reflect now and then on some of those memories. One of my fondest escapes is when up until we moved out of Brooklyn, I would have an early breakfast at home, then walk five houses down the block and have breakfast with Grampa. He would always wait for me and get upset if I didn't show up. I did this every day, rain or shine.

Another fun time was walking with him in the evening to get a bucket of beer. The saloon was only a block away, but to me it was a grand outing. Of course I was not allowed in the bar, but I can remember peeking through the mail slot in the door and seeing and breathing nothing but smoke. Boy did I think I was something special helping Grampa carry that full bucket of beer all the way home. Of course the bucket only held about a quart or so but to me it was gigantic.

I guess this drifting back in time is part of the aging process, which could be the reason my Grandfather suddenly changed.
Oh, he was still loving, but as I mentioned, appeared withdrawn.

Having moved further out on Long Island I did not get to see him too often as is the case with most people. Of course as a teenager my interest's changed.

I eventually joined the Marine Corps and was away and missed his passing, but believe it or not there are times he is with me holding my hand, walking to get a bucket of beer.

I really do believe this is the period my Grandfather drifted into. Except for my own few memories of being with my Grandfather, which in reality was a short lived period, I did not know him. The real man I mean. I knew nothing of his life. Let's face it, as a child you are not interested in such mundane topics. I don't even recall my Mom talking about his life other than that he was a good man. That much I already knew.

I know it seems like a long lead in, so let me get to the real story.

Chapter 2

As I noted earlier, my Grandfather passed in the mid fifties, My Dad in the late sixties and my mom in the mid nineties. As is the way of all families, "Stuff" gets passed on. This "Stuff" was now mine. Now twenty years after my Mom passed, and me in my mid seventies, I had decided perhaps it was time to look into some of that "Stuff".

I set aside an afternoon for a session in the basement. Two and a half hours of sorting, and looking produced satisfactory results. I had a throw out pile, a give away pile, a give to my children pile and a keep for me pile. Why I needed more "Stuff" I can't answer. I guess I'm just an old sentimental fool. There was one box, however, that had me intrigued. It was approximately two feet square and about eighteen inches high. It was sealed, and I mean sealed. Double taped on all sides with a type of tape I had not seen since I was a child.. Dust, dirt and scrape marks gave testament to it's constant moving and storage. But what attracted me the most was the label on the top of the box. In faded ink on faded paper was written James Jacobson.

I had no idea why, but I just sat there staring. Warm fond memories flashed through my mind. James Jacobson, that was my Grandfather. Shaking myself awake, I neatened up my mess and very carefully carried the special box upstairs settling it on the floor next to my favorite chair, my curiosity burning inside of me. Prolonging my agony, I went to fetch myself a cold Guinness first. Finding my pocket knife, I very carefully cut the tape along the top seam of the box. I had to laugh at myself for treating an old box with such reverence. After my careful box surgery I hesitated in removing the top. Not really afraid of what the contents were, but again playing mental games with myself in dragging out the suspense.

I took a sip of my dark brown liquid and almost timidly opened the lid. I wasn't expecting a jack in the box, but I wasn't expecting what I saw either. Looking up at me were sealed boxes and closed leather bound journals. The journals themselves were an average book size, you know about six by nine inches.

A bit perplexed by this I reached for the top book. The dark brown leather was securely latched with a similar colored strap and brass buckle. The leather itself still had that distinct perfume that only real leather gives up. I set it on my lap and studied it for a while. Perhaps at last I would learn something of my Grampa's life.

"Stop being melodramatic and open it." I scolded myself.

Gingerly I opened the buckle, one would have thought too carefully, then again someone else did not have the emotional attachment that I did. The inside pages were heavy grade and slightly rough in texture and gave off the aroma of their age. The first page was blank and felt inviting as I touched it. The second page was a total surprise. I was viewing handwriting as I never saw before. Cursive script done to perfection, indented paragraphs, upper and lower case letters that could have come out of an instruction manual. The black ink, slightly sepia with age, remained more than readable. It was asking to be read.

I gazed at the title line.

"This is the journal of Jim James Jacobson. Aug. 1897."

There was a space of about two inches before the start of the first paragraph.

"I joined the Army today and decided to keep a journal of my time and places traveled. I don't even know why I'm doing this. I'm not a writer by any means and I'm certainly not going to publish a book. I figure it might be fun to look back on when I'm old and gray. That is if I survive that long."

I never knew my grandfather was in the Army. I wonder why I was never told ?

My Dad was in the Marine Corps and I knew all about that. He was part of the reason I joined. I just did not understand the mystery of my Grandfather.

Oct. 8, 1897 - "We finished our basic training with absolutely nothing in particular that I felt was noteworthy. Some journalist I am."

Dec. 1897 - "Received word today about some young Major looking for volunteers for some kind of special outfit. I think his name is Roosevelt. It sounds interesting so I think I'll volunteer. I always did want to ride a horse."

This is going to be an obviously long train ride. I just found out we're heading for Texas. Oh well, there is no one to blame, I'm the one who volunteered.

Almost three weeks have passed since we arrived in Texas and this is the first chance I've had to even think about this journal.

Training here has been hard and continuous. This Roosevelt is some tough character.

On closer observation there is an interesting mix of volunteers here. Rich college boys, average Joes and kids from the wrong side of the tracks. We also have some real cowboys here. It's nice to learn how to ride from real pro's. In fact most of the men are from the Southwest. There are quite a few Indians too. I'm glad they are on our side for a change. Surprisingly there are many Buffalo Soldiers also. These are the free black men who made themselves a reputation in the Civil War. They sure are darn good fighters and soldiers.

I must say this is sure one mixed up outfit. Everyone

is calling us the "Rough Riders". Teddy Roosevelt's Rough Riders. Although the official name is "The United States Volunteer Cavalry" but the Rough Riders sounds more exciting.

My own imagination was starting to take over on it's own. It took some control to harness it. This was my Grandfather's story, not mine. It was exciting to think back on.

I asked myself again, why wasn't I told ? I glanced down at the box once more. There were five more journals and three sealed boxes and of course my curiosity got the better of me. Putting the first journal aside I reached for another. The first page was another shock, so to speak.

Nov. 1917 - "I tried to reenlist in the army again because of the Big War. They politely told me I was too old. That and the fact that I was married and had five children. It's probably for the best though, because I did not ask or tell my wife. I'll just keep this my own secret.

I did not go any further at this time, a burning urge to peek at the others was pushing me on. I opened the third and read nothing of consequence on the first page.

Those Brooklyn Bums lost another game. - I don't know what's happening to them this year. They even lost to the Giants. How bad can things get.

I can see Grampa was back to his baseball again. It's now pretty obvious I'm going to have to read the journals in full to find any information about Grand Dad. I guess I'm just being too anxious. I think I'll leave the boxes till later and get on with some reading. I went back to the first journal still thinking about the contents of the boxes, but decided I would be patient.

June. 1898 - We loaded onto trains at San Antonio, Texas for our trip back east. We weren't headed for New York though. Tampa, Florida was our destination.

We're now getting ready to embark aboard transport ships, both men and horses. Word is we're heading for Cuba. Major Roosevelt sort of rushed ahead to board the ships. Other officers complained that we were going out of turn. Roosevelt pretended not to hear and aboard we went and were soon underway for Cuba.

I'll say again, this Roosevelt fellow is one strong willed, dedicated soldier. I'm pleased with myself now for having volunteered. I wish us all luck.

I rested the journal on my lap, my mind swimming with disappointment. The same question kept coming forward. WHY ? Why wasn't I told these things before ? Of course I received no answer, and the worse part of that was that there were no relatives left to ask.

I made up my mind then to leave as much information about my own life as possible for my own children. I would hope it would give them a sense of belonging or maybe comfort or possibly even pride.

Resuming reading I could almost feel my Grandfathers excitement of a Cuban adventure. His notes of the voyage were the usual, some spotty rough seas, over crowding of the ship, and time passes slowly. There was barely a half page of entries. Then the excitement started again.

Our training was short but we felt, as did Major Roosevelt, we were ready. There had been a lot of criticism of the Rough Riders for lack of complete training compared to regular Army training. It was our officers opinion that as long as we could ride well and shoot well that was all that was necessary.

Our equipment was poor, we had no luxury items, only basic field equipment and even that was leftovers. Between some of our regular higher ranking enlisted men and a few of our officers we were very well outfitted by the time we embarked for Cuba.

I can remember learning about the Spanish American War in both grade school and high school but never this kind of detail. I now contemplate sometimes how accurate the school history books actually are. My mind drifted back to my youth and the good times I had with Grampa. Grampa, that sweet, loving man that I thought I knew, now I realize I never really knew.

How unique and interesting it is to learn these kinds of things. It makes me kind of wonder how many others go through this same scenario. You know, not knowing interesting history of close relatives or even friends for that matter. Perhaps if more people kept journals a more detailed and accurate history of the world would be known.

I'm letting myself drift now which has nothing to do with my Grand Dad. Now that I think of it, I feel privileged to be witness to actual first person accounts of a piece of history.

Now that I brought myself back to Cuba, I continued reading.

Our first encounter with the Spanish Army was mostly on foot. The jungle was so thick, the horses almost became a liability. This battle took place in an area called "Guasimas" It was quite a fierce battle but short lived. The fact that we were greatly outnumbered meant nothing. Our determination and leadership put the Spanish on the run in quick order. Roosevelt himself seemed fearless and believe it or not that attitude was contagious.. I stuck to him as close as possible. He even used me as a runner a few times.

Again I rested the journal and allowed my imagination work this new stimulation. I was beginning to feel that I knew Roosevelt myself.

The more I thought about it I actually had chills run through my body. How about that. Me and Teddy Roosevelt. How's that for an ego trip. Enough silliness, back to the war.

July 1, 1898 You could see Roosevelt was getting frustrated. He had finally received the order to advance but could not get through to the front. Other units either did not get the word yet or ignored it. Finally the mounted Major and a few of us who followed, pushed through. There were very few of us. Seeing this, this ultimate soldier returned to route the men. He was so successful that even men from other units followed him. United we charged up San Juan Hill following our fearless leader and totally routed the Spanish regulars. I think fear alone at witnessing our determined charge scattered the enemy. Soon after this was total capitulation on the part of the Spanish.

We camped and rested in Santiago.

I tried to imagine what it was like, charging up San Juan Hill side by side with Teddy Roosevelt. Daydreaming seems to be a habit with me lately but who cares, it's not every day you get to ride with the Rough Riders.

I just found out my man is now a Colonel. He deserves it if anyone does. Not that we're best of friends but we have nurtured a close relationship albeit professional. It seems like such a short time but we're headed home.

The Rough Riders, or should I say The First United States Volunteer Cavalry, were disbanded at Montauk Point,

Long Island.   We were only in existence four months but our service time was considered complete.

I'm now headed back Brooklyn.   At least the train ride is not as long as going to Texas.

That's funny, I don't remember in school learning that this conflict was so short lived. That was a good thing for my Grandfather though. I wonder what's in store for him next.

I've been back home for a while now.   I was gone for such a short time most people did not even know I was away , let alone in the Army.   I think I'll leave it just that way.

Putting the book aside while I refreshed my brew, I thought; *"Now there's a clue."* Perhaps it was my Grandfathers choice to keep this part of his life secret. I can respect that, but I'm glad I found these journals. I wonder if any other family members have read them. I never did get my beer. I realized I was neglecting other chores. Reluctantly I put the diary aside and tended to my other responsibilities.

My mind was so preoccupied with San Juan Hill that time flew by and my day's obligations were finished. A quick supper and back to my box of goodies. I retrieved the diary I was reading and flipped pages to where I left off. The next few pages were blank, then suddenly it was 1901. I guess not much happened of worth for three years. I became puzzled again by the next short entry.

1901. - - - T. R. Now President.   I'm proud to have been a small part of that.

Exactly what Grand Dad meant by that I have no idea. The next four pages were also blank. I suppose he had his reasons. My spirits perked a bit when I turned the next page.

1904. - - T. R. contacted me again today in the usual manner. He asked if I would be up for another assignment. He should know by now he need not ask. I accepted the assignment and would contact him within the week.

The rest of the page was blank. How interesting I thought. This is even more intriguing than the Cuba thing. Obviously some mystery involved.

It took a while but I managed to find the necessary information for him. Will follow up at Oyster Bay next week. It's nice to get out of Brooklyn once in a while.

Grampa really had me guessing now. I wish I knew what the big secret was. I guess I'll just have to read on.

I reported aboard the USS Mayflower at Oyster Bay today and finished up the final details of my assignment. Will meet with T. R. tomorrow in Manhattan.

WOW! I thought. Grand Dad was really someone.

Our meeting today was quite successful. I even managed to receive lunch with T. R. out of it. We reminisced about the

Heights and even had a few laughs.

Now that the Oyster Bay thing is finished I can stay back in Brooklyn and relax.

The next couple of pages were again empty. After those few was a newspaper article pasted in:

1905 - It referenced a peace accord reached between Japan and Russia (Russo - Sino) brokered by Theodore Roosevelt aboard the USS Mayflower.

A separate article announced the Nobel Peace Prize was awarded to T.R. for that effort.

On the following page was pasted a short note;

Jim,

Thanks for your help on the Oyster Bay project. Will be in touch soon.

T.R.

Who would have thought my grandfather actually had a part in the history of this country. I felt a slight touch of pride swell within me. Then the wrong side of me started thinking of a monetary value of hand written notes by Roosevelt. I quickly scolded myself for even contemplating such a thing. These were very personal things of my grandfather. He chose to keep these secrets, therefore it was not my place to go against his desires. These journals would stay just as they are. I promised myself I would never think along those lines again.

I didn't realize how late it was. I was pleasantly tired and wanted to let my imagination have free reign, so off to bed I went.

I slept late the next day which was unusual for me. Letting my imagination run amuck the night before I guess wore me out. No matter though, I treasured my time once again with my grandfather. As anxious as I was to return to the diaries I took my time with breakfast while revving up my already overactive flight of fancy. With a second cup of coffee I grabbed the leather bound book of last night and turned to where I left off to find many more empty pages. The next to last page, however, was another pasted in note.

The surprises never stop. John M. Hay, that was Roosevelt's Secretary of State and here he is calling Grampa by his first name. There was no recorded answer in the journal. I presumed this will also remain a mystery. With mixed emotions I put aside the first book and reached for the second.

Anticipating additional excitement I felt disappointed once I opened it. The entry's were rather mundane every day occurrences. A trip to the park with the kids, a Dodgers ball game, comments about his job and other remarks of no real interest to me. At least after Roosevelt and the Spanish - American War.

Reassessing my view of the second journal I decided it really did have some value. It showed the private thoughts of an ordinary, dedicated family man.

Who would have known he actually had a small part in the making of history.

All three journals that followed pertained to family and his private life. Perhaps not text book history, but history nonetheless. Private family history, hopefully to be passed on for generations.

I took a short break to refill my coffee mug and returned to the boxes. I became anxious agin wondering what treasures I would find. I don't know why I do this to myself. I let my imagination take over my common sense and then disappointment sets in when I don't see what I expect.

The boxes were no exception. Cuff links, tie clasps. Wallet

pictures and a few coins. The usual men's trivia. I was about ready to put it all away when I noticed a cloth bandana laying flat on the bottom. My curiosity winning out, I picked it up only to be surprised by it's weight. Carefully unwrapping the cloth I discovered two military medals, both naturally from the Spanish / American War.
Also included was a neatly folded paper.

I opened it excitedly and read.

To James Jacobson,

Jim,

Sorry for not having the normal honor ceremony, but your active service was so short we did not get the opportunity. T.R. wanted you to have these. He said you deserve them if anybody does considering what you did for him at the Heights. Not everybody is a quiet hero.

Congrats,

John Hay

Each medal came with it's own certificate and seal. You know the above and beyond duty stuff. Unfortunately a detailed explanation of the event was not given. So the mystery remains.

I'll never know, but that does not dampen my pride in the least.

As proud as I am about my Granddads hidden heroics exploits, the thing I remember the most and Don't ever want to lose is how my Grampa is, was and always will be just my loving Grampa.

The End

Atlantis ?

by

K.J.Goss

ATLANTIS ?

     Having worked through out the Carribean for quite some time I always enjoyed my free time snorkeling or SCUBA diving. The not often seen coral reef's are absolutely breathtaking to behold. Swimming with schools of fish is something I highly recommend everyone try at least once. My work, to my regret, of the last five or six years was such that it kept me away from those magnificent blue waters.

     I was long overdue for a vacation so when I heard my wife won a trip to the Azores, I was elated. I had never been there and therefore never dove in the North Atlantic waters before. My excitement was quite obvious.

     Five weeks was not really too long before our departure of mid August, but it had been years since I dove and I was letting my anxiety take over my mind. My wife Karen, with her usual efficiency was washing, ironing, and packing for both of us. You know, the "be prepared" for anything routine. I chose not to take my SCUBA equipment knowing that where ever there is beach and water, I can rent whatever I need. I caught up with my present work load and finally departure day arrived. Friends drove us to the airport and we were on our way. I believe I was more excited than my wife.

~ ~ ~ ~ ~ ~

     While my wife settled herself back with a headset and a movie I had no interest in, I relaxed gazing out the window watching clouds and ocean change shape and color. I periodically glanced at the GPS tracking on my TV monitor watching the miles slowly inch by.
I almost could not believe I was on my way to the Azores. It's amazing how many people do not have the slightest inkling as to their location. The name Azores is all the familiarity they have. Myself, being an unofficial history and geography buff and very familiar with the mapping industry, knew of the location, but up till now had no idea of their beauty. The major thrust for tourists is either the Carribean or the South Pacific. Now that we were approaching them, I thought why not the Azores. We had descended from thirty three thousand feet to fifteen thousand and the beauty of the mountains

and beaches could already be seen. The atoll lay some eight hundred miles due west of Portugal on a latitude somewhere between Baltimore and New York.

We were headed for Lisbon first then transferring to a smaller craft for the journey to the isle of Flores, one of the western most islands of the atoll.

On our relatively short flight to our island destination one could almost make out the volcanic depression area of the atoll as if the sea were actually lower in this area. The history of the islands beginnings is said to have been volcanic activity eons ago. They were, according to the experts, only populated by humans in comparatively recent years. Perhaps that is why these islands have maintained their natural beauty, the lack of civilization's drastic incursions. But I go on too much.

I am now doubly anxious to see them up close. I could feel my anticipation building again.

We touched down and once my feet hit the tarmac I could feel myself torn between the green of the majestic mountains and the blue of the North Atlantic waters. Now I must choose which should be first to investigate.

~ ~ ~ ~ ~ ~

It's usually the woman who wants to do this, that or the other when on vacation, particularly when visiting exotic isles. My wife, being the loving and giving and understanding woman that she is, put her own desires aside to let me fulfill my wishes. Without hesitation I took advantage of her generosity and we both headed for the beach to look for boat rental's. While I chose not to bring my own SCUBA equipment, I was very partial to my own face mask and snorkel tube which we carried with us as we strolled the docks. I worked out a satisfactory agreement on a multi-day rental of boat and motor and soon we were skimming our way to an off shore reef. The day was perfect, not a cloud to be seen in any direction with the temperature holding in the mid seventies.

We arrived at a flag marked area indicating the reef and diving grounds. There were a few other boats whose occupants were already snorkeling. My wife and I soon joined them in the surprisingly warm waters.

It felt good to be back in the deep. Karen, who was not as avid a fan of the water as I , was enjoying herself immensely. She kept mentioning how beautiful everything was. She was definitely right about that. I dove on many reefs but somehow this was different. I couldn't quite put my finger on it, but something was definitely different. The overall structure of the reef perhaps. I decided to leave the heavy thinking for now and just enjoy the sights. I retrieved a small camera from the boat that I had rigged for under-water use, and proceeded to record some vacation shots to show folks back home. Karen was even playful enough to star in some photos, more like being a clown, I think.

While looking for the right composition of scenery and light I began to study the overall reef again. There was some sort of enchanting quality about it. I made a mental note of a section I wanted to explore in more depth but not now, another day perhaps. Today I was with Karen and I wanted to be with her the full day. After all, it was her vacation.

~ ~ ~ ~ ~ ~

The day had been truly wonderful for both of us. Almost the entire time was spent in or by the water with a light lunch break in between. After lunch, while Karen soaked up some sun on her towel, I walked the beach. The shore line was not all beach front. Volcanic rock cliff's shot up from the water hundreds of feet, separating sections of small beaches. The beach we were on presently was approximately a half mile long before being interrupted by fallen rock and rock cliffs. I made another mental note to make it a point to search out other stretches of mixed colored sands, both by walking them and viewing them from offshore. From what I saw from the plane the rising cliffs outlined by the lush green mountains would make some breathtaking photos which I'm sure have been done before. You never know, but another angle and a different eye could still produce that perfect captivating image.

Back to the sleeping beauty and another short dive to keep me sated, at least for the day. We topped off the perfect day with an impeccable meal accompanied by just the right bottle of wine. It was a day we did not want to end but we knew we could look forward to a few more tomorrow's.

~ ~ ~ ~ ~ ~

I sipped my coffee as I gazed in awe at the early morning blue-green glow of the water from the hotel window. I could not believe our good fortune for Karen having won this surprise vacation. We had been here only one day and I already knew we could not have picked a better place. A casual breakfast on the outdoor shaded terrace added to our already relaxed sense of being. We lingered more than we ever had before. As anxious as I was to dive again I couldn't resist this mood provoking atmosphere.

We finally broke the magic spell and decided to take a short driving tour to fill out the morning and I would dive in the afternoon.

A winding road carried us up the mountainside amid those lush shades of green interspersed with volcanic rock born in fire who knows how long ago. The driver was kind enough to stop as I asked to take advantage of photo ops. He also mentioned a lot of caves most likely formed by the eruptions. He particularly referred to the ones that only have access from the sea. That intrigued both Karen and me but obviously would have to wait for another day. The view of the sea from the top of the mountain was spectacular. We stood in silence, inhaling the stunning beauty of the scene. The driver chose another road down from the peak which was just as wonderful to view and soon we found ourselves back at the hotel. We quickly changed and went straight for the docks.

Our reserved boat was ready for us and I aimed for the same location as the day before. Karen and I dove and swam right to where I left off yesterday. The same enchanted feeling overcame me as we neared the formation. The volcanic rock was encrusted with coral, sea growth and vegetation, but somehow I just got the feeling that there was much more. I was about to move closer when I was distracted by Karen pointing to something and making a motion she wanted some pictures taken. I moved to her and saw a school of varied colored fish that was quite striking. After many shots and spending more time than I wanted, I returned to the coral encrusted wall. Moving as close as possible I gently scratched at the wall loosening some of the growth revealing a relatively smooth surface. I knew water could smooth rough stone yet there seemed to be a different quality here. I was about to look further, when suddenly the light dimmed. Karen was nearing to get my attention and pointing upward. We both ascended to an almost overcast sky. A sudden storm front had moved in.

We made it back to the docks before the rain and luckily even back to the hotel. We settled in the small balcony of our room and watched the storm run it's course. Even the rain had an inviting quality about it.

The storm and dark clouds were short lived, and the forced rest was welcomed. We treated ourselves to another memorable dinner and spent the evening enjoying the soft night air, each other and good Cognac.

~ ~ ~ ~ ~ ~

The evenings relaxation carried over to the following morning and we caught ourselves sleeping late. It was about ten forty five by the time we arrived at the reef. I wasted no time. One last minute equipment check, waved to my wife and fell over backwards letting my oxygen tank carry me under. Righting myself and getting my bearings, I swam for the spot where I ended yesterday's exploration. Soon I was on my way deeper, following the outside of the coral. I could not identify this particular coral. It was nothing like it's Carribean cousins. I kept going deeper and of course the light was dimming. I stopped my descent to equalize pressure and caught movement off to my left. Thinking nothing of it I continued to study the coral moving ever so slowly downward. I sensed a disturbance near me again to my left. I turned to see what kind of fish was curious about me. To my surprise it was a man. It was nice to see someone else partake in the beauty of this reef.

Something odd struck me about the diver, but I couldn't

quite put my finger on it. I don't know why but I decided to pursue him. It was then I noticed, except for a small thong type swim suit, he was otherwise naked. Then I realized the odd thing that disturbed me was , there were no oxygen tanks. I was catching up to him but when he realized it he sped away as if I was standing still. It was as if he were part fish.

I gave up the chase recognizing the fact I could not catch him but mainly because my air tank was running low. I made a purposely slow ascent wondering about my almost encounter. Perhaps I was lower on air than I thought. I could have been hallucinating. Oxygen starvation can do strange things to a person. I eventually made it to the surface. I rested a bit and removed the mouthpiece. It shouldn't have made a difference but for some reason it just felt good to breath air not provided by a machine or device. I located my boat about fifty yards away and slow stroked toward it.

Once relaxed aboard I replayed my encounter several times in my mind and still could not make sense of it. I figured I better keep this one to myself. My wife deeply engrossed in her book hardly noticed my return. Luckily I was not bothered by this because it gave me time to reflect on the experience I just went through. By the time she was released from the book's spell I was almost back to normal myself. Polite chit-chat with Karen asking if I discovered anything new today. Of course I said no, just the usual pretty things.

"Did you get any good pictures today ?" she inquired.

I laughed and told her I totally forgot to even bring the camera.

"Some wildlife photographer you are."

She laughed as I started the motor to head back to the beach and our hotel.

We had a leisurely late lunch after which we hired a cab for a further tour of the island. It was like a tropical paradise without the coconut trees. The mountainous terrain was surprising for such a small island. The cab driver spoke in broken English but his speech was more than adequate for an informative conversation. I inquired about the reef diving as innocently as I could. I found his remarks about the reef intriguing. He spoke of how you can get beautiful pictures of the varied and colorful fish and other sea creatures. Then his voice suddenly changed. It turned deeper and more dramatic when he warned me to stay away from the southwest section of the coral reef. When I asked why, his eyes caught mine in his rear view mirror.

" There are bad things there." His eyes looked frightened.

That was all he said and changed the subject by pointing out a particularly old building and it's unique architecture. I was going to pursue the reef when I felt my wife's hand on my arm. I turned to her as she indicated with her eyes not to go any further for now. It was obvious she was upset and therefore I heeded her warning. Deep inside I wanted more information. I knew it would just have to wait.

~ ~ ~ ~ ~ ~

Early that evening, while my wife was showering before dinner I took the opportunity to go to the hotel bar hoping to ask questions about the reef and perhaps get answers. While sipping on a glass of local Sherry, quite good by the way, I casually asked about the local diving. Information was easily given until I asked why I never saw any boats on the southwest side of the island. Both bartenders instantly changed expressions. That same frightened look the cab driver had was now evident.

"You do not want to dive there Sir. The waters are too dangerous." was all either of them said. They chose not to talk to me any more.

I took the obvious hint, finished my drink and left. My curiosity was now boiling over. What was the big secret ? What was everyone afraid of ?   It just seemed incongruous in this day and age to be afraid of "The Boogy Man." I realized these islanders are not in the mainstream of today's computerized, fear nothing world, and age old terrors and fears do exist to them. I just wish I knew the story behind the fear. I dare not dive there until I have a plausible reason not to.

I returned to the room as Karen finished dressing. I then took my own quick shower and we made a beeline for the dining room. As the previous night, dinner was absolutely delightful, as was the wine. We skipped dessert for a Cognac on the terrace. The night air was refreshing further enhanced by a strolling violin player. Soft, sweet and romantic were his themes. We talked about our days of fun and how much we looked forward to the rest of our stay. It was then I spoke of my encounter with the barmen. Although she was concerned, it was not as drastic as I expected.

"Perhaps we may find someone tomorrow." she said optimistically.

Her optimism I found contagious and it uplifted my own spirits. We then sat back to enjoy the night, the cognac and the romantic music.

~ ~ ~ ~ ~ ~

Even though it was after midnight when we finally went to bed I was up with the sun. I relaxed on the small veranda and quietly sipped my coffee. Karen was still in dreamland which allowed the quiet time I so wanted and needed. Naturally my mind went to diving again, particularly that one reef. Who or what was that figure I saw. I was convinced it was not a fish. I'm sure it was a man, but it swam as good as a fish. If it was just another man, then where were his oxygen tanks. Never mind the oxygen I don't recall seeing even a mask or snorkel tube, and I had to be down at least

forty feet or so. Then there is the mysterious taboo of the southwest reef.
Why shouldn't I dive there ? What is so dangerous ? Maybe Karen is right,
we'll find some one to talk to today.

I went for a second cup of coffee just as Karen was stirring.

"Are you planning on sleeping the day away ?" I asked.

"I just may." was her yawned answer.

"Come on kid." I urged. "It's already past seven and we have
a full day ahead of us."

"No, you have a full day ahead of you, I'm taking a lazy day
and just reading and soaking up some sun" Karen answered smiling. "I'll go
out in the boat with you if that's what you want."

"That would be great. But first breakfast."

~ ~ ~ ~ ~ ~

After breakfast we leisurely strolled to the docks. At the end of the street just
before the wharf was a single cottage with a small yard fenced in by an old
rustic picket fence with many slats missing. A few chickens were roaming the
yard pecking at the bare ground. An old man, obviously native to the island,
sat mending a very worn fishing net. His eyes were soft and wary, his face a
golden tan with many wrinkles. The working hands showed his at least eighty
years, the veins, bulging and many, calling attention to his life's roadmap.
Smoke curled from an old dark and well chewed pipe which appeared to
satisfy him.

Karen suggested we ask him about the diving. We stopped
and flagged his attention without his eyes leaving his handiwork.
Unfortunately he did not speak or understand English. We were about to
leave when the cottage door opened and a woman, probably in her early
sixty's pleasantly asked if she could be of help. Her English was broken yet
quite understandable. Her voice was soft and pleasant. I explained I wanted
to inquire about diving the southwest part of the reef and was warned by three
people to stay away, but no reason was given. I guess my curiosity is getting
the better of me. The woman smiled softly and said that we came to the right
person. The old man before us was her father who was in his ninety second
year and probably had more knowledge of the island than anyone else. She
knew of the warnings we were given but like us, did not know the reasons.
She herself was not a diver, therefore had no first hand knowledge.

It seems her father has lived here his whole life and had never
left the island. He had no formal schooling yet maintains a wisdom far
beyond his generation. He know's of things not yet in the history books and
has not ever left this small community.

She volunteered to speak to her father and proceeded to do
so. The old man's hands went still and slowly he picked his head up and
studied us with questioning eyes. Those eyes sparkled brightly as a youth in

his twenty's, but even that twinkle did not hide his obvious wisdom. He took his time studying us as if gaging our sincerity or honesty of purpose. Slowly he smiled and answered his daughter who in turn translated.

"Strange things have happened in the past." she said.

"What kind of strange things." I asked curiously.

My question was relayed. The old man continued to study me while his hands went back to his repair work. The hands moved effortlessly never missing a stitch and all the time the eyes stayed with mine. He mumbled something quite fast to his daughter all the time still smiling.

"People have disappeared never to be seen again." she translated.

He continued to speak, pausing for her to interpret as he went along.

"It has been going on since before he was a boy. When his grandfather spoke of these incidents he would make the sign of the cross as if in fear. Someone did come back once and told of strange happenings. People considered him crazy. He eventually wandered off up into the mountains. That was the last he was ever seen. It is now referred to as *"de agua day Diabo"* the water of the devil."

That much I understood myself from my limited Spanish, since the two languages are very similar in many ways.

The old man's eyes were twinkling again as he broadened his smile.

"You should go and see for yourself, you will learn many things."

His daughter continued with her translation.

I asked one final question of the old man.

"Have you ever been down there yourself ?"

When he heard the question his eyes lit up as if recognizing an old memory. His smile grew broader, if that was even possible and he answered with;

"You should go and see for yourself. You will learn many things."

He then lowered his head to his netting work while the smile was no more. He puffed on his pipe watching his hands do their weaving. The daughter, who said her name was Theresa, smiled and quietly apologized.

"I'm afraid that is all you will get from him today, which is more then I get from him some days. He seemed to like you, which is rare.

Karen and I said a thankful and polite goodbye and continued on to the boat.

"Are you really going to dive there like the old man said ?" Karen asked.

"Are you afraid." I countered.

"A little I guess " Karen answered. "But somehow after

talking with the old man I'm not as fearful as I thought I would be."

"**I** had the same reaction. There was something about him that enhanced my confidence, it did not lesson it. My curiosity is still bursting, so yes, I think I would like to dive in the "de agua day Diabo." I said in a dramatic, exaggerated voice. "Would you care to join me ?"

No, I think I'll sit this one out. I already told you I just want to soak up the sun today. Maybe this time you will remember to take the camera. You never know what kind of monster you will meet and want to pose for photographs." Karen looked at me with a silly childish grin.

~ ~ ~ ~ ~ ~

After arriving at the dock, Karen went straight to the boat while I retrieved the SCUBA gear. I chose a double tank system this time to ensure myself plenty of time. I'll have to admit I was a little nervous or maybe I should say, more anxious than nervous. With everything now in working order I rejoined Karen at the boat. Her usual efficiency showed it's hand again, all I had to do was start the motor and go. This time I pointed in the opposite direction from the reef. Karen looked at me with question marks in her eyes.

"Just a slight detour." I said. "It shouldn't be too far to those caves and waterfalls the tour driver mentioned."

Her eyes lit up and I swear actually sparkled with delight.

~ ~ ~ ~ ~ ~

Fifteen minutes later we sat mesmerized. Natural waterfalls, which had to be some one hundred to two hundred feet high, were cascading from the luxurious green topping the volcanic cliffs splashing with a thunderous roar in front of caves evolved eons ago from underwater upheavals. I occupied myself for close to forty minutes taking pictures from all angles, as much as the small boat would allow me. I even dared to enter the cave and shoot out through the misty waters. Karen was drenched but absolutely thrilled by the experience. As we left the sun dried us off in no time and were soon on our way to the *"Devils Waters"*.

~ ~ ~ ~ ~ ~

Rather than call any unwanted attention, we anchored approximately the same place as before. I would swim underwater the necessary distance to my destination. Karen smiled as I prepared my gear. She was already prepared with her radio, book and suntan lotion and a small umbrella just in case. We blew each other kisses, she handed me my camera and over the side I went. After righting myself and getting my bearings I swam strongly to the wall where I encountered my human fish. I stopped at the wall and checked my oxygen levels. Camera first, I started a slow descent. A strong overhead sun provided an enormous amount of ambient light.   I would swear it was almost getting brighter the deeper I went. The vegetation clinging to the wall was changing, not only it's color but it's lushness. I continued down but now at a much slower pace. I stopped to equalize pressure and as before felt a presence. I did a three sixty and saw nothing . Shrugging it off I resumed my descent. The wall was now a bit rougher in texture and started to jut out by about ninety degrees.   I moved to accommodate the barrier, if you will, and found myself face to face with the human fish. I was startled but luckily did not panic, nor did the creature before me. Effortlessly he moved back a few feet which put us at a distance of about six feet. I remained as still as I could to hold my position. I was right about my quick assessment the other day. He had no oxygen tank or breathing gear of any kind, yet he was breathing normally without straining. The figure was clothing free except for what looked like a jock strap like garment. The manlike creature turned sideways as if to move and then I was really shocked. I saw what looked like gills on his neck just below the chin line. Impossible, I thought. People don't grow gills. This was definitely a man with gills. I don't know why but a thought flashed into my mind of something an uncle told me about years ago. There was a comic book hero who was a man with gills and could swim with the speed of a fish. He was called Sub Mariner. Wow! Talk about a reality check.

We both held our positions, gaging each other for what seemed like an eternity. My Sub Mariner made the first move. He turned, very slowly, and started to swim away. Turning his head to look back at me, he all but stopped swimming. It was as if he wanted me to follow.

"Why not. " I thought. *"That's what I came for wasn't it ?"*

I leveled off and kicked to start me moving. As soon as my water partner saw me move he swam a bit faster, but nothing I could not keep up with. He checked periodically to make sure I was still there. We moved further to the west while descending all the time. Believe it or not the deeper we went the lighter it got. Now I was getting confused. How can this be ? I suppose I should have been frightened but the opposite was occurring. I was becoming more excited all the time. We rounded the western most part of this volcanic wall only to be confronted by a cave. An underwater cave with light radiating from deep within. Without hesitation I followed the man fish into the cave. It grew narrow as we went deeper, but still with adequate light. Where it came from I had no idea. We stopped at what appeared to be a dead end. My swim partner put his hand to the wall which opened like an elevator door.   The cavity beyond the door was brightly lit. In and up we swam and broke the surface of the water. I was looking at what could have passed for a Carribean beach front, again lacking the Palm trees. Suddenly I found I could touch bottom and stand. My companion indicated I could remove the mask and shut off the Oxygen I did so hesitantly, took a breath and found the fresh air quite acceptable. We walked to the beach leaving the water where my guide turned and introduced himself."

"My name is Athos." He said, extending his hand.

I reached out to receive his hand and was surprised to see he reached further up my arm to clasp. This I recalled was the hand shake of long ago. His grasp was firm and warm in spite of having just left the water. He spoke in perfect English. I, in turn, introduced myself. He followed with

"We have been expecting you."

The look in my eyes obviously showed my confusion. Athos smiled and said.

"The old man told us."

I was still confused but said nothing further.

"Here comes your host." he said.

I looked inland from the beach observing a tall, lean, distinguished figure walking toward us. He was wearing a white robe or gown of sorts, tied at the waste with a black sash. His face was weathered, but carried an intelligent expression, sporting a close cropped pure white beard.

He approached, his arm already extended. I in turn, did the same. I received the same firm grasp as given by Athos.

"I am called Antilino, and you are ?"

My name is Kirkland but most people refer to me as Kirk."

"Kirkland it is then." was the reply. "Welcome to our fair land. Follow me please."

I took my swim fins off and ran a few steps to catch up. Just past the tree line of the beach was an open plaza filled with people going to and fro all dressed in similar attire. I guess I would liken them to Greek or Roman toga's. Men and women alike all dressed the same. The only break in white monotony was varied colored sashes. I wondered if there was any significance to the color designation. Before entering the plaza itself he stopped at a small shelter-like, shell shaped structure.

"You may put your equipment here. Not to worry, it will be perfectly safe."

After divesting myself of my diving gear I was handed a toga garment.

"This will keep you at an equal body heat reading."

I did as he asked. It felt a little strange at first until I realized everyone else was dressed exactly the same. Reading my mind Antilino addressed my thought.

"We have found over the centuries that this is the most practical type of garment for all climes, both for comfort and body temperature regulation. After a time you will also agree."

I put the garment on, not knowing what to say.

When satisfactorily clothed we continued across the plaza and up the steps of a flat topped pyramid shaped building. Before entering a portal I turned to view the plaza, which was the size of at least two football fields, the perimeter of which was outlined with similar structures. I hesitated upon entering and started thinking again.

"Where am I ? I'm underwater, yet dry, walking around a large city of who knows where. That's it! Where am I ? Maybe I should ask myself who am I ? This is crazy."

My thoughts were then interrupted.

"You are not crazy my friend, a bit mixed up perhaps because of the situation, but you are not crazy. Yours is not an uncommon reaction."

My host was answering my thoughts once again. I looked at him directly and asked.

"Where am I ?"

Antilino smiled for the first time.

"You mean you have not figured that out yet."

I just stared at him stupidly.

"Welcome to Atlantis."

I continued to stare probably with my mouth hanging open. Antilino was patient and remained quiet awaiting my next question. Finally able to function I stuttered out;

"At—lan—tis ? But Atlantis isn't - - -"

I was interrupted before I could finish.

"Atlantis is now, and always was real." said Antilino proudly. Perhaps later with wine I can give you the real story.

"What do you mean later." I thought. "I've got a wife to get back to. I guess this is what they refer to when they say people just disappear. Then again, if the old man made it back I guess I can also. I'll stick this out a little while longer.

"I looked at Antilino and he smiled slyly as if he heard my thoughts, which I'm sure he did. My curiosity was overpowering my better judgement.

"Come, come with me. All will be revealed in good time."

Like a lost puppy I just followed as he entered the building. We passed through a small marble columned hallway only to enter a large sparsely appointed room.

"This will be yours while you are here with us."

"What do you mean while I am with you. I can't stay here."

I smiled and said this would do just fine.

"I'll leave you for now to get adjusted. I will send for you later."

Before I could object he was gone. I stood there staring at an empty portal, my mind in a state of mass confusion. I tried to make sense of all that was happening, but my mind took a vacation. Nothing in my head was

working. I was here to get adjusted. Adjusted to what ? The fact that I'm
under water and dry, in a dark cave but it's daylight. In a place that is myth,
yet I'm here. Men that have gills and swim like fish but talk and walk. This
whole scenario is not possible and here I am in the middle of the impossible.

  I took a deep breath, moved to what I assumed to be a bench
and seated myself.

  "What now." I whispered aloud. For once I received no
answer. I checked the time. I had only been gone forty two minutes. I still
had roughly an hour and forty minutes of air left. Karen would not be worried
yet. She knew how much I loved to explore. That fact allowed me to breath
a little easier.

  Relaxed somewhat I decided to have a walk around the room,
as it was, and sort of survey the accommodations. There were no windows but
there was an opening overhead the bed, at least I was guessing it was a bed.
 I assumed there was a way to close it in case of rain. Yeah, if they had any
rain.

  Along the far wall were bathing facilities, I hoped.   I'm sure
its workings had a simple explanation.

  Overall the was sparse but the necessities were taken care of.
I settled on the bed, which appeared to be rock hard from it's looks and was
truly astounded. However it was like Great Grandma's old fashioned feather
bed. I just thought about getting comfortable when I heard a soft gong outside
the portal. And a portal it was in the absence of a door. Seconds later a young
woman appeared. She was stunningly beautiful, with long flowing blond hair
that hung just below her waist.

  "Atilino will see you now. Please follow me.

  I stood up as she turned to go.

  "What name do you go by." I sought.

  "I am called Antilina, I am Antilino's daughter. Please come,
You are expected."

  She turned and vanished around the portal. A few long strides
and I was in step with her. Trying to be friendly I inquired.

  "If we are still underwater what is the source of light ?"

  "That will all be revealed in good time."

  "As far as I'm concerned, now is a good a time as any." I
thought.

  "That may be alright for you Kirkland, but Antilino will
decide when the right time is." she answered in my mind.

  "Does everyone read minds." I asked myself.

  "All but outsiders." she answered aloud. "We are a people far
more evolved than what you consider humanity. I have said too much already.
All will be revealed when the time is right."

  I was beginning to get sick of that statement. What ever I
thought obviously didn't count. I resigned myself to go along with this a

while longer and then demand the explanation I felt I deserved.

On thinking that, I detected a slight smile on Antilina's face.

After turning some corners and ascending a few extremely wide, marble steps, I found myself in what I guessed to be a banquet room. Luxuriously simple in its design yet exuding an inviting warmth about it. The table held a bounty that would please kings of old. Antilino moved to meet us with a genuine smile and a warm handshake. He lovingly kissed his daughter on the cheek and led me to the chair of honor at the table. As if by a silent signal people appeared carrying platters of food to add to the table. After each delicacy found it's place on the table the servers also took a seat at the table. My look of confusion must have been showing which Antilino answered immediately. There are no servants here or anywhere in Atlantis. We are all equal and share everything. Yes, we all have our own speciality, but none is more important or better than the other. The citizens of Atlantis heard of your coming and wanted to meet you.

Introductions were then made of names I couldn't even pronounce, never mind remember.

Antilino, being the perfect host, raised his glass of wine, directed it to me and said;

"This is an official welcome to Atlantis."

Mumbles were heard all around as each guest tipped their glass to me and in turn, drank. I answered their toast with thanks and sipped the wine. It was a white wine I had never tasted before. I can't begin to describe its perfection. The pleasure of the wine must have been written all over my face fore all the guests smiled.

"It is quite good, isn't it." remarked Antilino. "Please partake and enjoy." he added with a swing of his arm across the whole table. When all had served themselves and were relaxed, eating, Antilino took the opportunity to speak directly to me.

"And now my friend, answers to your questions and confusion."

He certainly had my attention with those words.

"You see Kirkland, Atlantis always was. Our people always were. Our civilization predated anything you have ever learned or read about. We, ourselves do not know when our beginning was. Our oral history tells stories of our existence when the world was just one land mass. Today you have given it the name Pangaea. This was approximately two hundred million years ago. We Atlantians, if you will, have been evolving since then, both physically and mentally. That is why we may appear somewhat different than you are today."

"If I may ask a question Sir." I inquired.

"Of course Kirkland, we welcome them.

"Well, Sir."

I started but was stopped with a polite wave of the hand.

"Antilino, please, we should have no formality between us."

"As you wish." I answered. " And thank you."

He acknowledged my thanks with a nod of his head.

"I started to say what ever stories or information we have about Atlantis are considered myth and that if Atlantis did exist at one time it was completely destroyed by volcanic eruptions and vanished in the depths of the ocean thousands of years ago. People have searched for centuries only to find nothing. And now you say this is Atlantis. How can this be ?" Antilino's and other faces were now adorned with smiles.

"That my dear Kirkland is a very logical question and I'm sure has led to many mysterious misconceptions." Antilino answered softly. "Relax, enjoy the food and drink while I give you a brief history of our unique civilization which I hope will enlighten you and allow you to believe in us."

I did relax and smiled. I then felt a certain calm come over me and actually was eager to hear his story.

After a short hesitation and a long sip of wine, Antilino found a comfortable position in his chair and proceeded.

"At one time we also appeared as what you simply refer to as cave men. Our evolvement, however, was much faster than your present day civilization. To use a mathematical equivalent, it would be something like thirty or forty thousand to one. Our brain development alone advanced so fast, we almost could not keep up with it ourselves. But we learned the use of moderation and patience of thought."

A pause for a taste of wine, Antilino smiled as he resumed the story.

"Putting that aside for the moment, that fact will become more evident as I go along. Our advancement in the arts and sciences was so startling, we did not have the time for confrontation. We learned early on that confrontation only led to destruction. Nothing productive was ever a result. We mastered the art of co-existance in total harmony and that harmony benefitted all. We sent out missionaries, if you will, not for religious conversion, but the advancement of knowledge so that peaceful existence would take precedence over war and destruction. The urge for power is just not in our makeup. One might say it was bred out of us over the course of our evolution. Some of those missionaries, whose names are still known today, tried to influence others outlook on destructive behavior, but to no avail."

I politely interrupted Antilino, who graciously took my question.

"You spoke of your representatives whose names are still known today. Would I know these names ?"

"You most certainly would my friend. We have our own designation for them but you will recognize them by more familiar names. Such as Quetziquatl, or the Feathered Serpent who walked among the Mayans, also Mohammad, Buddha, Jesus Christ and quite a few others. Even in your lifetime you had Ghandi."

   I sat there dumbfounded by this revelation. I was at a total loss for words. My mind became a merry-go-round with thoughts thrown about into nowhere. Shaking myself back to reality to be able to organize thought, I finally found my voice again.

   "**O**kay, I understand what you just said, hard to fathom, but I understand. That was in the past. What about the present, the here and now. Can you explain the fact that I'm here under water but dry and in daylight ?"

   Antilino gave a soft chuckle.

   "**O**f course Kirkland, I am not here to frighten or confuse you. If you remember, I mentioned earlier our advancement in the sciences. Over the millennia we have grown to a point where our technology allows us to duplicate almost anything nature has provided. So here, now in our present world, as you can see, we have duplicated Earth's atmosphere, weather as we need it, day and night as desired, and yes all under ground."

   There was a renewed wine pause, this time for both of us.

   "**W**e realized." furthered Antilino, "Many centuries ago, that our way of life was not being entertained or accepted by the less evolved people. It was then decided that this situation presented a danger to us and an even greater danger to those who would seek to control us or worse yet, destroy us. We chose to protect our way of life and with that decision, approved by all our people, manufactured for ourselves this world you stand in today. What you say is true, Atlantis disappeared into the depth's of the ocean, but as you can see, not destroyed. By our own design we engineered the volcanic eruptions to show our destruction. This small act freed us from a world we no longer wished to be part of. We survive and continue to evolve in hopes that someday the world, as you know it will quit their insanity and learn what we already enjoy. We continue on quite content in our artificial world. We, of course still have access to your world and of course still have no desire to be part of it. Our observations tell us the upper world is getting worse not better with time. Our major concern is it's destruction, which will be caused by the few power hungry. It is totally unconscionable that these few care to risk such total annihilation for little or no gain. Your technology has come a long way in recent decades but it is being used for personal gain and not for the betterment of mankind. We have all that your world desires and it happened without individual greed. One did not try to better the other. One did not try to destroy the other. Improved ways were found and given to all, not selfishly used to control others. As you can see we are a quiet content people and wish it for all."

   "**A**nother question, Antilino, if I may."

   "**A**sk, my friend, we harbor no secrets."

   I hesitated a moment rethinking my thoughts so as not to offend.

   "**I**f your technology is so advanced why do you not put a stop to my worlds misguided ways."

"I knew you would be coming to that."   Antilino responded. "That question has been asked many times before."

"And what is your answer." I pushed.

"That is one of those "easier said than done situations." Believe me, Kirkland we have been assessing this problem for some time. We are not a big nation. We have no standing Army or Navy. If word of our advances were to get out before your world's crisis was solved, we also would be in great danger. Misuse of our technology in the hands of such power mad people would certainly mean indescribable world wide catastrophic upheaval. Most likely the total annihilation of the planet. That in turn would affect the synchronisation of the whole galaxy. I think you can see why it is a course we choose not to take."

Reflecting on his words I felt self consciously humbled. I had not allowed my limited thinking to go that far. I sat back with another sip of wine.

"I know you have other questions Kirkland, please don't hold back."

"To get away from the disaster issue for the moment, Is there any truth to the rumor of people disappearing. The locals on this island are actually frightened and even fear to talk about it.

"The answer my dear friend is both yes and no."

I questioned his response with my eyes.

"Let me explain." continued Antilino. "Others have made dives ,as you did, and were invited here, again as you were. They were not harmed in any way. As for their disappearance from the upper world, this is true, only because they chose not to return. They knew what they were giving up but still made an unprecedented, conscious decision to become part of Atlantis. Many of our citizens are from your world by choice.

Over time we have had many survivors of your wars who we had rescued from the sea. Some were returned safely but most elected to stay with us."

"Those that returned to the upper world, do they not jeopardize your secrets."

"We have a method that will erase all memory of their time with us. In fact we do not exist."

"Will I be subjected to this ?" I asked.

"Not necessarily. There have been some who live above and still maintain our secret. For instance the old man you recently spoke with."

I smiled at this exposure, remembering the old man's words.

"We can usually ascertain who is worthy and who is not. You, my dear Kirkland have the character we so value. And if you so choose to return to the upper world you will maintain your memories and we hope stay in contact with us.”

A swell of pride rushed through me and I felt my face flush crimson. Feeling embarrassed and I’m sure looking the part, I addressed Antilino.

Perhaps if I were not married I would stay to learn, but I can not leave my wife like this, not knowing. So I must return to the surface,”

Looking at my watch I added.

“And soon.”

Antilino looked at me warmly.

“We knew that would be your answer and it is just that character that we so admire and trust. Go my friend. I sincerely hope we meet again. We have much to share.”

All the guests bade me a warm farewell and Athos led me to where my SCUBA gear was.

“I will guide you out and back to the area of your boat. Good luck Kirkland.

I ascended slowly, looking forward to seeing Karen as the last hours’ events rushed through my mind.

~ ~ ~ ~ ~ ~

“I thought you were going to cut the grass, not take a nap.” interrupted Karen.

“Huh- - -What - - - Oh, where are - - - ?” was Kirkland’s answer.

“Boy you must have been really out of it, sweety.” she said with a smile.

“Huh, Oh it’s you.”

“Well thanks for the great and loving recognition.”

“ You’re lucky to have me here.” Kirk said strangely.

“I know that.” Karen answered hesitantly. “Are you alright ? She followed.

“Yeah, I guess it will take a few minutes. I was in a deep sleep or something.”

Kirk shook his head trying to get rid of the groggies.

“Didn’t you say a while ago that you took a chance on a trip to the Azores or something ?”

“Oh yeah, that was months ago, they had that drawing last week. Somebody from out of state won that.” Karen answered from the kitchen.

~ ~ ~ ~ ~ ~

The End

"LIFE"

By
K.J.Goss

LIFE

"Whatcha doin Grampa ? What are you staring at ?"
Asked the inquisitive young boy.

"I'm looking at the forest." answered the kindly old man.

"Why ? It's just a bunch of trees."

"It's more than just trees. It's life."

"What do you mean it's life ? There's no one living there."

"Perhaps not people, but everything there is living."

"I don't see the trees moving except when the wind blows."

"That's because you're not looking or listening. Sit with me a while and I'll show you life that you're not seeing. Real life that is part of us all."

"That's silly Grampa, I'm not part of a tree."

"Maybe not, but a tree is part of your whole life. So is everything else in the forest. Life isn't just people. Life is everything you see or hear, even when you don't see or hear."

"How can something be alive if I don't see it or hear it."

The old man was now smiling.

"Let me try and explain. Where's your Mom right now ?"

"In the kitchen baking cookies."

"Is she alive ?"

"Of course she's alive, I just saw her in the kitchen."

"But now you're here with me on the porch. Can you see or hear your Mom ?"

"Nooo - - - -"

"Then how do you know she's alive."

"Now you're confusing me Grampa."

"You're right, I probably am. Let me explain it another way. Do you have time for a story ?"

"**I** always have time for one of your stories Grampa. I like your stories. They're a lot of fun."

*"**G**ood, then sit with me and I'll tell you a story of the forest. It will be a little different then my other tales, but if you listen real carefully you just may learn something."*

"**O**kay Gramps, but a story about trees doesn't sound very interesting to me."

*"**B**e patient boy, be patient."*

"**D**oes it start with once upon a time ?"

*"**A**ctually it does not. Just be patient and listen. That forest that you see is a whole life unto itself."*

"**B**ut it's just a bunch of trees Grampa."

*"**I**s it really now ? Just a bunch of trees is it. Look again Tim, look real hard and listen."*

"**A**ll I see is trees Grampa. Some big ones and some not so big."

*"**L**et me help you Tim. Let me help you see what I see. Look at that pine tree over there. The one your Mom has her clothes line attached to. Can you see the top of it ?"*

"**W**OW ! That is big. I can barely see the top. It's way up there mixed with all the other trees. And look Grampa, look how straight it is."

*"**N**ow you're seeing things Tim."*

"**H**ow big is it ?"

*"**I** didn't measure it Tim, but I'd guess it to be about eighty feet."*

"**W**OW ! You could make a whole house with just one tree."

Laughing, the Old Man answered:

*"**N**ot quite Tim, but it sure is a lot of wood. How do you think it became so tall ?"*

"**I**t grew I guess."

*"**T**hat's right Tim. It grew, just like you do because it's a living thing. That particular tree is probably over forty years old."*

"**W**OW ! That's really old."

Again Grampa just smiled silently.

"**H**ow does it grow so big."

*"**W**ell, just like you he gets food and nourishment."*

"But who feeds it ? What does it eat ?"

Now we're getting somewhere thought the Old Man

"The forest feeds it. Everything in the forest feeds each other.*"

"What do you mean by everything, Grampa ?"
"Everything you see or even not see in the forest is living and growing."

"But where does the food come from ?"
"The trees take turns going to the supermarket."
"GRAMPA !" said Tim in a scolding manner. Trees can't do that."

Then he noticed the smile on the older man's face and in turn smiled himself.

"I'm serious Grampa. Where does the food come from ?"
"Well let's see, we'll start with the easy part first. What does your mother do to help the flowers and house plants grow ?"
"She waters them once in a while."
"That's right. Very good. She waters them because they are living things. So what about the trees ? Do they need water ?"
"I guess so, cause you said they were living,"
"Right, so how do they get it."
"I don't know, Oh wait, I know. The rain. The rain waters everything."
"Good, now you're catching on Timmy. Now what else can you tell me ?"
"I thought you were supposed to be telling me Grampa."
"I guess I am, Tim, I guess I am. Okay, you asked me how do the trees eat. Well to start with..."
"Wait Grampa." Tim interrupted. "I asked you how do they get the food."
"So you did, Tim, so you did. I stand corrected. Let me see now, how can I put this. The whole forest is living and the whole forest is their food."

Tim looked up at his story teller with a puzzled look.

"HUH." He said.
"It's okay Tim, just listen and I'll explain."

Young Tim sat back staring intently at his Grandfather.

"I'm going to put this in story form like I promised. Let's see now...., as I said the whole forest is life. Just about everything is alive. —— Remember in the fall when the leaves fall off the trees. Well that's when they stopped being alive."

"**B**ut Grampa, you just said everything was alive. You're confusing me again."

Smiling the Old Man patiently answered.

*"**I** know I did Timmy, but please listen patiently and I'm sure it will all become clear to you very soon."*

"**O**kay Grampa, I'll try to be quiet and listen."

*"**G**ood boy Tim."* answered Grampa as he reached over and gently rubbed Timmy's head messing up his hair a little more.

*"**N**ow where was I, Oh yeah, The leaves. All the little leaves were happy to fall off the trees because they could now do the other job they were meant to do."*

"They have jobs ?" commented the boy. "Oops, sorry."

*"**T**hat they do my boy, that they do. It's part of what they were grown to do. You see once they fall off the trees they all get together and cover the ground. That's their first winter job. They protect the ground from the deep freeze. This helps the roots stay warm for the winter so they can grow again next year. Then they start their second job. They slowly start to decompose."*

"**H**UH !" said Timmy. "What's decompose ?"

*"**T**hey start to rot."* smiled Grampa. *"They dry up and fall apart. The rain now plays his part by pushing the dried up pieces into the dirt. Then the bugs and worms that live in the dirt eat the rotting leaves and turn it into fertilizer. In other words food for the trees and bushes and grasses."*

"**W**ow ! the forest sure is a busy place." Tim remarked in wonder, his eyes showing new interest.

"The leaves have yet another job to do."

"**R**eally ! said the young boy. "I didn't know leaves were so important."

The Old Man smiled to himself knowing his young grandson was suddenly learning a new respect for nature.

*"**Y**ou're right Timmy, they are important and their other job is just as important."*

"**W**hat is it Grampa.?" Tell me! Timmy asked excitedly.

*"**S**helter and housing."* answered Grampa.

"Houses." repeated Timmy. "I never saw a house made of leaves."

"Oh, but they are all over the place. How could you not see them."

Timmy started searching in earnest.

"I still don't see anything Grampa."
"I guess they are a little hard to see." Grampa admitted. *"Look over here with me."*

The Old Man knelt down on one knee and gently moved some dried leaves aside exposing a cluster of beetles burrowing deep into the soil.

"WOW ! Look at all them bugs." Exclaimed Timmy.
"They also are doing an important job. " said Grampa.
"Digging holes in the dirt is an important job ?" questioned young Tim. "I do that all the time."
"It's more then just digging holes. They loosen the dirt and let air in. They also fertilize it as they go. They put food into the soil. Food that will feed the trees and bushes next spring. The dead leaves and twigs are also used by the birds, squirrels and other critters for their nesting and bedding and protection in the winter."
"Boy, Gramps you sure know a lot. How did you learn all that stuff ?"
"By looking and listening Tim. By quietly watching everything around you."

The pair became silent for a while, looking and listening. Tim finally glanced up at the Old Man and whispered;

"It sounds like there's a bunch of birds in the tree."

Smiling to himself, Grampa reached for the young boy's hand.

"Come with me Timmy. I'll show you one of my favorite spots."

Hand in hand they wove in and around trees until they lost sight of the house.

"Let's rest awhile on that log. " said Grampa.

They sat on a fallen tree next to a brook, the moving water glimmering with the sun's highlights as it moved in and out of the tree shadows. Grandfather and grandson remained silent as the forest came alive with sound.

"I thought a bird was a bird." whispered Timmy. "So far I've seen five different kinds and they all have a different sound."

"And they all have different names also."

"Do you know all their names Grampa ?"

"No, but I wish I did. I'm still learning, just like you."

"But you're old. You should know everything by now."

"Why thank you for that young one, but one should never stop trying to learn. That's what keeps us going no matter how old we are. Now back to the forest my boy. What else do you hear ?"

"I was just watching a couple of red squirrels chasing each other. Boy, they sure make a lot of noise don't they ?"

"They sure can. Did you know the forest feeds them too. This is their home. The trees give them nuts and berries and nice tender buds to eat. Twigs and dry leaves help to make their nests. The nests are high in the trees to protect them. What about the trees Tim ? Did you notice anything special ?"

"Yeah !" Timmy answered excitedly.   "They're all different. I thought trees was trees."

"I thought trees <u>were</u> trees Tim"

"Oops ! Oh yeah – sorry Gramps. I didn't know they were all different."

"That's because you never really looked before."

"I guess I didn't. Do they have different names too ?"

"You bet they do, and they all have different jobs. The main thing is that they all share the forest and keep it alive."

"It sure is pretty, ain't it."

"You mean isn't it, don't you."

"Yeah I guess so, I mean, yes I guess so."

"Yes Tim, it is absolutely beautiful."

"WOW, look at those butterflies Gramps. Ain't they pretty, I mean aren't they pretty. I guess they live here too."

"Yes they do Timmy."

Suddenly Tim turned his head.

"What's that noise Grampa ?"

"That noise, my young friend are the frogs that live in that pond over there."

"Can we go see them ?"

"We can try boy, but they usually jump in the water when you get near them. But we can try."

The pair stood and advanced toward the pond as quietly as they could. Sure enough three frogs disappeared under the lily pads. Grandfather and Grandson stood hand in hand silently.

"Listen to that Grampa, the trees are talking to each other."
"What do you mean son ?" said the older of the pair quietly smiling.

Young Tim pointed to the tree tops swaying gently in the breeze.

"Each tree is making a different sound. I guess that's because they have different kinds of leaves, but it sounds to me like they are talking to each other."

The Old Man smiled, pleased that his Grandson was now seeing.

"They probably are Tim. We just don't understand their language."

"Maybe if we listen long enough we can learn it."
"Perhaps we can Tim, perhaps we can. We better head for home now." Said Grampa. *"Your Mother might be wondering where we went. We don't want to worry her."*
"Okay Grampa and thanks."
"Thanks for what Timmy."
"For showing me life like you said you would."

The Old Man smiled to himself again feeling good inside.

~ ~ ~ ~ ~ ~

Sitting back on the porch with cookies and lemonade and starring at the forest young Timmy said;

"You know Gramps I really liked being in the forest. It's so alive with so many things. Can we go there again sometime ?"
"Of course we can Tim, any time you want as long as your Mom says it's okay. Perhaps next time we can see and learn about some of the animals who also share the forest."
"That would be great Gramps, I want to learn everything

about life, everything about the forest. I want to know things just like you."

The Old Man sat back and sipped his lemonade

The End

The Miniature Railroad

by
K.J.Goss

The Miniature Railroad

The puffs of smoke curled upward when the old steam locomotive slowed down as it neared the small station at Kentville. It switched to the small track extension to the backside of the depot leaving the main track open for the main liner from the big city. Among the flatbed and hopper cars was a small passenger coach just before a tiny red caboose. Used mostly by the locals, it was a convenient and very inexpensive form of transportation.

The main travel route of this antique train was between two villages about thirty miles apart with many unscheduled stops at local farms in between.

There was nothing formal about this quaint rail run from Kentville to Jeanstown and back, and that's just the way Kent designed his miniature rail road layout. Years in the making, this H O gage railway and the two towns, were just about complete now, as were all the farms and industries making up this little world. This had been a dream of Kent's since early childhood and now after sixty plus years was a reality. His beloved wife of forty five years had passed on a few years back. He missed her dearly but was able to fill his time with his favorite rail road towns. Jean had shared his love of these make believe towns but with slightly less enthusiasm or so he thought in the beginning. They were devoted to each other for those many years, now his only real pleasure to pass time was the dream town of make believe.

Since he retired, Kent had expanded his layout to pretty much fill his basement. His sophistication went so far to have automatic timers to change from day to night, each giving it's own atmosphere to his world of make believe.

The details of the hand made world were precise, reflecting his every wish and desire for what he wanted in a community. A dream, I'm sure, many of us would like to decorate.

The little village of Kentville had a town green he constructed with loving care that he took particular interest in, especially at Christmas time with lights and greenery decorating the gazebo. The town itself had everything a town should have. There was no need to leave the area to shop at a mall. Shopping malls were a taboo in his eyes. You name the store or activity and it was incorporated in his village or in Jeanstown. The towns were individual but shared in everything. This of course kept the small steam railway busy all the time.

There was about one hundred and sixty feet of track which made a good separation between the two sister towns and including much open farming space and small industrial areas. This was Kent's perfect world.

~ ~ ~ ~ ~ ~ ~

He had no children of his own, but occasionally a niece or nephew, or both would visit him. In evitably they would find him in his fantasy world. Though he appeared happy and content they were becoming concerned that this fantasy was consuming every waking moment. His conversation was only about the make believe towns and the people in them. He knew the names of every person that lived in the made up world. These metal or plastic figures, no more than three quarters of an inch high and painted in minute detail, all had names and personalities according to Kent. These were now his only friends and spoken of as family.

Visits by the younger relatives became more frequent because of their concern for their uncle. He appeared perfectly normal in every way except for the obsession for his little world. His food pantry and refrigerator had not changed in months yet there was no apparent weight loss or loss of energy. His answer to these type of questions was always the same. He ate with so and so or what's his name in Kentville or Jeanstown. He really believed this and there was no way to convince him otherwise.

Seeking professional help, they became frustrated when told

it was a harmless pastime and he was hurting no one.

~ ~ ~ ~ ~ ~ ~

Month's passed with no change in Kent's behavior until one day Kent was no where to be found. The first place checked was, of course, the basement train layout. The trains were running but again, he was not to be seen. As the two younger people were ready to leave they heard his voice in the distance.

"**H**i there, I thought you might come by today. Wait in the kitchen, I'll be right with you."

They both looked around and at each other confused. Are we missing something they each thought independently.

"**D**on't worry." they heard again. "I'll be right there."

The niece and nephew waited in the kitchen no more then five minutes when Kent appeared up from the cellar.

"**W**e were just there. We didn't see you down there." said the niece.

"**I** was on the train coming from Jeanstown, I had to wait until we got to the station." answered Kent.

Though shocked, the young ones said nothing. The rest of the conversation was normal and after tea and cookies they left. Nothing further was related to other family members out of embarrassment. Kent's nephew figured it was just a play on words and that he was probably under the table fixing something.

A few more month's went by and both niece and nephew received a phone call from Kent. It was a direct invitation to come to dinner. He had a proposal for them. Peaked with curiosity, they arrived together at the appointed date and time. Kent had a wonderful dinner prepared including a bottle of wine. He casually mentioned how Jan Hewlett from Kentville prepared most everything for him that morning.

Still harboring strange feelings, yet again saying nothing, the two family members anxiously awaited Kent's proposal.

With dinner over and the dishes rinsed the trio relaxed with the wine.

"**N**ow my dears." Kent started. "I'm sure you are wondering

-213-

about my proposal. It may sound confusing to you but please hear me out before you make any judgements or decisions. I'm going away for a while. I don't exactly know for how long but I'm asking the two of you to look after the house."

Before he could say more, Kent's nephew interrupted.

"You can't go anyplace. You don't have any means of transportation, and you don't drive."

"Where are you going ?" added the niece. "This is all rather sudden, isn't it ?"

"We're going to forbid it." said his nephew sternly.

"Oh dear!" answered Kent. "I thought you might react this way. It is because of this that I almost didn't tell you. I am going. It's something I want to do and you are not going to stop me. I will be perfectly okay."

"Where are you going ?" asked the niece again.

"Just to visit some friends, and that's all you need to know, now please let me finish." Kent emphasized firmly.

He paused, looking directly at both of them.

"Now as I said, I'm going away for a while and want you to look after the house, and do not, under any circumstances disturb my train layout. Which means more directly, to not interrupt the electricity to the basement. Do I make myself clear?"

The two could tell he was obviously becoming upset and chose not to push against him any further. They agreed to his wishes, finished their wine and departed, still concerned for their beloved uncle.

Two days later, Josh, the nephew, stopped by Kent's house to have one more go at talking him out of traveling. Entering the house he noticed the dishes had been cleaned, in fact the whole house was neat and orderly.

Hearing a distant humming Josh decided to check on the cause. With nothing obvious upstairs he headed for the basement. All was dark except for the layout tables, and a train was moving slowly along the back mountain range.

"I wonder why he kept the train running." he said aloud. Josh walked to the control station to shut it down, then remembered his uncle's caution. "Do not disturb the train layout." Josh laughed to himself. "Oh well, it's his electric bill." and returned upstairs leaving the train running. He checked the rest of the house, making sure all was secure and left, thinking no more about the basement.

Another week zoomed by and Josh having not heard from his uncle called his cousin Susan. She also had not been in contact with her uncle, so Josh made plans to check on uncle's house again. He arrived early evening after work to find the house totally secure both inside and out. Before leaving he decided to check the basement one last time although he did not expect anything to be different. Descending the stairs he did not hear the hum of the train. The cellar was dark but the train layout was lit up for evening and night time.

"How wonderful and magical it looked." he thought. "It almost looked real."

He reflected on endless hours of dedication his uncle must have spent to realize the detail now displayed. The electrical wiring alone must have taken weeks. Josh had not seen the layout at night before and now gazing at the intricate lighting system, was fascinating in it's reality. Varied houses and business's were lit, street lamps were working, some blinking, some constant. Even the traffic signal lights were working. The control panel alone was impressive. Obviously everything was on some kind of timing system.

Turning to leave, he noticed the old train, the steam engin, was stopped at the depot in Jeanstown. Josh accepted the fact that this also must be on a timer.

"I guess if it makes the old man happy, then what's the harm.

He locked the door as he left still thinking how beautiful the miniature train layout was. It contained everything one would like for the perfect place to live.

"It is amazing what detail these hobbyist's get into for their craft." he thought as he drove away.

Another five days went by when Josh received a call from Susan. She was at their uncle's house.

"I thought you said the trains were not moving ?" she questioned.

"They weren't." Josh replied. "It was parked by the depot at Jeanstown."

Suddenly Josh thought; "Now he's got me talking about toys

as if they were real."

"**I** wouldn't be concerned, it's probably on a timer just like the lights."

"That's not all." Susan continued. "I get the feeling other things have moved. I can't say for sure but something is just not right. I would feel better if you would come over."

"**O**kay, give me about thirty minutes, in the meantime don't touch anything."

They ended their conversation and Susan sat at the kitchen table to wait for Josh.

Her visit to the basement was really the first time she observed the layout at length. She also was taken by the realness of the design. She now understood how someone could be taken with a hobby such as this.

She heard Josh's car and felt more comfortable now that he was here. She met him at the door, and joking, Josh asked

"**H**ow long have you been seeing things?"

"That's not funny, Josh. I really felt there's something strange about these trains. Perhaps not the trains so much, but the two towns Kent made."

"**I** don't know if I would call them strange. They are beautifully designed, and they are Kent's dream town." Josh answered.

"**I** know that." countered Susan, "and I agree they are beautiful, yet I have this feeling inside that there's much more that we are not seeing or understanding."

"**O**kay." Josh said, "Let's go down and look at the layout and see what we can find."

He said this to humor Susan and to help her relax though he admitted to himself he was curious also.

The steam train was parked on the siding of Jeanstown depot, while the newer diesel passenger liner was on the main track heading for the same depot.

"See." Susan exclaimed, "The train is running except earlier it was the other one.."

She looked slightly upset.

"That's what I was trying to tell you before." Josh

interrupted. "Everything is run on a timer. Come here I'll show you."

Josh walked her over to the large electronic control panel. Various colored lights were blinking. Each was labeled for a different function. " This blinking blue light shows that the express train is running. These other lights represent the night time lights, etc."

Susan looked at him still obviously upset.

"**B**ut why is he letting this run for weeks when he is not here.?"

"Good question." replied Josh. "We'll make it a point to ask when we see him again."

"**W**hy don't we just turn everything off ?" Susan queried.

"**W**ell, I for one would rather respect his wishes. If you remember, he was rather emphatic about not touching anything."

"**W**ell, I don't exactly agree with you and I still think something is not right, I just can't put my finger on it. Okay let's get out of here, I'm beginning not to like it here."

Smiling, Josh stepped aside to let her go up the stairs first. One last look at the train, which was now stopped at the station, and he followed her upstairs. Susan said her goodbye and hurried out the door leaving Josh alone in the kitchen. He listened as she drove away and decided to have another look at the layout.

The old steam engin was now chugging along, puffing out little clouds of smoke on it's way to Kentville. Josh had never really studied the track layout before and was now fascinated at it's intricate meanderings, through mountain tunnels, over bridges, through farmland and skirting mountain sides. It was as real as could be. He stopped closer to the Kentville end of the spacious layout. His eyes took in the wonderful detail of the village. It was laid out like a giant oval, the village green occupying the center, with a few side streets splayed out like wheel spokes. The village green contained both a band stand at one end and a beautifully constructed gazebo at the other, with meandering pathways throughout and sundry benches placed strategically here and there for the comfort of the townspeople.

Suddenly the movie theater caught his attention. The marque had blinking lights but more importantly there was a line of people at the box office. Josh had not noticed this earlier, in fact he didn't ever recall a line *there*.

"I guess I'm just imagining things." he thought.

As he turned to leave he saw that the steam train was now stopped at the Jeanstown station. He walked to the other end of the layout to Jeanstown. The town was planned a bit different but maintained the same inviting warmth of a small friendly village. The several shops, as in Kentville, provided all the necessities of life needed in a rural community. The village green, although smaller than Kentville, also contained a bandstand. If you listened carefully you could hear music. A speaker inside the bandstand, he assumed.

Josh looked at his watch noting it was time to leave if he wanted to keep his appointment. Moving toward the stairs he passed the Kentville village end of the layout. He stopped abruptly when he noticed there were no people figures at the movie theater. He shook his head as if to clear it.

"How can this be." he thought. He looked again bending over to get closer. Not only were there no people in line but the light was now out in the box office.

"This is not possible, I must have been mistaken before."

He left taking the steps two at a time. Driving to his appointment he recalled Susan's remarks about something feeling strange and not right.

Josh waited a few days before contacting Susan, more out of embarrassment than anything else. He had no clue as to how to broach the topic with her, she was already upset with the whole thing. He felt it would be better to talk to her about it before she should discover it herself and get freaked out. His mind now made up, he called her. They arranged to meet for coffee at Uncle Kent's place mid-afternoon Saturday. This at least gave him time to come up with the right words so she won't be too unsettled.

~ ~ ~ ~ ~ ~

"You can't be serious ? That's not possible ! They're toys !" was Susan's reaction.

"I'm glad to see you're taking this calmly." Josh said with a smile.

"This is nothing to laugh at." Susan said looking straight at him. "First Uncle Kent and now you. You're both balmy."

She started to get up to leave but Josh gently put his hand on her arm.

"Please Susan, wait till you hear me out. There has to be an explanation and I think together we can work this out."

Susan shot Josh a disgusted look but did sit back down.

"I'm sorry." she said. "All this just seems spooky to me."

"I know what you mean but I did not think this is one of those spooky things. For all we know it may be Uncle Kent playing tricks on us."

"I never thought of that. That would be just like him too." replied Susan.

"Okay then, to satisfy our mutual curiosity let's go down to the trains and study what we think is not what it should be."

"I guess you're right." she replied, "I know I'm probably being silly about this whole thing.

As they descended to the basement they could hear the trains running, actually both the steam and diesel engines were running pulling their mutual loads. Josh and Susan turned the corner at the bottom of the stairs and physically bumped into their uncle.

"Hi there you two, I was just going to call you. I'm glad you're here."

A bewildered look appeared on both of the younger faces.

"Surprised you, didn't I ." Kent said.

"When did you get home ?" asked Susan.

"Oh, a while ago." was Kent's answer,

"Then why didn't you let us know ?" followed Josh. "We were becoming concerned.. We do care for you, you know."

"I know you do ." replied Kent. "And I really do appreciate it. I thought I could have some fun with you."

Josh looked a little confused.

"How did you like the line of people at the movie theater? Had you going there, didn't I ? "

"We thought it might be you playing jokes." put in Susan. Josh however, looked closely at the face of his uncle and thought he detected a certain look. A look that told Josh there was more to it than just a joke, but he chose to remain silent. He did not want Susan going off the deep end.

Josh answered; "You sure did have me there, Uncle Kent. I

thought I was seeing things and maybe losing my mind.”

Kent also saw something in Josh’s eyes that lead him to believe he was more aware of things then he showed. He also chose to remain silent for now.

To keep the mood light, Kent went over to Susan.

“How did you like my little make believe world, now that you have had a closer look.”

“I think it’s quite beautiful Uncle, but forgive me if I don’t get as enthused about it as you are.”

“That’s quite alright my dear, I know not everyone follows my interests as passionately as I , but it fills my time and I enjoy my little villages.”

Susan smiled and gave him a one armed hug.

“Well now that we know that you are alright.” Susan said cheerfully, “If you will forgive me I have other things I have to attend to.”

She kissed her uncle’s cheek and turned toward the stairs, “See you later, Josh, call me.”

~ ~ ~ ~ ~ ~

Josh and his Uncle were now alone.

“So I really had you fooled with the theater line up, eh.”

Suddenly Josh felt angry and serious.

“You can quit the act now Uncle Kent. Susan is no longer here.”

“Why I don’t know what you mean, Josh. What act am I supposed to be taking part in ?”

Josh smiled to himself, thinking, “I wonder how long he’s going to keep this up ?”

“You know exactly what I mean Uncle. You never went away at all. You’ve been here all the time. You seem to be under some sort of spell as if you were hypnotized and I think it has something to do with these trains. Am I correct ?”

Kent, looking directly at Josh, smiled. A very big warm smile.

“You are almost correct, Josh. It doesn’t have something to do with the trains, it has everything to do with the trains.”

Josh, now somewhat befuddled and at a sudden loss for words, continued to stare at his uncle.

"Perhaps it's time I told you the whole story, come, sit with me and be prepared for something unbelievable."

The older man headed for upstairs and directed Josh to make himself comfortable at the kitchen table while he prepared some coffee. Not a word was spoken until the coffee was ready and Kent sat himself down across from his nephew.

"I can hardly believe it myself." Kent started. "It all happened just after Jean passed. She loved these trains, or should I really say the two towns, almost as much as I did."

"What happened ?" Josh interrupted even yet sounding serious.

"Be patient my boy, I think it's best I tell the whole story from the very beginning."

"I was quite distraught after her passing. I was lonely, angry and in general I was feeling sorry for myself. I did not go out for many weeks and refused to talk to anyone. We used to play with the trains together always speaking of the perfect place to live, our perfect place. A town the way we wanted it. The design of the layout I credit to her as much as to myself. We spent many weeks together talking of what we thought would be the ideal place to live.

Jean, unbeknownst to me was writing down every detail we mentioned. Again, we spent countless hours physically drawing out on paper, forever readjusting sizes of property or the placement of stores and business's. She pretty much took care of the towns while I laid out the track ways accordingly.

Then one evening Jean joined me with a glass of wine stating her perfect town, our perfect town, was now complete. All that was left was construction. I had never seen her so happy."

Kent paused for a sip of coffee and a tissue to blot his eyes. Josh had no idea his aunt was so involved with the toy trains. It never dawned on him that she would be so taken in with make believe. He felt his heart warming as his put on seriousness melted away. He wanted to ask questions, yet at the same time, did not want to disturb the world his uncle had entered. Josh silently sipped his coffee.

A few minutes passed and Josh could tell his uncle was lost

in memories. As abruptly as he stopped he started again.

"The construction of our dream world took a long time. Of course we were both still working then, so our time was limited. All in all I guess it was close to three years to see what you now see and we both enjoyed every minute, actually every second of it's making.

After dinner each night we would go downstairs with a glass of wine and proudly toast each other and our creation.

We modified some things as we went along because new ideas would present themselves or it just appeared to be a better way. I must say though," Kent laughed out loud. "Jean always had the last say. She was so proud and very protective of her two towns."

Uncle Kent paused anew a few seconds, obviously reflecting on a sudden memory.

"Nearing the constructions end, she occupied herself with buying the people figures that you see. There was a time I thought we were going to go broke." Kent laughed again. "But she swore all the people were necessary for our towns."

Uncle Kent looked up and smiled directly at Josh.

"Did you know it was she, who actually gave each and everyone of them names.

Kent jumped up from the table and hurriedly moved to a desk drawer in another room. He returned with a brown, ten by twelve envelope containing many pages. He placed them in front of Josh.

"Here, take a look at these." He said.

Kent refilled the coffee's and reseated himself.

Josh emptied the contents of the envelope and there before his eyes were page after page, in Jean's hand writing, of names paired with jobs and occupations. There had to be hundreds. Josh was dumbfounded as he gazed at his smiling uncle.

"And she painted the majority of them. I helped but she was very fussy about the colors and style of the clothes."

Josh, surprised anew at his aunts dedication to this project, smiled to himself thinking, "I guess you really don't know other people." He silently apologized to his uncle for earlier accusing him of living in a fantasy world.

"She truly loved her new world and was totally consumed by it." Kent continued.

"And that's what I was accusing you of." reflected Josh silently.

"I guess we both were consumed by it I mean, but It didn't matter though. We were together and that's all we wanted."

Kent looked at Josh. "Are you still with me or am I boring you to death ?"

"I'm still very much here and I find your story fascinating and to anticipate your next question, yes, I believe you." Josh answered.

"Good."said Kent, emphasizing the word with a nod of his head. "Because now comes the unbelievable part."

"When the whole layout was finished we naturally had more free time to pursue other things. I thought that would be a break for both of us. That was not to be though. Jean still preferred the trains and our little made up villages. She got to know the control panel well, so much so that, she programed most of the daily activities. I did take care of our household needs, you know, food shopping and the like and run the normal errands. It even got to the point that she would eat her meals downstairs."

" One day I returned from town, the real town, only to find her missing. I searched throughout the house, naturally the basement was the first place I looked, but no Jean. I just assumed she was over at a neighbors for tea or something so I went about my day. I had some cleanup work to do in the garage. Before I knew it my watch said five fifteen and still I had not heard from Jean. I went back inside the house and called her name. On the second call I heard her distant answer. The voice came from the basement. Just as I got to the foot of the stairs Jean met me all bubbly and happy.

"You'll never guess where I just came from." she exclaimed. She didn't wait for an answer.

"I was in Kentville. I didn't get a chance to go to Jeanstown. Perhaps next time. I'll just have to get to Kentville earlier to catch the train."

"Whoa, slow down Jean." I said, "What's all this about ?"

"I had such a wonderful day." she went on. "Being in the town was even better than when we were planning it."

"She would not stop talking. I finally put my arms around her hoping to quiet her. She was actually trembling, she was so excited. I lead her upstairs and all the while she just babbled on. I guided her to the living room and managed to seat her on the couch, and I must say, that was a chore. She paused for a deep breath to continue and I took the advantage to speak.

I told her to just relax and I would fix her a cup of tea. She answered that a glass of wine was preferred and wouldn't I please join her. I did as she asked.

"**R**eturning with the wine, I could see she was still very excited. As soon as she saw me she went right on with her story. She told me of Jan Hewlett, and what a wonderful cook she was. She ran the diner, you know, the one only a block away from the depot."

Josh, recognized the name Hewlett, Uncle Kent mentioned it himself earlier. "I wonder where this story is going to lead." he thought.

Kent took a mouthful of coffee and sat back in the chair a smile on his face, recalling more fond memories. Having refreshed himself, Kent slid right into his tale as if he had not stopped.

"**J**ean was a non stop recording about now, so I just let her go. She went on and on about other people assuming I was familiar with all who lived there.   You remember Al Miller, he's the one I had to paint twice because I was not pleased with the colors I first used. Well anyway, he's running the hardware store now, he didn't like where I put him at the switching station. And do you remember the drug store we put at the corner of Main and Maple streets ? They serve the best ice cream soda's there. Phil Crowley is the pharmacist, such a nice man, you just have to meet him. Well of course you will as soon as you get there."

Kent paused again to catch his breath. "I'm sure you get idea by now."

He spoke more slowly now; "Jean went on speaking about the town and it's people for close to an hour.   She hardly touched the wine I poured for her."

"**I** guess she finally ran out of steam because she slowed down and actually looked at me."

"So when do you want to go ?" she asked..

"**I** was so taken by surprise by her question that I answered with the only thing that came to mind."

"**A**nd what was that ?" asked Josh.

"**G**o where ?" Kent stated.

Josh laughed as did his uncle.

"Jean looked at me with an unbelievable stare and said;

"**W**hy to Kentville of course. Haven't you been listening to anything I've said? "

"**F**or a minute there I did not know how to answer her. Then

I took her hands in mine and as calmly as I could said Jean, these are toy trains, toy buildings and make believe people. You just admitted yourself that you painted the small people figures. Perhaps you were dreaming. Sometimes dreams can appear to be very real."

She continued to look at me with a shocked expression.

"You don't believe me ! You think I'm crazy !" she stated.

"I don't believe any such thing." I answered trying not to upset her any further. I think she saw I was concerned and she softened both her look and her voice.

"It was real Kent. It is real. I was there. Not in my mind but in reality."

Josh looked at his uncle somewhat saddened by what he was hearing.

"I had no idea Uncle, that you were having such difficulty with Aunt Jean. It must have been very trying for you."

Josh himself was shocked by Kent's answer.

"Not at all my lad. It wasn't trying at all, in fact, just the opposite. It was an eye opening, unbelievable event."

Now Josh was the one confused.

"But you just explained to her that these are toy trains.

"That I did Josh, that I did. Before you go any further, be patient a short while longer and I'm sure you will understand all."

"Okay, I'll wait but I do have a lot of questions."

"I'm sure you do lad, Just let me finish my story and I'm sure you will have your answer." Kent smiled saying this.

Josh accepted his smile and returned in kind. He knew he would have to wait. Kent himself was now excited and was anxious to continue his mysterious tale.

Kent refilled their coffee's knowing he was dragging out the suspense for Josh.

"Would you like some cake or cookies with your coffee." He asked before reseating himself.

"No, I'm fine." Josh replied. "Just go on with your story, please."

"**O**f course, Josh, of course. Now, let's see where was I ."
He mumbled. "Oh yes, Jean was saying it was real because she was there.
So to humor her, I asked how did she get there. Suddenly there was total
silence. She looked a little disoriented and answered quietly."

"**I** don't know." she said. "I was standing by the layout
and then the next thing I knew, I was in it. I could look up and see the
ceiling light over the control panel. Then suddenly Jan Hewlett was talking
to me. She wants very much to meet you and talk with you, after all, you
are the mayor of Kentville. You have an office in town hall and
everything."

"**S**he caught herself babbling on and on and stopped. Am I
alright Kent ? Am I going crazy ? I really thought I was there."

"**I** assured her she was not crazy and suggested we go back
downstairs and reenact what she remembered. Hesitantly she agreed."

Josh could now feel himself becoming anxious. He was
himself now starting to think of impossible things as he was drawn into
Kent's story.

Kent helped himself to a few cookies and placed some in
front of Josh. The nephew took one of the offered cookies and queried.
"And? "

Kent was pacing now obviously filled with excitement
which transferred itself to Josh. He repeated his query, "And ?"

"**O**h yes, Josh, sorry. We returned to the basement and
Jean directed us to the spot she said she last remembered standing. We
stood quietly for a minute or so and nothing happened . Not wanting to
disappoint Jean too much I would humor her and wait a while longer. Still
nothing. Taking her gently by the arm I said. Let's sit and rest. She did not
want to move. "I don't understand." she mumbled, "I'm doing exactly as I
did earlier." So what's different ?" I asked. "Nothing." she said. "I was
standing here in the same spot, thinking, how lovely the town was and how
I wished I could be there."

Kent now looked at Josh directly with a broad grin.
"That's when it all happened."
"That's fine." Josh commented. "But what happened ?"
Kent now spoke softly; "Jean just faded away from me.
She disappeared from my arms. I was now alone. I was stunned. I didn't
know what happened. I just stood there. I couldn't move. Then I heard
my name. Someone was calling my name. It sounded far away or a very
weak voice. I looked around and saw no one. Then there were two voices
calling me, still from a distance. I tried very hard to concentrate and finally
could make out the words. "Down here." they said. 'Down here."

        "Not really knowing what I was doing I looked down at the
layout. After a few seconds I noticed some of the people figures actually
moving. I could not believe what I was seeing. I probably looked just the
way you look now. Total disbelief."

        Josh shook himself out of his shock and half smiling said;
"I don't believe what I'm hearing."

        "I didn't believe it either, my boy, and I was there replied
Kent. I rushed over to my work bench and grabbed a large magnifying
glass. Back at the table I looked more closely at the moving figures and to
my further wonderment one of them was Jean. The other I didn't know.
Then a man joined them. He too was telling me to come on down. I knew
him as the station master because I had painted him. Of course then he was
just a lead figure."

        Josh interrupted once more with an unbelieving half smile.

        "You expect me to believe that Jean just disappeared from
your arms and suddenly she was up on the train board, reduced in size and
was moving and waving at you ?"

        Kent sadly gazed at his nephew;

        "I know it sounds hard to fathom, but it's true Josh. It
really happened. I have no reason to mislead you. I found it hard to
believe myself yet I was there watching it happen."

        Josh was silent. He just sat there looking at Kent's face. It
showed genuine sincerity. He wanted to believe his uncle but this seemed
so far fetched. People just don't turn into toy lead figures. It was
preposterous. Josh felt Kent looked so sad and hurt right now, he thought
he would humor him a bit longer and let him go on with this ridiculous
fable.

        "Go on." he said quietly. "What happened next."
        Kent's spirit perked up a bit.

        "Well, as I said I was somewhat stunned by the events
unfolding I continued looking through the glass, listening to all three now
shouting for me to concentrate. It dawned on me then, remembering what
Jean had said about thinking how she would like to be there and all at once
she was."

        Josh looked skeptically at Kent thinking to himself, "Here
it comes now." but he remained quiet. Kent, so wrapped up in his tale ,
was not even watching Josh as he continued.

        "So I did as Jean asked, which wasn't hard because I really
did want to be part of my dream town. It didn't take long either. Before I
knew it I was standing next to Jean. She was so happy for me she gave me
one of her special loving hugs. It was then I realized where all her

excitement came from, because I was now feeling it myself, and it was wonderful."

"**H**e's really believing himself." thought Josh. "What do I do with him now, poor man ?"

Kent went on for another ten minutes without pausing. He was doing exactly what he said Jean had done, talking of everything that went on, in detail, in the town. He finally stopped talking and with an embarrassed look, apologized to Josh.

"**F**orgive a crazy old man, please. I know I got carried away with my own story. Perhaps you will also get to live the experience that Jean and I have had. Think about it Josh, living in a dream town, living a dream life, having everything to give you total happiness. You and your special someone. I wish everyone could share in this perfection. Although I do know, not everyone shares the dream of the same things."

Kent became silent. He was now lost in his memories. Not wanting to disturb him Josh quietly got up to refill his coffee. He starred out the window trying to sort things out. "Except for this train fantasy, he's perfectly normal." he told himself. " Perhaps if I review this with him downstairs at the train layout I can convince him of his folly."

Kent, now out of his memory trance, was all happy and smiling again.

"**N**ephew, you don't look as pleased for me as I thought you would."

Josh gazed at his uncle not knowing how to answer without hurting his feelings.

"**I**n fact," continued Kent, "You actually have a look of disbelief about you."

Josh could feel a flush of embarrassment come over him.

"**I**t's okay my boy, no need to worry. I know it sounds a bit strange but I assure you, all is right with the world. I apologize for getting carried away with my story. Bare with me a short while longer and your doubts will disappear."

Josh felt he owed that much to his uncle so he relaxed in his chair.

"**A**s you wish Uncle."

"**G**ood." said Kent, "Now where was I, oh yes, I started all this I believe with a statement about Jean passing. It wasn't long after my first trip to Kentville that Jean passed. By the way that's where she is buried. The quiet hillside cemetery just out side of Kentville."

Josh again had a look of extreme doubt written on his face.

"**A**s I said earlier I felt lonely, hurt and angry and after the burial I chose not to go back there again. Many month's passed when I did not even go down to the basement. I finally out grew the feeling sorry for myself bit and realized how truly happy I was living with my trains. I returned to the world of make believe and that's where I'll stay. You and Susan are the only family I really have in the real world which is why I'm still here part of the time. But not for too much longer. You see I want to stay in my dream world for my remaining days. I also want to be buried there alongside my Jean."

Josh abruptly stopped his uncle.

"That's enough Uncle Kent. Now you are getting much too carried away with all this foolishness. I think perhaps we should visit a doctor."

"Nonsense, my boy, I'm as sane as you are." was Kent's reply. Not waiting for Josh to answer he went on talking. "Now Josh, my skeptical friend, I think it's time we visited my basement world."

Josh did not resist and followed his uncle to the basement knowing that this whole foolish matter would be put to rest. Kent stopped at the Kentville side of the large train layout. Gently pointing, he turned to Josh.

"This is the lovely cemetery I was talking about. It is such a perfect setting." Without hesitation and moving a few steps, he again pointed to a small white farm house. "This is my house. I do hope you can visit sometime. Jean did such a wonderful job of decorating."

Josh, now becoming upset, spoke harshly.

"That's quite enough, Uncle Kent, I'm not going to listen to any more of this."

"As you wish, my boy. Just grant me one more thing. Keep your eyes on the corner of the Kentville station house."

Josh moved to look for the depot and then turned back to his uncle who was no longer there. He quickly scanned the room to no avail. Kent was not to be seen.

A faint noise caught his attention. It almost sounded like his name. It was his name when he heard it the second time. The call was still distant but clearer. Remembering what his uncle said he looked down at the station house. A figure was moving and waving. Very soon the moving figure was joined by others. Going to the work bench he found the large magnifier. Using the glass he identified the waving figure as his uncle because of the red and black plaid shirt he was wearing.

"Now do you believe me. This is all real." His uncle said.

Josh heard the old steam engin start. It was headed for Jeanstown. The whole layout seemed to come alive. Figures were walking, cars were moving, it was business as usual for the two towns.

An alarmed Josh looked away and shook his head and rubbed his eyes. Returning his gaze, nothing had changed, both towns were still alive with movement.

"This is not happening." Josh told himself. "I'm hallucinating now, just like Uncle Kent." He sat down with his head in his hands trying to make everything go away, his confused mind going in circles."

"Are you alright, my boy." said Uncle Kent as he gently placed a hand on Josh's shoulder.

Jumping a bit from the shock of the touch, Josh stared at Kent still in disbelief.

"It's okay, son, I know what you're going through having been there. It is a bit shocking."

Finding his voice again Josh answered.

"I know what I just saw but I still don't want to believe it. How is this possible ?"

"I can't answer that and I don't even try any more. It is what it is and it makes me extremely happy, as it did Jean."

Both men were silent for a while.

Josh, hesitantly spoke, almost stuttering.

"I'm not sure I accept all of this yet, but if I did, I am really confused about the burial thing. I still think the whole thing is impossible and in particular, the burial. How can you be buried in a one inch thick piece of wood ?"

"I had my doubts about that also in the beginning. The answer, which was not really an answer, appears to be, that when you are in that miniature world, everything is as possible as it is in our larger world. In actuality when you are in that world as long as I have been, you start wondering which is the real world. Are we being reduced to their's or are they being enlarged to ours."

Josh was now even more confused than before, yet accepted Kent's explanation, if that's what you wanted to call it. He decided to give up on any kind of an explanation. He was witness to what happened and still did not believe it.

"Susan." He thought. There was no way Susan would ever accept this, whether she saw it or not. She would absolutely freak out and probably run away screaming.

Kent agreed with this, so it was decided she not be in on the secret.

~ ~ ~ ~ ~ ~ ~

The next really big question Josh put forth.

"When it comes time, however long that will be, and you pass, what do we do with the layout and trains ?"

"Very good question, son, very good." Kent answered.
"I thought of the very thing a few month's ago, so I discussed it with the folks of both towns. Believe it or not they had a simple and logical answer."

Josh in the first time in the last few hours sat up and was genuinely interested.

"It would be nice to have one thing make sense today." He thought. "And what would that be Uncle ?"

"Well the trains, buildings and accessories can be taken apart, put away or sold including the figures of people. The cemetery, on the other hand contains the remains of real people. This part of the layout should be cut out and preserved in one complete piece and buried in a proper place."

"That is really simple and logical." Josh remarked. "What happens to the other figurines ?"

"They go on just being inanimate lead or plastic figures until another train layout is set up, then they continue their lives or not. That all depends on the person and his attitude about the trains and make believe villages."

Josh began to feel better about this whole crazy mess. At last something made sense. Recovering some of his normality he asked Kent for another demonstration of miniaturizing. In fact they did it twice. At least Kent did it twice. Josh wanted no part of it. Though he witnessed two more transferences, he still did not believe in it one hundred percent.

~ ~ ~ ~ ~ ~

Life went on as usual for all concerned for almost another year. Susan and Josh saw their uncle full size a few times and Josh alone was witness to a few functions taking place at the two make believe towns. He never took an active part in their size nor had the will or desire to do so.

Uncle Kent was happy in his life in the miniature world he chose and actually built.

As with all of us his time was up and he passed away. Fortunately for Josh, Susan was out of state so no explanation had to be rendered.   Josh, through the magnifying glass attended the funeral and burial. He was truly happy for his uncle for having the life he wanted his last few years.

He disassembled the layout and stored it in his own attic although he had no idea why. He wanted no part of the miniature world. The cemetery from his uncle's made up world he preserved lovingly and buried it properly. He would miss the old man but not the world of make believe.

The End

The Wander

by
Ken Goss

The Wander

Chapter 1

The culmination of two months planning and preparation were now at hand as the happy mother bid farewell to her father and her son. She wished them luck and a safe journey. The pair disembarked from the SUV with their packs and equipment they considered necessary for the two to four week hike through the eastern mountains of the Adirondack range. Pre-made arrangements would allow for them to call to be picked up at the time of their choosing once they decided to end the wandering through nature's gift.

Dan Harper, at only sixty three years young was probably one of the most physically fit grandfathers you will find anywhere. At five foot eleven inches he stood tall, his muscular build holding him erect, the perfect companion for his athletically active thirteen year old offspring. Neither of them was expecting anything but good male bonding during their long awaited excursion.

Dan took a GPS reading of their entry point to the forest recording it in his notebook.

"Okay Chuck, do you still want to do this?" Dan jokingly asked.

"Are you kidding me, after all this planning, you bet I do!"

They entered the green woodland and instantly were refreshed by the coolness given up by the interior wilderness. Within minutes the disturbing sounds of the outside world faded and were replaced with the sounds of silence. This pleasant silence was an old memory to Dan, yet for Chuck a whole new experience.

"Boy. It really got quiet in here didn't it? Yet the sounds I do hear are almost comforting and relaxing."

"Not almost," commented his grandfather, "They are comforting and relaxing."

Dan smiled to himself happy to see his grandson pick up on nature's serenity.

It had been quite a few years since Dan had the luxury of wandering in the forest and he vowed to himself then and there not to let time slip by again.

The din of the forest, so unlike the man made world they just left, caused both human intruders to unconsciously lower their voices. It was the natural thing to do out of respect for the pristine curtain that now enveloped them.

"I have always been intrigued by your stories of unexplored forests and jungles Gramps but never imagined it was this beautiful." Chuck whispered.

Again Dan was pleased his young grandson was learning a different view of nature, nature as it once was.

As they penetrated deeper they became aware of the trees growing taller, thicker and more prolific. Their steps also required additional effort to compensate for the incline they now encountered.

"If you need to stop and rest, don't be ashamed to say so Chuck. We are in no hurry to get anyplace. The idea of this outing is for us to enjoy ourselves." Dan remarked.

"No need for that yet Gramps, I'm feeling great. I'm so busy looking I wasn't even thinking about being tired. How about you?" Chuck returned.

"I'm doing just fine son, in fact I'm feeling better with every step." He smiled back.

Dan's mind was reliving past experiences of wilderness treks in all parts of the world. He already knew this one would be extra special because of his young companion.

Chuck would pause every now and then for a more thorough study at a particular tree or flower or rock. This was a whole new world to him and his Grandfather delighted in his enthusiasm and continued instructing the lad when the opportunity presented itself.

A hurried glance at the GPS confirmed they were ascending. They were already some four hundred plus feet above their starting point. The terrain abruptly steepened and slowed their progress and additional effort was required, but the pair took little notice. After all, the challenge of the journey was what they set out for. By four PM they had ascended to about eighteen hundred feet which included some rope assisted climbs. They came upon a somewhat level tract partially covered by a rock outcrop and decided to make camp for the night, another original experience for young Chuck. They chose not to assemble the tent this night and to use sleeping bags with the outcrop as overhead protection. The excitement of the day, this first night under the stars, the start of the journey, and the expectation of adventure had Chuck so wired with excitement he could not keep himself contained. Dan's patience was truly put to the test on this first night yet he did manage to rein in the young ones enthusiasm with other stories of adventure and discovery, each with it's own lesson of coping with the environment and survival techniques based on the given situation of place and time.

It was not till elevenish that both grandfather and grandson were settled enough to think about getting some sleep. You could see Chuck was tired but did not want to lose the thrill of the day, however, even he realized tomorrow would be just as exciting. As he crawled into his sleeping bag he looked at Dan and unembarrassed said;

"Thank you grandfather for this dat and our journey to come. I love you."

Dan, also feeling an inner contentment, could feel himself choking back a tear as he returned the sentiment.

"I love you too, boy, now try and get some sleep."

He laughed quietly to himself as he watched Chuck out like a light as soon as he was in a prone position. He then stretched out, hands folded behind his head and gazed at the stars. It was almost a full moon and both it and the stars were twinkling their messages between the high leaves and pine needles. *"A perfect ending to a perfect day"* he thought, as he felt himself succumb to the gentleness of sleep.

Chapter 2

As was his bent, Dan was up with the sun. There was something about this time of day that he found satisfying. It was like a religion to him. Rain or shine the first light was sacred, particularly at times like this when he could breathe freely the unpolluted air of the forest. As he stood there contemplating everything he saw, but nothing in particular, he became aware of another presence. Young Chuck was standing beside him quietly studying the surrounding terrain, a half smile on his face. They stood side by side for upwards of ten minutes, not uttering a word. There was no need as they were both in total harmony with each other and their surrounds.

The spell, finally broken by a doe and what was probably her six or seven month old offspring. The four carefully observed each other, unafraid, until the deer, satisfied of her safety moved on as if the humans did not exist. Silently, Chuck and Dan returned to the outcrop and set about fixing breakfast in the quietude.

Half way through the bacon and egg feast Chuck's youth took hold again;

"I never had bacon and eggs taste so good before. It must be the magic of the woodland."

Dan, laughing in answer said;

"Everything is better when done in cooperation with nature, my boy. This is truly the way man was meant to live."

"I'll have to agree with you there gramps, this is the best ever." Chuck answered with enthusiasm.

Cleanup after breakfast ensued with Chuck a bit on the rushed side. Dan, his usual patience showing again calmly corrected his young grandson with the wisdom of experience. He spoke of the destruction of forest land by carelessness of humans always in a hurry. He instructed Chuck in proper outdoor behavior so that no trace of their presence remained. The way they found natures beauty is the way they should leave it. Chuck valued these words and proceeded to carry them out to the letter and then some. By the time they were ready to continue their climb not a trace of human presence was to be found. Dan even thought it was a bit overkill but said nothing that would dampen the boys spirit. It was obvious Chuck was proud of himself.

Choosing what seemed like a decent path they commenced their climb. An hour and a half passed quickly only to find themselves on a small plateau, not the top of the mountain yet but a good resting place. The day was clear and the view opened up for miles north, east and somewhat southeast. Chuck was absolutely speechless as he gazed at what lay before him. A distant spec caught his attention as it circled lower and moved closer to their vantage point.

"Gramps, is that what I think it is?"

"It sure is Chuck, our national symbol right before your eyes. He's bidding you welcome to the natural world."

"I never saw an eagle before only pictures in books."

"And seeing it this way is something you will never forget."

As Chuck continued to follow the flight of the eagle Dan surveyed the surrounding countryside. Something did not feel right. No matter which direction he looked he saw no trace of civilization, not a house or roadway in sight. *"That's odd."* he thought, *"I guess it's just the angle of view from this precipice."* He dismissed his thoughts after a minute or so.

"What do you say sport, you ready to go on."

"I feel like I'm on top of the world." Was Chucks smiling answer.

"We're not there yet, we still have a ways to go." said Dan pointing up and to the right.

"Then what are we waiting for?" answered the youngster grinning from ear to ear.

Up and up they went the rock edges becoming sharper and hand holds less frequent. Trees and foliage all but vanished by now. It was a difficult but not impossible climb with even young Chuck being able to overcome this small challenge.

The summit at last, with the three hundred sixty degree perspective even more dazzling than the night before. Here they rested awhile with Chuck taking pictures of the full arc of the horizon.

Dan, still with nagging thoughts, could not yet see signs of roads or houses, forest and occasional meadows were all there was to identify. He took a GPS reading to record the latitude and longitude to be plotted on a proper map at a later date. These feelings were to be kept to himself for now. Why spoil the kid's adventure.

Rested and ready they chose a southerly direction to start their descent. It was somewhat steep yet easier than the upward climb. It was not too long before they found themselves in tree cover and the cooler air was a welcome commodity. The lower they went the thicker the overhead canopy became. Just after eleven they stopped for lunch though the available light gave the appearance of very late afternoon, almost evening like. Chuck, in his usual upbeat mood thought this was a wonderful thing as he made notes in the journal he was keeping of his magnificent adventures with Gramps.

It was a fast lunch, Chuck being eager for more discoveries. Dan always willing to accommodate let his grandson take the lead. Having gone no more than a half hour Chuck stopped and back tracked about ten feet his eyes carefully scanning the stone mountain side. With Dan drawing closer he excitedly yelled;

"Look gramps, it looks like a cave or a tunnel, maybe both."

"Careful son, don't just go barging in."

Chuck turned to his grandfather with questioning eyes.

"First rule of the forest is caution. It may be inhabited by who knows what, so check it out first."

"How do I do that without going in?" Chuck asked seriously having already learned to listen to his grandfather.

"That's easy." replied Grandpa. "Throw a stone in first and listen carefully."

"What do I listen for."

"You will know when you hear it." smiled Dan. "You can also poke a long stick in there. Remember you are now in a world unfamiliar to you, but that doesn't mean it is uninhabited. There is bear, bobcat, and snakes just to name a few possible residents."

Chuck carefully stepped back from the entrance just to be on the safe side. He followed Dan's instructions to the letter to satisfy himself there were no present occupants of this high mountain home.

Dan nodded approval and with flashlight in hand Chuck slowly entered the cave. The interior was small and the floor held a few small critter bones, other than that it appeared to be nothing special. The interior walls were fairly smooth but not man made smooth and was about thirty feet deep. Toward the back not quite aligned with the entrance was another opening barely wide enough for a man. Both studied this carefully with Chuck finally saying;

"Do we dare see how far this goes?' He asked the question in a positive way hoping to get his granddad's approval. Without too much hesitation Dan agreed on a short exploration.

It took a little doing to get through the opening because of the packs and all, but once past the first five or six feet the passageway widened. The crevice they were now walking in was at least twelve to fifteen feet high, probably caused by terrestrial plate movement who knows how many eons ago. Dan did detect the faint odor of carbon or charcoal, faint enough not to be recent, attesting to a former occupation. They followed the semi-serpentine rock crevice for awhile, coming upon what appeared to be attempts at rock art scrapings on the wall in crude but identifiable likenesses of deer, bear and even an owl.   A short span after the drawings Chuck commented;

"My flashlight battery is running out, Gramps."

"I'm afraid mine is too Chuck. Tell you what, stick close to me and turn yours off.. We will just use mine for as long as it lasts."

"I never realized this cave was so deep. Do you think we should turn back?" inquired the thirteen year old.

Chuck Townsend had been looking forward to this hiking trip with his grandfather for months and he certainly did not want it to end it now when they only embarked on their journey yesterday.

"That's up to you. You're the one who wanted to explore it." answered the older man.

"Naa.., let's keep going. It shouldn't be too hard to find our way back even in the dark. We seem to have been going in a pretty straight line, even with the small bends."

"That may be Chuck, but have you not noticed we are also descending slowly."

"I did notice something, I just dismissed it as a little dip."

"I'm afraid this is more than a little dip. We have been going down steadily."

Suddenly all was black.

"Damn, there goes the light." old Dan muttered annoyingly.

"That's okay." Chuck offered, "I still have a little life left in mine."

"We may not need it." returned Dan. "Look up ahead."

A dim glow could be seen, not enough to light up the passageway but enough to follow. Slowing their pace so as not to stumble the pair headed for the distant light. It became apparent they were still descending. The faint glow they were following failed to increase in its intensity but did periodically disappear. This is when the pair would run into the cave wall then realize the pathway turned. Sighting the glow once again they continued on not uttering a word to each other except for the occasional "Ouch" when the foot would find a large stone in the path.

"Hold up a minute Chuck." the older man broke the silence.

"What's up Grampa?" Chuck asked.

"Turn your light on a second."

Doing as he was asked, the darkness faded, momentarily leading to involuntary squinting by the two. Dan held his watch to the light.

"We have been following this glow for almost fifteen minutes and we are not gaining on it which I can not understand. Do you want to continue?"

"I guess so." replied Chuck. "We've come this far and it's still only a little after eleven. We have lots of time before it gets dark."

"What do you mean before it gets dark?" chided Dan. "We have been in the dark for the last twenty five minutes."

"You know what I mean Grampa, before it gets dark outside."

"It's okay by me if you want to continue. I just didn't know how you felt." Grampa offered.

"To be perfectly honest I'm really getting curious now." Chuck said excitedly.

"I'll have to admit I am also." remarked Grampa.

They carefully stumbled on, feeling the walls as they went. The passageway became narrow, not significantly but enough to put them on alert. The walls were now more jagged and dampness made itself known. Dan knew from experience the wet walls were a sign they were deeper underground where there was less airflow. He did not want to alarm his young companion yet he felt from here on they would, or at least he would, have to be alert for rushing water. He was sure during heavy rainstorms it could prove disastrous.

"That's strange." thought Dan, *"The light they were following did appear more brilliant every now and then but just as quickly would dim again."*

As if on the same wavelength Chuck commented;

"If I didn't know better I would say I would say that it was moving. Every once in a while it radiates more and seems a bit larger, then it fades again like it was moving away from us."

"You may be on to something Chuck, my boy." said Dan light heartedly. You know about fireflies don't you?"

"Of course Gramps, everyone knows about them."

"Well I seem to remember reading once when I was about your age."

Dan was instantly interrupted here.

"You mean they had books way back then." wise cracked Chuck.

A thump was heard as Dan smacked his grandsons pack.

A low laugh came from Chuck as he struggled to keep his balance.

"As I was saying." continued Dan, "I read about a cave moth that would project an illumination while flying just like fireflies. The reason for the glow has yet to be determined. I thought perhaps this could be one of those rarely seen bugs."

"If it is, I hope he's leading us to an exit." Chuck shot back followed by a loud thump and a verbal "Owww..." This certainly is a sharp turn and narrow too."

He snapped on his flashlight as dull as it was it illuminated the passageway enough to show the confining walls. Not far up ahead though could be seen a wider stretch and they chose to go ahead.

It took a bit of a struggle but they managed to conduct themselves through. They ended up in a spacious cavity roughly ten foot square. Here they rested.

"I just remembered Gramps, I have new batteries in my radio that will fit my flashlight. He rummaged through his pack then cried "Bingo" as he pulled out the radio. Twenty seconds later light once again illuminated their surroundings.

They were both spellbound. This cavity under the mountain had obviously been occupied previously for who knows how many years.

"Wow!" cried Chuck, "Look at the size of those bones. This is not your everyday small animal."

He leaned over to pick one up until his grandfather's caution.

"Try not to disturb too much Chuck. If this cache is what I think it is, it is best to leave as much "in situ" as possible."

"What do you mean Gramps?" questioned the youngster.

"Well take a good look around you. Someone or group has been living here or at least using this cave for many, many years, and not recently either."

"You mean we discovered something old and valuable." stated Chuck excitedly.

"Valuable yes, but historically not financially." answered Dan. "Take a look at the overhead, that blackening is smoke residue of fires over many years. Just behind you is where the fire base was. That carbon and charcoal are the remnants of the very last fire used here. It could be a few hundred years old, perhaps older."

"Wow!" was the only thing the grandson could utter.

"**G**et your camera out and take some shots. I know the lighting is not the greatest, but try and do the best you can."

"**I**sn't that a torch on the wall Gramps?"

Dan directed his attention to where the lad was pointing. Sure enough it looked like one but he figured it would be dry from years of non use. As he approached the wall he could already smell an oil of sorts not readily identifiable. *"It's worth a try."* he thought. Reaching into his pack he pulled out a cigarette lighter and with a few attempts it caught fire and slowly reached full burn illuminating the cavern.

"**W**ow!" again came from Chuck. "Look at all this stuff."

Dan also taking In the view remarked;

"**I**f I didn't know better I would say this room is still being used."

"**H**ow can you tell that Gramps, just from looking around?"

Smiling, Dan answered;

"**F**irst of all the place is clean, nothing has dirt covering it. Who ever it is they are good house keepers. I'm sure if we look hard enough we will find a niche in the wall well covered. In it you will find food stuff."

"**W**ow!" was repeated as Chuck's favorite remark. "How do you know all this stuff Gramps?"

"**I** won't go into all that right now, suffice it to say I learned many things over the years; just as a reminder try not to disturb too much. Another fact just occurred to me, if this cave is still being used we should not be too far from an entrance, so if you are finished with your pictures and are rested enough let's be on our way. We want to be out of here before it gets dark outside."

"**O**kay, I'm about set. How do we kill the torch?"

"**I**'ll take care of that." said Dan reaching for it. He removed it from the wall and smothered it in a small hole at the edge of the wall close to the floor, then replaced it on the upper wall. Flashlight in hand he led the way out of the cavern into the narrow passageway. Following the craggy walled path with it's many turns Dan halted shining the light more directly ot the upper wall motioning to Chuck;

"**H**ave a look at this."

Carved into a smoothed section of rock was an obvious large cat.

"**T**hat looks like a mountain lion or maybe a cougar."

"**C**ould very well be and from the looks of the grooves it was scratched out a long time ago."

Chuck hurriedly took a picture of the carving.

Redirecting the light the pair continued their outbound journey. Every now and then they came across other crude wall scratching, identifiable but the renderings were quite primitive.

Chuck continued his picture taking. If nothing else he could use them as memories of his journey with his Grandfather.

Another half hour finally brought a hint of daylight and the welcome scent of fresh air. Now spurred on with renewed vigor the pair carefully negotiated the snake like and ever increasing narrowness of their escape route achieving their goal of total daylight and fresh air; an air that somehow smelled different to the senior of the two adventurers. For some unknown reason the atmosphere's aroma appeared cleaner. Not mentioning it to his grandson he easily dismissed it as being too long in the stagnant air of the mountain tunnels.

"That was quite the experience." volunteered Chuck. "But I have to admit the fresh air feels good."

"I can't disagree with that Chuck, but you are right it was an experience to remember."

They slipped off their packs and sat resting against some trees. *"These trees were noticeably old for this area."* thought Dan to himself.

Chapter 3

    While resting and refilling their lungs with fresh mountain air Dan retrieved his GPS to record their exit point.

    "**T**hat's funny." he said aloud.

    Chuck turned toward his older companion.

    "**W**hat's funny."

    "**N**othing really." answered Dan unconsciously. "I'm not registering my readings. I know the batteries are good because the functions are working. I'm just not getting a satellite signal."

    "**M**aybe it's not reading the satellite because of the forest and mountain blockage. It's happened before. They had a thing on TV not too long ago explaining the movement of the satellite and how there can be loss of signal for a short period of time because of mountainous terrain."

    Dan accepted this and smiling at Chuck said;

    "**Y**ou're not really as stupid as your mother said you were. You do know something."

    Feigning hurt feelings Chuck replied;

    "**T**hanks Gramps and here I thought you were my friend."

    "**B**ut I am Chuck, I wouldn't insult a stranger like that, I wouldn't want to hurt his feelings."

    Still pretending hurt Chuck turned his back to Dan.

    "**S**ee if I take you hiking again."

    Both were laughing now.

    "**Y**ou're probably right kid, I'll wait a few hours and try again. Okay sport; choose a direction, north or south?"

    "**I** was just thinking about that, these woods look so thick, dark and interesting, let's head north for a while."

    "**S**ure thing sport, perhaps you can get some good pictures."

    They entered the dark forest heading north. Ten minutes went by and Dan paid close attention to tree size. His earlier feelings were being confirmed. This particular woodland had not been cleared or even conservation forested for some time. If he had to guess from his own experience he thought at least two to three hundred years. He didn't think there was any pristine tree stands left, especially in this areas of the Vermont / New York border and as before he chose not to alarm Chuck.

"I wonder how long before some greedy money maker discovers this and clear cuts the whole area." Dan reflected.

"Boy it's sure is geeing dark in here and would you look at how thick some of these trees are." Chuck noted.

"At least the kid is learning how to observe for himself." thought Dan. *"This whole trip may turn out to be a great experience for both of us."* his thoughts rambled on.

Chuck was in the lead choosing his way carefully and intelligently Dan observed. His pride in the boy was growing by the day. Their meandering eventually led them to a small creek. Here they stopped to rest and refill the canteens. The refilling finished they rested on the creek bank where there was natural clearing only to have their silence interrupted by the sound of young girls laughing. Dan and Chuck gazed at each other then in the direction of the giggling voices.

From a thick stand of hardwoods on the other side of the creek emerged two young girls, apparently teenagers. Each was dressed in soft deerskin dresses of a sort, their satin sheened black hair flowing past their shoulders with their glowing skin a well tanned color. Each girl carried a vessel for holding water. They spotted the two adventurers and froze, fear filled their eyes. Chuck politely waved and called a cheery hello. The startled girls spoke something that was unintelligible to the men, turned and ran back to the trees dropping their water vessels as they went.

Chuck turned to his grandfather a flush of guilt spread across his face.

"I didn't mean to scare them Gramps, honest, I was just trying to be friendly."

"You did nothing wrong Chuck. They were frightened by our unexpected appearance. They were genuinely afraid of both of us."

"But why? We didn't do anything."

"I know son, but I don't expect they get many strangers in these mountains. I'm sure they were just startled."

Dan did not really believe that himself. Right now he was confused with feelings he was not accustomed to.

"What language were they speaking Gramps? I didn't understand what they were saying, did you?"

"So he did pick up on that." Dan's thoughts continued.

"I'm not exactly sure Chuck; it had the sound of old Native American of a local people, which tribe I did not hear enough to determine."

They were dressed like Indians, maybe there's some kind of summer near here." Chuck suggested.

"Perhaps you're right, but for now I think we should be moving on."

Dan took the lead and purposely took off in the exact opposite direction of the girls. His thoughts, running wild, stirred his imagination beyond that which he normally allowed. All he knew was that he wanted as much distance as possible between them and where they encountered the girls. He mentally scolded himself for even allowing the thoughts he had to tale over his imagination.

"What's the rush, Grampa? I thought we were supposed to be enjoying a slow leisurely pace." questioned Chuck.

"I wanted to find a nice campsite before nightfall." Dan lied. "Up on a ridge someplace where we can overlook the area."

"Sounds like a good idea, maybe I can get some good pictures to show Mom."

An hour or so of hard moving Dan decided to rest. There was a small stream with clearing enough to see blue above. He carefully scanned the area and determined all was clear. Chuck was already topping off his canteen.

"This water is about the best tasting and clearest looking that I have ever seen."

"I can't disagree with you there Chuck."

"To bad all water wasn't like this." added Chuck.

"This is the way it used to be." Dan thought.

Looking   upstream   Dan   noticed   a   higher   knoll overlooking the stream. It should be no more than an hour to reach he figured.

"That looks like a good spot Chuck. See that small rock outcrop upstream, it shouldn't take too much effort to reach. What do you think? Should we try it?"

"I'm game." Chuck answered while securing the canteen to his pack.

"Good." Dam mumbled to himself. *"We should be safe there."*

In just over an hour they stood looking down on the stream.

"It sure was a narrow trail to get up here." commented Chuck matter of factually.

"Good, an added safety feature." whizzed through Dan's mind.

Feeling a little more comfortable he paid attention to setting up a proper camp. As a repeat of last night they chose to go tent less an such a warm night. Dan also avoided making a fire, choosing to eat prepared cold food instead.

Once settled and rested Dan decided to challenge his grandson's mental acceptance of out of the ordinary things which could have a big influence on their future travels.

"Tell me Chuck, what you think of science fiction stories?"

"I think they're pretty cool as long as they don't get carried away with twelve eyed monsters and other silly kid stuff. Why do you ask?"

"Nothing special." Replied Dan. "Just conversation. Ever read anything on time travel or things like that?"

"As a matter of fact I have and just recently too." Chuck answered animatedly. I read a book called "The Time Machine" which I really loved. In fact, I saw the movie also. We were able to rent it from Net Flix. I often thought it would be neat to go back in time but know what we know from our time."

"Do you believe in things like that? You know Sci Fi stuff?" Dan queried.

"Not all of it obviously, but I do think there has to be something to myths and legends you always hear about."

"What about time travel? Do you believe in that." Dan further asked.

"I think I do, I just don't know how or where to go about learning more. Do you believe in it Gramps?"

"Well, just like you, I have always had my doubts and suspicions. Dan paused, then added; "Until now."

"What do you mean, until now?"

Dan suddenly captured all of Chuck's attention. He hesitated for a moment trying to put his thoughts into words correctly not to panic his young grandson. Right now though, it appeared that the boy's thinking was mature beyond his years. He convinced himself the youngster could handle such information.

"Look around you Chuck, what do you see? Or more importantly, what don't you see?"

While Chuck was trying to make sense of his grandfather's mysterious questions Dan's mind kept on going.

"Am I wanting this too much? Am I putting the wrong ideas into the kid's mind? Is this all just wishful thinking on my part? I've always been accused of having too much imagination or too wild an imagination. Is this situation further evidence to prove what people have said about me? Perhaps my overactive imagination is just getting the better of me."

Chuck, looking quite pensive addressed his grandfather;

"I think I know what you mean Gramps. All day long it's been rather quiet. I haven't heard any airplanes or even seen any con trails. All day has been nothing but forest and streams. It's almost like being back in time. I imagine this is what it could have been like a couple of hundred years ago,"

"You don't see or feel anything more then that?" asked Dan.

Looking confused but interested Chuck finally spoke his mind.

"Meaning no disrespect Grandpa, but why don't you say exactly what's on your mind instead of going on with riddles?"

"The boy is wise for his years." thought Dan. "Okay, you're right. Look around you and think about all day. What didn't you see?"

Chuck stared out over the precipice in thought. He turned back to Dan, a half smile on his face.

"Roads, we saw no roads today, not even used trails. No sounds of cars or trucks."

Dan excitedly interrupted; "And most importantly, no houses or barns or other buildings of any kind." As he was talking he was unfolding a map of the area. "Look here." He said inviting Chuck to where he laid out the map. "This is where we started when your mom dropped us off, right here on the west side of Buck Mountain." He then pointed to another red X. "This is where we spent the night. You saw this morning we couldn't get a GPS reading but I figured we came out of the cavern passageway about here." moving his finger to the east side of Buck Mountain.
From this position it's about six miles to fort Ticonderoga and only about half that to Crown Point to the north. It's not a heavily populated area but it is occupied."

Here is where Chuck finished his sentence. "Then where are all the houses or buildings?"

Pleased with Chuck's answer Dan remarked "Exactly"

Chuck's mind was now racing with excitement.

"Do you think we really experienced a time shift? If we did it would probably have something to do with the cavern passageway through the mountain."

Dan, now smiling to himself, thought his grandson grasped ideas rather quickly. *"I hope I'm not leading him astray."*

"Okay Chuck, before we both get too carried away we need some sort of conformation of our speculative theory."

"At this point I don't think that should be too difficult." Chuck said enthusiastically. "You pointed out the tree size for one thing. There has been no car noise, no airplanes, and no modern structures. Why don't you try the GPS again? We're on a high point with a good line of sight."

"Good idea." Said Dan reaching into his pack. The device powered up showing the various functions yet received no reading from the satellites.

Chuck was having a difficult time controlling his excitement.

"Let's not get carried away just yet Chuck." Dan cautioned, there may be a simple explanation for all of this which totally excludes our Sci-Fi fantasies."

Chuck was laughing now, mostly at himself for letting his imagination take control of his common sense.

"I'm sorry Gramps, I should know better."

"Not to worry son I kind of led you astray with my own mental wanderings. But, and it is a big "BUT", something tells me we should still get some sort of confirmation of the questions we raised."

The evening light was waning as they watched the sun drop behind the western mountains. Getting serious Dan suggested Chuck try and get some sleep while he stood watch.

"I'll wake you at midnight then you can watch for a while."

"Okay Gramps, I realize you know better about such things. Please be careful." Chuck answered showing his concern.

He settled himself in the sleeping bag while Dan located a position giving views to both the trail up and oversee the stream corridor below. Looking back he could tell Chuck was almost in dreamland so he made himself comfortable and rested, but not too comfy because he dares not fall asleep.

Dan felt a little guilty for not revealing all his true thoughts about where they might be. Not the geographic location but the time period. He had read a sizable amount on the theory of time travel and had by now convinced himself that it was feasible yet up till now had not experienced it. *"Until now."* he thought. His first guess, judging by how the young Native American girls were dressed, would be late sixteen hundreds or early seventeen hundreds if they were back in time at all. And if they were, he realized it was a big "IF", he would have to be on the alert for small war or search parties. This was the time period when the European settlers were moving and settling on land that was not rightfully theirs by treaty. *"It sure is a help knowing of history before it happened."* He thought amusingly.

Those two young girls would surely tell of the two white strangers they encountered and the possibility exists that a small group of warriors set out to investigate.

The realization that he and Chuck were virtually defenseless save for a hunting knife each also weighed heavily on his mind.

"Part of me would love to be thrown back in time but at the same time I would be jeopardizing young Chuck who has his whole life in front of him yet."

Dan tried to overcome his negative thinking by remembering how mature he thought Chuck was and how accepting he was of any situation. *"I guess the only thing to do would be to wait and deal with whatever problems arise one at a time."*

Dan refocused his thoughts on their adventures to come as if nothing had occurred.

It was one AM when Dan decided to awaken Chuck who arose full of enthusiasm.

"Oh to be that young again." Dan told himself. "I'll relieve you at four o'clock, then you can catch a few more hours of shut eye." Dan explained.

Chuck immediately protested, saying he was fine and could stand watch longer because he was concerned about his grandfather. Dan, of course would hear none of his reasoning and Chuck retreated instantly bowing to Gramps' will and experience.

He assumed the same spot Dan occupied and was looking forward to his guard duty with his imagination weighing in. Dan lay down facing Chuck and watched for a few minutes then allowed sleepto overcome him.

Chuck, now alone with his thoughts, succumbed to his teenage hormones and let his mind drift to the young girls of the afternoon. They both were cute he thought but one more so than the other. The long, Satan sheened hair really caught his eye. Her smile and laugh were extremely inviting. He guessed their age to be about the same as his. He also realized the chances of running into them again were probably one in a million. Though he dismissed the idea of seeing her again the image of her face and smile refused to leave his head.

Chuck let his mind drift to the idea of time travel once more. He was attempting ti logically weigh the pros and cons of such a fantasy. Both sides, he decided, carried equal weight. The knowledge part of such a scheme was intriguing with the scale again balanced for both arguments. The knowledge you could bring to the past or return with from the future would appear as comparable results. Laughing to himself he thought; *"Since when did you become such a philosopher of life."*

He gazed up at the stars listening to the sound of the night some of which were entirely new to him.

"Sure sounds a lot better than where I live." he thought.

Chuck snapped himself out of the trance he felt himself drifting toward and concentrated on his actual purpose of being awake. He watched the beauty of the moonlight dancing on the shimmering water of the stream below. It was like bits of diamond dust reflecting many colored lights. The lonesome time allowed him to appreciate how lucky he was to have the grandfather he had. His watch alarm quietly signaled four AM and he moved to grandfathers sleeping bag.

"I'm awake Chuck." he heard him say, "I have an alarm also but thanks for following my instructions."

"I always will Gramps because I trust in you."

They both smiled as they exchanged places. Chuck being totally relaxed and content barely lay down when sleep overcame him.

Dan picked up where Chuck left off by gazing down at the stream only this time he was not looking at pretty water sparkles, he was searching for movement, human movement all the while hoping he would detect none.

Time passed quickly and soon rays of the sun were climbing over the eastern hills. The daylight had a comforting feel about it and Dan noticed some tension leave his body as he nudged his young companion awake.

Chuck was completely awake within seconds and went about cleaning camp without being asked. They both had a quick breakfast, once more without fire. Before putting his pack on Chuck jokingly said;

"Excuse me for a moment, I have to go to the men's room." As he headed off into the trees some thirty feet away.

Chapter 4

Returning to his Grandfather Chuck found a bit of a surprise. There was Dan standing there, hands at his side with two men behind him rifles at his back, a third man in front but off to the side some sort of club in his right hand. A forth man was at his side facing Dan about twelve feel away. Somewhat startled but not frightened, Chuck stopped in his tracks. His eyes took in the scene before him then settled on Dan's.

"I guess this counts as the confirmation you were looking for." Chuck said quietly, half smiling.

He then felt a hand on his back pushing him. He turned to see two more men urging him forward towards his Grandfather. He complied willingly and stopped at his position, turning to face four of his visitors. Dan amazed yet again, at the boys calm demeanor, said quietly;

"Don't worry, it will be alright."

The six uninvited guests were all bare chested, wearing deer skin loincloths and calf high foot wear laced full length with thin strips of leather. Two wore beaded arm bands; one had a lone feather dangling from the back of his hair. All were rather muscular without being muscle bound.

"Just stay quiet." Gramps whispered while Chuck nodded his assent.

Two of the strangers were conversing quietly looking at their captives periodically.

"Iroquois" Dan whispered, "Probably Mohawk."

The one with the feather started giving commands and before they realized it Chuck and Dan each had a length of coarse rope around his neck with leads attached. Signals were given for each to pick up their packs then were yanked by the collar leads to a slow trot as the now group of eight moved down toward the stream.   They took up a southerly direction continuing with the slow running pace for the next half hour.

Chuck found it very interesting that out of the eight people moving through the woods Dan's and his were the only footsteps that were really heard, his own more so than his Grandfathers.

"No wonder they were able to find us unheard." He thought. *"I thought I was in pretty good shape but even I'm getting tired."*

He tried whispering to Dan;

"**H**ow are you doing Gramps."

He was rewarded with a grunt of some unintelligible word and a rifle butt into his ribs. He staggered but did not fall, Dan helped steady him anc caught a jab in the ribs himself.

Within ten minutes they finally stopped allowing one man to continue on alone, while the related pair of captives were forced to their knees. Speaking with their eyes only they assured each other all was okay. Dan still marveled at his grandsons tolerance.

The much needed rest was soon interrupted with strong yanks on the neck ropes. Struggling ti their feet Dan and Chuck once again took up the trotting pace keeping in step with their captors. Another quarter hour brought them to a walking pace, a fast step, but walking. Chuck noticed smoke rising above the trees, in fact various plums of wispy smoke. Dan managed a one word whisper, "Village". An additional ten minutes walking and they entered a rather large clearing. Before them lay a well planned community; a central clearing occupied by mostly women and children in various acts of work, their daily assignments so to speak. This community space was surrounded by long houses. Well built lodges both wide and long were home to many families, each with their own space and fire spot.

Dan and Chuck were slowly walked through the open clearing as men, women and children made threatening gestures and physically poked at the two innocents. They were brought to the end of the village and were tied with their hands behind them to a tree. Satisfied the bindings were secure they were left alone but not out of sight.   Young children came in groups to stare and throw stones and sticks while yelling. A few brave ones would run up to and touch the pair with a stick and just as fast run away to the cheers of others. The novelty wore off within a short time and the curious stopped coming.

Now that they were alone Dan and Chuck felt they could safely speak. With sincere concern in his voice Dan said;

"**A**re you alright son? Are you hurt?"

"**I**'m fine Gramps." he said with a smile. "I was worried about you."

"**T**hanks but no need. We have to try and figure out what is the time period we're in, then we can plan accordingly."

"**P**lan what?" was Chucks curious return.

"**G**etting out of here and where to go." Dan stated.

"**A**t least now we know for certain." Chuck remarked.

"**K**now what?" was Dan's retort.

"**T**hat there is such a thing as time travel." Chuck was laughing this time.

"I really did not to learn about it this was though." answered Dan. "I'm sure these people are Iroquois, I just don't know which nation."

Their attention was diverted by two young girls walking towards them each carrying a small gourd type vessel. They were being escorted by a male brandishing a rifle, a menacing was club slung across his back. One of those things you did not want to see flying through the air aimed at your back.

It was them, Chuck realized excitedly, it was the same two girls from yesterday at the creek.. Unnoticed by their escort the girls were whispering to each other. As they drew closer, the one that caught Chuck's attention at the creek made eye contact with him ever so shyly. It did not go unnoticed by Dan who smiled quietly to himself. *"Oh to be that young again."* he thought. He watched as the favored one edged out the other girl to get to Chuck. The water was offered ever so gently which Chuck drank without moving his eyes from her. Dan admitted to himself that she was rather striking with that long black hair. He thankfully drank the water the other girl offered. He had not realized how genuinely thirsty he really was. The guard impatiently urged the girls away the disappointment showing in both Chuck and his new found friend.

Alone again Dan cautioned Chuck not to allow himself to get involved; it would only cause problems later on.

"I know you're right Gramps, it's just that I have never seen anyone that beautiful before."

"I complement you on your eye for beauty young man but right now I would rather have you thinking about getting us untied."

"You're right Gramps and I apologize."

Dan smiled to himself and answered;

"I understand Chuck; just remember we're from another world."

Refreshed by the water they both went to work on the ropes again.

The sun was swallowed by the western horizon when once again the trio of visitors made an appearance. This time they were accompanied by a fourth, another young male carrying a rifle. Dan sensed a no nonsense attitude in this new addition and quietly alerted his young grandson to be extra cautious. The girls were carrying warm food as they waited patiently to one side before approaching. The new man remained about ten feet away while the younger one advanced with additional bindings.

Dan was the first to have his feet bound, not only together but also to the tree and only after being secured thusly were his hands released. Dan unconscionably rubbed both wrists t ease the discomfort of the restraints. The same was repeated on Chuck. The girls were then allowed to approach with the food. Chucks lady friend almost spilled the bowl she carried because her eyes were in constant contact with his, therefore tripping on a tree root. This of course sparked an angry reaction from the newest guard. She answered him almost apologetically but when she was sure no one was watching she smiled warmly at Chuck and whispered a word which of course meant nothing to him. She slowly backed away almost repeating the tripping action again, her eyes remaining locked with Chuck's. She was roughly grabbed by the new man and pushed aside with her friend and apparently ordered to sit. Dan quickly gazed at Chuck awaiting his reaction and was relieved not to see any.

Grandfather and Grandson ate quickly using their fingers. Neither found the food unpleasant even though it was not identifiable. The girls were ordered to their feet and retrieved the now empty bowls. Chuck managed to whisper "thank you" at which the young girl, barely, but warmly smiled. The girls were immediately urged away while the two men redid the wrist bindings behind the tree. These new wrist securities were even tighter than before. The guards satisfied with their efforts returned to the village area.

"Looks like we're here for the night." remarked Dan casually. "It may be difficult but try to get some sleep."

"It's not the most comfortable I've ever been but I'm alright Gramps. I just know things will be better tomorrow." returned Chuck.

"The boy certainly knows how to keep a positive attitude." thought Dan.

Sleep did not come easy for either of them, sitting on gnarled exposed tree roots, back against rough tree bark with hands behind the tree in leather bindings. These were not exactly creature comforts being endured by the family duo. Sheer exhaustion finally overcame them in the wee hours of the morning and an uncomfortable sleep took hold.

Just after sunrise the rustling of a few women starting their daily routine awakened the captive pair. Dan noticed a figure with a rifle did come close enough to ascertain that the prisoners were still there.

There was not much that could be done by either of them. They would have to wait to see what fate had in store for them.

The leather bindings on the wrists proved to be an overwhelming challenge. Trying to pull them apart only made it tighter. Both captives resigned themselves to waiting.

Noon brought the two young teen girls with water along with a very uninterested guard. This lack of interest allowed for more verbal contact between young Chuck and his hearts delight. Words were exchanged, each not understanding the other. Dan suddenly noticed their back packs were sitting against a tree probably no more than one hundred feet away. He quietly mentioned this to Chuck who then took it upon himself to point this out to his dark haired friend. Whether or not she completely understood he did not know because the guard became impatient with the girls dallying and rushed them away.

"At least you tried son." Said Dan once the guard was out of hearing range.

Chucks positive spirit slightly diminished once the girls left which showed on his face. Dan noticed this but let it pass for the moment putting his concentration on escape plans.

Some time passed before Chuck broke the silence.

"What do we do now Gramps?" His tone was not as upbeat as he had been Dan took note, however he knew it would change soon enough.

"Well for one thing we have some time on our hands now and I don't believe we are in danger of losing our lives. At least not yet."

"What makes you say that Gramps? How can you be sure?"

"Let's call it an educated guess, but why would they take care of us and feed us if they were going to kill us. The Abenaki on the other hand would be a whole different story. Enough of that for now, back to the matter at hand. How much did you observe about this camp when we were brought here?"

"You mean the layout and stuff?" Chuck asked.

"Exactly." Dan answered. If I'm correct the stream is behind us, it's just well hidden by the trees."

"Yes, I saw that." Chuck responded. "And most of the long houses are facing away from the water."

"Good observation." Dan Commented. "And that's the direction we head once we get out of these bindings. When we get to the stream we can walk it to help cover our tracks. I've made a little progress with my wrist restraints, but we'll have to wait for the cover of dark anyway."

The discomfort grew as the day dragged on. There was only so many positions to shift the body into because of the bindings, while the heat of the day was also taking it's toll.

The setting of the sun signaled the return of the *"Meals on Wheels"* crew. The three original members made a repeat performance, but the forth was new. The hand release routine was repeated only this time the armed guard appeared almost disinterested.

"Perhaps this is a good thing," thought Dan.

They knew they should behave themselves for now.
Chuck, of course could not keep his eyes away from his raven haired beauty. He also noticed, more closely this time, her dark and tantalizing eyes.

The hands now free and the feet double checked for security the two young maidens were allowed forward with the food.

"Looks and smells like venison stew." Dan whispered to his young companion.

Chuck barely heard him being so enamored with the girl approaching him. In accepting the bowl, which was quite full, he observed the dark eyes were rapidly moving between his eyes and the vessel. This action was repeated numerous times. Not really understanding the meaning Chuck smiled and nodded his head. The girl smiled and let him take the food. She backed away slowly and joined her friend off to the side.

A few minutes passed and when she felt the guard was not paying attention she made a noise as if she were clearing her throat. Chuck's eyes instantly trained on hers. After double checking the guard she made a motion with her shoulders at the same time shrugging her shoulders. Dan understood the meaning right away and nodded his head in confirmation. With another motion of her head she indicated behind where she was sitting. With renewed spirit Dan and grandson ate heartily. When almost finished Chuck hit upon a hard object in the gravy, or whatever the juice was supposed to be. Thinking it to be a bone he almost discarded it until he discovered it was a piece of sharpened stone, very sharp. He looked over to dark eyes who returned his gaze with a smile from ear to ear. *"So that's what she meant before."* he realized.

The guard started to show his impatience yet Chuck did manage to secret the stone behind him under his belt. The impatient one mumbled something and the girls arose and went to retrieve the bowls. Chuck was all smiles and as the day before managed to whisper "Thank You". As his young lady took the bowl from him her hands touched his and even her bronzed skin could not hide the flush that grew on her cheeks.

The girls were then ordered back to the village while the captive's hands were re-secured behind their backs. A secondary rope bound them to their respective trees. The guards, now satisfied, also took their leave.

"She must really like you to assume these risks." Dan said quietly.

Now it was Chucks turn to wear a crimson flush.

"She risked more than just our back packs." Chuck was quick to reply.

Looking puzzled Dan asked;

"What do you mean?"

"A knife was buried in my food. Well not exactly a knife, but a sharpened stone." Chuck answered.

"Well, where is it?" Dan pushed.

"I'm using it as we speak." smiled Chuck in return.

"Not so fast." cautioned Dan, "Yo know they will check on us at least on more time before they retire for the night."

"You're right Gramps. Sorry, I guess I'm just a little anxious."

Just as Dan predicted the village activity slowly faded and two men armed with rifles appeared out of nowhere. Chuck faked sleeping so they only checked Dan's bindings. One mumbled something and they both laughed and walked away. Dan waited a good ten minutes before attempting to speak. Keeping his voice as low as possible he addressed his grandson.

"Okay Chuck, I think it's safe enough to continue now."

"I started a few minutes` ago and I believe I'm almost through." was Chuck's equally quiet answer. "This may be only a hunk of stone but it sure keeps a sharp edge. This thing cuts better than my knife."

By the time he finished speaking his hands were free. Pausing and listening before moving, both he and Dan scanned the area as much as the darkness would allow. Satisfied they were alone; Chuck leaned forward and cut free his feet. Keeping low he crawled quietly as possible to his Grandfather and worked his amazing stone blade on the bindings. Now that they were both free, Chuck kept watch while Dan retrieved the hidden back packs. Chuck gathered all the binding material together to take with them. Without further words, the captives made their way to the stream moving carefully to avoid making any noise.

It took longer than expected but once they reached the creek they somehow felt safer. Entering the water, which retained a winter's chill, they took up a downstream direction.

"We'll stay with the water for a while to help hide our tracks." Dan whispered. "Do you think you can deal with the cold for a while?"

"No problem Gramps, as long as you're all right."

Dan smiled to himself always amazed by the youngsters concern.

An hour plus whizzed by with Dan feeling his feet getting numb yet there was not a single complaint from young Chuck.

"Okay sport, I think we can take a break now but stay alert."

The pair left the water at somewhat of a clearing and proceeded to sit and remove their footwear.

"With a little bit of sun later these things should dry off in no time." commented Chuck positively.

As an afterthought he mumbled,; "I sure wish I had taken a picture of that girl."

Dan smiled to himself. *"I can remember the days when I felt like he is right now."* he thought.

"Okay what now Gramps? Where do we go from here?"

"We head south from here. If I recall correctly Fort Ticonderoga should be six or seven miles from here. Of course we have no highways so it will take a while to get there."

"We'll be safe with the British then I guess." replied Chuck.

"Perhaps not." Dan responded. "It depends on what year it is."

"How far back in time do you think we are?" Chuck asked.

"I'm not quite sure, from what I've determined so far we may be in the middle of the French and Indian war. Mind you that's just a guess, but if that's the case we will be heading for Fort Carillon."

Chuck looked at his Grandfather, obvious questions in his eyes. Smiling, Dan explained that the French built the fort long before it was called Ticonderoga.. "Carillon was blown up buy the French when they withdrew in July of seventeen fifty nine. The British rebuilt and repaired sections of the fort and renamed it Fort Ticonderoga; Ticonderoga being the Indian name for that area or place."

Chuck was the one smiling now. "How did you get to know so much about history Gramps? Especially about old history of this area."

"I've always liked our history, ever since I was a small child. I find it fascinating to learn of our past. I think we can learn a lot from our past if we just take the time to pay attention to it."

Chuck then thought about what his grandfather said and inquired;

"Well, if the French are there now, why are we going there? Shouldn't we be looking for the British?"

"**M**aybe so my young friend but again that depends on what year we are in. My guess is that right now we have more to fear from the Indians than the French. The French will protect us. They are not inclined to indiscriminately kill people, especially if they think we can be of value to them. I believe our best bet will be to head south to the fort no matter who has control of it."

Both were silent for a moment, each contemplating their plight. Dan looked at his young companion, concern in his heart, then hesitantly spoke again.

"**T**here is still another option."

Chuck was now staring directly into Dan's eyes, silently questioning.

"**W**e could go back and find where we entered this time warp and hopefully return to where we started."

"**N**o" Chuck rushed to answer with a very serious expression. "I know there are a lot of unknowns and we may be facing many dangers, but I would like to see this through. We have been here such a short time and we really haven't seen anything yet. This may not even be the French and Indian time period, and if we truly are in history I would like to be a real part of it by seeing it first hand, not just reading about it."

Dan put his hand up in a slight pushing motion to indicate a halt. He started to speak slowly and quietly.

"**S**low down sport, I'm not trying to push you into anything. I don't disagree with anything you have said. I was just covering all out options. Frankly, I'm kind of excited about this whole thing myself. You're also correct about the dangers we may be facing, and the unknowns."

"**S**o on we go then?" asked Chuck, anticipation in his voice and doubt showing in his eyes.

Hesitating for only a few seconds Dan answered straight forward;

"**W**e go on."

With a big smile of relief the younger one cheerfully stated;

"**S**ome of our things are almost dry, even without the sun"

They rested for a short while longer then resumed their journey southward. The sun finally poked its head above the tree line and the pair changed direction slightly leaving the stream behind. Their chosen trail was an up and down jaunt over hills occasionally crossing a small open area.

Two hours of silent walking brought them to a low waterfall that filled a rock-lined depression with cold inviting water. Here they paused to listen to the surrounds before speaking. Deciding they were alone they grabbed the opportunity to catch their breath and refill the containers they carried. Dan, going by instinct, figured they were going in the right direction. Looking at Chuck he announced they should have Ticonderoga within sight by nightfall. This news excited Chuck even more than he had been. He was anticipating actually meeting the historical figures he had only read about.

This time I will remember to tack pictures." he mumbled to himself letting his mind drift again to his young Indian maiden. Hearing Dan's voice interrupted his thoughts.

"We better get a move on if we want to get there before dark."

Feeling a bit embarrassed and half smiling Chuck answered;

"I'm right with you Gramps."

Picking up his pack he hurried to catch up.

Trailing Dan by ten yards or so and dat dreaming as he went Chuck's reverie was suddenly interrupted by a loud human grunt. Turning to the direction of the sound he saw two figures just about to collide; his grandfather and a very fierce looking Indian, war club at the ready. Sensing also a presence near himself he took off in a run toward the now wrestling pair. As he neared them Dan was now on his back with a knee on his chest, a hand at his throat and his enemy's free arm in a downward motion his war club aimed at his grandfathers head. In an unthinking motion Chuck hurled himself at the attacker, his arms catching at chest level rolling them both off and away from Dan. By this time the second Indian was also wrapped in the mix; one hand holding a hand full of Chuck's hair the other hand closing in with a knife at scalp level.

"WE HAVE INFORMATION FOR YOUR FRENCH FATHERS ABOUT THE ENGLISH." Dan shouted in French.

All motion stopped while the two Indians looked at Dan. The original assaulter questioned in very broken French.

"YOU ARE NO ENGLISH."

"NO" answered Dan instantly.

By now the three bodies were untangled with Chuck sporting an expression of both freight and anger at the same tome. Not getting up he rolled to his grandfather.

"TAKE US TO THE FRENCH FORT." Dan stated firmly and with authority.

The two natives were mumbling to each other glancing at Dan every now and then. The same brave spoke again in poor French.

"WHERE FROM YOU?"

It took Dan a few moments to decipher and hoping he was correct answered;

"ALBANY"

Apparently he guessed right because the glint of recognition appeared on two faces.

Chuck in the meantime remained very still not taking his eyes from the two Indians. His heart pounding in his chest, his breathing was rapid and forced causing flared nostrils. His anger was obviously stronger than his fear when he realized he was not shaking even though his body remained overly tense. Dam managed a whisper;

"Do not talk no matter what."

Chuck understood and nodded in compliance.

The two Indians discussed this situation no more then twenty seconds then approached Dan and Chuck indicating they stand. From out of nowhere each produced a length of leather roping. A noose type knot was fashioned and looped around the neck of both grandfather and grandson. With leashes in place and packs picked up the party of four took to the trail south bound again. Dan was hoping it was toward Fort Carillon, though he did not know how ho would explain their appearance or language. Their pace was fast and non stop, and the leather leash extremely uncomfortable. They had to keep up or literally chock themselves.

The sun was disappearing into the western mountains when the fort came into view. Dan recognized it's shape right away as Ticonderoga or Carillon from pictures and drawings he had come upon in his readings of the early history of New York and New England. It was only now that their captors slowed down. They approached the first heavy wooden gate shouting something unintelligible and were answered in kind. Dan had finally figured out, or at least made an educated guess, that these two Indians were Abenaki.

He had forgotten that the Abenaki along with the Huron were allied with the French. In the area just before the gate the quartet was met by several other similarly dressed Indians who proceeded to push, pinch and generally harass the two prisoners until an armed French soldier interceded. He yelled a few harsh remarks and unhappy Abenaki backed off mumbling remarks of their own.

The main gate now opened and grandfather and grandson were escorted inside. The two viewed these environs; Dan with an eye for study and information while young Chuck gazed at everything with awe and excitement. He could feel his heart pounding again not really wanting to believe this was happening. His thoughts went directly to the movies he had seen depicting this time period. It amazed him how accurate the Hollywood sets were now that he was viewing the real thing. Dan also was soaking up the surrounding complex, more like studying it for amount of troops, canon and placement and the most fortified areas. He realized this would all be for naught. He remembered he was back in time, in history, and you can not rewrite history. He caught himself smiling for being so naive.

They were eventually met by a young Lieutenant along with a sergeant. The Lieutenant ordered the neck leash off. The sergeant complied immediately throwing the leather strapping at the two Indians. Angrily speaking in their native tongue they reluctantly turned and walked away.

For the first time since their arrival the prisoners were spoken to directly.

"WHO ARE YOU AND WHY ARE YOU HERE."

With some hesitation Dan at last managed the words;

"I HAVE SOME INFORMATION THAT MAY BE OF USE TO YOU."

The lieutenant slyly smiled and with narrow eyes answered with; "DO YOU EXPECT ME TO BELIEVE THAT." His gaze then moved to Chuck who showed no emotion but continued to star back at the officer. "WE HAVE SOUNDLY DEFEATED ABERCROMBY AND HIS ARMY AND SENT THEM RUNNING TO WHERE EVER THEY CAME FROM." The lieutenant continued.

This was just the information Dan wanted to hear. He could now put a year to their travels. General Abercromby withdrew his remaining troops in July of Seventeen Fifty Eight. This was now September. It would be ten months before General Amherst would be here, but he had to say something convincing.

"THIS HAS NOTHING TO DO WITH ABERCROMBY, THERE IS ANOTHER LARGE ARMY BUILDING RIGHT NOW."

Dan tried to sound sincere and convincing. These last words caught the Lieutenants attention. Turning to the sergeant he said;

"LOCK THESE PEOPLE UP UNTIL WE CAN GET TO SEE THE GENERAL."

"BUT GENERAL MONTCALM IS AT CROWN POINT." Replied the Seargeant.

The Lieutenant, looking and sounding angry instantly replied;

"DO AS YOU ARE TOLD SERGEANT." then turned and stormed away.

The sergeant signaled for two soldiers armed with rifles and bayonets to escort Dan and Chuck to the guard house with him leading the way. Dan smiled at Chuck who smiled in return excitedly loving this whole experience never once considering any dangers.

Chapter 5

The lower level of a corner blockhouse was used as the prison facility. The walls were double logged at more than two feet thick. The interior consisted of seven rooms or cell blocks if you will, each with iron bar doors. The individual bars were at least an inch and a half thick to ensure no escape. At present time Dan and grandson were to be its only guests. Dan was thankful for it would enable them to talk freely, that way young Chuck would be kept informed of Dan's French conversations.

They were pushed into the same barred enclosure which also pleased Dan because of his protective instincts over his young charge. The door was locked and the three uniformed men exited the blockhouse leaving Grandfather and grandson breathing more easily. Chuck began speaking as soon as the outer door closed.

"I don't know what you were saying back there but I did understand the name Montcalm. Are we going to get a chance to meet him?"

"There's a strong possibility that we will Chuck but I'm still concerned about our believability because of the way we talk and dress," Dan replied showing that concern in his voice.

"Yeah, I guess we do stand out a little." Chuck remarked. "Ah heck, just tell them we've been here so long that this is the way they dress back in the woods."

Dan chuckled at his simplicity and proceeded to explain the details of his previous conversation in French.. He complimented Chuck on his demeanor and what appeared to be his lack of interest and that he should keep up his lack of facial expressions.

"That's easy." said Chuck. "I just think of that Indian girl and I forget everything else."

They were quiet for a moment till Chuck grew serious.

"I've been thinking Gramps, about our struggle back in the woods. We made it through alright, but what if we didn't? What if one or both of us had been killed? Are we really dead or do we return to our own time? The other question is, can we return to our own time? What would happen if we chose not to return?"

"Whoa, slow down boy, you're living the past and the future both at the same time and letting them get to you. I've considered some of those same questions myself and frankly I don't have answers. I don't know if we ever will but I'm not going to let that frighten or take control of me. Let's just live, enjoy and learn from now on no matter what world we are in. Survival is instinctive, but thought and planning can go a long way in helping to ensure it."

Chuck listened to what his grandfather had to say and genuinely heeded his council.

"Thanks Gramps, I know you're right, forgive me for being so foolish."

"Nonsense Chuck, there is nothing to forgive. You reacted perfectly normally."

"By the way." Chuck interrupted changing the subject, "I didn't know you could speak French so well. When did you learn?"

Dan smiled, answering;

"I had two years in high school; the rest just came with my travels. Luckily I used it often enough not to forget it."

"Okay, so where do we go from here?" inquired Chuck.

"Obviously not for a walk." quipped Dan standing and gazing around. "Let's try for some sleep tonight and wait for Montcalm. At the moment we can't plan for anything." When Dan noticed Chuck sit on the edge of what passed for a bed he followed with; "Go dream about your little Indian maid and while you're at it see if she has a grandmother for me."

They laughed as both lay down. Sleep was restless because it was not the creature comforts they were accustomed to.

Both were up early and as they stretched out the kinks an elderly woman was allowed to enter the cell with a tray of food and cups of water. She was obviously frail but maintained a wary smile and had kind eyes. She put the tray on the floor and was hastily escorted out. Chuck and Dan were quickly at the food since they had not eaten since noon the day before.

Chuck thought it was not his mom's cooking but all in all it wasn't bad. Afraid to show his ignorance he chose not to ask Dan what they were eating. The water is what really surprised him with its lack of chemical taste. He found it quite refreshing. He noticed Dan was quiet and obviously deep in thought. He tried to be quiet himself so as not to disturb him. His own mind was at work;

"Perhaps we are safe here with the French, safer than out in the woods with hostile Indians, yet I felt a great excitement out there. Well at least we know the British defeated the French so maybe we should search out the British to be on the safe side. I'm guessing now that Indian girl with the beautiful Raven hair was Mohawk and they allied with the

British. Maybe I can... ...Naa-a...stop being such an idiot, you're from another time. There's no way possible we could get together."

There was a quiet voice behind Chuck;

"What's the matter sport, why so down?"

Looking embarrassed he answered;

"Nothing really Gramps, I'm suddenly realizing that we're from a different time and I have to forget that girl we saw."

"Wise decision my boy, welcome to the adult world, now perhaps you can keep your mind on our mutual problem." Smiling and feeling better Chuck asked;

"Do you think we'll be locked up for long?"

"I don't really know but I think once we get to see Montcalm we should be okay. The question is when we'll see him is still unknown."

Their temporary housing left a lot to be desired, they did not even have a window. If it was not for the watches they were wearing they couldn't tell if it was night or day. They took turns pacing the ten by ten cubicle. The thickness of the walls prevented outside sound from penetrating. Their boredom was interrupted around noon when the Lieutenant entered the guard house along with two soldiers.

"WE HAVE NO NEED OF YOUR PERSONAL BELONGINGS MR. HARPER. WE HAVE SEARCHED YOUR PACKS AND DID HOWEVER REMOVE THE KNIVES. YOU HAVE MANY THINGS THAT HAVE TEASED OUR CURIOSITY YET SEEM HARMLESS ENOUGH. YOU MAY HAVE YOUR POSSESSIONS. I'M SURE THE GENERAL WILL NOT MIND.."

The two soldiers placed the packs down inside the cell and as all three prepared to leave Dan stood and questioned;

"WHEN WILL WE GET TO SEE THE GENERAL?"

"THAT IS OF NO CONCERN OF YOURS MISTER HARPER, UNTIL HE RETURNS FROM FORT SAINT-FREDERIC (the fort at crown point) I TAKE MY ORDERS FROM CAPTAIN DESANDROUIN. HE MAY CHOOSE TO SEE YOU THIS AFTERNOON, IN THE MEANTIME ENJOY YOUR STAY WITH US."

These last words from the young lieutenant were voiced in a sarcastic and a demeaning way.

Alone again Dan and Chuck looked at each other while Dan repeated his conversation in English. Each retrieved his own pack checking it carefully.

"At least they didn't take anything other than the knives." commented Chuck. He held his small camera in his hands, smiling he asked;

"How about it Gramps? One for posterity and my memoirs when we return home. It will be a good keepsake of our journey. How many people do you know that have a picture of themselves in the original Fort Carillon?"

Dan happily posed one arm around the bars of the cell. He then gladly reciprocated with his young charge as star of the picture.

They chose not to try either of the radio or GPS, knowing neither would work. At least they still possessed them, for now anyway. The rest of the afternoon and evening passed slowly. Chuck occupied himself writing in his small journal while Dan consulted various maps of the area which proved to be difficult not having the actual roads that showed on his maps. It was early evening when the elderly Indian woman entered with dinner. Chuck automatically and politely said "Thank You." Much to the surprise of both he and his grandfather the weary featured woman answered in English, "You are Welcome". Her eyes sort of sparkled as she looked at them before she was escorted out. With his eyes Dan cautioned Chuck not to speak or react until the guards were out of ear shot. Assured they were now alone Dan, speaking quietly, said;

"That was a strange turn of events."

"Why so." inquired Chuck.

"I believe that woman is savvy to more than most would suspect."

"You mean because she said "You're Welcome." furthered Chuck.

"Of course not." Dan replied. "I've watched her before. She is not one of them. She's probably here more for survival then anything else. Most likely a captive of the Abenaki or Huron and here at the fort is a safe haven for her. She is too old to travel the forest alone and most likely does not know where her people are. She could be of help to us so let's not rule it out. In fact I would suggest you try befriending her. I know they don't allow her much time here but perhaps a few more kind words would help her and us."

"No problem Gramps, I'll do what I can."

As it turned out they remained alone and in the stockade another three days before Montcalm returned. Chuck took advantage of every opportunity to get close to the aged Indian woman and after a while the guards ignored his closeness to her. She eventually identified herself as Silver Cloud and was of the Seneca Nation. Dan went on to enlighten

Chuck that the Seneca people were of the Iroquois Confederacy but were the western most nation, the area we now call Ohio and western New York.

Chuck grew quite fond of Silver Cloud. Her demeanor reminded him of his own grandmother on his fathers side though his relationship with her was short lived before her passing. The warmth that grew between Chuck and the old lady did net him some more and better food for which he was grateful. Those short interludes were the only brief respite they had in the boredom of their waiting. The long awaited moment was now at hand. The Lieutenant and his usual two man guard entered the blockhouse with much fanfare of his importance. Silver Cloud was there to collect the food plates and in his ignorance he attempted to push her out of the way. Before his hands could actually touch her Chuck was between them and took the brunt of the Lieutenants force. Chuck said not a word but stood his ground. The two guards slowly moved to intervene when Dan firmly spoke.

"LEAVE HIM BE. LEAVE THEM BOTH ALONE."

Dan slowly stood but did not advance. The guard's eyes moved from Dan to the Lieutenant. The Lieutenant, with an almost frightened expression nodded his head and the two men stepped away. He paused for a moment as if collecting his thoughts, then yet again with the sly smile and attitude Dan and Chuck were informed of General Montcalm's request to see them. With a soft smile towards Chuck, Silver Cloud made her way out of the cell with no further interference from the guards.

Chapter 6

    Chuck found General Montcalm's office very unassuming. HE WAS EXPECTING THAT A MAN OF SUCH REPUTE WOULD BE BASKING IN LUXURY OF well appointed surrounds. This was truly not the case. One side of the room was set aside for maps and battle plans; his desk was no more than a solid wood table and a straight back chair. There was a scattering of military books on a table behind the operating desk which also held some glasses and a few bottles of wine.

    Dan noted the Generals appearance as commanding yet understanding. He took this as a good sign that may help their plight. He still did not have a planned strategy of the reason for them being here.

    With the wave of a hand Montcalm dismissed the two guards leaving the Lieutenant smiling and chest puffing.

    "MY GENERAL." HE STARTED, "THESE TWO..·..." pausing he turned his head casting a disgusted look at Dan and Chuck, "THESE TWO PEOPLE SAID THEY HAVE INFORMATION FOR YOU. THEY WERE CAPTURED BY A FEW OF OUR LOCAL FRIENDS."

    The General interrupted.

    "'IM SURPRISED THEY WERE NOT MURDERED AND LEFT TO THE SCAVENGERS."

    The Lieutenant not the slightest bit disturbed by the Generals comment answered with;

    "PERHAPS THEY SHOULD HAVE BEEN." as he finished the sentence he again glanced a reproachful look at Dan. Dan in turn glared, tight lipped, at this verbal antagonist. What he really wanted to do was to grab and throttle him, but because of Chuck he thought better of it.

    This did not go unnoticed by Montcalm, who, asserting himself sharply spouted;

    "YOU ARE DISMISSED LIEUTENANT." and turned his attention to Dan and his Grandson. He waited for the younger officer to close the door behind him then relaxed and sat down.

    Speaking in English, albeit slightly accented, he addressed Dan.

    "What is this information you have for me Sir?"

Dan also calmed somewhat replied in French;

"MUST WE BE LOCKED UP LIKE CRIMINALS GENERAL?"

"That is such a harsh word Sir and that is for me to decide upon hearing what information you may have." the General continued in English.

"BEFORE I GIVE YOU THAT INFORMATION I HAVE WILL YOU PROMISE ME TO AT LEAST LET THE BOY GO. HE HAS DONE NOTHING AND CAN AND WILL DO NOTHING." Dan replied in French knowing his words were not entirely true.

The General smiled a knowing smile.

"YOU MUST REALLY LOVE THIS BOY VERY MUCH TO PROTECT HIM THIS WAY."

This time he answered in French.

Now it was Dan's turn to smile. He realized he and the General were on the same wavelength and aware of the same game being played. He further relaxed and decided to tell the General about Amherst. This time he spoke in English.

"The British are planning an attack."

Smiling calmly Montcalm answered almost amused;

"Of course they are Mr. Harper, as we are. We are at war Sir and that is what adversaries do. Why should I be concerned? General Abercromby already tried and was soundly defeated."

"But Sir, this is a different General. A General Amherst and he is forming a new army now, a very large army; one that will outnumber you many times over and with much artillery at his disposal. If I am not mistaken Sir he is planning this for the coming spring or late spring." Dan paused here feeling he had already gone too far. The General, not seeming disturbed by what he was told shifted his glance to Chuck who continued to play his part well showing no emotion at all. His eyes remaining on Chuck he asked Dan how he knew of such information.

"We were in Albany and heard of General Abercromby's withdrawal to Lake George. This news greatly disturbed the British." Dan answered trying to sound convincing. Now contemplating directly on Dan, Montcalms question was repeated.

"And how Sir were you privy to such information."

Feeling caught in his lie Dan hesitated trying to come up with an answer. The General now pressed his advantage.

"And you Sir, are you a deserter?"

It was more of a question then a statement. These words caught Chuck completely off guard as he was quick to speak out.

"He is no deserter."

Suddenly realizing what he said he gazed at his grandfather, his eyes asking forgiveness and inwardly praying he did not jeopardize their situation any further. Montcalm smiled warmly.

"It is obvious the boy loves you as much as you he."

Growing serious once more he continued;

"I almost want to believe in your sincerity Sir but feel you are not telling me something. Now Sir is the time for complete truth."

Dan felt awkward and threatened not knowing where to go from here. He was suddenly silent. Montcalm started to get up from his chair when Chuck, even against his own wishes, became vocal again.

"We are not British." he said firmly avoiding his grandfathers eyes.

The General retained his seat and addressing Chuck questioned;

"You say you are not British yet you speak English. What are you then?"

Without hesitation Chuck blurted out rather proudly;

"American." He thought of what and how he said it and respectfully added "Sir."

General Montcalm maintained his bearing regarding first Chuck then Dan and back again. The silence in the room suddenly became deafening. Dan's mind was in high gear searching for the appropriate words of explanation. Nothing was forthcoming. Chucks innocence of youth showed in his simplicity of words. He could see his grandfather struggling with his thoughts so he decided to speak out again but was saved from embarrassment when Montcalm broke the silence.

"If you are as you say "American" then what you really mean then is the rebels we hear so much about. You wish only to answer to yourselves, yet inevitably you will be under the flag of "France." He paused here, then smiled, "Or perhaps the British flag."

At this point Chuck thought to remain quiet rather than upset Dan any further.

"I do believe you sir, but I must ask again how came you by this information." repeated Montcalm.

Dan was abruptly Dan again, out of his confused state. Chuck sensed this and felt relieved. Dan, with his renewed confidence gazed at Chuck as if to say *I can take it from here kid."* Then turned to the General;

"You are right Sir, I have been avoiding some of the real truth and only because it may sound so out of tune with reality."

Now it was Chucks turn to look perplexed, *"Was his grandfather going to reveal the secret truth?"* He asked himself. He mentally started to prepare himself to have Montcalm throw the two of them in the loony bin. *"So much for our adventure."* He thought quietly. Dan resumed after a short pause;

"The information you refer to, I read about it."

"And how came you to such private papers." the General inquired.

Dan gave a quick peek at Chuck and could read his approval.

"They were not private papers, it was from a book of history."

Here Dan paused observing Montcalm's facial expression. One of surprise and astonishment, not of shock and disbelief. Quickly recovering Montcalm inquired of Dan;

"Ah! So you are a student of ancient warfare and you came across a similar situation of the past?"

"No Sir." Dan answered. "It was a history book of this war."

Chuck felt himself grow tense and apprehensive, not knowing what was to come and awaiting the Generals reaction. Montcalm, however remained quiet and pensive, his hands folded, elbows on the desk and his chin resting on the folded hands. He was sort of gazing at nothing in particular. Dan and Chuck looked at each other anxiously wondering what was going to happen next but not wanting to disturb the silence.

After a very long two minutes the General slowly settled back in his chair and brought his eyes to bear on Dan and surprisingly without malice. In a calm and soft voice he began;

"I do not know what it is about you Sir, but I find both you and your young charge a fascinating pair. What you are saying does not really make any sense yet something inside of me wants to believe you. You are not like other people of this area. You both carry an air of confidence these other people do not possess. Your bearing is different, you appear to be well educated, your dress is obviously not of this environment. Your speech, though it is English, is not the English we are accustomed to hearing."

He paused here collecting his thoughts. "Who are you Sir? Where are you from? Most importantly, what do you want?" Here Montcalm paused again smiling a half smile. "I truly would like to know Sir."

Chuck was all smiles now awaiting Dan's answer.

"With all due respect Sir, let me try to explain. You are obviously a well educated man of the world and I believe I can count on your open mind. Please, before you make any judgement, allow me or us, to finish our complete story. The General, with an expression of sincere interest nodded his head as acceptance of Dan's words.

"For many years, more than I care to count, people have been talking about time travel. It has been discussed and argued by some of the greatest minds of civilization long before either of our times."

Here the General softly interrupted.

"I am familiar with the subject of which you speak. My own readings of the great minds that preceded us have reflected on that very subject. It has been referenced by the likes of Aristotle, Plato, and Archimedes. It was also thought to have been noted in books residing in the great library of Alexandria."

Astonished with his knowledge and acceptance of the subject Chuck's respect for Montcalm doubled. Dan was similarly disposed. Resuming his story Dan explained;

"We are not scientists or pursuers of time travel, but happened accidentally to come upon a portal which brought us back in time to here. We originate in the year twenty fifteen. We are not only viewing history but living in it. This was not our choice but we are not regretting the opportunity."

"Nor would I Sir." the General offered. "Can you find this portal to return where you came from?"

"We only hope that we can Sir but we have to be free to do so."

Smiling again General Montcalm remarked;

"You are either a very good liar or a very lucky man to be going through such an adventure. I want to believe the latter but you must admit your story does pose a lot of unanswered questions. I do not suppose you have any tangible evidence to prone what you are trying to convince me of."

Dan's face took on an expression of sudden defeat and answered;

"Unfortunately we do not, you will just have to accept my word." As an after thought he added, "I can also understand your position of doubt. I also would feel the same."

An excited voice rang out from further back in the room.

"Your watch Gramps, show him your watch."

"I noticed your timepiece on your wrist. What a cleaver idea and unique way to carry it." The General suggested. "But that hardly counts as proof that you are from another era."

By now Chuck was up at Montcalm's desk, his enthusiasm bubbling.

"The battery Gramps, show him how it works."

Dan took the boy's clue and proceeded to remove the watch from his wrist before an extremely interested onlooker. Dan demonstrated that the small clock was working. He then removed the back and battery. He handed the now stopped watch to Montcalm.

"Check it yourself, it is no longer working and will not work until I replace the power source."

The procedure apparently fascinated him because he repeated it himself a few times.

"As astonishing as this is I can not accept this as fool proof evidence of your amazing story. I do have a position to uphold."

"Again I do not disagree with you General. At this point I do not know what else I can say to convince you of my sincerity."

"I also understand your predicament, but what about your young charge here. He appears to have a number of ideas and is not shy about them."

Montcalm was smiling as he said this while looking directly at Chuck..
"Well Sir!" he spoke right up, "I do not have it with me, it's in my pack at the guardhouse, but I do have a flashlight I could show you, at least that's what we call it, I don't know what you would call it in France, probably a torch, and it works the same way the watch or time peace does with what we call batteries or an external power source and if I had it here I would show you, if you let me I will go get it and bring it back."

Here Chuck stopped to take a breath while he noticed the two adults were smiling. He was confused by this until his Grandfather spoke.

"Whoa boy, slow down, do you realize you have not stopped to let anything you said sink in. The General and I are still back at the guardhouse."

Joining the conversation the General proposed a temporary solution.

"His enthusiasm alone adds credence to your story my friend. Mind you it is not a one hundred percent final solution but it is ths best I can do right now. I must have more time to consider other things. I will have to return you to the guardhouse for now."

Dan was about to speak up when the General held up his hand to stop him.

"And to anticipate your next question, yes the boy will have the run of the compound but cannot leave."

Chuck's eyes became brighter and his thoughts went instantly to Silver Cloud.

"Fair enough General, and I thank you. You will not regret your decision." Dan stated as he extended his hand. He and Montcalm shook hands and a feeling of mutual respect passed between them. The General walked to the door, opened it and asked the guard to come in. He was soon followed by the young Lieutenant. Addressing no one in particular Montcalm ordered that the gentleman be returned to the guardhouse. A conquering smile flashed over the Lieutenant's face as he grabbed Chuck's arm not to gently pushing him towards the door.

"NOT THE BOY." Montcalm spurted out rather harshly.
"JUST MR. HARPER AND YOU WILL TREAT HIM LIKE A GENTLEMAN. IS THAT CLEAR, LIEUTENANT?"

"YES MY GENERAL." Answered the lieutenant sharply.
His eyes said otherwise.

"Thank you again Sir." Chuck replied as he passed through the door. Once outside he addressed Dan.

"See you later Gramps, I'm going to try and find Silver Cloud."

"Careful son and behave." Dan answered knowing he did not have to add the last part.

Chapter 7

Returning to the guardhouse was of little concern to Dan. He still felt confident enough that he would be released. What he was not prepared for was the loneliness he faced without his grandson. He knew he would see him periodically but his love for the boy was greater than he imagined. His protective instincts suddenly appeared as overwhelming. He knew it would take a lot on his part to, first not to show it and second have faith in both his grandson and Montcalm.

It did not take Chuck too long to locate the cook house and was thankful he guessed correctly. Silver Cloud's soft smile was a warm welcome to this young stranger from another time. She embraced him gently and said she was happy the great French Father released him. She noted that she thought the General to be a fair man.

"**C**ome, you will stay with me until your grandfather can be with you."

She took his arm and led him to a small corner of the stable area. Here she directed Chuck to climb the ladder finding himself in a deerskin and blanket walled room roughly six foot by eight foot. The old lady had made herself a comfortable in spite of the conditions surrounding her. Her few meager possessions were well taken care of. She told young Chuck the General looked after her which kept the others and their negative attitudes away from her. She, right away set up some robes and blankets in a corner area telling him this was where he was to sleep. Chuck found her English surprisingly good. Her actions along with her words made herself quite understandable.

"**C**ome you help me cook, make food for Haksod."

Looking confused at the word she used he asked what it meant.

She smiled warmly and explained that in her language it meant Grandfather.

Chuck felt totally at ease with Silver Cloud and knew he was more than welcomed.

On the return to the cook house they passed the lieutenant among other officers. Total annoyance and dislike flashed across his face.

Silver Cloud spoke softly;

"**S**tay away from that one. He not a nice man. Do not trust him. Trust only Great Father. Stay by me, he no bother you."

She squeezed his hand lovingly signaling her sincerity.

Chuck was intelligent enough to heed the old woman's words till he got a better feel for the place. He promised himself a walk around the compound at another time to fulfill his curiosity. He decided then not to mention the small incident to Dan or Silver Cloud's words, at least not yet anyway. He willingly helped her prepare the General's meal and some extra goodies for his Grandfather.

Silver Cloud also prepared part of the officers meals and delivered them in the evening. He had already seen his Grandfather so he volunteered to assist his new found friend.

The junior officers building was as unassuming as the General's office. He followed the old lady and helped in setting the table.
At the opposite end of the table Silver Cloud was portioning out some stew when his not so favorite lieutenant pushed into her causing a spoonful of the stew to spill onto the table. Yelling at her and pushing again caught Chuck's attention. He rushed around the table placing himself between Lieutenant Brissot and Silver Cloud. The lieutenant's evil eyes seared into Chuck's and in surprisingly good English said;

"What are you going to do squaw boy? You want to hit me Go ahead, I dare you."

He took a step closer to the boy when at last a few of the other men interceded, stopping the Lieutenant from moving any further towards the boy. They were talking French and rather fast and of course Chuck did not understand what was being said.

Silver Cloud calmly wiped up the small spill and continued her serving. The Lieutenant was put under control and although appearing calm now continued to glare at Chuck with obvious hatred.

Chuck was proud of himself for not getting too carried away and was even more surprised at his lack of fear.

Silver Cloud was soon finished and she and Chuck carefully exited the building making a point to avoid the Lieutenant.

"Thank you my son for your help. It was not really necessary; I'm accustomed to his manner. He is the only one like that."

"That may be." answered Chuck, "but no one should treat a woman like that."

"I think there is something wrong with his head." She demonstrated her words by pointing her index finger at her head making small circles. Again she warned Chuck;

"Do not trust him."

Once back at the stable he was very comfortable in his corner sleeping area. He lay down with the flashlight nearby. He missed his Grandfather and hoped he would be released soon.

The next day he was up early and accompanied the old woman on her daily chores; firewood, water and to the cook house was her routine. He found it hard to believe how spry she was. True she moved rather slowly but her strength had not waned with age. He attributed it to her natural way of life. He knew for a fact very few women of that age living in his time maintained that level of strength and agility. He wanted to know her better.

The morning meal, in fact the day went well and without a sign of Lt. Brissot. Chuck was able to see the whole fort in between the two visits to his Grandfather. Most of the men were pleasant and accommodating. He was even permitted access to the wall and canon emplacements. The camera was , unfortunately, back in his pack with Dan. *"Wouldn't it be great if it was a digital or even a Polaroid."* he thought. *"I bet that would really blow their minds."*

He also thought about how hard it must be for the men to be so far from home and loved ones yet this is the way it has always been and most likely always would. The young lad actually felt sorry for them and could relate with them in the every way.

He noticed there were very few Indians inside the walls and except for Silver Cloud, they were completely absent at night. Various reasons passed through his mind but concluded it was really no concern of his. Overall Chuck viewed the fort as a substantial structure. No wonder it has lasted all these years.

Having satisfied his curiosity he returned to his Grandfather and then his evening chores with Silver Cloud. He learned from Dan there may be possible good news tomorrow. This re received directly from Montcalm who had visited him while Chuck was touring the fort.

The working part of his evening came and went without notice. His free time with Silver Cloud was pleasant and relaxing. She told stories of he r people and that she was mother to a chief. She was a clan mother. Chuck had no idea she held such high status. He was growing to love this old lady as his own Grandmother. She was eager to share her stories as her affection for Chuck was apparent. Her goodnight words were charming and left no room for argument.

"It is time young one we must allow our bodies to gather strength for another sun. Good things will come to those who honor the Great Spirit and live according to the rules He set down."

"What are these rules?" the young one inquired respectfully.

"Another sun will bring more time child, now we become one with the peace of the night."

Silver Cloud lay down and said no more. As Chuck cuddled under the blankets his thoughts reflected on her tales of old until he was asleep.

Chapter 8

The sun was already warming the air when Chuck awoke to the sound of much commotion on the parade ground in the center of the fort. He quickly got dressed realizing Silver Cloud was already up and gone. He climbed down the stable ladder and made his way as stealthily as he could to the center area hoping to learn what was happening. He could not interpret the French but did pick up on the English being spoken. There were seven men, their hands tied behind their backs. To Chuck they did not look like soldiers. He assumed they were settlers turned militia men. There were four Native Americans among the group guarding the men. He recognized the one who almost scalped him. He made it a point to stay out of sight. He watched a while longer but learning nothing new he made his way to the guard house. Along the way he noticed Lt. Brissot was escorting the General to the new prisoners.

Once with Dan, he relayed the events that had transpired. His Grandfather was pleased with this information. The General had mentioned a prisoner exchange; perhaps this was to be part of it.

Chuck had to eventually leave before the seven men were brought to the cell area. He went straight to the cook house knowing the old lady would have extra work.

Silver Cloud was happy to see him and teased him somewhat for sleeping late. This jovial mood continued through the morning. A midday meal was provided for the soldiers that just returned from the field for which they were grateful but then there was Lt. Brissot again. Chuck had been occupied with table settings and when he turned around he was facing the only man he could ever remember genuinely not liking. The Lt. Only about two feet away, stared, not moving, a sneer showing on his lips. Not a word passed between them. With much self control Chuck sidestepped uttering "Excuse me Sir." and crossed the floor to the prep room.

"You did right, my son, do not play onto his selfish tricks."
Silver Cloud had watched the whole thing from the doorway. "Just avoid him." she advised. "He will attempt to agitate you, to make you do something rash. Do not let him get inside your head. You are too good for that."

She touched his shoulder softly and smiled. The tension he was feeling faded quickly at her touch.

The next couple of days proved to be quite interesting. Other English prisoners from various outposts were brought to Fort Carillon. This grouping was varied to say the least. The many soldiers were accompanied by civilian militia men and added to the mixture were regular settlers including some women. The latter group were from Indian settlements. The French were able to convince their native allies that they were of more value alive.

Montcalm, through his intermediaries, had set up a prisoner exchange to be held at Fort Ann. Fort Edward was to be the final destination for the captives and freedom, while the actual exchange would be made at Fort Ann. As plans for the journey and exchange were being made the General met a few times to talk with Dan. The meetings took place in his office for privacy. Montcalm was pretty well convinced of Dan and Chuck's tale of time travel; enough, at least, to warrant the freedom for them to return to their own time. He explained, however, of other circumstances that had to be considered. He wished them free but that part would have to take place with the English. He did not foresee any problem; it was only a matter of the travel time to Fort Edward. He sincerely apologized and wished both travelers a safe and successful journey.

Dan accepted Montcalm's position without ill feelings and decided a few more days mixing with people of the period would be of great educational value for both Chuck and himself.

Young Chuck had his own unique way of persuading the General of letting Silver Cloud go with them. It was his intention that she would have a more successful chance of being reunited with her own people through the English. The General yielded to the arguments of his new young friend admitting he would miss her cooking.

Chuck could hardly contain his joy at the final decision and ran to tell Silver Cloud. She accepted this wonderful news with much enthusiasm and thanked Chuck with a big motherly bear hug. When the initial celebration was over Chuck could see a tear caught in her eye.

"The great French Father has been very good to me and treated me well. I shall miss him."

Feeling her sincerity Chuck promised himself he would arrange a private farewell meeting for the old Lady and the General.

It required another two days of preparation before leaving for Fort Ann at a distance of about thirty miles. This was a lot further south than Dan planned on going originally but right now he had no control over the situation. Neither he nor Chuck divulged ant information about their origins only that they lived in the hills east of Champlain.

There were thirty on persons in the exchange group to be escorted by eighty plus regular French soldiers commanded by a Captain and two Lieutenants. Unfortunately one of Lieutenants was Brissot. It was only now that Chuck made know to his Grandfather the incidents between he and Lt. Brissot. This of course included involving Silver Cloud. Dan, as would be expected, was a bit perturbed with his Grandson for not revealing the truth when these happenings took place. Dan did not chastise Chuck but made know his disappointment. Silver Cloud exercised a very good motherly instinct during this exchange between the two. Both Dan and Chuck succumbed to her charm and wisdom.

Luckily time was found for one last talk with Montcalm in the presence of Silver Cloud. It was easy to see why she was a clan mother and leader of the Seneca.

The General, obviously disturbed with this news, promised to talk with Captain DeGrasse about Lt. Brissot. He could not, however replace him in the escort detachment. His military priorities took precedence. The Captain would be instructed accordingly. Dan was again satisfied with the outcome. By eight o'clock the next morning the detachment was already on the way flying the white flag of truce. Normally they would fly a red flag signifying truce because their uniforms were white, but since they were entering British territory they used what the British used, white.

Fort Edward was to be the final destination and freedom while the actual exchange would take place at Fort Ann. After an hour's march additional escorts joined the march. These were all Native Americans, most of whom did not carry a friendly bearing. The soldiers themselves were more on the alert hoping there would be no antagonisms. There were still eighteen or so miles to go. The troublesome Lieutenant was nowhere to be seen and this first day although Chuck though he saw him early in the evening with his ever present two man armed guard. The night passed quickly with Chuck staying very close to Silver Cloud and his "Haksod" as she called Dan.
For some unknown reason young Chuck did not feel safe in this group of over a hundred soldiers as he did when it was just he and Dan. He did sleep but sort of with one eye open as the expression goes.

On their way the next morning he stayed close to the old lady in case she needed help. Yet at times it was she who was helping him. During the trek he was mentally comparing the women he was with to those of his own time. These women appeared to be stronger and with a lot more endurance; obviously the results of the lifestyle of the time.

The pace of their march this second day was steady and at times relatively easy because of the terrain. It was apparent that parts of the trail were well traveled which allowed for a faster pace than the day before.

There was only two and a half miles to go when they stopped for the evening. The Captain chose not to chance the forest at night. Arriving at Fort Ann mid morning the next day would do just fine.

Later in the evening before going to sleep Chuck saw Lt. Brissot again looking at where he and his Grandfather were in the crowd. This time he did tell Dan who confirmed what he saw having noticed the Lieutenant himself.. Silver Cloud, in her usual unassuming way quietly mentioned;

"The Scorpion attacks from the front but it is what is behind him that is most dangerous."

She just smiled and continued poking the fire. The rest of the night passed with no irregularities and with the morning appeared a welcoming sun.

Dan and the two under his care were toward the rear of the march of captives as were both of the two body guards of Lt. Brissot. They took turns yet were far from being inconspicuous. Silver Cloud, unnoticed, meandered her way forward in line and lost herself among the other women.

"Just as I thought." talking to herself, *"It is not me they are interested in. I must watch out for my new young friend and his Haksod."*

Fort Ann finally sighted, the captives were filled with renewed hope. The fort itself was not very impressive compared to Carillon but was suited for this prisoner exchange. The Captain met a British officer of equal rank and they exchanged military courtesies. They entered a building to further the protocol of the exchange, paper work, signatures and the like.

More than one hundred French soldiers were lead to the center of the fort all appearing to be of good health, battle wounds having been properly administered to.

It was during this activity Silver Cloud spotted Lt. Brissot conversing with a few other British officers, and periodically pointing to the rear section of the prisoners they had escorted here. Alarmed by this she moved as fast as she could to find Dan and Chuck. Being an elderly Indian woman actually helped her pass through the many people at the fort. She sighted Chuck and went to him almost out of breath.

"Where is Haksod?" she asked hurriedly.

"I don't know." Chuck answered with questioning eyes. "He was here a minute ago. We were talking to those settlers." he said pointing.

"We must find him now."

Chuck spotted Dan just as Silver Cloud finished the word now. An officer and three soldiers were just putting him in irons. Chuck started towards his Grandfather but was held back by the elder lady.

"Too late my son, we must find French Captain."

Weaving through the crowd to find the office their attention was diverted by the French formation moving out with Lt. Brissot at the front moving the men as fast as he could.

They finally made it to the office just as Dan was being pushed onto the guard house. Chuck did not understand what was going on. Silver Cloud had not had time to explain what she saw as of yet. The office was empty. Stopping a sergeant he asked;

"We need to fond the French Captain right away. Have you seen him?"

"He is with Captain Archer. They were heading for the stables."

Chuck faced the stable area as both Captains rode out the gate to follow the French detachment. He was out of luck for the moment. He knew Captain Archer would return and he would just have to wait. But it was Captain De Grasse he needed to talk to otherwise his Grandfather was in serious trouble, perhaps even himself. For the first time since he left on this journey he was experiencing helplessness. He wanted to cry but dared not. He sat down on the step of the office shack, face blank, eyes moist.

"A young warrior who has a true heart never shows despair. To be a man he must accept disappointments yet look beyond them. An answer is always there. Despair hides it from the heart." Silver Cloud, her hand now on his shoulder, her eyes understanding, quietly added, "Come."

Not understanding why but he felt compelled to follow this motherly figure. They weaved their way throughout the yard and exited the main gate and walked toward the Indian encampment. Under ordinary conditions Chuck would have been intimidated by the fierceness of some of the warriors they passed but with Silver Cloud no such fears appeared. She stopped at a specific long house apart from the others and uttered many words of a language unknown to the young man. Soon they were facing two other woman and many men both young and old. There was an exchange of many foreign words. Chuck observed a change in most of the new audience. There was no bowing or any physical exhibition of honor but a veil of respect shadowed the people. Apparently the old woman's honored position was recognized. A short discussion ensued an a conclusion appeared evident with a half dozen warriors being singled out. With final instructions by Silver Cloud, she, Chuck and the six men started north. Two men broke into a run and were soon out of sight. Chuck recognized the trail as the one they had taken to Fort Ann. With an expression of confusion he inquired of Silver Cloud;

"Why are we leaving my Grandfather, we have to help him."

"That is what we are doing young one, Keep going while I explain."

Chuck somehow knew this was right, for his trust in her was unquestionable. Still amazed at the elder woman's stamina he attentively listened as they walked briskly onward.

"I sent the two runners ahead to caution the British Captain of our plight. He will meet with us so we can speak of your Grandfather."
Chuck politely interrupted her.

"I'm sorry to stop you like this but that's the part I do not understand. Why did they put my Gramps in the guardhouse again?"

"I'm sorry my son, I was in such a rush I failed to tell you the reason. I saw Lt. Brissot talking to a young English officer then quickly go away. That is when your Haksod was taken to the guardhouse. I do not think Captain De Grasse knew of this. The Lieutenant then rushed the French soldiers out to march home. I do not believe the two Captains knew of this either.   When the English Captain is caught up with the runners will go on to catch the French Captain. We will continue this way until we can meet with both."

"I sure am glad I'm on your side." breathed Chuck.

"It is not a matter of side's young one. It is what is just and fair. There are always those who do not believe in the fair way of things. They are the ones who must learn what is just for all."

At this point Chuck considered himself fortunate to know this great lady of wisdom.

The fast pace continued a while until Silver Cloud called a halt. She admittedly needed a rest. She urged Chuck to go on but he chose to stay with her. It was not long when the sound of many horses was heard. Captain Archer, two guards and a rider less horse appeared. Chuck, at the urging of Silver Cloud, put forth the story of Lt. Brissot and his Grandfather in the guardhouse, adding that Captain De Grasse could expound on it in more detail. Chuck and Silver Cloud were encouraged to mount the spare horse. The five rode north to catch the moving French unit.

Chapter 9

Just at noon Captain Archer came in contact with the rear guard of the detachment and word was sent forward. With the troop at rest Captain De Grasse met with his British counterpart with a full account of the story told. The French Captain assured Captain Archer there was no need for Dan Hanson to be in the guardhouse. Whatever Lt. Brissot may have said was untrue. Lt. Brissot was summoned to appear. The Lieutenant arrived with his usual self importance on display until he saw Chuck and Silver Cloud. Hatred and fear crossed his face, his pallor went gray. He approached the pair of Captains trying for proper military decorum.

"YOU SENT FOR ME MON CAPITAIN ?"

"YES I DID LT. AND WE WILL SPEAK IN ENGLISH FROM HERE ON."

"It seems we may have a conflicting story situation here. What light can you shed on this for us?"

With a feigned expression of surprise he answered;

"I have no idea what you are talking about Captain."

"Then let me enlighten you Lieutenant. Did you or did you not speak to the English officer and have Mr. Harper put in the guardhouse against the Generals specific orders ?"

"I did no such thing Captain. Are you going to take the word of a wild savage over an officer of good standing." The Lieutenant spurted out.

"I made no mention of any accusation Lieutenant. Why are you looking at Silver Cloud ?"

"I will not stand for such attacks on my character." he shouted as he turned his horse away. He started running, not toward his position with the troops but toward the forest thicket.

Captain De Grasse turned to the rear guard ordering;

"BRING THAT MAN BACK HERE."

Two soldiers instantly assumed pursuit. A few quiet words by Silver Cloud released two of her escorts who joined the chase. All five figures were now out of sight. Within two minutes a man's scream was heard. Moments later a soldier returned for rope. The Lieutenant had slipped off a precipice and was hanging by a tree branch over what was a severe drop. Rope in hand, the guard ran back to the forest. The Captain sent a few more men to help. The quiet was again broken by a more distinct scream.

Chuck, along with the pair of officers started towards the trees. It was then Chuck noticed Silver Cloud was missing. Arriving at the cliff he saw Silver Cloud off to one side returning a knife to a hidden place in her deerskin dress, a thickened waistband at the small of her back well hidden by her long silver Grey hair. It was reported by one of the soldiers that the branch broke. On closer inspection Chuck could see where the branch had been slashed with a knife. The two warriors carefully helped the gentle old lady back to the waiting detachment. Captain De Grasse assured Captain Archer things here would be properly taken care of. For a second time they bid their farewells both satisfied the situation was resolved. The English and French Captains amicably parted, each going their own way.

A few men managed to climb down to retrieve the body. Death was most likely instantaneous; The Lieutenant's head was smashed on a rock.

There was no question of his guilt after his reaction to the initial question. Captain Archer had assured young Chuck that Dan Harper would be released as soon as he returned to Fort Ann. Silver Cloud stayed to herself yet as Chuck looked to her she smiled humbly. The elderly clan mother chose to walk back attended by two young braves, so Chuck accompanied her. It was obvious they were fond of each other and as far as Chuck was concerned, she was family.

Silver Cloud remained silent for most of the return to Fort Ann. Chuck chose not to pursue what he witnessed. He was happy his Grandfather would be freed. When there was conservation it was light and kept tp generalities, yet even these generalities were of great interest to Chuck. There was always something to learn from someone like Silver Cloud. Chuck did not ask about what he had seen, nor did Silver Cloud volunteer any comment. *"No matter."* thought Chuck, *"What's done is done and with positive results for all."*

~ ~ ~ ~ ~ ~

They arrived at Fort Ann late afternoon greeted by Dan who gave a genuine warm hug to Silver Cloud. It was hard to tell but it seemed as if she was blushing. She politely asked to be excused and she joined others outside the gate.

Chuck and Dan strolled to a quiet corner and sat on an old log bench. Chuck then, with some anxiety, outlined the day's exciting activities in great detail for his Grandfather. Dan let him have his moment understanding what it was to be an impressionable young teen. When Chuck finally ran out of words, Dan confided that once he was released from the guardhouse, he and Captain Archer spoke at length of the day's events. Captain De Grasse's instructions from Montcalm were also shared and it was determined that Lt. Brissot was acting solely of his own accord most likely out of meanness. Their chat ended with Dan excitedly announcing that they were free to go anytime.

"Can we stay the night at least?" Chuck asked.

"Of course we can sport." Anticipating his motive Dan offered, "We'll make sure Silver Cloud is well looked after before we leave. Fortunate for her, and for us, Captain Archer has a great respect for the Native Americans, the Iroquois Nation in particular.

They both had dinner that night with Silver Cloud who also supplied them with some travel food. Chuck was further assured of her well being and safe return to her own people in western New York. He took great comfort in her words as they parted company.

"Be true to your own heart my son, and you will never have regrets in your life. Truth is the only real path to happiness."

Silver Cloud hugged Chuck warmly and upon release said;

"May the Great Spirit keep you safe on your journey."

Without further fuss she turned and entered the long house.

Young Chuck was not prepared for the abrupt ending and remained still, staring into nothing.

"It's better that way sport, let's go. She will never forget you, nor you her. It is their way."

Dan extended his arm around Chuck's shoulder guiding him away.

Just after sunup and a very peaceful night the time travelers, as they now referred to themselves, were making last minute preparations before leaving Fort Ann. Dan managed a short meeting of thanks with Capt. Archer. Back packs in hand, equipped with new knives; The pair gave one last look at Fort Ann's gate and started north.

Chapter   10

The freedom of movement was a wonderful feeling for both.
Not since their first day did the serenity if the first capture their attention as it was doing now. The fresh air, as clean as it was the first day, smelled and tasted even better. They wandered care free though still maintained a northerly aim.

A mid morning break found them at a small creek of fresh, cold, fast running water. Chuck passed o few moments munching on some flat bread provided by Silver Cloud, and watching a brook trout meander from rock to rock following the current. Dan, ever alert from experience was attuned to a noise missed by Chuck. He, moving slowly to get his Grandson's attention had his finger to his lips signaling quiet. The searching eyes of the pair suddenly locked on the same spot. There before them was the biggest bull moose either had ever seen. Nature's large monster both saw and smelled the intruders. Dan knew something was antagonizing the animal to make him appear this dangerous. The brown giant pawed the ground violently, swinging his head with angst. That's when Dan saw the two arrows well seated just behind the left shoulder. Ordinarily he knew this would have brought down any normal deer or smaller moose. The thought of his rifle quickly rushed across his mind. This thought was quickly replaced with the safety of Chuck. Calling as loud as he dared;

"Chuck, when I shout go, you run across the creek and climb that big oak tree. Do not argue."

Chuck knew when not to argue with Dan, and this was that time. A shot rang out, the moose bellowed in agony, ran about four yards and fell, blood gushing from the ear. Not too many seconds later four Indians stepped out of the forest; two with bow and arrow and two with rifles. Dan guessed correctly that they were Iroquois. Remembering a greeting word Silver Cloud had spoken he repeated it as best he could. The four warriors turned their attention to Dan and by this time Chuck was also standing. One of the four advanced toward them weapon at the ready.

"You English?" he inquired.

"Yes." Dan answered confidently.

"You are long way from fort. What are you doing here?" was the return.

Surprised by the proper retort Dan was momentarily at a loss for words. In a very friendly voice he replied;

"You speak English very well. You have lived with the white man but you choose your own people. You are obviously a man of honor."

A slight smile crossed the lips of the bare chested figure.

"And you Grey one are obviously not from around here. Where are you heading?"

"North to the Champlain."

"But why? That is the land the French claim?

"We live a great distance east of the big water and are trying to get home." explained Dan.

"I ask again, what are you doing here?"

"We were captured by the French and were freed here as part of an exchange of prisoners. We just want to go home."

The young brave nodded his head in understanding and turned to consult with his comrades. Addressing Dan again he smiled saying;

"We can help you but first you must help us."

Dan showed confusion but agreed.

"What will you have us do?" He asked anxiously.

Still smiling, knowing Dan was uneasy, he proceeded to explain;

"This meat will feed us for some time. You will help carry it back to our lodge." Chuck was the first to answer.

"When do we start." he said excitedly. "I never butchered a moose before."

Weapons were put aside while a prayer was offered to the spirit of the great moose who would now help feed many men, women and children. The four hunters began the skinning process with Chuck eagerly at their side. Quite a few hours passed with all six working together not only in the butchering but in making sleds for hauling the meat. Not really a sled but a triangular shaped slide from two saplings and cross bars that can easily be pulled by a man.

The meat was equally divided among the skids which made Chuck proud to be considered an equal. A little over an hours haul found the small hunting party at a village. There were many long houses and people. In thanks for their assistance Dan and Chuck were naturally invited to stay, eat and rest overnight. They accepted without hesitation.

Chuck was in awe of the peace, harmony and cooperation of the villagers. He marveled at the fact he was witnessing living history.

Even at his young age he wondered why all people could not be like this. These people worked as a community. You could still be an individual but your neighbor was never forgotten. A good hunter shared with all. The elderly were taken care of and respected. They spoke of Silver Cloud whose wisdom was known throughout all the nations of the Iroquois.

The next morning came sooner than Chuck wanted though he did understand that they had to go. As promised, the English speaking Mohawk and a companion escorted the pair north on a trail that probably saved miles and time. By noon they reached a parting point where the Iroquois would turn back. Dan with an instinctive sense of direction continued north with Chuck. He already recognized the shape of some distant mountains and hills. He figured they could be there by the next morning. But what's the rush. He promised Chuck some time in the woods and decided one or two more days would not hurt. But also to be on the safe side they would stick close to the portal.

Despite the dangers they had faced and the potential dangers ahead Chuck was still riding a high of excitement. He would really have liked to spend more time among the Indians yet accepted the fact it was not possible. For reasons unknown, he felt comfortable with their lifestyle. He even teased himself thinking how much better it would be if he could see his Indian maiden again. His Grandfather was saying something that he didn't hear that broke his daydream. Smiling Dan repeated;

"How about we camp here for the night?"

"Sure thing Gramps." Chuck answered eyes searching. "How about up on that knoll? It looks clear and we can see more around us."

"Good call." Replied Dan pleased that the boy was learning.

"After this trip I guess we can't call him a boy anymore." thought Dan.

Slowly they meandered up to the chosen knoll and set up house for the night. Dan cautioned, though unnecessarily, that they still faced some possible threats from various groups both Indian and White. During a relaxed supper they reflected on the events of the past week, good and bad. They laughed about the fact they could tell no one of these happenings.
Who would believe such wild tales. This would be their own bonding secret.

Just to be on the safe side they took turns keeping watch that night. Chuck chose the morning shift from two AM to sunrise. He found a comfortable spot that overlooked quite a range. Dan had already pointed out distant fire specs most likely from an Indian encampment. Chuck estimated them at about one and a half miles distance, which to his pleasure was confirmed by his Grandfather.

The youngster sat with his back against a tree while his mind instantly went to the experiences he had just lived through. Who would have believed one could relive history coming from some two hundred sixty years later. To actually see it happening before your very eyes, not just reading about it. Meeting and learning about the other people who helped write this history but were never named in the history books. Only a very few received credit for deeds wrought by so many others. That was the real history, the unknown history. Right away familiar names flashed through his mind; Capt. Archer, Silver Cloud, Capt. De Grasse and even Lt. Brissot. They played important parts in the making of history but their names were unrecorded.

"I suppose that is typical even today." he thought. *"We are surrounded by history makers but only a few are recognized and remembered."*

It did not feel like he was keeping watch for very long when he became aware of the sunrise. It did not present anything spectacular but because of the situation Chuck found it beautiful and comforting.

He stood, exercising arms and legs enjoying it's warmth. He decided not to disturb his Grandfather; he knew he was tired and he was sure to enjoy a little extra sleep. Chuck walked to the edge of the knoll and stood there taking in the undisturbed beauty before him. *"It's a shame."* he thought to himself, *"that mankind evolved to the point of destroying nature instead of living with it. Progress and inventions were all well and good but they cost a tremendous amount of natural beauty that is lost forever. Instead of being calmed and soothed and relaxed by the world us, we, ourselves created stress and conflict and are reaping self destruction upon mankind and the innocents around us.*

Chuck's thoughts became so overwhelming he could feel himself being saddened and distressed. He changed position slightly so he could view upstream a bit more. It was then he detected movement below out of the corner of his eye. Instantly he dropped to his knees to make a smaller target keeping his eyes on the disturbance that followed the stream. He knew he had not been seen because of the distance and he also knew he did not want to be seen until he assessed the exact cause of the disturbance. He threw some pebbles toward his Grandfather hoping to awaken him without scaring him. The small stones worked and Dan was not shocked awake. His eyes found Chuck right away who had his finger to his lips indicating silence. Seeing his Grandson crouched he followed suit in his approach to the edge of the precipice.

"**W**hat's up?" he asked quietly.

"**M**ovement down by the edge of the stream." Chuck answered in a similar tone. "I have not determined who or how many just yet."

The two waited patiently counting men as they came into view from around the curve of the stream. Sixteen in all appeared to be the final count.

"**T**hey all seem to be white men though many appear to be wearing native attire." Dan whispered.

"**I** wouldn't mind having a set of deerskins to wear. They look pretty cool." answered Chuck. They continued watching the patrol of obvious scouts of some sort follow the stream. Both were suddenly startled.

"**A**lright you Frenchy's, turn around slowly."

A lone man with a rifle and pistol pointed at the pair stood before them also attired in buckskin garb, including moccasins.

*"**N**o wonder we didn't hear him."* thought Dan. "No need for the weapons young man we mean you no harm. As you can see we have no guns."

"**Y**ou don't need guns to spy on people. What are you doing hiding up here." was the quick reply.

Being accused of spying annoyed young Chuck and he answered quickly without thinking.

"**A**nd what are you doing sneaking up and spying on us." By now Chuck was standing in a definitely defiant pose that was not really his usual manner. He suddenly realized what he had done and was embarrassed bu his unusual behavior and turned to his Grandfather silently asking forgiveness.

The intruder, startled by the young boy's action responded;

"**C**alm down boy, I'm not here to hurt you. I can see now that you are not French, but your actions do seem a bit suspicious."

"**I** can explain sir, if you give me a chance. I take it you are part of the Rangers with Major Rogers."

Dan took a lucky guess, more of an educated guess remembering his readings.

"**R**ight you are sir, but not many people would know that." the stranger answered accompanied by a confused look.

Continuing, Dan further explained; "We were just set free in a prisoner exchange at Fort Ann and are on our way home. We live east of the Champlain. We noticed the movement down by the stream and thought it might be Indians that we are trying to avoid."

"It being a good thing trying to avoid them blood thirsty savages; our patrol is doing just the opposite. We're hunting them down, if we can catch them." commented the ranger. Dan noticed the look of disgust on Chucks face knowing how he felt about Native Americans; Luckily Chuck held back his comments this time.

"Seeing that you are one of us I know you're not spying on us. Be careful with that young boy, them savages would just love to kidnap someone like him. Good luck in getting home. You may want to think about traveling only early morning or just before dark. That might be your safest time." volunteered the deer skinned figure. He turned and disappeared into the forest as quietly as he had come. Chuck looked down from the knoll only to see the last of the men fade into the woods around the curve of the stream.

Still thinking of his blunder the youngest of the pair looked at Dan;

"Sorry Gramps for getting carried away before."

"That's okay sport, no real harm done. Actually it did work out to our benefit."

Chuck was now all smiles and felt better. More than better, he was feeling great.

"How did you know that they were Rangers Gramps?"

"It was a good guess on my part but I remembered my history readings of years ago. It just made sense to mention it."

"I sure am glad you did. Getting thrown in jail again for spying was not my idea of fun." replied Chuck smiling still.

Both Grandfather and Grandson relaxed somewhat as they prepared a leisurely breakfast. As they ate Chuck's curiosity again overwhelmed him.

"Tell me more about this Major Rogers. I don't recall hearing about him before."

"Rogers Rangers were a special regiment with the British. They were not drilled soldiers. They trained in forest warfare and fought as the Indians did. In most cases they were even more savage than the Indians because of their indiscriminate brutality. Why the Abenaki's themselves called him "WOBOMAGONDA" which loosely translated means "White Devil" His method of warfare put even the Abenaki to fright."

"Wow! That doesn't sound very civilized to me." Chuck remarked. "Didn't the British try to stop him?"

"Apparently not, they just wanted to get rid of the Indians."

The young lad pondered this while he finished his meal.

After breakfast Chuck performed one of his miracle *"make man disappear."* cleanups.

"Ready to go home sport?" inquired Dan.

"Part of me wants to say no Gramps, but to be practical I think we can both use a break."

"Good, then let's get going. I think we can make it to the cave in about two hours or so unless of course you run into any more Indian maidens."

Chuck's cheeks flushed a bit but he knew Gramps was only ribbing him.

In just under two hours he recognized the rock formation hiding the portal, the entrance to modern times. Neither had his full heart into entering the cave. It meant the end of excitement and a lifestyle they both wanted to pursue down deep inside.

An unexpected vision of a small band of Abenaki with a tethered prisoner quickly made up their minds. Chuck was first to enter. He did so as quietly as possible not to attract attention. Dan was close behind. They dared not use flashlights just yet. Barely inside and out of sight had both frozen in place when they heard voices at the cave entrance. Not moving even an eyebrow Chuck felt his heart pounding. He was afraid even that noise would give them away. He knew this to be ridiculous thinking., but for the first time on this adventure he was really frightened. Dan and the boy remained motionless for five or six minutes before Dan indicated they continue very slowly with the slightest push on Chucks back.

Obviously the Indians had not discovered the portal entrance and were only gathered near the outside. Dan wasn't positive but he thought he recognized the voice of the ranger that had discovered them earlier that morning. Unfortunately there was nothing either he or Chuck could do. He did not mention this to Chuck.

It was slow going in the caves serpentine passageway since they were going uphill the whole time. To be on the safe side they gave themselves ten minutes or so before they began to use the flashlights which aided in the avoidance of stumbling. Some quiet conversation also resumed. The pair chose to continue the slow journey until they exited to the fresh air even though it was now dark. Setting up a quick camp they ate silently and both exhausted, climbed into their sleeping bags for a safe and restful night.

Chuck awoke early to the sound of a distant train whistle.

"I guess we took the right tunnel." he teased himself.

There was blue sky and sun but the air was definitely different. He could not pick out any one particular thing, it was just different. He could see the con trail of a jet liner high above and hear the distant whine of the wheels of the long haul trucks from the far off superhighway. As the sun climbed higher the haze of pollution became evident.

"Welcome back to my own world." he said to himself disgustedly.

"What was that you were mumbling sport?" asked his Grandfather shaking off the sleepies.

"Oh, nothing Gramps, I was just mumbling to myself."

Dan half smiling knowing what he was feeling commented;

"I don't want to be back either son, but we do have obligations in our own world."

"I know." Chuck answered thinking of his Mom.

Chuck fixed a quick breakfast while Dan pulled his GPS from his pack and pushed the ON button. Sure enough within seconds the Lat. And Lon, readings registered. Dan silently laughed to himself staring at almost the exact same readings they started out with.

Breaking camp they headed for the nearest convenience store to call Chuck's Mom. Knowing they had at least a three hour wait they made themselves comfortable at a picnic bench and happily reminisced about their adventure of two hundred sixty plus years in the past.

On the ride home they made up stories for Chuck's Mom, of their outing knowing they could not tell what actually took place. They didn't dare tell the truth. Who would believe them?

~ ~ ~ ~ ~ ~

Months passed while Chuck became an avid colonial history buff devouring every book he could get his hands on, agreeing with some and not with others.

His second semester American History class proved especially interesting to him. A transfer student joined the class. Chuck sat there staring with his mouth open. She was the spitting image of his Indian maiden of long ago. He did not get a chance to approach her until after the last bell. He noticed her walking away from school and hurried to catch up. He boldly but politely introduced himself. They spoke in the generalities of their generation until Chuck could no longer contain himself.

"I don't mean to be forward or rude but you strike me as being of Native American ancestry, Mohawk to be precise."

Warmly smiling her reply;

"Yes I am. How did you know? No one ever believes that when I tell them."

"Let's just say I've had some interesting relationships with the Mohawk people in the past years.

They became fast friends. Chuck was not going to let her get away this time. He couldn't wait to introduce her to his Grandfather.

The End

(of the past or the future ?)

Bibliography

Return to Eldorado   The Search for Eldorado
            By Walker Chapman

Family History   Life of Washington
         By Washington Irving Vol. II, III,IV,V
   Trenton - Vol.II pg.470-485
   Morristown - Vol. IV pg.1
   Valley Forge - Vol.III pg. 332,377,404
   Farewell Address - Vol. V pg. 370
   Hessions - Vol.IV pg. 469, Vol.III pg. 3, Vol. Pg. 322
   Benedict Arnold - Vol.IV pg. 131
       George Washington
       By William Sterne Randall
        Pg. 76-80

My Grandfather

    Theodore Roosevelt, an autobiography Copyright 1913
       Pub. By The Macmillan Co.
    The Autobiography of Teddy Roosevelt
       Centennial edition. Copyright 1951
       Pub. By Charles Scribner & Sons, N.Y.
    Wikipedia
    Potus

Atlantis
    World Map & Wikipedia.

The Wander
    White Devil
      By S. Brummell
       Pub. By DaCapo Press

The western Abenaki of Vermont.
By Colin G. Calloway
Univ. Of Oklahgoma Press
Time Travel in Einsteins Universe
By J.Richard Gott   Pub 2001
Time Machines
By Paul J. Nanin Pub 1998&99
Light Years and Time Travel
By Brian Clegg   Pub. 2001
Ticonderoga   1758
By Rene' Chartrand Osprey Publishing.
The War that Made America
By Fred Anderson
Pub. By Penquin Group.

<u>*Also by Author*</u>

Simple Short Stories
(To tingle the Imagination)

Simple Short Stories II
(To further tingle the Imagination)

The Dead Living Mummy
(An epic story of a lost city that ends with a lost mind)

The Innocent Murder
(The tranquility of an English Manor upset by a sudden death)

The Ancient Ones
(Another adventure with Eric Dexter)

The Librarian Checked Out
(Murder by the Book)

The Jury is Out
(Why the Jury ?)

The Other Planet Earth
(The Possibility Exists)

The True Cost of Ignorance and False Judgement
(How one Lie can destroy a person)

<u>*Children's Stories*</u>
<u>*(A series of ten adventures with Squiggy the Squirrel)*</u>

1-The Garden Mystery
2-The Christmas Garland Mystery
3-The new Land
4-New Friends
5-Squiggy and the Bear
6-Squiggy and the Storm
7-The Next Generation
8-Squiggy's Maine Vacation
9-Squiggy and the Virus
10-Suzette Squirrel